We don't make glass

by

Hugh Chare

Publication data
We don't make glass © Hugh B. Chare 2022

Book and Cover design by Hugh B. Chare.
Cover based partly on an image from iStock credited to Yoric.
ISBN: 978-1-940012-66-7

 Kilihune Books

The James Martin series
African Encounter
Across the Zambezi
Just off the Great North Road
Well, there you go!
Back to Africa
We don't make glass
The Sagitta Mishap
Flight 5 to Johannesburg

Marieke Englebrecht mysteries
Death in the Mopane
Revenge after twenty years

Other books
The journal of Jan Englebrecht
British Spy in the Bushveld
Federica

Preface

This is a work of fiction. Names, characters, businesses and incidents are fictional except for obvious references to historical figures, companies or events. Any resemblance in the featured characters to actual persons, living or dead, is purely coincidental.

The company James & Brown, which is featured in this work, is wholly fictional. It has no relationship with the automobile maker James & Browne, which produced cars in England in the early 1900s. Waterford Industries is also wholly fictional and has no relationship with the well-known Waterford company that makes famed crystal glass products. There is no relationship between the fictional character, James Martin, who appears in this book and in earlier novels, and James Martin of Martin Consultants, author of *Surface Mining Equipment*.

In the early 1980s, Namibia was still under South African control, so it is referred to in this novel as South West Africa.

Contents

Waterford Industries

The acquisition of Waterford Industries by James & Brown went through in June of 1982 with the minimum of difficulty. There was no market concentration to worry about, no reduction in competition, just a simple diversification on the part of James & Brown, entering into a new field, aerospace, industrial gearboxes and other sundry products, but no mining or construction machinery. James & Brown, more commonly referred to as simply J&B, had been flush with cash and had engaged a well-known consulting group for advice on what to do and had been directed to Waterford by the investment banking house of Goldrich Faber, a well-known firm that dealt a lot with mergers and acquisitions. There had been a short bidding war, but one that, fortunately, did not drive up the price too much, and then it was just a question of paying out to the shareholders of Waterford, who all now had appointments with the Internal Revenue Service to discuss their newfound fortune. James Martin sat back and thought about the acquisition, couched as a merger, but in truth a straight buy. Waterford came with six companies, all registered as separate companies under the umbrella holding of Waterford Industries. The largest of the companies was headquartered in Tustin and built actuation systems and gearboxes for commercial and military aircraft. Next in size was the industrial gearbox company, based in Santa Ana. Then there was the marine company, based in Georgetown, a suburb of Seattle, that made things marine for the Navy and for oil companies, there was another aerospace company that made structures for aircraft, and that was based in Albuquerque, there was a company based in Tulsa that made hoists of all kinds, large and small and finally an aircraft cargo handling company in Pueblo, all in all a revenue base of some $278 million.

James had been part of the due diligence team that had scoured through financials, sales projections, personnel records and anything that might give comfort to the decision to buy. It had meant long days and weeks for James as the data had been secured in an office in Irvine and he had spent almost a month poring over reports, projections and comments. The acquisition done, he had wondered what his next project would be. He had come back from South Africa, where he had run J&B Africa for two years, then had spent the past three years looking at product development, market research, mergers and acquisitions and latterly the Waterford Industries acquisition.

"It's all done," he told Katrina, his wife, that evening as they sat down to dinner.
"Well, I'm glad, at least you'll be home now," she said. "What's next?"
"I've no idea," he said. "I can't ask John, Hank Miller is really busy these days, so I suppose I'll just have to wait and see."
"I'm so sad about John and Bobby," she said. They were talking about John Williams, who had been the vice president of sales for J&B until he and his wife, Roberta, had been killed in an avalanche while on a skiing trip to Utah.
"They didn't have to leave us anything in their wills," James said. "I'm surprised they did."
"It was a surprise," she agreed. "But I'm glad that their estate went to fund research for breast cancer. I'm sure that was Bobby's idea."
"Shame to lose a mentor though," James said.
"Hank Miller seems to like you," she pointed out.
"I suppose there are worse things than having the CEO like you," James laughed.
"I think he likes you because you tell him the truth," she said.
"It hasn't always been the smartest thing to do," he said.
"Maybe not, but you can hold your head high," she said.
"I'm glad we exercised our stock options when we did," he said. "At least we made a little out of them. I see the stock price dropped back to where it was when the option was granted, so the fact that the last shares won't get us much, if anything, is not too bad."
"Why didn't the stock price go up with this acquisition?" she asked.
"Not sure," he admitted. "Maybe Wall Street doesn't see any benefit in J&B buying something else and stepping away from their expertise."

James learned what his next assignment would be when Hank Miller called him down to his office.

"James, I want you to go out to California and join Bob Decker at Waterford," Hank said. "I've brought Bob in to run Waterford while we look at the structure and the management."

"This would be in Long Beach?" James asked.

"It would," Hank confirmed. "As you know, there's the small corporate office for Waterford there by the airport, and we need to know how much of it we need. We'll relocate you to California and pick up your house here if you can't sell it."

"What would I be actually doing?" James asked.

"We had debated whether to put you into the battleground of manufacturing or the bloodbath of accounting, but decided that you might best serve as business development manager, keeping your eyes and ears open for the business and what goes on at each division," Hank replied.

"I didn't meet Bob Decker, where's he from?" James asked.

"Bob and I worked together some years ago, and he took an early retirement, and I persuaded him to come out of retirement and run Waterford for a while, until we've taken a good look at the people that run the place," Hank explained. "He came on board the day of the close and is out there now."

"I should talk to Katrina," James said.

"You should," Hank agreed. "Come and see me tomorrow."

"They want us to go to California," James told Katrina that afternoon.

"Relocate to California?" she asked.

"Move there, yes," he confirmed. "They'll pay to move us out there and pick up the house here, if we can't sell it."

"Where would you work, where would we live?" she asked.

"I'd be working for a new chap, Bob Decker, I gather that he and Miller are old friends. The office would be in Long Beach, by the airport, but I suspect that I'd spend time at Tustin and the other divisions," he replied. "Two of them are in Southern California, so I suppose it makes sense to live there."

"Are they going to give you a raise to go there? I gather that houses cost quite a bit more than they do here," she said. "Plus, mortgage rates are running at between 16 and 17 per cent, and we bought this house when they were 8 per cent, that's a big differential."

"It is," he agreed. "I'll talk to them about that tomorrow."

"I'd like to go out on a house-hunting trip," she said.

"We should go," he agreed. "Can you get some time off work?"

"Of course," she said. "They won't miss me for a couple of days."

"I'll be sorry to give up this house," he said. "I like it here, I like the space, the trees, but I won't miss the snow and ice, California would be a nice change from that."

"It would," she agreed. "Will they let you keep the car?"

"I should ask, but I can't see why not," he said.

"I'm going to keep my Jeep," she said. "Maybe out there, we can take the top off more often."

"Do you feel like cooking, or should we go out?" he asked.

"Let's go and get some Italian," she suggested. They drove to a small Italian restaurant in South Milwaukee that they had patronised for years, after discovering it when they had first moved to the States and were living in an apartment building by the shore of Lake Michigan.

"Hey, folks, back again," the waitress, Vittoria, said.

"Back again," James echoed. "What's your suggestion tonight?"

"Veal," Vittoria suggested. "Veal patties cooked with red wine, really good, have with a glass of Barbera."

"Done," James told Vittoria, and she left to get the wine and place the order for the veal. "I suppose when we move to California, we'll have to find places to eat, doctors, dentists, all that sort of stuff all over again."

"At least we've had a couple of years since we got back from Jo'burg, so we're not going through the same things too soon," Katrina said. "We'll have to find a new bank, new insurance agent, all that."

"We'll manage," he said. "We've moved a couple of times now, and we've managed."

"Here you go, folks," Vittoria said, bringing plates of veal patties, with vegetables and other fixings, and a bottle of wine.

"Are you driving, or me?" Katrina asked.

"I'll drive," James said.

"So, James, can we count on you to go to California?" Hank asked.

"Yes, of course," James replied. "We'd like to take a house-hunting trip and see what we can afford."

"Good," Hank said.

"There are a couple of issues," James said.

"Fire away," Hank said.

"Mortgage rates are very different now than when we bought here a few years ago, and we understand that house prices in California are higher than here. We were wondering what might be done about that," James said.

"We thought about that," Hank admitted. "What we propose is a mortgage differential that is the difference between your current payment and what you'll face in California; that differential will decline over five years to zero, and we will gross it up for tax purposes."

"I see," James said, or at least he thought he saw. He would need an actual example to see how the differential would actually work.

"Ray Pierce has details for you," Hank added. "You should hang onto the car you have now and when you're ready, arrange with Traffic to have your household belongings moved to your new house."

"I should probably go out to California soon to meet with Bob Decker," James said.

"The company plane is deadheading out on Monday. Why don't you and Katrina take it to Long Beach?" Hank suggested. James thought about that and almost smiled; a suggestion from the CEO was as good as an instruction.

"We'll be on it," James said.

"Good, I'll tell Bob you're on your way," Hank said. "Keep me up to date with things, and if you notice anything at Waterford that you think I should know, tell me."

"I will," James promised.

"We'll, of course, bump up your salary from where you are now, and there'll be another round of stock options soon," Hank added. "So, let me know next week how things are at Waterford."

"I will," James said.

"The plane will bring you back on Sunday, so I'll expect a report on Monday morning," Hank said.

"Can you get a couple of days off next week?" James asked Katrina later. "We can take the company plane out to California on Monday and take a look at some houses."

"No problem," she assured him. "I've given my notice, and they just paid me out the two weeks, so I don't have to go in there any more. Where will we stay?"

"There's a Marriott near the Long Beach airport, I thought we'd stay there, then I can meet Bob Decker and we can find a realtor to help us find a house," he said. "They're talking about a mortgage differential. I've got the details here, if you'd look through it for us."

"I see," she said, scanning the pages. "I can use this; it makes sense, it helps us in the short term, and who knows where we'll be five years from now. If we buy out there, will the company pick up the house if they move us in less than five years?"

"I'll check with Ray Pierce," James said. "They said they'd pick up this house if we can't sell it, so probably would do the same there, if they move us."

"So what do they want you to do out there?" she asked.

"It sounds like be the company spy," he said. "I'm going out as the business development manager, whatever that means, and Hank told me to keep him informed of anything I see at Waterford that I think he should know about."

"I wonder if this new *ou*, Decker, will appreciate that?" she asked.

"I wouldn't," he said. "But maybe they know each other well enough that Decker will tell Miller everything anyway, so no need for me to report on anything."

"What sorts of things does Waterford make?" she asked.

"Bits for aeroplanes, industrial gearboxes, marine transmissions, industrial hoists and aircraft loading machines," he replied.

"A bit different from mining," she commented.

"A bit," he agreed.

"I'm sure you'll work it out," she said, confidently. "You always do."

"Mr. Martin, Mrs. Martin, nice to see you again," Bill said. Bill was one of the pilots that the company employed to fly their planes.

"Nice to see you, Bill," James replied.

"If you're ready?" Bill asked. "We're taking the 55 today." Bill was referring to the new plane that the company had just taken delivery of, a Lear 55, larger than the previous plane that they flew and capable of flying to really high altitudes; in fact, it had a service ceiling of 51,000 feet, so far above where regular commercial planes would fly.

"This is bigger than the other plane," Katrina said as they climbed aboard. "You can even stand up."

"We like it," Bill said. "We'll be going out today at 46,000 feet, so it should be a nice, smooth ride, and we'll have you on the ground in Long Beach at 8.48."

"Thanks, Bill," James said. He and Katrina took their seats and buckled up, then they taxied out and were gone. It did seem a long time before they levelled out, but then they had climbed quite a way past the altitudes normally used by commercial flights.

"Breakfast?" Chuck, the co-pilot, asked.

"Thank you," Katrina replied. Chuck handed out breakfast trays and tea; he knew that they both preferred tea in the morning from past trips they had taken.

"How do you like this new plane?" James asked.

"It's really nice," Chuck replied. "It handles well, it's got legs to do coast to coast, and the higher ceiling gives us more flexibility. Just give us a yell if you need anything else."

"Thanks, Chuck," James said. He tucked into his breakfast, a seven in the morning wheels up meant that they had to be there by six-thirty, so it had been an early morning with no time for breakfast. The country rolled by, over the Midwest and its extensive agriculture, then over the Rocky Mountains, with snow still clinging to the north slopes, then over the deserts of Utah and Nevada and on into the Los Angeles basin.

"Look at that smog layer," Katrina said, pointing out of the window. It did indeed look daunting, a reddish grey haze that hung over the basin that they soon descended through and began their approach into Long Beach. They flew out over the ocean, past the port of Los Angeles, then came back inland towards the southeast and landed. There was a bit of a taxi to the fixed-based operator that they used, but it had the benefit of being almost adjacent to the office that Waterford maintained. There was a rental car waiting for them, and James suggested to Katrina that they go and introduce themselves to Bob Decker, then check into the hotel and go their separate ways. They had found a realtor who said that she would be happy to work with them, and apparently, who already had a selection of homes for Katrina to look at, so that she could get a better idea of what they would like and what price range they were working in.

"James Martin, come in, come in," Bob Decker said as they were announced by the secretary who guarded his door.

"Mr. Decker, this is my wife, Katrina," James said.

"Great to meet you, Katrina," Bob said. "What can I get you, coffee, tea?"

"Coffee would be very nice, thank you," Katrina replied.

"Megan, would you please get us some coffees?" Bob asked.

"This is an interesting view," James commented.

"I like looking out at planes coming and going from Long Beach and the occasional one from the MacDac place over there," Bob said. "It's more interesting than a parking lot or a railroad yard. So, James, ready to get to work?"

"It will be interesting to see how different, if at all, the operations are to what was given to us in the data room," James replied.

"I'm sure it will," Bob said. "So, Katrina, any ideas on where you'd like to live?"

"Not really," Katrina replied.

"If I may make a suggestion, try looking in the City of Orange," Bob said. "It sprawls a bit, but on the eastern edge, it goes into the hills and isn't quite as built up. Where are you staying for now?"

"The Marriott, just down the road," James replied.

"Good idea," Bob said. "Great, coffee's here, thanks, Megan."

"Where do you live, Mr. Decker?" Katrina asked.

"Call me Bob," he said. "I've got a place in Sedona in Arizona, and I plan to commute, go home on the weekends. I've got my own plane, so it's about two hours, give or take. I can park my plane right next door here, so I can be out of the door and in the air in fifteen to twenty minutes."

"I should go and check in at the hotel and meet the real estate lady," Katrina said. "She was going to pick me up at ten. Where is the hotel?"

"You stay on Spring outside the door here and go east, towards the hills you can see in the background," James said. "You'll see the hotel on the right not long after you go under the runway."

"I'll drop James off at the Marriott when we're done here," Bob said. "I took a long-term rental at a place not too far from there. Say, why don't we have dinner tonight, and we can get to know one another a little better. I've seen your file, James, so know what you've done for J&B, and Hank told me a bit, but I'd like to get to know you a bit better."

"So, James, where shall we start?" Bob said.

"Perhaps with this office," James said. "During the due diligence process, I met some of the people here, but we never got to see the different divisions. Hank and some others did, but I didn't."

"We'll fix that in the next couple of days," Bob said. "I got Hank to send the plane out so that we can zip up to Seattle, land at King County, and then out to Tulsa, Albuquerque and Pueblo. We can fly out to Tulsa and pick up either Pueblo or Albuquerque on the way back, so let's say a day for Georgetown, another for Tulsa and Pueblo, then one more for Albuquerque, and the two here we can drive to and do both in one day. If we leave tomorrow, we can do Georgetown, then fly on down to Tulsa, then the day after, we can hit Tulsa and

Pueblo, then zip on down to Albuquerque, see them and come home and do the two home plants on Friday. How does that sound? Will Katrina be okay for a couple of days?"

"We can ask her tonight," James suggested.

"Back to your question about this office," Bob said. "I get that we need a legal department, government contracting is complex enough, then we've got the industrial products and any time someone does something dumb, they want to sue anyone with a nameplate on a piece of machinery. Finance, we need, why we have a quality guy here, I don't get. The marketing guy is more of a government relations guy, but I'm not convinced that we're big enough to ever get a prime contract, so not sure what he buys us. The engineer, I could go either way, the guy's clearly a really good engineer and probably serves a useful purpose, but I think we should look at who he does most of his work for."

"There are three lawyers here, and I only met one of them?" James asked.

"Three, and as best I can tell, all pretty good," Bob said. "They got a paralegal between them and a secretary each, the finance guy has an assistant, but she does numbers for him, HR, he's got a secretary, and I think we need to hang on to the HR guy, just to keep some continuity across divisions and keep an eye out for pensions and health care. Like I said, the quality guy, don't know what he does, maybe he troubleshoots if there's a problem, we should ask him and also ask the divisions who they would use."

"I got the impression during due diligence that Ralph Thompson, the quality guy, wasn't really a quality guy, but a troubleshooter for the corporate office," James said. "I also got the impression from Adam North, the engineer, that Thompson was prone to jumping to quick conclusions and not doing a thorough engineering review of issues."

"Interesting, I forgot that you'd probably met the corporate staff during due diligence," Bob said. "Maybe we'll sound out North a bit more. We'll do it carefully so he doesn't think he's dropping Thompson into it, but I'd like to know more. Shall we take a walk, and you can meet all those who are here?"

They stopped first at the office of Henry White, the Vice President of Human Resources, guarded by Becky White, his secretary, no relation.

"Becky, Henry, do you remember James Martin?" Bob asked.

"Of course," Henry said. "Good to see you again. When you were out here before, we never got the chance to just chat. Have you been with J&B long?"

"Seven years," James replied. "I like this office better than the data room I was cooped up in for so long."

"Bob has the best view," Henry said. "I guess we'll be transferring you to the payroll out here."

"That's what I understand," James said.

"I'll have forms for you to sign, beneficiaries for you to name, all that sort of stuff," Henry said.

"Thank you," James said.

"We've just switched from the defined benefit pension plan we had to a defined contribution plan with a 401(k)," Henry said. "You need to let me know what your contribution will be, and we'll match fifty cents on the dollar up to five per cent, and you can add more unmatched up to ten per cent, all pre-tax. Anything over ten per cent is after tax. I've got plan details here, take it away and read it and let me know. Health care, we're Blue Cross Blue Shield. I'll get you and your wife cards. Vacation, we'll count your existing service with the company for eligibility, so you're up to three weeks paid."

"Thank you," James said.

"If there's anything else, I'll find you, or Becky will," Henry said.

"Great, thanks, Henry," Bob said. "We should go and meet the rest of the office."

"James, good to see you again," said Jim Beatty, the lawyer that James had met during the due diligence process. "You should meet the others, guys, this is James Martin with J&B, he's one of the guys that was out here in the data room, James, this is Pete Willis, and over there is Greg Norman, then out here we've got Anthea Phillips, Belinda

McBride, Cathy Finch and Eleanor Williams, this is James Martin from J&B."

"Nice to meet you all," James said, filing away names and faces and hoping that he would remember them all.

Next, they met with Ralph Thompson and spent some time trying to understand what he actually did. James had been right; he had been a corporate troubleshooter, sent in to look over products that had failed to meet specifications for one reason or another. James thought it would be interesting to see if the various companies felt that he had been of use over the years, or if he had just been someone the corporate office trusted to give them unvarnished reports on issues. Adam North was more forthcoming on Ralph Thompson and pointed out more than a few instances where Ralph had leapt to conclusions that were disproven in time. Clearly, there was no love lost there, but who had the right of it. That was something they would have to test at the companies to see who was the most value to the company. Adam did tell them that he planned to retire in the next month. He was of an age to do so, but did indicate that he would be happy to consult on a case-by-case basis. Next on the list was Mike McKane, the finance man, someone James had spent a lot of time with in the weeks up to the close. Last was Charles Newman, the VP of Marketing, who essentially couched himself as government relations. James had also met him and had been less than impressed as Charles did not have all the government program details at his fingertips, the way James thought he should have. He spent more time talking about political connections, and James had wondered how much those connections played into the decisions that the prime contractors that Waterford typically contracted with made. When they left his office, Bob was also less than enthusiastic about Newman. They did learn, however, that the company retained the services of an employee in Paris and one in London who helped with contacts with Airbus and the other European aircraft companies and consortia. The Parisian was Paul Sykes, who apparently had become more French than the French, and the Londoner was Graham Finch.

12

"So, there we are, James, 19 of us all told, with you 20, how many we actually need, we'll see," Bob said, when they were back in the quiet of his office. "I think we should sound out each company as we go, and what their views are and how much help they get from this office."

"Does each of them need a secretary?" James asked.

"Well, Mike McKane has his assistant who does numbers and as far as I can see, she's pretty darned good, Becky White does a lot for Hank White, she's basically the administrator for the plans, I don't know that Adam needs his own secretary, but that's going to be moot when he retires next month, I don't see you needing a secretary so there'll be no need for Judith Walls. More to the point is, do we need all those guys?" Bob asked.

"Do we need a rep in Washington?" James asked.

"That's a good question," Bob said. "We're not a prime, so most of our work comes from the primes; whether or not political influence will cause a prime to throw contracts our way is debatable. My sense is that they're just going to go for the lowest bid, unless we have something they really want, even then, they'll try and get it for next to nothing."

"You don't have a high opinion of them," James commented.

"They didn't get to be prime contractors by being nice guys," Bob said. "In my view, they succeed financially by screwing their suppliers, some worse than others, and if you challenge them, it's, we've got more lawyers than you do."

"If that's the case, why do people like Waterford stay in the business?" James asked.

"Because if you do it right, you succeed despite your customers," Bob said. "Waterford is one of the go-to places for actuators and gears; they've become pretty good over the years. Plus, we're pretty good at controlling overhead, which is why it's important to figure out how many of the guys here we really need. They're all straight overhead. Let's go and get some lunch and plan out the week."

"So, all told, you have twelve direct reports?" James asked.

"Thirteen with Megan, fourteen with you," Bob replied. "It's a lot, but I'm leaning towards thinning that down a bit by looking closely at this office, do we need a quality guy here, and what does the marketing guy do for us. I can see the guys in Paris and London, expensive as I'm sure they are, but here, I've my doubts, and if we do need one, I don't think Newman is it."

"How was your day?" James asked Katrina later when Bob dropped him at the Marriott.

"Busy," she replied. "Angela is pretty good, she listens and has already scrubbed four houses that were on the list for tomorrow and added two more. How was your day?"

"Busy too," he said. "Bob wants to take a trip over the next couple of days to look at the companies. We'd leave tomorrow morning and be back Thursday afternoon."

"That's fine," she said. "By then, I'll have a short list that you and I can look at over the weekend."

"Any possibles?" he asked.

"Not really," she said. "But, Angela is adjusting the list, so maybe those we look at tomorrow will be better."

"Can we afford anything?" he asked.

"Oh yes, depending on where we want to live, we can easily afford some houses, but do we want to live there?" she replied. "We can go quite a bit higher than we did in Oak Creek, and I know it's scary, but I've looked at lots of numbers, and we can manage. That bequest we got from John and Bobby will provide a down payment. What time are we meeting Bob for dinner?"

"Six-thirty," James replied.

"Do I need to change?" she asked.

"I don't think so," he said.

They met Bob at a restaurant on Atlantic Avenue.

"Katrina, how was the house hunting?" Bob asked.

"Busy," she replied. "The agent scrubbed four for tomorrow but added some others, so we'll see. It's all a little overwhelming."

"One thing you should get yourself is a Thomas Guide," Bob said. "It's basically a street map book of LA and Orange counties, and no self-respecting Angelino would be without one."

"That must have been the map book that the agent kept referring to today," Katrina said.

"So, James, your file says that you worked for a mining company in Zambia. What did you actually do?" Bob asked.

"I started with them when I got my degree," James replied. "I was in training for a while, then took over a production section as a first-line supervisor, with about thirty men. I progressed up the ladder to the next level and took over three more sections, so about 120 men in all. After we took some leave, I was offered the chance to start up a new surface mine, which we did, and I ran that until the mine was closed down due to falling copper prices. I took a buyout of my contract and came to work for J&B as an application engineer, then Hank moved me back to Africa to run J&B Africa in Jo'burg, which I did for two years, then we moved back, and I joined the marketing, product research group that became the mergers and acquisitions group."

"So, you've had P&L experience," Bob mused. "No manufacturing per se, but production experience of a different kind, and what did you do in Zambia, Katrina?"

"My folks ran a transportation business until they sold up and retired, then we moved to the new mine and I got a job selling industrial minerals. When we went back to Africa, I got a job as a financial analyst for a conglomerate in Jo'burg," she replied. "Since we came back, I've been working as a financial analyst for a large transport company."

"You'd probably have no problem getting a job out here, if you want to," Bob remarked. "So, James, how big is J&B Africa?"

"Sales of a little over 5 million Rand, mostly in the sale of machines for construction, parts and service, and a fee for managing the sale of larger mining machines, 50 people all told," James replied.

"How big was the mine?" Bob asked. "The mine you ran."

"We had 500 people, between the open pit and the concentrator," James replied. "It was essentially a cost centre, because we had no sales, we were just given production targets to meet."

"So, no legal department, no sales and marketing?" Bob asked.

"Not at the mine, no," James agreed. "At J&B Africa, we used an outside solicitor for legal issues, but we did have our own HR and accounting and sales and marketing."

"Makes sense," Bob said. "What do you know about Waterford?"

"Only what I've read in the Data Room and in public reports," James said. "I could list products, but I've not seen many of them in the flesh. I know that over the years, they picked up each of the companies and have kept them as separate companies, all wholly owned by Waterford Industries."

"I haven't seen any of the companies yet either," Bob said. "So, this week will be instructive. So, let's plan for wheels up at seven in the morning. Do you want me to just swing by and pick you up on the way?"

"I would appreciate that," James replied.

"No problem," Bob said. "So, sorry to drag James away for a couple of days, Katrina, but I'll have him back here late Thursday afternoon."

"I'll be busy for the next couple of days," she told him. "Just as long as James is here to look at a short list on Saturday."

"I think we can pretty much guarantee that," Bob said. "So, see you in the morning, James, bring safety boots if you have them."

"He seems nice enough," Katrina said to James when they got back to the hotel.

"At first blush," James replied. "I'll have a better sense by Thursday afternoon after we've been to the companies."

"At least you get to fly around in the company plane, so you're not trying to work out how to get to all those places," Katrina said. "Will they let you take pictures?"

"I don't know," he said. "I'll try and get some sales literature that has pictures of the products. Do you want to take the camera to take pictures of houses?"

"I don't think I need to," she replied. "I'm sure the flyers for each house will have pictures."

"Where did you look today?" he asked.

"Santa Ana, Garden Grove, and parts of Anaheim," she replied. "We could afford any that I saw today, but nothing appealed. I'll keep looking."

"How much can we afford?" he asked.

"Anything up to about $190,000," she replied.

"That's quite a jump from where we are now," he said.

"It is," she agreed. "But the mortgage differential makes it possible."

"Even though it runs out in five years?" he asked.

"In five years, maybe even less, I expect you'll be running Waterford," she said confidently. "So, I'm betting on pay increases that will cover the decline in the differential."

"You've got faith," he laughed.

"We've managed so far," she said. "And, I think I'll look for a job too, and that will help. I'm going to have a shower; the bath here is far too small for two."

"I'll come and watch," he said.

"I doubt you'll see much," she laughed. "The door will be all steamed up, like you."

James was in the lobby of the hotel at six-thirty the next morning, in time to see Bob arrive.

"On time, I see," Bob said.

"When you get cages to go underground, you learned to be on time, or have to explain yourself to the bosses if you missed the early cage," James said.

"So, what do we know about the Georgetown operation?" Bob asked.

"Mainly marine products," James replied. "Pipe laying and cable laying machinery, positioning winches, anchor winches, US Navy stuff, they also do some hoists for ocean drilling barges and rigs."

"Who's in charge?" Bob asked.

"Chap by the name of Paul Rose," James replied. "According to his file, he's a mechanical engineer from Georgia Tech, been with the company since he graduated. Started as a design engineer with Waterford Gear, the industrial gearbox company, then moved to Waterford Hoists as

17

engineering manager, then moved to Waterford Marine six years ago and took over as the President two years ago."

"The division is nicely profitable," Bob commented. "I wonder what the future holds for them."

"Well, deep ocean oil exploration is on the increase, the Cold War is still here, so we'll be spying on the Soviets for a while, and that means submarine cables," James commented.

"Okay, here we are," Bob said. They pulled up to the fixed base operator, and Chuck saw them.

"We're ready to go whenever you are, Mr. Decker," he said.

"Okay, bathroom break, then we'll be right out," Bob said.

The flight to Seattle took two hours and forty minutes, and they were given a wonderful view of Mount St. Helens and the destruction caused by the eruption two years earlier. From the airport, it was a drive of less than ten minutes to the factory, which was on the waterfront on the Duwamish Waterway.

"Hey, guys, welcome to Waterford Marine," Paul said when Bob and James arrived.

"Morning, Paul," Bob said.

"I've got my team ready," Paul said. "Maybe you'd like to take a look at the plant first, then we can get into presentations. What time do you want to leave?"

"We'd like to be out of here at a quarter of two," Bob said.

"That'll give us plenty of time," Paul said. "Let's just give you some hard hats. Did you bring safety boots, or do we need to get some?"

"We have," Bob said.

"Okay," Paul said. "Well, we do some fab here, a lot of machining, some gear cutting and of course assembly. Let's start in the fab shop."

"How much do you make here, and how much do you buy?" James asked.

"Depends on what it is," Paul replied. "Obviously, we buy ropes; we also buy sheaves, no point in us putting in our own foundry, cable drums we'll spec out and buy the casting from a foundry we normally deal with and cut our own grooves here, or we'll roll steel and fab up a drum. The steel work we'll fab up ourselves and the gear elements we make most, but buy some from the guys in Santa Ana."

"Is that done at market price or a transfer price?" Bob asked.

"Transfer price," Paul replied. "The guys in Santa Ana would rather just sell us stuff at market, but the finance guys in Long Beach told us that sales between companies would be done at transfer prices."

"What's that over there?" James asked.

"Pipe payer," Paul replied. "We buy tracks and track drives from Cat and modify them for our use."

"Who buys pipe layers?" James asked.

"Mostly oil guys," Paul replied. "But once in a while, some big water line needs to get put down, and we've sold a couple there."

"How much of this is Navy and how much commercial?" Bob asked.

"Most of the cable stuff is Navy, but occasionally we get something from the phone guys who need to lay or replace submarine cables. Nearly all the pipe layer stuff is commercial. Winches can go either way, unrep ship stuff is all Navy," Paul replied.

"Unrep?" James asked.

"Underway replenishment at sea," Paul explained. "Oilers, ammo boats, supply boats, all need to transfer stuff at sea, and that takes the right kind of equipment."

"Who are those winches for?" James asked, pointing to some large pieces of equipment being readied for shipment.

"Positioning winches for a drill barge," Paul explained. "Once you've started a hole, you want to stay as close as you can to right over it to avoid stressing the drill string. The trick to that is all in the control system and managing the tension of each winch to hold the barge where it needs to be."

"Many of the big winch drums look like the kind of things that J&B uses in draglines and shovels," James commented.

"Same thing really," Paul replied. "The biggest difference is the length of rope stored on the drum; these are more like mine hoist drums."

"That was going to be my next comment," James said. "The mine I worked at had winding engines with a few thousand feet of cable on them."

"Only real difference is cable size and control systems, were yours automatic?" Paul asked.

"No, we had winding engine drivers who sat at the top and drove the hoists; the hoists were all Ward Leonard, but thirty years ago had been steam," James replied.

"Mining hoists is a specialised market," Paul said. "There's already a field of suppliers, and it would take a bit to break into the market, and it's not really big enough to support another supplier."

"Your total sales are what, $40 million or so?" James asked.

"Last year, $41,200,750," Paul replied. "Net before tax, $5,750,000."

"And 500 or so people?" James asked.

"509 last count," Paul replied. James did the arithmetic and came up with just under $81,000 per employee, not bad, really.

The tour continued with Paul pointing out various items that would eventually finish up as parts of winches, drums or other things. The place was busy and in some ways, it reminded James of the J&B factory in Oak Creek, with the same smell of weld rod, the same huge bins of blue steel chips and the size of some of the drums. James did wonder if it would make any sense for Paul to bid on doing drums for J&B shovels and draglines, but saw issues of territorial protection being rampant there. Back in the offices, Paul took them to a conference room where his management team was waiting. Introductions were made, then Paul gave a brief overview of the company, its markets, its competitors and the prospects for the future. He then let his finance man take over, and they went through the results of the past five years, plus the projections for the next five. James noted that the bottom line numbers did match those that were presented in the data room. After finance came sales and marketing, then engineering, then manufacturing and finally human resources. It all made sense, provided that the sales projections held up. James looked to Bob and asked him if it was all right to ask questions. He got the nod to proceed.

"Paul, what happens if the offshore oil market dries up, or cuts back sharply in the next few years?"

"We've done some thinking about that," Paul said. "If we look at the projected sales and earnings, we've done some risk analysis, and we'd have to cut back on people by about fifteen per cent. We'd look for other markets that use the kind of equipment we could make, drums, hoists, anything like that, or even remotely like that. We're probably a little too early in the game, but if windmills for electricity ever really take off, we'd be well set to do the gear elements for wind power."

"I see," James said. "Conversely, what happens if the markets you serve grow a lot faster than you project?"

"We'd have to think carefully about expansion," Paul replied. "What we would want to avoid is over-expanding and then having a large empty factory to fill in the out years."

"This property is owned?" James asked.

"It is," Paul replied.

"Are there any plans by Seattle to do anything on this waterfront?" James asked.

"Not that we've heard of," Paul said. "I've seen nothing in the city plans or proposals that would affect us in any way."

"What about our suppliers, the people we buy sheaves from, the foundries?" James asked.

"We have three possible sources for sheaves and two for major castings, including brass and bronze in case we get a mine sweeper job," Paul replied.

"Should we buy any of them?" James asked.

"I wouldn't," Paul said. "Having two or three possibles is good, if we bought any one of them, I'm not sure their order book would stay as good, they also sell to competitors."

"Are they good at segregating work?" James asked.

"So far, no complaints," Paul said.

"Who in the Navy do we sell to?" James asked.

"Sea Systems Command," Paul replied. "They buy and we ship directly to the shipyard for new construction or to one of the Navy yards for refurb and repair jobs."

"And cable laying?" James asked.

"Same," Paul replied. "We work closely with Western Electric, who do the listening equipment."

"Who are your biggest competitors?" James asked.

"For positioning winches, Skagit," Paul replied. "For the other things, we have a list here."

"What do we do with waste?" James asked.

"Cuttings, offcuts and other metals we have a scrap dealer," Paul replied. "For cutting fluids and oils, we've got a licensed waste collection firm, and for office waste like paper and cardboard, we shred the paper, then we have a compactor to bale it, and it goes to the dump."

"Thank you, Paul," Bob said. "This has been most useful, thanks, guys, for the presentations and the information. Do you think we might have a few minutes with Paul?"

The others all left, and Paul looked to Bob for his questions.

"The guys in Long Beach, how much value do you get out of them?" Bob asked.

"Bill Willis handles any legal issues we get into," Paul replied. "We don't get much out of Ralph Thompson. The one time he came up here looking at a casting problem, he got it all wrong. Adam North stepped in and saved the day. Newman, he doesn't do a thing for us, spends all his time schmoozing the big defence contractors and his friends in the Air Force."

"Thank you, Paul," Bob said. "Let's turn the tables here, what can we tell you?"

"Any plans to split up the company and sell us off piecemeal?" Paul asked.

"Not that they've told me," Bob replied. "My remit is to make sure the whole company stays profitable, grow it if we can. We'll try and keep visits from James & Brown guys to a minimum, but there may be some. I think there are things to be learned here."

"I don't know that much about James & Brown, except that I have seen some excavators in the street," Paul said. "The main business is big mining machines?"

"James," Bob said.

"It is," James confirmed. "We make electric mining shovels, blast hole drills and walking draglines in the mining division, and backhoes, crawler cranes, rough terrain cranes, hydraulic excavators and truck cranes in the construction division. We've got factories in Oak Creek and Pittsburgh, and overseas subs in Brazil, South Africa, Australia and England. I ran the South African operation for a while."

"What did the South African sub do?" Paul asked.

"We sold construction machines, we managed the local sales contacts with the mining companies and organised erection services, we also sold parts and service," James explained.

"We sell some parts," Paul said. "But I wouldn't call it the major part of the business. Did you source everything from the States?"

"No, a lot of the construction machines we got from England, we had a few parts made locally, but not too many, I was reluctant to give too much away of our technology," James replied.

"I'd fixed up some lunch with the guys, do you have time?" Paul asked.

"Of course," Bob said. "We don't have to leave for a while."

Over lunch, James learned a little about Bob's background, and he learned more about the others on Paul's team. Most of them really only wanted to know what the plans for the company were, and would they be left alone or subjected to all kinds of corporate scrutiny. Bob assured them that there were no plans to sell off bits of the company, and that there would be no legions of people from Oak Creek second-guessing their every decision and move. There might be some changes in reporting styles for accounting, as their financials had to be rolled up into the Waterford financials, and similarly, the Waterford financials would be rolled up into the James & Brown financials.

Tulsa

"So, what do you think?" Bob asked James when they were on the plane on the way to Tulsa.

"It's an interesting business," James replied. "A lot is going to depend on the offshore oil industry."

"That's the way I see it," Bob agreed. "So, downvotes on Thompson and Newman from Paul."

"I asked the engineer about the issue that Paul referred to, which was a casting that had not been cooled properly to give it the properties they needed. Once they adjusted that, all the other castings were fine," James said. "The problem was that Thompson is not a metallurgist and doesn't understand castings. Adam North worked it out in one visit."

"I wonder how often they get asked if they make glass?" Bob said.

"I would think not that often," James said. "I imagine that most of the likely customers know who they, we, are and know what they make. It would only be a cold call from a potential glass customer who would be confused. My impression of the factory was ordered and as neat as such a place good be, not a lot of junk lying around."

"Do you have any numbers on lost times?" Bob asked.

"The last report I saw was half a million man-hours since the last reportable accident," James replied.

"Good questions, by the way," Bob commented. "So, what do you know about these guys in Tulsa?"

"It's the hoist business, all kinds of small hoists, a lot used for window cleaning on buildings and other industrial applications, sales of about $28,000,000 all told, twenty-four in the US, two in the UK and two in France," James replied.

"I can see that being a lawyer's dream or nightmare, depending on which side they're on," Bob commented. "I can see all kinds of issues around hoists used by cleaning and painting contractors. I doubt that they have the best safety records. Ever been to Tulsa?"

"I have," James replied. "Tulsa is the home of Unit Rig, who make large mining trucks, and I went there a couple of times to see them."

"Tulsa to me is oil and oilfield equipment," Bob commented.

"Can I get you gentlemen anything to drink?" Chuck asked as he came aft from the cockpit.

"Scotch and soda if you've got it," Bob said.

"Rum and Coke, please," James added.

"Coming right up," Chuck said. "Touch down in Tulsa at seven on the dot, any sense of when we might leave tomorrow?"

"Let me think about that, Chuck, I'll let you know by eight in the morning," Bob replied.

"No problem," Chuck said. "We've got some dinner on board. Let me know when you want to eat."

"Come to think of it, Chuck, tomorrow, let's do wheels up at twelve-thirty, that'll put us into Pueblo about twelve-thirty local time, that about right?" Bob asked.

"Right enough," Chuck confirmed. "It's only a short hop from Tulsa to Pueblo, hardly enough time to get to altitude before we're coming back down."

"Okay, then let's have lunch on board tomorrow, that should put us at the Pueblo company by one, do a wheels up out of Pueblo at five-thirty, that would put us into Albuquerque when?" Bob asked.

"Just after six," Chuck replied. "Even shorter hop there, just over the mountains."

"Let's plan for that," Bob said. "Could we do dinner now?"

"No problem, I'll just heat it up and be back in five minutes," Chuck said.

Dinner was beef, not too bad considering that it was airline food. The pilots sourced meals from essentially the same people who supplied the airlines, so choice was limited. They flew over the Rocky Mountains in Wyoming, not the dramatic peaks of Colorado, but some 13,000-foot mountains all the same in the Bridger Teton National Forest. They cut across a very small corner of Nebraska, then over nearly all of Kansas, before starting down into Tulsa. There was a rental car waiting for them, and Bob drove them to the hotel where they would be staying.

"Breakfast at six-thirty?" he suggested as he and James checked in.

"I'll be there," James replied. They went their separate ways, and once in his room, James called Katrina.

"Hi, honey," she said. "How was your day?"

"Interesting," he replied. "And yours?"

"One possible," she said. "Five more to look at tomorrow, three in Orange, one in Villa Park and one in Anaheim. I'll show you on the map when you come back."

"Can we afford the possible?" he asked.

"We can," she assured him. "It's pushing the limits of what we can afford, but it is still possible."

"A little scary, isn't it, committing to a huge mortgage?" he said.

"It is, but with the differential, we'll be fine for the first two or three years; after that, we'll see how we're doing," she said. "We had lunch in this great Mexican place in Orange, Moreno's, we should go there when we move in."

"What did you do for dinner?" he asked.

"I am going to eat in the restaurant here at the hotel," she replied. "And you?"

"We ate aeroplane food on the plane," he replied. "Wasn't too bad. Tomorrow we're going to see the place here in the morning, then in Pueblo in the afternoon, and we'll stay tomorrow night in Albuquerque, then fly back to Long Beach Thursday afternoon."

"That all sounds like a lot of hopping around," she laughed.

"It is, from here to Pueblo is only about an hour and from there to Albuquerque is even less, just over thirty minutes, so up down, up down," he said.

"I should let you go to bed," she said. "It must be getting late there."

"Not too late," he said. "We're two hours ahead of you, it's just gone eight."

"Well, go and have a bath or shower and get a good night's sleep," she instructed. "And be awake and alert for your session tomorrow, it sounds like a busy day. Love you, sleep well."

"Love you," he replied. Before going to sleep, James pulled out the notes he had made on Waterford Hoists during the due diligence and refreshed his memory of the people and the products.

James was seated for breakfast a few minutes before six-thirty and had just ordered when Bob joined him.

"Morning, James, ready for today?" Bob asked.

"Ready," James confirmed.

"Who's the boss here?" Bob asked.

"Chap by the name of Edward McIntosh," James replied. "Been in the business since it was acquired by Waterford ten years ago, rather the creative genius behind a lot of the hoists' concepts, based on all the patent filings."

"Okay, and the rest?" Bob asked.

"I've only had the HR files to read on the direct reports, not all glowing histories, but that probably means they're honest, if they were all glowing I'd wonder, three new people in the direct reports in the last two years, and before that two more, so seems to be to be a high turnover, maybe McIntosh is hard to get along with," James replied.

"Worth taking a look at," Bob said. "Keep that in mind when we talk to them, see if he lets anyone else answer questions. Paul was here for a while. Did he say anything?"

"Only that McIntosh runs a tight ship, whatever that means," James replied.

"When you ran J&B Africa, would you say you ran a tight ship?" Bob asked.

"In the sense that I tried to make sure that we all had the same aims and goals," James replied. "I didn't interfere with the various parts of the company, left them to it, but made sure that we were all on the same page as we say in the US."

"And on the mine?" Bob asked.

"I was given a staff, some of whom I would have liked to change, but again, once the goals were set and we all understood what we needed to do, I left the concentrator chap alone, while I ran the mine itself," James replied. "We had more problems with higher-ups than with our own people. We had one chap who interfered and messed things up for a while. Fortunately, we recovered, and the main office in Kitwe told him not to come to Mkushi any more and not to issue directives without first clearing them through the Superintendent, who dealt with technical issues."

"Sounds like fun," Bob said. "So, ready to go and see what hoists look like?"

The factory was a short drive from the hotel, situated among other industrial enterprises, most of which were related to the oil industry. They found the hoist business easily enough, identified by the scissor lift hoists in the yard.

"Good morning," Bob said as they entered the foyer. "We're here to see Edward McIntosh."

"Oh, Mr Decker, isn't it? Ed is expecting you, let me show you in," the receptionist said. She led the way to a conference room where Ed, they had just learned Ed, not Edward, and his staff were already gathered.

"Good morning," Bob said. "I'm Bob Decker, and this is James Martin. We're here to learn a little about the hoist business."

"Thanks for coming," Ed said. "We're all a little anxious about what's going to happen to us."

"I can assure you that there are no plans to sell off the business or send armies of accountants and others from James & Brown to second-guess you," Bob said. "James & Brown, as you probably know, is more focused on large mining and construction machines, which is where their expertise lies. We're here to learn."

"Okay," Ed said. "Well, I'm sure you know the basics about the hoist business, we make scissor lifts, capstan hoists, swing stages and other access equipment under the brand name of HighRise, we've got the place here and a small sub in France and another in England and we've got a captive insurance sub in the Grand Cayman, a good chunk of our operating expenses are insurance premiums and retentions."

"I suppose that's inevitable given the nature of the business," Bob remarked.

"You wouldn't believe the things people do," Ed said. "No matter how much we try and build into the systems to make them idiot proof there's always one out there who will find a way to surprise you."

"Do you sell directly or through distributors?" James asked.

"A little of both," Ed replied. "We mostly sell direct in those places where the demand is really high from our own outlets, for the smaller cities, we've signed up with a national equipment rental company. Educating them has been a challenge. We've got a strong business in the engineered solutions, so we'll fix up a permanent system in a new building and work directly with the architect and builder on those projects."

"How much of the product do we make here, and how much do we buy?" James asked.

"We make most of it here," Ed replied. "We buy electric motors, batteries, diesel engines, hydraulic pumps and valves for the scissor lifts, but for the hoists, we pretty much make it all, except for the motors, which we buy. The swing stages and other work platforms we also make up here. We buy ropes and hardware and other readily available common items, like wheels and tyres for the scissor lifts."

"Do you think we might take a look around?" Bob asked.

"Sure, I'll give you the tour and we'll meet back here in an hour, okay, guys?" Ed said. He handed out hard hats and led the way to the factory.

"I thought we'd start at the shipping and receiving dock and work backwards," Ed suggested. "That lot over there is going to a high-rise in LA, that lot another one in Chicago, they're both custom systems designed for the buildings that are now going up. There'll be a permanent mount on rails on the roof and channels in the mullions that the swing stage will run down."

"Who does the actual installation?" James asked.

"The contractor, but we'll send one of our engineers out when they tell us they're ready to start," Ed replied. "Even if the installation drawings and instructions are as simple as we can make them, there are times when the contractor screws it up."

"I recall from some of the materials I saw before that we rent hoists and swing stages as well as sell them. How do we manage the proper use of them?" James asked.

"We send out each rental package with new hardware and step-by-step instructions, using mainly only pictures, so that even a ten-year-old could put it together," Ed said. "By doing that, we've dropped the accident rate a lot, and we're still looking at ways to make it more idiot-proof."

"You've got a pretty jaundiced view of your customers," Bob commented.

"I suppose I have," Ed said. "I like the business, I love the products, and it bugs me when people can't use them properly. We make really great things, equipment to make people's lives easier. Why not read the manual and use it properly? It's your life hanging on the end of the rope."

"It's like buying a Christmas present for your kid," Bob said. "Some assembly required. Who reads the instructions?"

"You're right," Ed agreed. "Anyway, that pile over there is a returned rental package, worse than usual. They usually come back with most bits, often covered in paint or dirt, so we pull them all apart, run the structures back through sandblasting, cleaning and painting, overhaul the hoists and put the package back together. Moving along, this is where we do the final assembly and where we pull together the custom packages."

"In a custom package, how much unique customisation is there?" James asked.

"Depends how quickly we can get to the architect and engineer," Ed said. "If we get to them at the start of the project, then we can help them spec out the mullions and the roof rails; if we're called in after the fact, then we have to engineer it to fit what's there."

"How do you manage risk?" James asked.

"Our safety engineer looks at every way he can to stick his hands where they don't belong, to not rig the hoists right and we then take that information and build it into our designs, we've taken a leaf out of the aviation industry and essentially send out hoist worthiness directives if we spot something that we'd never thought of before," Ed explained. "It's a challenge, people seem to be incredibly creative when it comes to hurting themselves."

"Which of our lawyers do you use the most?" James asked.

"Greg Norman," Ed replied. "He does most of our stuff, and he also handles the loader business, the scissor lifts and conveyor loaders that we make for the airlines. Similar issues in both."

"What does Charles Newman do for you?" James asked.

"Not a blamed thing," Ed replied. "All we get is a back-charge for him. He's never even been here."

"And Ralph Thompson?" James asked.

"Nothing useful," Ed said. "We had a problem with a capstan drive once, and Thompson came out, poked around a bit, then handed the problem over to Adam North, who worked out why the motor was overheating. Before you ask, Hank White helps us a lot with HR stuff, and Mike McKane just tots up the numbers at the corporate level."

"You have a fabrication shop here?" James asked.

"Sure do," Ed said. "That's the next stop." He led the way into a building that had metalwork of all types going on, from cutting of aluminium and steel plate to forming and welding, and a machining centre that was full of drums, gears and other components.

"What's the reject rate like with the machined parts?" James asked.

"Less than 5%," Ed said. "We've been working it down and to really knock it down, I'm going to put in a capital request for a new machining centre and a new gear cutter, ones that have tighter specs than these old machines we have."

"Can the rejects be reworked, or do they go to scrap?" James asked.

"Mostly we can rework them," Ed said. "It's not often we have to chuck something, unless there was a latent defect in the part blank, then we hit up the supplier for a new piece."

"The aluminium platforms, I assume, are the swing stages, and the steel parts go to the scissor lifts?" James asked.

"Sure do," Ed confirmed. "Want to keep the suspended load as small as possible, so stages, rails all aluminium, not so important on the scissor lifts, there we want a low centre of gravity, so steel frame, running gear and lift mechanisms are good."

"What happens to actual scrap, cuttings and other waste?" James asked.

"We've got a dealer we work with who takes it all, steel, aluminium, oils, cardboard, paper, you name it," Ed replied.

"And it goes where?" Bob asked. "I don't want us to land up with our name attached to a Superfund Site."

"Incinerator, metal recycler, water treatment, we're a small contributor compared to the oil guys," Ed replied. "I've checked them out a couple of times, and I know the EPA has, and they've been clean."

"Might we meet the rest of your staff now?" Bob asked.

"Sure, we're just about at the end of the tour, let's go and join them," Ed said.

Back in the conference room, Ed introduced his staff and then turned things over to James Verville, his finance man.

"Okay, sales last year were $27,850,000, next before tax, $3,335,000, up from the year before. We expect this year to be slightly up on last year, but not by a lot," Verville started.

"Cash positive?" James asked.

"We were," Verville confirmed. "I have the year-end income statement and balance sheets here for the US company and for the Brit and French subs." He passed copies over, and James noted that it was the same that he had seen in the data room. Good to know that all was apparently above board with the offering memorandum. Bob and James asked questions about material and labour costs, then got into the overhead. As Ed had pointed out before, there was quite a figure for insurance premiums and retentions. Verville also had copies of the captive insurance company in Grand Cayman.

"The legal fees that Greg Norman incurs, those are charged directly to you?" Bob asked.

"They are, we use proportionately more of his time than the others, so we pay for his time, by the hour," Verville explained. "We also use an outside firm for court appearances, and we have used some private investigators when we get the feeling that we're being shaken down. It hasn't happened often, but it has happened."

Questions and answers continued until Bob thanked him and asked if they could talk about the markets served, competitors, and projected growth, both of existing markets and new opportunities. Ed asked Greg Nauman, his sales and marketing man, to take over.

Greg took them through the markets served, projections for the coming years and then who the competition was and how HighRise stacked up against them. To James, it was in many ways similar to the construction machine business he had run in South Africa. Bob asked most of the questions, and James was surprised by his depth of knowledge of the industry. Greg also talked about the differences in the British and French markets and how their approach to selling varied by country. At least they were sensitive to that and did not just have one solution to every problem. Next up was engineering, then manufacturing, followed by quality, then safety. Safety was quite a long discussion as they talked about the risks of the business and what steps they were taking to mitigate that risk. As Ed had commented, a lot of it involved dreaming up bizarre ways that people could stick their hands where they did not belong, despite all kinds of warning labels, and simply not following the simplest of instructions when setting up hanging swing stages, or the total lack at times of common sense. The French and British business tended to have fewer lawsuits, but then the legal systems in those countries were quite different to the US and if one brought a civil suit and lost, the loss usually came with a bill for expenses for the other side, something that was rare in the US. It did have the effect of reducing civil suits to those that were possibly viable and removed most of the frivolous suits. Last on the docket was the human resource manager, who talked about employees, turnover, quits and terminations. He also talked about the attempts that had been made over the years to unionise the workforce. None had succeeded largely because HighRise paid fairly and offered good benefits. The managers who had left in recent times had all gone on to bigger and better things: Paul to the marine operation and the others to various oil field companies that proliferated in Tulsa. As far as Ed knew, none had gone to competitors, and he made a point of trying hard not to recruit from competitors. His view of that practice was that it devalued the product because customers saw a sales rep in January who represented one company and who extolled the virtues of their

33

products, only to have the same man come back in March and extol the virtues of another company, so what was the customer to think?

At eleven-thirty, Bob turned the tables and asked if anyone had questions for them. There were some, and like with the marine company, they were mainly along the lines of, will we be sold. Bob was able to assure them that there were no plans to sell off any bits of the company, provided, of course, that they stayed profitable and cash-positive. He also assured them that they would not be invaded by hordes of James & Brown people all wanting to tell them how they should run their business, but did make the comment that they might want to look at the distributor network that James & Brown had for its construction machinery line and decide if there would be any benefit to them to use that network. James provided the contact names and telephone numbers for that, and Ed said that he would look into it. Bob made the same comment he had made in Seattle, that there were things to be learned at their operation, so they might get a few visitors.

Bob thanked Ed and his team for their time, and he and James left for the airport. They were on board and ready to go at twelve-thirty, and Chuck handed them two cold lunch plates to hang onto before they even took off. As he explained, they would be busy in the cockpit as the flight was so short.

"So, impressions of the HighRise business?" Bob asked James as the plane sped down the runway and lifted off.

"I would agree that Ed runs a tight ship," James replied. "But I didn't get the impression that he stifles input from his people."

"I would concur," Bob said. "I was watching him closely while his guys were making their pitches, and I got the impression that it was not scripted and that he let them say what they really thought."

"Downvotes on Thompson and Newman," James commented.

"I can understand that," Bob said. "Newman with his supposed contacts with the government wouldn't be of much value to them, if any, and it sounds to me more and more that Thompson isn't really the troubleshooter that we were led to believe he is."

"How much similarity will there be between the HighRise company and the Waterford loaders?" James asked.

"I would say that with the scissor lifts used for containers, there would be a lot," Bob commented. "For the conveyor loaders, less, but still some of the same safety issues with guys sticking their hands where they don't belong."

"I wonder how much of the airline fleet uses containers and how much loose bags," James said.

"Well, the bigger planes like the 747, 767, DC-10 and L 1011 will all use containers, but the smaller ones like the 757, 737, 727, DC-9 and others will use conveyor loaders," Bob suggested.

"So, maybe the big question for these chaps is where do they see the fleets going?" James suggested.

"I'd agree with that," Bob said. "One thing about the marine company and HighRise that I noted, no women in the management ranks."

"I suppose if I think about it, there are none in the James & Brown executive office or the tier below that," James said.

"I'd have thought to at least find an HR person or an accountant," Bob said. "I know finding women engineers is a challenge, but I think we should look a little harder than maybe these guys have been doing in the past."

"I'll make a note of that," James said. "I also thought that both companies are pretty lily white."

"True," Bob agreed. "Let's face it, we all go with what we're comfortable with and for some, the idea that someone black, Asian or Hispanic could be as good a bet as someone white is a tough one."

"My experience in Zambia showed me that it doesn't matter what colour you are, there are those who are good and those who are not," James commented.

"Were they many blacks in the senior management where you worked?" Bob asked.

"Not yet," James replied. "The colonial government had done nothing to educate the local population, and it was only after Independence in 64 that significant numbers of students were sent to schools around the world to get degrees. For first and second-level supervisors, they were mostly black Zambians, and I knew of three third-level managers who were line managers, not HR people."

"Well, we should take a look at the structure of the company and get involved with hiring decisions for the top levels and see if we can't get some diversity," Bob said. "It may have to start at the first level, but it should start."

"It's interesting," James said. "My sister-in-law is a chemical engineer and worked for the explosives factory in South Africa. When she first started, she got no support, but over time, people began to realise that she could really help them, and she got a lot of support."

"What does she do now?" Bob asked.

"When she had her daughter, she left the explosives factory and now does bookings for travel, I think with a view that she and my brother will start up their own safari business," James replied.

"That sounds like an adventure," Bob said. "Good luck to them."

"Ten minutes to landing," Chuck called back from the cockpit.

The Pueblo Memorial Airport catered mainly to general aviation, but it did have rental cars and other services available. Bob took care of transport to the company by asking the manager of the fixed-based operator if he would just drop them off at the company. It was questionable whether it was worth renting the car, as they could have probably walked to the factory, which was in a small industrial estate just west of the airport. Waterford Ground Support was easy to spot; there were scissor lifts and conveyor loaders in the yard, visible from the road.

"What can you tell me about these guys?" Bob asked James as they stood outside for a few minutes before going in.

"The company was an acquisition of a small start-up that decided to go into the ground support equipment business to service airlines," James replied. "Chap by the name of Nick Jarman was inspired by the inventions of Joe Cochrane and started up his own company. I was told by some of the Waterford people that Joe Cochrane was the chap who first came up with the idea of the conveyor loader."

"Sales of how much?" Bob asked.

"Thirty million, give or take," James replied. "Four hundred and two people all told."

"Company manager?" Bob asked.

"Chap by the name of Morris Whitaker," James replied. "I've never met him."

"Well, maybe we should go and see what this place is like," Bob said.

"Are you Mr Decker and Mr Martin?" a receptionist by the name of Kathy asked.

"We are," Bob replied.

"Morris is expecting you," she said. "Please come with me." She led the way to a conference room where the management team was assembled, and by the look of it, had just finished lunch.

"Mr Decker?" Morris asked.

"The same," Bob said. "Please just call me Bob. This is James Martin, he's a transplant from James & Brown."

"Can we get you some lunch?" Morris asked.

"We're fine," Bob replied. "We ate on the plane, coffee would be nice though."

"Kathy?" Morris asked.

"Of course," she replied. "How would you like it?"

"Just black, thanks," Bob said.

"Some milk or cream with mine, please," James added.

"Well, this is Waterford Ground Support," Morris said by way of introduction. "We make a line of ground support equipment for the airlines, lifts, loaders and trailers. Sales last fiscal year of thirty mil and a hundred and fifty thou, net before tax, one mil five hundred thou."

"Do you think we could tour the factory and then come back and review things?" Bob suggested.

"Sure thing, you're the boss," Morris said. "Okay, guys, meet back here in an hour or so."

"Your coffee," Kathy said when she returned.

"Do we own this facility?" Bob asked as he sipped his coffee.

37

"Lock, stock and barrel," Morris said. "We were one of the early people in this development. We've got ten acres here, hundred and forty thousand square feet under roof, so plenty of room to expand."

"We saw some equipment in the yard," Bob commented.

"That's all waiting on disposition by the Material Review Board," Morris said. "The customer wouldn't accept them as built and wanted us to fix some items."

"Expensive items to fix?" Bob asked.

"Expensive enough," Morris said.

"May we take a tour and see?" Bob asked, putting down his coffee cup.

"Sure thing," Morris said.

The first impression that James had when they walked out into the factory was one of chaos and disorganisation. He presumed there was order somewhere, but it was hard to see.

"This is where we assemble everything," Morris said. "We've scissor lift loaders over there, conveyors over there, stairs here and container trailers over there."

"How much do we make and what do we buy?" Bob asked.

"We buy hydraulic cylinders and pumps, plus the diesel engines to run the machines," Morris replied. "We buy steel rollers and motors for the live decks and the basic elements of the control panels."

"Those machines over there, they seem to have been sitting a while," James commented.

"We had a couple of issues with them, so we pulled them out of line to let others go by," Morris replied. "We'll get back to them as soon as we can."

"How are deliveries?" Bob asked.

"For the most part, we can deliver on time," Morris said. "Sometimes it takes extra effort, tiger teams and overtime to get them finished."

The tour continued with, at least to James, more chaos and confusion until they finished back at the offices. The rest of the team was already there, apparently all sitting in sullen silence, or at least that is what it felt like when they joined them.

The meeting was interesting, James noted, the byplay between Morris and his managers bespoke a lack of trust and ill feeling. It was a very uncomfortable session because each time one of the managers started to say something that might indicate all was not well, Morris interrupted and took over. The numbers all matched the numbers that James had seen in the data room, and those numbers were less than stellar. It was quite a different session from the ones they had had with the marine operation and the HighRise team; those had been very cohesive teams with a common message, this one was fractured, to say the least. James could see that Bob was getting frustrated, but he controlled it well and gave away nothing to Morris and his people. When it came the turn of Bob to answer questions, they were the same as the other two: would they be sold and could they expect hordes of accountants and auditors from James & Brown. Bob assured them on all fronts that things would remain the same, for now, but that they might get one or two visitors looking to learn from them. When asked about help from Long Beach, Morris actually sang the praises of both Thompson and Newman, which surprised James. The meeting finally ended at five, and Bob thanked Morris and his team for their time, and then asked Morris would mind just dropping them back at the airport. Morris said he would arrange it and asked Kathy to do it for him.

"Thank you, Kathy," Bob said as she dropped them off.
"I hope you'll come again," she said. "We could use a little direction, please don't let Morris know I said that, but we're all at each other's throats because there's no clear direction."
"We won't," Bob promised. "And we will be back."
"Good," she said. "I like working here, but it could be so much better if we all were working together instead of everyone trying to protect their back for when Morris is looking for someone to blame when things don't go right."
"Thank you for telling us this," Bob said. "We will not betray your confidence."

"Thanks," she said. "Well, here we are, have a good flight."

"Thank you," Bob said. "Hopefully we'll see you again before too long."

"I think dinner tonight to talk about the day," Bob said to James as they boarded the plane for the short hop to Albuquerque.

"If you guys would stay buckled in for the flight," Chuck said. "We'll be up and down so quickly. Sorry, no drinks or snacks on this hop."

"Of course," Bob said. "First impressions, James?"

"Whitaker needs to go," James said. "It was apparent to me that the team lacks any cohesiveness, and Whitaker is clearly not a leader."

"You don't think we can help him?" Bob asked.

"I don't," James said. "I may be wrong, but in my view, he should be replaced, the sooner the better."

"We'll talk about it more at dinner," Bob said. "Ever been to New Mexico before?"

"When I first joined James & Brown, I came out here to look at a mine site," James replied. "We flew into Albuquerque, then drove to Gallup and then to the mine site."

"Was the trip successful?" Bob asked.

"It was," James replied. "We sold some machines to the mining company."

"Good to know," Bob said. "I like the Rockies; always struck me as very dramatic. Do you ski?"

"We tried a couple of times, we prefer cross country to downhill," James replied.

"I like to ski, my wife and I usually drive up to Flagstaff and stay there," Bob said. "Nice place, and it's a fairly short drive up there."

"There wasn't much in Wisconsin the way of real hills, and obviously none in Zambia or South Africa," James commented. "We started cross-country skiing when we lived in Cudahy. There was a park next door, and in the winter it was a good way to get outside."

"We'll be landing in ten minutes. Please make sure you're buckled in," Chuck said over the intercom.

James was given the task of renting a car and driving them to the hotel, and Bob suggested dinner at seven.

"So, James, you were quick to say that we should replace Whitaker," Bob said as they sat down for dinner. "That's a very snap judgement. You don't see a chance to develop him as a manager?"

"I think the place will fall apart if something isn't done soon," James replied. "It may seem a little drastic, but I don't think we have time."

"Sadly, you may be right," Bob said. "Of the management team, did you see any of them who could actually run the place?"

"That's a little hard to gauge on one visit and just a few hours to talk to them all," James replied. "But none of them struck me as a natural leader who could take charge of the situation."

"So, we go outside?" Bob asked.

"We could," James agreed. "Or we could raid James & Brown."

"You have someone in mind?" Bob asked.

"Bill Evans, we went through the Executive MBA program together; he's a manufacturing type, and I think he'd do a good job with Pueblo."

"So, do I call Hank or do you?" Bob laughed. "He might not like us raiding James & Brown; he may have plans for this Bill Evans."

"That's possible," James agreed. "But this is a P&L job, it might be small compared to James & Brown, but there aren't many true P&L jobs in the parent, let's face it most jobs are cost centres."

"That's true," Bob agreed. "You'd have to be running all of the mining or construction divisions or one of the overseas subs to get complete P&L responsibility."

"I'd agree with that," James confirmed.

"Do you think Evans would go for it?" Bob asked.

"I can ask," James said. "Question is, do we run it by Hank Miller first, or test the waters with Bill and see if he's even interested?"

"Call Evans and see if he's interested, then I'll call Hank and get his blessing to approach Evans officially," Bob said. "If he takes the job, would he be able to assess the others and tell us if we keep them all or replace a few more?"

"I think he'd be able to tell us if he can pull the company together and make something of it in a week or two," James said. "Spending real time with each of them would give him the chance to size them up."

"Okay, call Evans tomorrow morning before we meet with the structures guys and see what he says, then I'll call Hank," Bob said. "So what about the business itself?"

"Not performing as well as it could or should," James replied. "But that's not surprising given the amount of scrap and rework and the number of people they have, $75,000 revenue per employee is a little low."

"How much of that is built into the union contract?" Bob asked.

"Some, I grant you," James replied. "But not that much, if they made things right the first time, they wouldn't need the number of people, plus their inventory would go down as their work in progress would go down, that would free up cash, probably at least as much as they might need for some better tooling."

"We'll work on that," Bob said. "Or should I say you will, whoever we stick in there, I want you to stay on top of them and see if we made any measurable improvements. Now, what do you know about the structures business?"

"They make access doors, engine nacelle cowl doors, almost anything that's made of aluminium," James replied. "As I read from the data room stuff, lots of sheet metal work, forming, shaping, machining and riveting."

"Who runs it?" Bob asked.

"Chap by the name of David Pratt," James replied.

"You've done your homework," Bob commented.

"The names are familiar to me," James said. "I saw them often enough when I was going through the offering memorandum."

"James, are you a citizen of the US?" Bob asked.

"No," James replied.

"We must get you into the process so that you can become one; you can't get a security clearance unless you are," Bob said.

"What do I have to do?" James asked.

"Get the appropriate papers and file them, then we'll see if Chuck Newman actually knows anyone in Washington and get the application fast-tracked. Meanwhile, you need to brush up on your US history, constitution and system of government. I'd get Jim Beatty to help you," Bob said. "When we get back, ask Megan to get the forms for you and set up some time with Jim for Citizenship 101."

"I'll do that," James said.

"Okay, well, breakfast at seven?" Bob asked.

"I'll be here," James promised.

James went to his room and called Katrina.

"So, how was Tulsa and Pueblo?" she asked.

"The Tulsa place is pretty well run, but Pueblo is a *gemors*," he replied.

"So, what does that mean?" she asked.

"Someone new fairly quickly," he said. "I'm going to give Bill Evans a call in the morning and see if he's interested in making a move, then Bob can call Hank Miller and get an official blessing to raid James & Brown. Pueblo itself is close to the mountains, not too far from Denver; believe it or not, there's a steel mill there."

"Why there, was there coal or iron ore there?" she asked.

"Not just there, but there was coal from a place called Trinidad, which is not too far south from there, and iron ore from another place not too far away, the steel mill was there to make rails for the railway companies," he explained.

"I know you've flown to Albuquerque before. What's it like?" she asked.

"We could live here," he said. "There are mountains close by, it's dry, but does have the Rio Grande River. I hope we'll see a little more of Albuquerque itself tomorrow and see if I really like the city."

"Funny name that, Albuquerque," she remarked. "I wonder what it means."

"I'll ask someone at the factory tomorrow and see if I can get a story for you," he promised. "I'll be back tomorrow afternoon, so how has the house hunting been?"

"Busy," she said. "We looked at more today, and I've changed my list of possibles a bit and have three that I think we should look at again. Angela took me for lunch today at this shopping mall, South Coast

Plaza, very fancy, makes Southridge look pretty second-rate. We looked at a couple of houses near there too, but too expensive."

"I suppose it would be easy to see a house, really like it and then try and talk yourself into affording it, even though you really can't," he said.

"It would," she agreed. "But I'm staying within the limits we set ourselves. We could get a nice place for less than we budgeted, but it would be quite a long commute for you in the mornings on the 91, to the 55, then the 22 to the 405."

"I'm sorry, what?" James asked.

"Oh, I'm getting to know the numbers of the freeways and from Corona, where one of the cheaper houses was, you'd have to take the Riverside freeway, the 91, west to the Costa Mesa freeway, the 55, then go south and then pick up the Garden Grove freeway, the 22, to the San Diego freeway, the 405 that would take you to Long Beach," she explained.

"Your realtor lady, Angela, looks like she's working hard for us," James said.

"She's definitely earning her money," Katrina replied. "She picks me up about nine, we tour houses, have lunch, tour houses, then she drops me back here at about four, must be a long day for her. I wish you were here."

"I'll be back tomorrow," he said. "The other two factories are local, so we can do those by driving."

"I wonder when Bob leaves for the weekend," she said.

"Probably sometime between five and six," James guessed. "We'll find out tomorrow. So, Saturday we'll look at houses, what shall we do on Sunday before we fly back?"

"Go somewhere quiet and have a nice breakfast," she suggested.

"I like that idea," he said. "Ask Angela where would be nice to go."

"I'll do that," Katrina said. "And I'll also find out where we can buy what we'll need."

"So, from what you've seen so far, could you live here?" he asked.

"In LA, absolutely," she replied. "There's a lot of people, far more than even Jo'burg, but you can get away from them, and the sun shines a lot."

"It'll be different," he said. "You remember how we used to say only in the US, now I'll bet we'll have another list, only in California."

"I'm sure we will," she agreed. "There's one I heard about already. There's this little town called Villa Park, it's right in the middle of the City of Orange, but they have a Christmas boat parade, apparently, they dress up their boats with lights and then tow them around the streets."

"Genuine?" he asked.

"Genuine, *ou* man," she confirmed.

"That is a first," he laughed.

"I should let you get to bed and get some sleep," she said. "Love you."

"Love you," he replied. "I'll see you tomorrow."

Albuquerque

Early in the morning, James called Bill Evans.

"Hey, James," Bill said. "How's California?"

"I haven't seen much of it yet," James replied. "I'm in New Mexico at the moment, touring the various Waterford companies."

"So, what's up?" Bill asked.

"I was wondering if you'd have an interest in running the ground support company, which makes scissor lifts and conveyor loaders for the airlines. It's in Pueblo and needs someone to actually lead it," James explained.

"Sounds interesting," Bill said. "How big?"

"Thirty million in sales, 402 people, it's a president position, total P&L and balance sheet responsibility," James replied.

"Definitely interested," Bill said. "Can you send me anything on it and fix up a trip sometime to look it over?"

"I'm sure we can," James said. "Bob Decker needs to talk to Hank Miller first and get his approval for us to raid James & Brown."

"What's the main problem?" Bill asked.

"Lack of trust all around, too much rework and scrap, no common goals in the company," James replied.

"And the current guy?" Bill asked.

"The sooner he's gone, the better," James said. "And I didn't see any of the managers that bowled me over, so my view is we have to go outside Waterford."

"How did it get that way?" Bill asked.

"Not sure," James admitted. "I'm going to have to do some digging with the HR bloke in Long Beach and read through his annual reviews again and see if I can't pick up on something I missed in the data room."

"Okay, James, let me know what you can as soon as possible and let me know when I can fly out and take a look," Bill said.

"Thanks, Bill," James said. "I'll talk to you soon."

"Evans is interested," James told Bob when they met for breakfast.

"Good, I'll talk to Hank after we've seen these guys today," Bob said. "So, remind me what does the structures company make?"

"We make aircraft parts out of metals, aluminium, steel and titanium," James replied. "A lot of metal forming, machining and riveting, mainly for aircraft doors, commercial and military, weapons rails, external stores racks, main deck floor panels, cargo handling systems and some other pieces, some that are euphemistically called stores racks, but are just racks for carrying bombs."

"As I recall, about $30 million in sales, what's the guy's name that runs the place?" Bob asked.

"David Pratt," James replied. "Texas A&M mechanical engineer, been here since graduating, moved his way up slowly, probably close to retirement age."

"So, no other parts of the company?" Bob asked.

"Not that I read," James replied.

"We need to make sure our managers have been in more than one operation," Bob said. "Make a note of that."

"I will," James said.

"Get a list if you can find one, or build one, of all the graduates we have in the company, where they went, what their degrees are and what their progressions have been since they joined us," Bob instructed.

"I'll do that," James said.

"Okay, let's go and see the guys here," Bob said.

They checked out of the hotel and drove to the factory, which was a little south of the airport and west of the sprawling Kirtland Air Force Base. David Pratt knew they were coming, so he was in the lobby of the building to greet them.

"Hi, Bob Decker and James Martin?" he asked.

"The same," Bob replied.

"Dave Pratt, come on through," Pratt invited. He led them to a room close to the entrance that clearly served as a meeting room. It had a large table and chairs all around, and had a projection screen and he had a projector already set up, and there were several others already in the room.

"Coffee?" Dave asked.

"Thanks," Bob replied. He got himself some coffee and handed James a cup as well. "So, Dave, introduce us if you would," Bob said.

Dave went around the room and identified everyone and what they did. Then he launched into a summary of the business, the major customers and the programs they were currently working on. That led to questions and answers and brought in some of the others in the room. After an hour, Bob asked if they could take a break and perhaps walk around the factory to see the items they had been talking about. Pratt produced hard hats and took them on a tour. What struck James was the general appearance of chaos. If he looked at something long enough, there was some kind of logic to it all, but it was not apparent.

"What are these red-tagged items?" Bob asked.

"They're waiting for a customer MRB to decide whether they can accept them," Dave replied. "They usually do, so it's just a matter of time before they're gone."

"There seem to be quite a few," Bob remarked.

"Well, most of this is for military customers, and the DCAS guy is really picky; he complains about the slightest blemish or paint finish that he can't see his face in," Dave said, referring to the military representative who covered them.

"Is he a resident inspector or itinerant?" Bob asked.

"I guess he's itinerant," Dave said. "He lives here in Albuquerque and comes when we tell him that there's something for him to pass."

"What's his pass rate?" Bob asked.

"About 40% first time," Dave replied. "Usually, as I said, things can be resolved and we only scrap about one or two per cent."

"How much inventory value is sitting waiting?" Bob asked.

"Well, we're not really worried by that because we can progress bill on the government programs, so there's not much left to bill when it's red-tagged," Dave said, sidestepping the question.

"Humour me, how much?" Bob asked.

"I'd have to check with Luther," Dave said. "I don't carry that kind of information around with me."

"Revenues are $30 million?" Bob asked.

"And change," Dave confirmed. "We're looking at a couple of big programs right now for engine nacelles that could drive that up quite a bit."

"Do you have the room?" James asked, looking around at the jumble of pieces, parts, assemblies and materials scattered about.

"We'll make room," Dave said confidently.

"Do you have enough people?" James asked.

"We might have to hire a few more," Dave replied. "But, I'm sure we can find some."

"And net before tax?" Bob asked.

"Two million and change," Dave said. "We had some odd one-time expenses that impacted us."

The tour continued, and they ended back at the meeting room and waited a couple of minutes for the rest of the team. Dave then asked Luther Harris, his finance man, to go through the numbers, including the breakdown of the work-in-process inventory. Even Luther had a difficult time answering the question that Bob had posed on the factory floor, and could only hazard a guess as to the value of stuff that was sitting waiting for someone to make a decision. As with the other companies they had gone to, they heard from all the managers, then gave them the opportunity to ask questions, and they were the usual ones about plans to sell off their operation. Bob assured them all that there were no deep, dark plans to break up the company, but pointed out that financial performance was important. Dave had obviously talked to Morris Whitaker and had things set up, and had coached his team on what to ask. By noon, both Bob and James were ready to move on, so they thanked Dave Pratt and his team for their time and drove back to the airport.

"I asked the pilots to be ready to go at twelve-thirty," Bob told James on the way to the airport. "So, first impressions of this place?"

"It's another mess," James said. "I don't understand why there's so much sitting waiting for acceptance, and the chaos of the place makes me wonder if they can find anything, and the one-time expenses excuses seem thin to me. I would imagine that there's always something that crops up that could be considered a one-time expense."

"And Pratt?" Bob asked.

"If it were my decision, I'd be looking for someone new," James said.

"Another snap judgment," Bob laughed. "But I concur, we need two new managers, and we need them quickly. Anyone else from James & Brown come to mind?"

"There are a couple, my choice would be Phil Johnson, Phil was another of us in the Executive MBA program and has been working in the Construction Machinery Division assembling machines," James suggested.

"How well do you know him?" Bob asked.

"Not as well as Bill Evans, but well enough to be certain that he'd do a better job than Pratt," James said.

"You have no compassion?" Bob asked.

"When it comes to this, no," James said. "When I worked on the mine, I saw what hanging on to people who were out of their depth could do. A friend of mine was killed because the manager two levels above him was incompetent and made an ill-advised decision."

"How many levels were there in this mine?" Bob asked.

"From first-line supervisor to the general manager of the mine, eight all told," James replied.

"How many people?" Bob asked.

"Probably about 15,000 if you counted everyone from the mine, the smelter, the hospital and all the services needed to provide housing for the workers," James replied.

"How many first-line supervisors?" Bob asked.

"I've no idea off-hand," James replied. "It would have to be quite a few as there was one for about every thirty workers, and if we say there were 5,000 who worked underground, that would be 160 or so just there, plus there was the concentrator and smelter, then all the ancillary services, like, stores, engineering, ventilation, surveying, geology, HR, housing, hospitals, schools."

"How long did you spend as a first line?" Bob asked.

"Just under a year," James replied. "Then we had a shuffle of people caused by the accident I mentioned, and I moved up a notch and had five first lines reporting to me. It would have been difficult to have many more as the mine was spread out vertically and horizontally, so getting to all the workplaces was quite a walk and a climb."

"Rather you than me," Bob said. "Okay, Chuck said he'd have lunch on the plane, so let's just check the car back in, make a pit stop and then we'll be off."

"Hey, guys, ready?" Chuck asked as Bob and James made their way to the aircraft.

"Ready to go," Bob replied. "Here are our bags."

"Great, I'll get them stowed and we'll be off," Chuck said. "ETA Long Beach one oh three, local time."

On board, Chuck went through the safety briefing, then left them to go forward to the cockpit. Although the Albuquerque airport was big, it was not busy as its size was driven by the air force base that the commercial traffic shared. There was a short taxi out to the runway, then they were off, headed almost straight west to Long Beach.

"I'm curious as to how two such ineffective managers survived so long in Waterford," Bob remarked to James as they climbed out to their cruising altitude.

"Are they related in any way to the previous owners?" James asked.

"Maybe, we'd have to check," Bob said. "If that were the case, it would explain a lot; if not, I'd have to wonder what kind of performance review system they had in place. We should talk to Henry White about that. Did you meet George Berg?"

"I did," James confirmed. George Berg had been the president and chief executive officer of the company before the sale and had departed on the day of the sale. "Berg did most of the presentations about the business, he and Mike McKane."

"Did you get a sense about him?" Bob asked.

"Not really," James said. "He was focused on the sale. Hank Miller spent more time with him than I did."

"When I talk to Hank about raiding James & Brown, I'll ask him about Berg and see if he has any insights," Bob said.

"Gentlemen, ready for lunch?" Bill asked. "Chuck's minding the store up front, so I'll do the honours today."

"We're ready," Bob said. "What were you able to get us?"

"We were able to get some salmon with rice pilaf, cauliflower and crispy pancetta, served with a garlic sauce, and to follow a vanilla cheesecake," Bill replied.

"Where on earth did you find that here?" Bob asked. "I wouldn't have rated Albuquerque as having a demand for better airline meals; most of their traffic must be short-haul."

"We tapped into the source that Continental used for its First Class meals on its Chicago flights," Bill explained.

"I should remember that," Bob said. "What to drink?"

"We picked up an Australian Chardonnay that our source recommends. Let me know what you think, and we'll get some more if it's any good," Bill replied.

"Thanks, Bill," Bob said. Bill handed out plates, opened and served the wine, then went back to the cockpit with two more plates.

"This Chardonnay is not bad," James said, after taking a tentative sip.

"The salmon's pretty good too," Bob said. "Full marks for Bill and Chuck. So, what's your plan for this afternoon?"

"I'm not sure," James said. "I thought I'd start on that list you asked for. I'm sure that Henry White has got some of the information, if not all."

"Don't bet on it," Bob said. "Okay, you work on that while I chat to Hank, then we'll see what Henry has to say about our two lame ducks."

"We'll be on the ground in ten minutes," Bill announced through the intercom. "If you'd make sure your tray tables are up and everything is stowed."

They were on the ground in ten minutes and taxied over to the fixed-based operator they were using.

"We'll be here to run you back to Milwaukee on Sunday," Bill told James as they left the plane.

"Thanks," James said.

"What time do you want to leave?" Bill asked.

"Let's say nine," James suggested.

"We'll be ready," Bill promised. "Any requests for lunch?"

"No, we'll take what comes," James said.

"Okay, James, got your bag, let's go and see what Hank and Henry have to say," Bob said.

At the office, James went to see Henry White and asked him about the personnel files and learned that, apart from the corporate office and the division heads, all other files were lodged with the various companies. James asked to see such files as Henry had, and Henry waffled a little until Bob joined them.

"Is it okay if James has view of the personnel files we have here?" Henry asked.

"He's working on a project for me," Bob said. "He has access to everything we have here. One thing we need to do is have him apply for and get accepted as a citizen, so could you get the relevant paperwork started and also get Jim Beatty to put together a citizenship 101 class?"

"Of course," Henry said.

"So, tell us a little about Morris Whitaker," Bob said. "What do his past few performance reviews look like?"

"They're fine, as far as George Berg was concerned, he was doing a great job, of course, it didn't hurt that he was the nephew of George's first wife," Henry replied.

"I see," Bob said. "And do you share George's assessment of Whitaker?"

"Not really," Henry said. "I always got the impression that he was skating through life hanging on to family coattails."

"Any other family relationships we should be aware of?" Bob asked.

"Well, Dave Pratt is Chuck Newman's cousin," Henry explained. "Other than those two, as far as I'm aware, there are none."

"And how do you view Dave Pratt's performance?" Bob asked.

"As far as I can tell, he's doing a good job," Henry said. "Gets new contracts, makes a profit and keeps us in with the airframes."

"Tell us about Paul Rose," Bob said.

"Doing an okay job," Henry said. "Doesn't appreciate the help we can give him from here."

"And Ed McIntosh?" Bob asked.

"Wedded to his hoists, lives, breathes hoists," Henry said. "He's got a passion for the business that sometimes makes him blind to corporate direction."

"Make him blind to corporate direction, how?" Bob asked.

"We wanted more defence contracts less commercial rentals," Henry explained.

"I would have thought that his business was mostly commercial," Bob remarked.

"Yes, but when we wanted him to develop a rescue hoist to mount on a helicopter, he kept pushing it off," Henry explained.

"Wouldn't a helicopter winch be a drum winch?" James asked.

"I don't know, I suppose so," Henry said.

"Aren't nearly all HighRise hoists capstan winches?" James asked.

"I don't know, you'd have to ask Adam," Henry said.

"I see," Bob said. "Well, thank you, Henry, if you could see that James gets the files he needs, I have him on a deadline."

"Sure," Henry said.

"That was instructive," Bob said as James went back with him to his office.

"You think we need to find a new HR person as well?" James asked.

"I'll see," Bob said. "So, both Pratt and Whitaker had family ties. I talked to Hank, and we have a green light to talk to guys at James & Brown. You're going back to Milwaukee on Sunday. When can you be back here?"

"I'll talk to Hank and see what I need to do there, then Katrina and I will work out a plan. We're going to look at houses on Saturday, she has a short list for me to see," James replied.

"Talk to Evans and Johnson and if they're interested organise a trip to Pueblo and Albuquerque and drag them along as interested parties from James & Brown, tell the guys there some bullshit story about wanting to learn from them, then bring them both on here and let me talk to them, we'll do that off-site, I don't know what back channels there are between here and the divisions," Bob instructed.

"I saw that Ralph Thompson and Chuck Newman are not that far from retirement," James commented. "Assuming the files are going to be filled with glowing performance reviews, would it make sense to offer them an enhanced retirement package to leave early?"

"I'll talk to Hank and Ray Pierce about that," Bob said. "My view is it makes sense, getting them to go voluntarily makes more sense than going through a couple of years of extra reviews to build a file to stave off lawsuits. Go through their files and see what's in them. I suppose Hank never told you what it is you're really doing here?

"He just said to learn the business and keep my eyes and ears open," James replied.

"He was never one for elaboration," Bob said. "My mission is to look over the management here, make whatever changes we need to make, then hand the reins over to you in a year or so, if I think you're up to the job."

"That's direct enough," James said. "So, I should spend as much time as I can at each of the divisions, learn their markets and operations and see if we have the right people."

"That's about it," Bob said. "My rule of thumb is that I spend about a third of my time looking at markets, trends and disruptive technologies, then another third on operational performance, P&L and balance sheet stuff, then the last third on do we have the right people in the right jobs at the right time. Those requirements will change depending on what the business is doing and what we want to do with it."

"I see," James said, thinking that he had a fairly big challenge ahead.

"So, do you need a ride back to the hotel?" Bob asked.

"Thank you, I would appreciate that," James said.

"Okay, we'll call it a day, I'll pick you up at seven in the morning, and we'll hit the Tustin operation first and then in the afternoon we'll swing down to Santa Ana," Bob said.

"I'll be ready," James promised.

James was at the hotel before Katrina came back. She joined him about five-thirty, ready for a break from house hunting.

"I'm glad you're back," she said. "I've missed you."

"I missed you," he echoed. "You've been busy again today?"

"We have," she confirmed. "Angela took me to six more houses, and that's it, I'm done, I'm taking tomorrow off."

"Did you see anything that we could live in and afford?" he asked.

"Three possibles," she said. "We're going with Angela on Saturday morning to look at them, one's in Villa Park, another in Anaheim Hills, and the last one is in Orange. I won't prejudice you with my favourite, we'll see if we both pick the same one."

"Can we afford them all?" he asked.

"We can," she said. "And I met with a mortgage broker today, they want some information from you, but I already gave them the basics, and they don't see an issue."

"Fancy a drink?" he asked.

"Thought you'd never ask," she laughed. "Let's go downstairs to the bar and get something, and maybe something to eat. Did you fire anyone else today?"

"I don't do the firing," he said. "But yes, the chap today needs to go."

"It never bothers you to send people on their bicycles?" she asked.

"It depends," he said. "Sometimes people are just in the wrong job and that's as much the fault of the company as theirs, but other times they just don't belong and need to go, and for them, I don't have much in the way of sympathy. I told the pilots that we'd leave on Sunday at nine, is that okay?"

"Looking forward to it," she said. "Another ride in the fancy plane. Then I suppose when we get home we'll have to put our house on the market and get it sold and try and manage sales and purchases so that we're not on the street waiting for the new one to close."

"I'm sure we'll manage, we're not the first to change jobs and move," he commented.

"Angela calls us relos, relocations," Katrina told him. "Apparently, the estate agents are used to dealing with people moving around the country."

"What time do we start on Saturday?" he asked.

"Angela said that she'll pick us up at eight for our first appointment at eight-thirty," Katrina said. "It's fairly easy to get there from here, and on Saturday, there shouldn't be all the traffic that we've been seeing."

"I haven't seen much of it, but I imagine that tomorrow when Bob and I go to the Tustin plant and then Santa Ana, that we'll see a lot, particularly coming back from Santa Ana in the afternoon," he thought. "Let's get some dinner and then go and get a bath and bed, we've got some making up for lost time to do," she suggested.

When Bob picked up James the next morning, James did have a smile on his face and a feeling that all was well with the world.

"Ready for this one?" Bob asked.

"This one was probably the most different for me, it's all aerospace, defence and commercial," James commented.

"Well, it's the biggest single company we have," Bob said. "Lots of gears and lightweight gearboxes and some high-density winding electric motors used in aircraft."

"I suppose everything that flies has weight issues," James thought.

"It does," Bob agreed. "The lighter the better, but it still has to hold up in service and not crap out after a hundred hours or so of use. It's going to take a few minutes to get there; the place is just east of the 55 on the Alton Parkway and Jamboree."

"Is there a reason why the corporate office is not located at the Tustin operation?" James asked.

"From what I've been able to gather, the previous owners didn't want to impose too much on any one operation," Bob said. "Let's face it, if our office were there, it would be too easy to just wander around and start asking questions; if I were the division head, I wouldn't be too keen about that."

"I understand that," James said. "I've seen it before, the division manager gets to feel that he's being second-guessed at every turn. Hank didn't see any of the division heads that he thought could run the whole company?"

"I think it's more that we want our own guy in charge," Bob said. "Someone you can be sure will tell you the truth, no matter how unpleasant it may be."

"Thinking about the corporate office, I assume our space is leased, given that the two California operations are in Orange County. Why isn't the corporate office in Orange County as well?" James asked.

"I think it had a lot to do with where Berg lived," Bob said. "As I understand it, he had a fancy house in Signal Hill, so less than ten minutes away on surface streets."

"Any reason why it can't be moved?" James asked.

"Closer to the John Wayne you mean?" Bob asked.

"If it was, there's probably more choice in and out of John Wayne than Long Beach," James said. "And it wouldn't be too far from the two divisions. One other thing I learned was that this building is owned by Berg, and the lease is up for renewal in six months."

"So, Berg is continuing to benefit from Waterford, even after the company is sold, to the tune of $4,800 a month. Where does everyone in this office live?" Bob asked.

"Two in Dana Point, three in Newport Beach, one in Laguna Niguel, one in Lake Forest, one in Huntington Beach, four in Fountain Valley, two in Westminster, two in Santa Ana and three in Costa Mesa, I had to look on a map to find out where all those places are, and they're all east and south of here," James replied.

"So, somewhere not too far from John Wayne is as good as here," Bob said. "I can fly into Santa Ana as easily as here. Get me a proposal of what and where, plan for a corporate office of say fifteen, between staff and clerical, conference room, break room, all that kind of thing, plus what the current lease conditions are."

"Okay, we're here," Bob said. "Remind me, who's in charge here?"

"Stuart Wilson," James replied, thinking that Bob surely knew and that this was just a test to see if he had read any of the documents. "Graduate of MIT, master's in aeronautical engineering, spent time here, then at the industrial gearbox company, some time in Seattle, then back here. Revenues of just over $100 million, net before tax of 12, 1,020 people or so."

"Okay, let's go and meet Mr Wilson," Bob said. They walked into the lobby, and a receptionist looked up and smiled.

"Good morning?" she said. "How may I help you?"

"Bob Decker and James Martin to see Stuart Wilson," Bob replied.

"Of course," she said. "I'll just buzz his office and they'll come and get you."

"Bob Decker?" a man asked as he came through the door only a matter of seconds after the receptionist had called. He had to have been waiting for the call. "Stuart Wilson, please come through."

"Thanks," Bob said. "This is James Martin; he's a transplant from James & Brown."

"So, welcome to the world of actuation and gearboxes," Stuart said. "Which of the divisions have you seen?"

"Seattle, Tulsa, Pueblo and Albuquerque," Bob replied.

"This will be a little different," Stuart said. "Everything we make flies on something, whether it's actuators or gearboxes, so everything is about weight, tempered with reliability."

"We're keen to learn about the business," Bob said. Stuart led the way to a conference room where his staff was already arrayed. He made the introductions, then launched into a presentation about the business, the market, the customers, the programs, the competitors and what he saw as challenges that lay ahead. James noted that acronyms were common and wrote down all that he did not recognise to ask about later. He also noted that programs were referred to by the type of plane the bits went onto, with the assumption that the listeners knew who made them. Whereas James was familiar with the names and numbers of commercial aircraft, some of the military aircraft were new to him. He could look them up later, as he had seen a copy of Jane's All the World's Aircraft in the office.

They took a break at about nine, and Stuart gave them a tour of the plant and pointed out components and talked about what they went into and for which program. James was struck that this factory was a lot better organised than the last two he had seen, and there were not a lot of items sitting with red tags on them. There was a hum of activity that was reassuring, and conversations were normal, no whispered asides by the workers. Stuart seemed to know everyone in the place, which was quite a feat as there were over a thousand employees all told.

"Any issues you're having?" Bob asked.

"Just the usual," Stuart said. "Customers complaining that we charge too much, that we don't deliver as fast as they want, even when they leave ordering to the last minute, getting good machinists and so on."

"But nothing insurmountable?" Bob asked.

"No," Stuart agreed. "Just all that you'd expect in a manufacturing business."

"How much marketing help do you get from Chuck Newman?" James asked.

"Nothing that I can brag about," Stuart replied. "He schmoozes in DC, but we're not a prime; we're a sub-tier, so the big contracts don't go to us, they go to the majors, and we get subcontracts. The guy in Paris is handy, he keeps us abreast of Airbus, and we've actually gotten some business from one of the consortium members for actuators, same is true for the Brit, he keeps us in with British Aerospace, and we've done enough business with them that it's worth keeping him on."

"And Ralph Thompson?" James asked.

"Waste of money," Stuart said. "He never solved a problem for us."

"Adam North?" James asked,

"I'd love to have him here full-time," Stuart said. "There'd be a fight for his time with the other divisions, but I gather from him that he's about to retire, so that'll be moot."

"Any questions for us?" Bob asked.

"Is Waterford going to be broken up and piecemealed off?" Stuart asked.

"No plans for that," Bob said. "Our remit is to build where we can."

"What about the overhead in Long Beach?" Stuart asked.

"That we are looking at carefully," Bob said. "If we can reduce it, we will."

"You guys staying here for lunch, or are you headed back to Long Beach?" Stuart asked.

"We've got a meeting scheduled at Santa Ana at one-thirty," Bob said.

"So, why don't we grab Pete and grab an early lunch close by and then you can go on over to Santa Ana," Stuart suggested, Pete being his accounting manager.

"Can we walk there?" Bob asked.

"Sure can," Stuart said. "The other guys all have commitments right now, so we won't be offending anyone."

Lunch was at a small restaurant close by, and they were able to eat outside away from the other diners. Stuart talked about the marketplace and the likely orders from Boeing, Airbus, McDonnell Douglas, Lockheed and some of the smaller airframe companies like Fokker and Embraer. To James, it was fascinating, and it seemed that it was really all about providing basic parts for the planes, with very little in the way of spare or replacement parts, unless you were in the wearing parts of the plane, like the brakes and tyres. He did wonder who did all the interiors, things like the luggage bins, the seats, the galleys, all the bits the passengers see. Bob was asked about his background, and James learned a little more about what Bob had done in his career. Then it was the turn of James, so he gave a quick summary.

"You mean you actually went down the mine?" Pete asked.

"Every day for the first three years I was there," James replied.

"Wasn't it scary?" Pete asked. "Wasn't it dangerous? You hear of mine accidents and they don't sound nice."

"We had our accidents," James replied. "But we didn't have the risk of methane like the coal, gold and salt mines do; it never bothered me."

"Rather you than me," Pete said. "So, will the format for financial reporting change?"

"Perhaps," Bob said. "We'll wait to see what Oak Creek wants, but I would doubt that there'd be much change. I'll be talking to the CFO in the next week or so."

"We'll add you guys to the system so that the corporate badges you have will allow access," Stuart said. "No need to stop at the desk and be buzzed in."

"Thank you," Bob said. "We felt that on our first visit, it would be polite to announce ourselves and not just barge in."

"Appreciate that," Stuart said. "If you're going to be at the Santa Ana facility by one-thirty, you should get moving."

"Thoughts?" Bob asked James as they drove away from the factory.

"He has a handle on the business," James replied. "And his team are all singing from the same hymnbook."

"So, what about the industrial gear place?" Bob asked.

"Waterford Power, $50 million in sales, 4.8 net before tax, 498 people, and run by John Trent," James replied. "Supply gearboxes for all kinds of applications, from sugar mills to telescopes."

"Tell me about Trent," Bob said.

"Mechanical engineer from Purdue," James replied. "Joined the company and worked at Tustin for a while, then Seattle, then back here to Santa Ana, took over running the company two years ago."

"Okay, we'll see what this place looks like," Bob said. "Here we are."

They were greeted at the door by a receptionist who quickly directed them to a conference room where they found John Trent and his staff.

"Good afternoon," Bob said. "I'm Bob Decker and this is James Martin."

"Nice to meet you," John said. "This is an org chart and I'll run around the table and put faces to names, and this is a basic product brochure, and finally, this is a summary P&L and balance sheet for the last close."

"Thank you," Bob said.

"Get you anything, coffee, water?" John asked.

"We've just had lunch, so I think we're fine, thank you," Bob replied.

John then made the introductions and gave a quick summary of the company, its products, markets served, current backlog and order book and a sense of pending potential orders. The situation looked fairly rosy; they were sold out for six months, and the potential orders would take them well into the next financial year. That done, he suggested a factory tour, then a reconvening in an hour and a half.

On the factory floor, there were gearboxes lined up, ranging from those that were almost finished to those that had yet to see any gear elements installed. The factory was split into the assembly area, a fabrication shop where the boxes themselves were made, a gear cutting area where there were all manner of machines cutting and shaping gears, a paint shop for the boxes, a steel yard with sheet and bar stock, a heat treat furnace or two and areas for other necessary processes. To James, this was close to some of the factories that James & Brown had, particularly in the Construction Machinery Division and the small gearbox companies that were in Kenosha and Beloit. The workforce looked industrious and greeted John as they walked around.

"It's interesting," John remarked. "Some of the machinists fret if they don't see eight or ten jobs piled up ahead of them, as though they think we'd lay them off if they did nothing for an hour or two. Personally, I would rather see them pull the next job they have from the previous process so that the whole thing flies through the factory with little or no time just sitting around. Keeps WIP down and lets us advertise short delivery times."

"If you have a six-month backlog, doesn't that rather play against that?" Bob asked.

"Victims of our own success," John laughed. "We're looking to see where we can speed things up, without expanding capacity. I don't want a big fancy factory that would accommodate the current backlog and then leave us scrambling to fill it next year. We've already identified areas where we can cut out the time pieces spend just sitting."

"So you're a student of some of the Japanese techniques?" Bob asked.

"We are," John confirmed. "We've been studying what they do and have attacked defects, process flows and other things. We've moved machines around for a better flow, we've involved all the shop floor in how to do this, but as I said, some of them still fret if they don't see a month's worth of jobs sitting at their workstation. We're aiming for flexibility so that we can react to any potential order. We've already upped the number of completed boxes we can get out in a month, so you'll see revenues climbing, and you'll also see WIP going down."

"So the easiest way to control costs is to get it built?" Bob asked.

"The longer a work order stays open, the more costs it collects," John said. "So, the quicker we can get it done, the better, and that means getting it right the first time, so no re-work, no MRB, no scrap."

"Do the design engineers come out here at all?" James asked.

"Absolutely," John said. "They didn't used to, but when we did some digging into things we found design specs that we just couldn't meet, so we got them out here to work out what we actually could do, and what we had to change in the way of machines to meet the specs, hence the fairly big capital spend bill over the past two years."

"Have you gone to CAD/CAM?" Bob asked.

"We're in the process," John replied. "We've been putting old designs onto CAD, and all new designs are done with CAD. We're also updating controls on machines so that we can use the CAM better. We've been dropping our defect rate steadily and are aiming for a six-sigma factory."

James had to admit to himself that there were things there that he needed to research, CAD/CAM for one, and the significance of being a six sigma factory, but rather than getting into a big discussion there, he thought it would be better if he just did some homework.

The tour ended in the engineering department, which actually looked out over the factory floor, and he saw some of the computer-aided design, CAD, in action. It made sense, have the designs on a computer so that everything could be easily checked and issues identified. Back in the conference room, John gave his various managers their heads and let them talk about their departments and what their challenges and successes were. Bob and James asked questions, and they were all fielded quickly and completely. When it came to their turn, Bob gave the now well-established reply that the company was not to be broken up and sold off in pieces. They broke up at four, in time to catch the Friday afternoon traffic. Fortunately, Bob had already planned his route back to Long Beach, but it still took a good forty-five minutes to get back to the Marriott, where Bob dropped James, which did give them the time to compare notes about the last operation they had seen.

"Call me on Monday with your schedule," Bob told James when he dropped him off. "Try and get your two guys out to Pueblo and Albuquerque next week."

"I'll do that," James promised.

"I've been talking to Hank about getting the smaller Lear transferred to us so it will make flitting around the different operations a little easier," Bob said. "Talk to him on Monday and find out where we are on that. Good house hunting tomorrow."

"Thanks," James said. "Have a good flight home."

"Busy day?" Katrina asked James when he went to their room.

"Busy, then sitting in traffic for the past forty-five minutes," he replied. "What did you do today?"

"Sat out by the pool and lazed the day away," she replied. "All ready for house hunting tomorrow?"

"You've done most of the hunting," he said.

"True," she agreed. "So we'll see tomorrow if you pick the same one I did."

"No clues?" he asked.

"None," she laughed. "These are the brochures that come with each house. Let's get a glass of wine and sit outside and just look through them."

"Sounds like a plan," he said. "I will be back here next week, I'm supposed to be taking Bill Evans and Phil Johnson to Pueblo and Albuquerque to see if I can get them to commit to taking the two jobs to replace the *ouks* that are there now."

"That's pretty quick," she commented.

"The sooner the better," he said. "Neither one is anything to write home about, and both operations show that."

"And the rest?" she asked.

"On the whole, I'd say pretty good," he replied. "No need to make any changes there that I can see."

"Did Decker agree with you?" she asked.

"He told me I had no compassion, but agreed it had to be done and done quickly," he replied.

"So any thoughts?" Katrina asked James after he had had a chance to read through the brochures on the houses.

"At first glance, I like this one," he replied, holding up the brochure for a house in the City of Orange. "It's in a nice spot, it's not far from the hills, access to the freeways looks fairly straightforward, nice-sized garden and the interior looks liveable."

"We'll see tomorrow if your impressions match what you see," she teased. "Angela will pick us up at eight, so an early start. With luck, we'll be done by lunchtime."

"The traffic here is going to take some getting used to," he said. "I had suggested to Bob that we move the corporate office to somewhere near the Orange County Airport, which would be better than trekking up to Long Beach every day."

"That sounds good," she said. "So, let's get an early dinner and go to bed early."

"Is that an invitation?" he asked.

"Command performance," she said. "It's been a busy week for both of us, so now it's time for us."

"Lead on," he said. "Room service or dining room?"

"Let's do the dining room, then there's no need to be disturbed in our room," she suggested.

Changes

Angela was at the hotel bright and early on Saturday morning and drove James and Katrina to their first appointment, a house in Anaheim Hills. It was in a cul-de-sac, nice enough but with nothing about it that was unique, like so many of the California tract homes. Of the three that Katrina had picked out, it was the least expensive, a factor to be considered, particularly as it was well above what they had paid for their Oak Creek house. Angela led them through the house, extolling the virtues of the open plan, the well-ordered and equipped kitchen, the Roman tub in the master bathroom, the landscaped garden and other features. The one thing it did not have was a view of anything; there were houses across the street, houses on each side, houses to the rear with no looming hills in the background, even though they were in Anaheim Hills, or surrounding trees as they had in Oak Creek. To James, it was certainly a possibility, but he would reserve judgment until he had seen the other two.

The second house in Villa Park was completely different. It was a single-storey older home set in a peaceful neighbourhood with a mature garden replete with tall trees. To James, it felt oppressive, hemmed in by the surrounding houses and the feeling that the neighbours would not approve of any activity that did not fit the norm, not quite the *Stepford Wives*, but it still had that feeling about it. All the gardens were well-maintained, even manicured; litter was noticeable by its complete absence, cars were parked in garages, not in driveways or on the street, and there were only glimpses of people once in a while. The house was elegant, if a little dated, and Angela did her bit, extolling the virtues and features of this house, as was her job. To James, the interior of the house seemed a little dark, and he tried to imagine living there and decided that the first thing he would have to do was redecorate to lighten things up a little. Part of the problem was that the windows were quite small, and they were well curtained, but even if the curtains were drawn well back, the surrounding trees and shrubs cut out a lot of the light. It was also the most expensive of the three that Katrina had picked, almost as if one were paying for the cachet that living in Villa Park brought with it. That house James placed lower than the first on his list.

Villa Park was an oddity, an enclave surrounded on all sides by the City of Orange, and it was back to Orange that they went for the final house. James liked it immediately. Across the road was an old gravel pit, which meant that it was open, with further development unlikely, at least in the short to mid-term. Across the open area of the gravel pits, some distance away, were low hills, and to the east were visible the hills and mountains of the Santa Ana range. The house had a garden that was landscaped in the front, but just plain grass at the back, with a slope up at the back leading to a wall that delineated the next house up the slope. The house was on a corner, so had neighbours on two sides, but not the others. Inside, it had an open feel to it with a so-called great room, a kitchen and dinette, then upstairs three bedrooms, the master of which overlooked the front, so had something of a view. It was priced between the two others, so affordable, at a small stretch. James put that one at the top of his list.

Angela took them to a restaurant for an early lunch and their verdict.
"Well, James," Katrina said. "Which is your first pick?"
"The last one," he said.
"Same as mine," she said. "Angela, what do we have to do to make an offer on the house in Orange?"
"If we go back to my office, we can write up an offer," Angela replied. "And I can present it to the sellers this afternoon."
"I'll leave you contact numbers," Katrina said. "It's possible that James will be back here next week sometime. Is there a need for me to be here to sign anything else?"
"Not until the close," Angela said. "You'll want to do a walk-through just before the close, but other than that, we can do it all with Federal Express."

"I need to look at moving the corporate office closer than Long Beach," James commented. "What would be the route I'd have to take to get to the Long Beach airport from Orange?"

"Katella to the 55, then the 22 to the 405 and off at Lakewood," Angela said, with all the confidence of a true Angelino.

"And if we were to move the office south of here?" he asked.

"I'd put it somewhere down Jamboree, then you could go east on Katella to Santiago Canyon Road, then down Jamboree to Irvine, somewhere around the Alton Parkway, then you'd be close to John Wayne," Angela suggested.

"So, what should we offer on the house?" James asked.

"I'd start at $135,900," Angela suggested. "I'm sure the seller will counter; we'll see how high and if there's an agreeable point in the middle somewhere. When are you flying out?"

"Tomorrow at nine," James replied.

"If I hear back this afternoon, can I reach you at your hotel?" Angela asked.

"You can," Katrina replied. "We've got no plans to go anywhere."

"Let's go back to the office and write up an offer," Angela suggested.

The offer was written up and Angela duly called the sellers, who, as she expected, countered at $150,000. James and Katrina moved up a little to $142,000, with another counter of $147,500, then they moved up to $145,000, and that was accepted. So, Angela then took over and laid out all the things that had to happen before closing, including the main item, which was James and Katrina getting a mortgage. James suggested that Katrina come with him the following week, and then she could work on a mortgage while he was busy interviewing. They would be looking to borrow some $125,000, which for them seemed horrible, but which Angela assured them was quite usual and, in fact, quite low compared to some. Fortunately, James's salary and the mortgage interest differential made it possible, and Katrina had every confidence that James would soon be running Waterford Industries with the salary and benefits that came with the job.

James and Katrina had an early breakfast at a small place that was actually in the flight path to the main runway. For all the planes that went in overhead, it was not that noisy.

"Did we do the right thing?" Katrina asked.

"I'm sure we did," he replied. "We have to live somewhere, and why not live somewhere that we both like? We'll find a way to pay for it."

"I'll look for a job when we move out here, that'll help too," Katrina said. "So, are we ready to go and get the plane? I have to say I like this idea of your own plane, being able to come and go on your time, not trying to fit things in with airline schedules."

"We shouldn't get too used to the idea," he cautioned. "I doubt that we're going to be able to use the plane at will."

"I know," she said. "But it is nice."

"Mr Martin, Mrs Martin, good morning," Chuck said as they arrived at the FBO. "All ready?"

"Let's just make a quick stop at the loo, and we'll be ready," James said. There was actually a bathroom on the plane, not quite as tiny as the one on the Lear 35, which took some gymnastics to use, but James preferred not to use the one on the plane if he could avoid it. The flight time back to Milwaukee was a little under three and a half hours, so not too much of a stretch.

"All set?" Chuck asked when they returned from the bathroom. He led the way to the plane, and they climbed aboard and took their seats. Chuck closed up the plane and went forward to join Bill, and then they taxied out and took off towards the Pacific, climbing and curving back around to go over the San Gabriel Mountains and the route home. When they reached their cruising altitude, Bill came back to offer lunch.

"We've got lamb today," he said. "Found a great source that does the BA first class catering."

"That sounds nice," Katrina said.

"What will you drink with it?" Bill asked. "We've got a really nice Pinot Noir, Chuck and I tried it out Thursday night after we got back from Albuquerque."

"We'll try that," Katrina said. Bill poured, and she and James sampled the wine and pronounced it excellent.

"If you need anything else, give us a yell," Bill said. He took meals forward for himself and Chuck, but no wine, just Sprite. The lamb was good, quite unlike typical airline food, which was constrained by the need to cater for large numbers, and to have it pre-prepared as galleys were meant for reheating, not basic cooking. Chuck came back and cleared everything away, and served coffee.

Monday morning, James reported to Hank Miller's office and had to wait a few minutes before he was called in.

"So, James, thoughts, impressions?" Hank asked.

"Interesting set of businesses," James replied. "As you know, we think that two of the division managers should be changed. There's tension in those businesses, and there's no cohesion in them."

"How did that get to be?" Hank asked.

"I rather think that it was family connections that got them the jobs to start with, and since then, poor performance and other issues have been overlooked. I know Bob told me that I had no compassion for them, but in the best interests of the company, the sooner we replace them, the better," James explained. "There's also quite a lot of working capital tied up in inventory because there's a lot sitting around for re-work or for decisions by a material review board. If we fix the manufacturing issues, we'll free up cash."

"So now you want to steal Evans and Johnson?" Hank asked.

"I think they'd both do a good job," James replied.

"I've talked about it to Bob, and we've agreed that if they want the jobs, we'll move them out to take over PDQ," Hank said. "I've also agreed with Bob that we'll transfer the Lear 35 out to you; it'll make getting to Tulsa and Pueblo a little easier. Anything else?"

"Based on our observations and discussions with the division managers, we think that we could do without Ralph Thompson and Chuck

71

Newman, and Adam North says that he'll be retiring soon, so we'll so down by six in the corporate office as each of them has a secretary," James replied.

"You don't see a need to replace them?" Hank asked.

"Thompson, I think, was the family man who reported any and all issues to the management. Newman schmoozes in Washington, but we're a subcontractor; we get few prime contracts, so political influence is debatable," James explained. "Adam North would be worth replacing, but I doubt whether any of the companies would willingly give up their chief engineer for a corporate slot. There is one other item that will come up in the financial reporting, the industrial gearbox operation has quite a large contract for gearboxes for the Middle East, they've been building to inventory, then relieving the inventory when blocks of gearboxes actually ship, but they've been making real improvements in their operations, so the standard costs have been going down, meaning that there is excess inventory that will have to get written down."

"But, because the costs are now less, we'll see better margins?" Hank asked.

"Yes, and next financial year, we'll see a lot less working capital tied up in inventory, along with the better returns," James confirmed.

"Good, we'll note the write-downs when they come and know the reason why. Did you find a house?" Hank asked.

"We did," James confirmed. "We made an offer and it was accepted, now we have to sell our house here and get a mortgage for the new one and then move."

"Get Ray Pierce to help you," Hank said. "This week, take the 35 and take Evans and Johnson and visit Pueblo and Albuquerque and let me know what they decide. Bob wants to make these changes quickly. He also talked to me about an incentive to get Newman and Thompson to retire early, so we don't have to go through terminations and all the problems that might come out of that. I've got Evans and Johnson and their wives here standing by, so as soon as you're ready, you can go, maybe even as early as tomorrow morning. Does Katrina want to go back out?"

"I think she'd like to see about mortgages," James replied.

72

"Okay, spend some time this afternoon talking to Evans and Johnson, find realtors in Pueblo and Albuquerque and set things up for the wives," Hank instructed. "Anything else?"

"I talked to Bob about moving the corporate office closer to the Tustin company, not close enough to become a nuisance, but close to the Orange County airport," James said. "Apparently, the reason the office is in Long Beach is that Berg lived close by, and I discovered that Berg actually owns the building."

"Bob mentioned that," Hank said. "I'll rely on you and Bob to get the best deal you can for space. I suppose the plane can stay there as well?"

"There's quite a lot of general aviation in and out of that airport," James confirmed. "So I don't see an issue there."

"Okay, well, get to it and keep me informed," Hank instructed.

James found Bill and Phil and told them what he could about the places they were going to see. He also got Ray Pierce to line up realtors for Tuesday and Wednesday. They discussed schedules and decided that wheels up would be at seven-thirty, which would put them into Pueblo at about eight-forty-five. That would give them plenty of time to tour the plant at leisure and give Amanda Evans time to look at some of the town and the type of house that might be available. James planned to hop over to Albuquerque that evening for an early start on Wednesday and give Susan Johnson a chance to at least visit Albuquerque, finishing up in Long Beach, ready for interviews with Bob on Thursday morning. Before they left for the day, James called Morris Whitaker and David Pratt and told them that he had two people from the construction division who were really interested to see the operations and see what methods and techniques they could apply in their own operations. Whether or not Whitaker or Pratt believed his story was neither here nor there, but each of them promised plant tours and time with the manufacturing, quality and engineering managers.

The flight out to Pueblo was with a fairly full plane, six passengers in all, so not much room. The pilots were Greg and Andrew, who normally flew the 35, but who, like Bill and Chuck, had been checked out on the 55. Amanda and Susan had questions, most of which James could not answer as he had never lived in either Pueblo or Albuquerque. Katrina described to them the challenges they had faced when they had moved to Johannesburg and back and how they had overcome each of them. Amanda and Susan were both quite excited by the prospect of a move to the Mountain West and the possibility of taking up skiing. Andrew served breakfast and picked everything up in good time for them to put down on Pueblo. There, there was a realtor who whisked Amanda, Susan and Katrina off for a tour of the town and a look at a selection of houses.

James got a rental car and drove the short distance to the factory, and introduced Bill and Phil to first Kathy, then Morris. Morris was joined by Fred Norman, his manufacturing manager, and they led a tour of the factory with Morris waxing lyrical about the splendid job they were doing. James had to give credit to Bill and Phil; they gave nothing away but trotted around after Morris, hanging on his every word. They also visited with engineers and learned about the demands of the airlines and how they wanted their ground support equipment to be configured. They learned about the issues with cold weather when machines would be called upon to work even though the outside temperatures could be many degrees below freezing. Morris excused himself as soon as he could and disappeared behind his office door. James did wonder what he might be doing and was a little surprised when Morris joined them in the conference room and told him that he was handing in his notice. He apparently either saw the writing on the wall or just did not fancy answering questions about the way the company was run. James asked the Human Resource manager, Tom Reed, to join them, then told him that Morris had just handed in his notice, and to escort him out and pay him off in lieu of notice. That done, he told Mark Brooks, the finance man, that he was in charge until a replacement could be named. He then called the rest of the managers together, told them what had transpired and that Mark would be in charge for the moment until a replacement could be named. He did invite those there who might have an interest in the job to give him a résumé before he left that day. James also called Bob Decker and told him what had happened and what he had done.

Kathy had organised lunch, and James did note a lighter tone to things, and little stories and anecdotes started to come out. Morris was not universally loved; in fact, James got the general feeling that most disliked him a lot, and many of them had been using the company as a potential stepping stone to better things. By the time James and the others left that afternoon, they heard laughter in the offices and saw smiles, something that had been noticeably absent when they arrived.

"Good day?" Katrina asked when they were on the plane headed for Albuquerque.
"We have to move fast," James said. "The incumbent quit today, so Bill needs to wow Bob Decker on Thursday. Amanda, what do you think?"
"I like Pueblo," she said. "I saw houses that we could live in, and we got a tour of the town."
"Any advice for meeting with Decker?" Bill asked.
"Just tell him what you saw here today and what you'd do about it," James suggested.
"What about the managers here, any that you'd consider?" Bill asked.
"It's hard to judge," James said. "Whitaker didn't seem to do much in the way of development of his staff, so there might be some really good ones, but it's hard to tell. One of your tasks would be to develop them and get them ready for assignments elsewhere, if they want them."
"I'm sure I can do that," Bill said.
"What can we expect tomorrow?" Phil asked.
"Lots of aircraft structure parts, lots of issues with cosmetic finish, lots of inventory sitting around waiting for MRB," James replied. "Dave Pratt is full of excuses why, so is his accountant, that always spells trouble for me when the boss and the money man are in cahoots."
"What's this guy Pratt like?" Phil asked.
"Sounds like a bit of a pratt," Katrina joked.

"Sorry?" Phil said.

"Brit slang," James explained. "Usually someone not very competent or worse."

"Do you really suspect something is going on?" Phil asked.

"No, I've no reason to, but it wouldn't surprise me," James replied.

Susan, Amanda and Katrina left with the realtor the next morning, and James took Phil and Bill to the Structures Division.

"Morning," Dave said when they arrived. "I gather you canned Morris yesterday."

"Mr Whitaker resigned of his own volition," James stated. "Any other comment is contrary to the facts."

"Oh," Dave said. "Well, I suppose we'd better give you the tour."

He led the way and showed them the factory floor, replete with all its pieces sitting waiting for decisions. James let Phil ask the questions, and they were good and to the point. He might have never built parts for aircraft, but clearly, he had built parts that were in many ways similar to those made in Albuquerque, certainly from a paint and finish point of view. The tour was extensive and lasted until lunchtime, when they joined his staff for lunch.

"Have you had the opportunity to think about how much is tied up in inventory because of MRB issues?" James asked.

"Are you still harping on about that?" Dave asked.

"I am," James replied. "There's cash tied up in those parts."

"We progress bill, so it's not an issue," Luther Harris interposed.

"I think it is," James said. "If we allow parts to sit because of some issue, do we miss delivery dates, do the parts acquire unnecessary costs?"

"I don't have to deal with this," Dave said. "I'm out of here. Morris was right, you assholes are just jerks."

"Do I understand that you are tendering your resignation?" James asked.

"Damn straight," Dave replied.

"Very well, Mr Willis, please escort Mr Pratt from the premises and make sure that he gets paid in lieu of notice," James said.

"If Dave goes, I go," Luther said.

"Very well, Mr Willis, also escort Mr Harris from the premises," James said. When they had gone, James looked to the rest with the obvious question. There were no further quits.

"I'd like you, Pete, to take charge temporarily until we have the chance to name a successor," James said to Pete Cranwell, the manufacturing manager. "If you'll excuse me, I should make a couple of telephone calls; perhaps you could give Phil and Bill a rundown of the customers and the business."

"So, James, what is it with you?" Bob asked when James called him with the news.

"It wasn't intended," James said. "I was surprised, first by Whitaker, then by Pratt. I would have thought that they would have stayed on and make us pay them out, so it makes me wonder if there's something they'd rather we didn't find."

"I'll call Hank and tell him I want an internal audit team at both places," Bob said. "When will you be here?"

"About five this evening," James replied.

"I'll join you all for dinner at the Marriott," Bob said. "Give me a chance to meet these guys and their wives. We'll need a new finance guy for Albuquerque as well. I'll ask Mike McKane for recommendations."

"Fine," James said. "I'll see you later this afternoon."

James rejoined the meeting, and there was a lively discussion taking place between the engineer, John Hill, and Pete Cranwell. It seemed that a chance question from Phil about process capability had set things off. As far as James could tell, the upshot was that parts were being engineered to tolerances that the factory could only hope to meet by random chance, so either the specifications had to change, an unlikely solution as they were dictated largely by the customers, or there would have to be improvements in the equipment used to make parts. James gathered that in the past, all capital requests for new machines had been shelved by Pratt, for whatever reason he was not able to fathom. Phil got them on the same page, as the saying goes, by asking them how they would set out the specifications of the machines required. That got them onto common ground, and James asked if they would write up capital requests for the needed machines and equipment.

When they left Albuquerque, the division seemed a little happier place, but they were all on tenterhooks waiting to see who would be named as the replacement to Pratt. Susan had had an interesting day with the realtor. She had shown them old town Albuquerque and newer parts of the town, including a variety of house styles and price ranges. The flight into Long Beach only took an hour and forty minutes, so they were there by five, five minutes to actually. James took them all to the offices, and Bob Decker and Megan Grant, his secretary, were still there. He said hello, and then he and Megan ferried everyone to the Marriott. Megan left, and Bob suggested that they get checked in and settled and then join him for dinner in half an hour. James and Katrina went to their room, then went back down to talk to Bob before the others came down.

"So, James, tell me about it," Bob said.

"We had a plant tour with Whitaker, then he disappeared for a few minutes, then dropped his bombshell," James replied. "I had Tom Reed, the HR person, walk him out, get his badge, keys and so on, then put the accountant in charge for the interim. I did ask for résumés of those who think they might like the job, but I don't see one that stands out."

"And Albuquerque?" Bob asked.

"Whitaker must have called Pratt because when we arrived Pratt accused me of canning Whitaker, I told him that Whitaker had resigned of his own volition," James explained.

"And anyone else there at the time?" Bob asked.

"Bill Evans and Phil Johnson and Fred Norman, the manufacturing manager and Chris Bishop, the engineer, were all in the conference room with me," James replied. "Pratt did the tour, then when I asked questions again about the amount of inventory tied up with MRB and rework, he got agitated and told us that he didn't have to put up with that and quit on the spot, as did Luther Harris, his finance guy, so I had them walked out and left Pete Cranwell the manufacturing chap in charge. The fact that Pratt and Harris both wanted out of there makes me wonder if they have something to hide."

"So, I've been thinking about this," Bob said. "If your picks are good and I approve, I'll fly back to Albuquerque tomorrow afternoon with Evans and Johnson. I'll put Johnson in charge of Albuquerque first thing Friday morning, then hop over to Pueblo and put Evans in there."

"Any word on audit teams?" James asked.

"They'll be out next week, oh, and Mike McKane recommended a young accountant from Tustin to go to Albuquerque," Bob said. "I've talked to Stuart Winter, and he's willing to let him go, so I'll take him along with me on Friday. Evans and Johnson can make their own way back to Milwaukee or Pittsburgh and get moves organised. I'll be back Friday afternoon, so you and Katrina can spend Friday getting your mortgage sorted out, then I'd like you to look into office space in Irvine or Tustin."

"I'll do that," James said.

"When I talked to Hank and told him what was going on, he laughed and said that you'd essentially done the same thing when you went over to Johannesburg," Bob said.

"He was due to leave anyway," James said. "All I did was ask him if he wanted to go early, and he jumped at the chance."

"So, Katrina, any insights into what Mrs Evans and Mrs Johnson think?" Bob asked.

"Amanda, Bill's wife, liked Pueblo, liked the realtor and even saw some houses that she'd like to look at again," Katrina replied. "The same was true with Susan, Phil's wife. I think if it were my choice, I'd pick Albuquerque over Pueblo, but if I were a skier, Pueblo would be better."

"So, both keen to give it a go?" Bob asked.

"As far as I could judge, yes," Katrina replied.

"When do you guys need to go back to get your house on the market and organise your move?" Bob asked.

"I think when we get a close date here, then we'll set up the move, hopefully by then the house will be sold, or the company will have taken it," Katrina said. "We should probably go back the middle of next week, get things started, then we can come back here."

"I need to talk to the two pilots as well about relocating here," Bob said. "They'll want to live somewhere convenient for the Santa Ana airport."

"I'm a little confused," Katrina said. "Is it Santa Ana, John Wayne, Orange County, which?"

"It's actually the Santa Ana airport, SNA," Bob replied. "But they gave it the name John Wayne in 1979, after Wayne died. It serves Orange County with commercial and general aviation; the only other airport in Orange County is Fullerton, which only does general aviation. Ah, here are the others. I booked us a private room, so more privacy."

Over dinner, Bob talked to both Bill and Phil, and not to exclude them, made sure he devoted time to talk to both Amanda and Susan. James was impressed by the way that Bob put them all at ease and managed to get them all to talk about themselves, their aspirations, misgivings, if any, about moving, their interests outside work and what Amanda and Susan might like to do for themselves. Susan and Phil had two small children, not yet school-age, so she was devoting her time to them. Bill and Amanda had no children, and Amanda was thinking of applying for a job with the Pueblo zoo. She had been working at the Milwaukee Zoo, so she felt that would put her in good stead for a job in Pueblo. After dinner, James and Katrina talked about what they needed to do.

"We should get our house on the market as soon as possible," Katrina said. "If we both go back for a couple of days next week, we can do that, then you can come back here and start work. See if you can talk Bob into trips home at the weekends."

"I'll do that," he promised. "I wonder when the close here will be?"

"I'll talk to Angela tomorrow while you're busy with Bill and Phil and get dates from her, then we can talk to George about moving our stuff," she suggested, George being George Whitehead, who was the Traffic Manager for James & Brown.

"I'm tired," James said. "Can we get a bath and go to bed?"

"I thought you'd never ask," she laughed. "When I've finished with you, you'll have a reason to be tired."

"We'll see," he laughed.

The next day, James left Katrina to entertain Amanda and Susan and got the hotel shuttle bus to drop him, Bill and Phil at the office.

"Hey, guys," Bob said. "I've set things up for you to talk to Mike McKane, he's the CFO here, Henry White, he's our HR guy and Adam North, he's the engineer, then I'll talk to you. Let's see, Bill, would you start with Mike here, and Phil, with Adam, here's a schedule each. James, could I have a few minutes of your time?"

"You wanted to see me?" James asked.

"Only to let you know that Newman had calls from Whitaker and Pratt whining about being let go, but I set Newman straight and told him that there were witnesses to the quits. After that, Adam got calls from the engineers at both Pueblo and Albuquerque who confirmed that both Whitaker and Pratt publicly quit and that they were delighted," Bob explained. "Mike is not unhappy about Harris going too, I think he'd rather have one of his own protégés in place."

"On a crass level, the thought did occur to me that the quits probably saved us long and drawn-out battles over terminations," James said. "You're right about that," Bob agreed. "But we won't discuss that outside this office. I've got Jim Beatty lined up to start you on your citizenship classes, Henry has all the forms you need to fill out, so see him sometime today and get that done, oh and Henry has some pull with the local congressional rep and has asked for help, so you'll get an early appointment for the citizenship test, so be ready."

"Thanks," James said.

By the end of the day, Bob had confirmed James's suggestions, and between him and Henry, they had established salaries and benefits, all the usual things. Bob had told them his plan, so they were both looking forward to going and taking over their new assignments. Bob also suggested dinner, this time at a nice restaurant in Irvine, a place called Pronto. Bob had arranged a minibus and had also invited Adam, Henry and Mike to join them, and from the two Southern California operations, Stuart Winter and John Trent. Bob cautioned the latter two that news of the appointments had yet to be made public, so to wait until Monday before telling their staff. Stuart commented that he had heard from Newman and that his story was that James had fired the two. Adam set him straight and repeated what the engineers had told him: the quits were voluntary and very public.

On Friday, James and Katrina were left to their own devices, so Katrina contacted Angela and arranged to meet at her office at ten to go through the details of what they needed to do next, and to meet with a mortgage broker about the loan they would need to buy the house. When there, James asked Angela if she knew anyone who dealt with commercial premises, as he was looking for office space to rent. Angela gave him a name and number and suggested that she set up a luncheon meeting for him. Then they sat with the mortgage broker and went through all the forms and provided all the documents that were required to prove that they could qualify for the loan. They did not actually need the mortgage differential to qualify, but it would certainly make life easier from a financial point of view when it came to making mortgage payments. The lunchtime meeting was close at hand, only a short walk from Angela's office. The broker's name was Carol Black, and apparently, she and Angela knew each other well.

"Carol, this is James and Katrina Martin; they're moving out here from the cold," Angela said. "James is looking for office space to rent. James is with Waterford Industries."

"How much are we looking for?" Carol asked.

"I've measured offices and the space we have now and think the 4,500 square feet should be more than adequate," James replied.

"Divided how?" she asked.

"The president's office, three next level down, another four below that, plus space for secretaries, a lunch room for say ten, a conference room for twenty, a couple of file rooms and a reception area, maybe to seat about five," James replied.

"4,500 feet would be a good, comfortable space," she said. "Any ideas where?"

"We were thinking of Irvine, somewhere close to the airport," James said.

"I have some space on the corner of MacArthur and von Karman that might suit," she said. "Would you like to see after lunch?"

"That would be great," James said.

"What does Waterford Industries do? Is that the Irish company?" Carol asked.

"We don't make glass, that's known as just Waterford," James said. "We make gearboxes and actuators for aircraft and industrial uses. We also make loaders for the airlines and some marine equipment. We've got a factory in Tustin, another in Santa Ana, then three more scattered about the country. We're currently housed at the Long Beach airport, but when I look at where everyone lives, down here be a shorter commute for all."

"This is nice," James said when they were looking over the space later. He tried to imagine it built out and not the empty space he was looking at.

"I would imagine you'd want your offices along the windows and the conference room, lunch room and other space on the interior," Carol said.

"That would make sense," James said. "How much would it cost to get the interior finished, and how long would it take?"

"Depending on what you want $30 to $50 per square foot," she replied. "And allow three to six months, again depending on what you want in terms of finish. I have a list here of six reputable contractors that I've used in the past that I wouldn't hesitate to use again."

"If we agree the space and the rent, is the owner looking for short, medium or long-term commitments?" James asked.

"The longer the term, the lower the rent, so 85 cents per square foot per month to a dollar ten," she said. That made sense to James. The market for office space was softening; he had just read an article about that in the Wall Street Journal, so now landlords were probably looking to fill space for a longer term rather than have it sit empty because there were no takers.

"So, who do we negotiate with?" James asked.

"I can help with that," Carol said. "I can set you up with the owner's property manager, and we can go from there."

"Any other properties of about the same size?" James asked.

"If you've got time, there are three more in the same general area," Carol said. "We can see them all in the next hour or two."

"That was interesting," James said to Katrina as they crawled back up the 405 towards Long Beach.

"It was, what was your choice?" she asked.

"I think the first one," he said. "It's the easiest to get to, has enough parking, it's not too far from the airport, best of all, easy for me to get to, but then they would all be easy, no freeways at all."

"What shall we do tomorrow?" she asked.

"Let's explore a little around where the house is," he suggested.

"I saw in the Thomas Guide a couple of parks," she said. "Let's see, there was the Santiago Oaks Regional Park and the Irvine Regional Park; we should check those out."

"Any preferences for dinner tonight?" he asked.

"I saw this place up the road a little, it's a golf course, but they have a restaurant, and Angela told me that it's pretty good," Katrina suggested.

"So, not too far to drive?" he asked.

"Five minutes," she replied. "Funny, here everything is about time, how far is it to Irvine from here, thirty minutes during the day, up to an hour in peak times, so no one talks in terms of miles."

"I suppose for the LA basin everything is about the car and getting around, so people are used to talking in hours and minutes instead of miles," he thought.

"Just as well it's not light-years," she laughed.

On Monday, Bob gave James a review of his visit to the two divisions and said that, as far as he could judge, Bill and Phil had been well received. There had been a little disappointment that none of the local managers had been selected, but Bob had then told them that part of the jobs that Bill and Phil now filled was to develop the managers so that they could be eligible for transfer elsewhere, if they desired that. He had also told them to expect internal audit teams to show up, which, in the case of Albuquerque, caused some smiles, which had bothered him a little, as it suggested that not all was above board.

"So, did you find us somewhere to move this office to?" Bob asked.

"I looked at a few places in Irvine," James replied. "The one I liked best is on the corner of MacArthur and von Karman. There'll be some build-out costs and moving costs, but the rent will probably be negotiated to be a little lower than here."

"And we won't be beholden to Berg any longer," Bob said. "Get Jim to help you and get a lease signed and a contractor, then we'll let Berg know we're not renewing. I'll get Megan to work on what the offices should look like as far as decorating goes. We'll take this furniture with us, so no need for new stuff there. What's your plan for the week?"

"I need to go back to Oak Creek for a short while to get the house sale going," James replied.

"Okay, do that, then get back here and we'll start going through who we have working where, and we need to get a better sense of the markets we serve and what's likely to happen in each of them," Bob said. "I also expect Ray Pierce and Keith Baird out here on Friday with packages for Thompson and Newman. Ray and Keith are flying out in the Lear; you might want to be on it."

"You'd rather have Keith as Corporate Counsel there than Jim?" James asked.

"I'd think it would be better to have the James & Brown guys here, keep Jim out of it, I don't know where his loyalties might lie," Bob explained. "It also gives them the idea that they're considered important enough to warrant corporate attention."

"Will Thompson and Newman take the packages, do you think?" James asked.

"My sense is yes," Bob said. "I think they've both come to recognise that they've reached the end of the easy ride and life from now on may get more demanding, a lot more demanding, so why do that, take the money and run."

"What about Henry White?" James asked.

"I've got someone lined up," Bob said. "Victoria Wilson, she used to work for me, crackerjack HR manager, she's interested you should meet her before we make any change."

"Thanks, anything else?" James asked.

"Yes, I would like you to think about how we divide up our time, my rule of thumb is spend some time on operational performance, not too much, that's what we have division managers for, and spend more time on strategic issues, generals do not plan attacks on hills, they lay out a broader scope for war, and to achieve success we need to know that we have the right people in the right jobs at the right time," Bob said. "So, get comfortable with the operational details, but think a lot more about the markets we're in and what our strategies should be for success."

"I will," James replied.

Move up

Six months on, James and Katrina had moved to California, the Waterford Industries office, now reduced in numbers, had been moved to Irvine, and Bill Evans and Phil Johnson were making real improvements in Pueblo and Albuquerque. David Pratt and Luther Harris had been rumbled and had been prosecuted for fraud and found guilty, and were serving time. Their big mistake had been to cheat on a government contract, so when that was uncovered, the Justice Department came after them. Henry White had been replaced with Victoria Wilson, and James had to agree, she was several steps above Henry in capability. Bob and James had talked to the Parisian and London aerospace representatives, and James had been sent on a flying visit to meet them. He reported back to Bob that both had their contacts in the European aerospace industry and knew what programs there were and what opportunities there might be.

James had also been trotting around the country with Bob, getting to know the markets, business and people in the United States. Katrina had a job; she had been taken on by a company that sold and maintained construction equipment. James had also had his test with the Immigration and Naturalization Service to determine eligibility for citizenship. The hearing actually only took a few minutes, and James had had to answer three questions: who wrote the Star Spangled Banner, what did he understand by inalienable rights, and what were the three branches of the United States Government. After that, he had been tested on his ability to read, write and speak English, and it was done. The actual swearing-in as a citizen normally took place at the Dorothy Chandler Pavilion with a cast of thousands, but James had been instructed to report to a Federal court in Los Angeles, where he had joined a much smaller group that included nuns, military spouses and a few others like himself. The nuns took an alternate oath of allegiance because obviously they would not bear arms to defend the Constitution. For the rest, it was the standard oath, and then the judge just talked. He talked about the changes he had seen over the years in who was becoming a citizen and then what he saw as the responsibilities of being a citizen. When it was all over and people filed out, they were able to pick up not only their naturalisation certificates, but also their new passports, which were part of the special session, as many of the military spouses were leaving shortly for Germany. One thing James had been amused by was that, as part of becoming a citizen, he could have selected a new name for himself and become Ronald Reagan or John Wayne.

After his citizenship was sorted out, Greg Norman, the lawyer who also served as the company security officer, then filed the necessary paperwork to get James a security clearance. The forms had seemed endless to James, and his greatest challenge had been remembering addresses from up to fifteen years earlier. Fortunately, his mother had kept all the old addresses he had had while he was at college, so he was able to complete the form. He also had to get yet another set of fingerprints taken; apparently, the Defense Investigative Service did not share information with the Immigration and Naturalization Service. Greg cautioned him that friends and neighbours might get odd calls enquiring about him and Katrina and their habits, how much they drank and so on. All that done, James then settled down to the business at hand, until one day in mid-December, when Bob called him into his office.

"James, we need to be in Oak Creek next week Wednesday for a board meeting," Bob said. "Bring an overcoat, I looked at the weather, and it's cold, no snow forecast, just wind and chill. Put together a presentation going over third-quarter results and current forecasts for the fourth quarter."
"I'll do that," James said. "Just the financials or a view of the markets as well?"
"Have those ready in case we get asked," Bob said. "Let's review things on Thursday and then if we have to make changes, we can do them on

Friday, we'll fly back on Tuesday and should be able to come back on Thursday morning."

James went to his office and started to put the presentation together. The first task was simple enough; they had the results of the third quarter ready to hand, and they were far enough into December to have a good view of what the year-end would look like. The second task took a little more time, putting into a simple form what was actually quite complex because of all the different markets they served, from aircraft sales to air travel demand and airport and aircraft configurations, to basic industrial markets, offshore oil development, and finally the construction and building maintenance industries. James took from the reports of each division and added his own perspective on what was happening and how it would affect them. By Thursday, he was ready and sat down with Bob and went through all the charts.

"Nice job," Bob said. "Don't see much we need to change here. Get these charts put onto overhead slides and make a dozen hard copies to take with us."

"No changes?" James asked.

"Don't see anything that I'd change," Bob said. "Will you be ready to explain all this and answer questions?"

"You want me to do the presentation?" James asked.

"Right," Bob said. "You've met the board members before; they'll listen, they might ask questions, and just between us, a couple of them might ask penetrating questions, but I doubt it. Hank will have done a good job of prepping them."

"Who do you think is likely to ask anything?" James asked.

"At a guess, I'd say that Collier will ask about building maintenance, that's his business after all, maybe Brant will ask about cash flows and assets, to a banker, that's the be-all and end-all," Bob replied. "The others, maybe one or two things about the airframes and the airlines, but I wouldn't expect too much. Eastwood may ask about industrial gearboxes; they're the most likely to be paired with the electrical equipment he makes. Remember, James, they're just guys who happen to run companies; they're no smarter than you, just longer in the tooth and with more experience."

James went home that evening and related all to Katrina, who was amused by Bob's comments about the directors, or rather his implied comments, almost as if he was saying that they were not that smart.

"Are you ready for them?" she asked.

"As ready as I'll ever be," he said.

"Just don't talk down to them too much," she cautioned.

"What do you mean?" he asked.

"Just because it's obvious to you doesn't mean that everyone else sees it as quickly," she explained. "Please don't ever say, it's so simple, it may not be to them."

"I don't think I'd ever do that," he protested.

"You would if they were being particularly dense," she laughed. "They're all probably expert in their own fields, but don't necessarily do well thinking about other industries."

"Well, it's all straightforward stuff, no leaps of imagination required, and the numbers speak for themselves, which fortunately have improved quite a bit since Bill and Phil took over the two lagging divisions," James said.

"Anyway, good luck next week, I hope you still have a job when you come back," she said.

"I've talked to these *ouks* before," he said. "They're not too bad, just a little slow sometimes."

"That's what I mean," she said. "They're captains of industry, but you think they're slow, so be nice."

"I will, I promise," he laughed. "Shall we go out for dinner tonight?"

"Why not," she agreed. "Let's go to the Orange County Mining Company. I like the views from there."

"Are you gentlemen ready?" Andrew asked when Bob and James went to the hangar at the Santa Ana airport.

"Quick bathroom break, then we can be off," Bob said. Andrew took their bags and stowed them, then waited until they came back, then closed up the plane after they had boarded. They had elected not to leave at the crack of dawn, but at nine, which would put them into Milwaukee at about two-fifteen that afternoon. They took off, out over the ocean, then turned left and climbed out and up to cross the Santa Ana Mountains, then the San Bernardino Mountains. There was actually snow by Big Bear.

"Been up to Big Bear yet?" Bob asked James.

"Not yet," James replied.

"You and Katrina should take a drive up there one day," Bob said. "Go and see how the Angelinos handle snow. There is a chain-up point on the road, so if you haven't got chains for your car, you might want to get some."

"I'll do that, I think for Katrina's Jeep," James said.

"Ready for tomorrow?" Bob asked.

"As ready as I'll ever be," James replied. "Do you want to review the material again?"

"No need," Bob said. "We've been through it enough, any more and we'll be making changes just for the sake of it."

"Mr Decker, would you like lunch now?" Andrew asked as he came aft.

"That would be fine," Bob said. "What did you manage to get?"

"A pretty good-looking salmon," Andrew said. "We've also got a good chardonnay to go with it."

"Thanks, Andrew," Bob said. "So, James, here's luck," he said when they had their wine in hand. "I'm impressed with the way that Evans and Johnson have taken on those divisions. Any more like them in the roster at James & Brown?"

"There are a few more," James replied. "Hank Miller set up a mentor program for a group of us, and he encouraged participation in an executive MBA program that the company paid for."

"That was far-sighted of him," Bob said. "Most companies would just let you muddle through and find your own ways. Who was your mentor?"

"Hank Miller," James replied. "Myself and Bill Evans. He gave us all kinds of things to research and report back on."

"Let's look at the roster for Waterford and see if we can't do something along those lines," Bob suggested. "Oh, I forgot to mention, you'll be left to your own devices tonight, I've got dinner with Hank."

"I'm sure I can amuse myself," James said. "What time in the morning?"

"Board meeting at nine, so we'll be there by eight, give you chance to check the projector," Bob said.

"How was your flight?" Katrina asked James that evening.

"Fine," he replied. "On time, no delays, so good. I was on my own tonight, so I went to the Italian place we like; the waitress there wanted to know where you were. I told her that we've been moved to LA, and she was jealous. It's bloody cold here right now. How was your day?"

"Busy," she replied. "We've just sold a fairly big lot of machines to a contractor who has a big sewer job, so we were busy getting them out. When are you coming home?"

"Bob said that we should come home on Thursday," James replied. "I suppose it all depends on how long this board meeting takes."

"Nervous?" she asked.

"No, actually not a bit," he said. "After the pep talk from Bob, I've no qualms about talking to these *ouks*."

"Well, stay warm, don't freeze your tootsies off," she said.

"I won't," he promised. "Love you."

"Love you," she replied.

"If you'll just wait here," Bob said to James the next morning when they arrived at James & Brown. "We'll call you in when we're ready."

James sat and twiddled his thumbs, wishing that had had the chance to check the projector and make sure things were in order. He waited perhaps half an hour, then he was called in.

"James," Hank said. "Good to have you here, let's hear all about Waterford Industries."

For the next hour, James went through financial reports and the market analyses that he had done. Bob had called it quite well on the questions and questioners, and he was able to answer all that was asked of him.

"Thank you, James," Hank said. "Gentlemen?" he asked, looking at the board members. They all nodded, which must have been some kind of signal or approval from them. "James, we'd like you to take over as President of Waterford Industries, effective immediately. Bob is happy with where you are, and we are too, so there is no need to delay any further."

"Thank you," James said. "I'll try not to disappoint."

"I'm sure you won't," Graham Brant said. "From what Bob has told us, you jumped right in and started sorting things out as soon as you got there, and these results speak for themselves."

"So, gentlemen, lunch?" Hank suggested.

"Good idea," Evan Eastwood said. "You seem to have a good grasp of the markets you serve, James. You must have worked hard to get all that done in six months."

"Bob was a good guide and mentor," James replied.

"Oh, we almost forgot, you'll be in the next option," Hank said. "We'll bump up the options to 10,000. We'll also put in place a change of control agreement that will kick in if all or substantially all of the voting stock in the company changes hands."

"Thank you," James said.

"So, let's go and have lunch," Hank said. He led the way to a conference room where lunch had been set up by a caterer.

"James, I'll be out of your hair on Friday," Bob said. "When we get back, I'll call the staff together and give them the news, then I'll turn things over to you."

"Thanks, Bob," James said. "This was a little unexpected."

"There seemed no point in waiting," Bob said. "We've bumped up your base to $70,000 and your bonus opportunity to 40% of base."

"What should I know about the change in control agreement?" James asked.

"We'll go over that on the plane. What do you feel about going home this afternoon?" Bob asked.

"That would be great," James said.

"Okay, I'll call Andrew and tell him wheels up at four," Bob said. "That should put us back into Santa Ana at about six-fifteen. Okay, you'd better schmooze these guys while they're still sober."

"I'll do that," James said, smothering a laugh.

"So, James, here's how a change of control works," Bob said when they were on the plane, later headed west. "In the event that the company is sold, then you get three times your annual salary, plus incentives, with some provisos. If you quit voluntarily before a change in control, then the company has no obligations; there is a non-compete covenant and a confidentiality covenant. If you're terminated for cause, then all bets are off."

"I presume the change of control means James & Brown," James said. "How does this agreement apply if J&B decides to sell off Waterford, there's no change in control there, and any likely buyer of Waterford is going to want their own man to run the place?"

"Good point," Bob said. "I'll talk to Hank and see if we can't amend your agreement so that if J&B sells off Waterford and J&B doesn't want you back into an equivalent position, then the change of control kicks in for you. Anyway, here's the agreement as it stands now. Read it through and let me know if you have any other questions."

"Who decides who gets these change in control agreements?" James asked.

"Hank and the board for Hank," Bob replied. "He can at any time end the agreements, so don't piss him off unnecessarily."

"What will you do now?" James asked.

"Go back to Arizona full time, fly more, paint, hike, enjoy myself," Bob said. "I promised Hank I'd do this until I thought you could take over, and there's no point in me hanging around any longer."

"If something comes up that I need advice on, could I call you?" James asked.

"Sure, just don't make a habit of it," Bob laughed. "Go with your gut, you've got good instincts, so don't be afraid to make a decision, even if it turns out not to be the best. The worst thing you can often do is waffle too long or get paralysis by analysis. I'll get together with Victoria and we'll cook up an announcement and send it out tomorrow."

James arrived home at seven, a surprise for Katrina, who was not expecting him.

"You're back early," she said. "That's wonderful, good meeting?"

"It was," James replied. "Plus, I've got news, as of this afternoon, I'm the President of Waterford Industries."

"Genuine?" she asked.

"Genuine," he confirmed.

"This deserves a celebration," she said. "Shall we eat in or go out?"

"Let's go out," he said. "I'll stay sober."

"We could always get a driver to take us," she suggested. "Let me check the Yellow Pages. Here's one, SoCal Limos, let's give them a call." Katrina called the service and they could accommodate even at such short notice. The next question was where to eat. They decided on the Orange Hill Restaurant, another restaurant perched on a hill looking over the valley and plains created by the Santa Ana River, replete now with buildings and attractions like Disney Land.

"Okay," James said. "Dinner at seven-forty-five and the driver will wait for us."

They had just enough time to shower and change before the driver came, and he delivered them to the door at seven-forty-five precisely. They had a table outside that gave spectacular views of the lights below and those twinkling in the hills to the east. They could actually see all the way to the coast and gathered that out there in the dark was Catalina Island.

"So, what do we eat?" she asked as they scanned through the menus.

"Pick whatever you want?" he said.

"*Pampoen, rys and vleis,*" she joked.

"Somehow I don't think that pumpkin, rice and meat are on the menu," he laughed. "But, you're right, this is a far cry from Kitwe or Calitzdorp and the dive your dad liked. We've come a long way."

"You have," she said. "I've just tagged along."

"I don't think so," he said. "Without you and your support, I wouldn't be in the job I have now."

"Good evening, folks," the waiter said. "Are we celebrating something special?"

"We are," Katrina said. "But we don't want any kind of fuss."

"What may I bring you to drink?" he asked.

"Bring us a bottle of the Rousseau Pinot Noir," James replied.

"The 1980?" the waiter asked.

"That would be fine," James confirmed.

"I'll be back to take your dinner orders," the waiter promised. He came back, served wine and took their orders for dinner, which was very good, and later, after they had been delivered back to their house, they celebrated again, this time in bed.

"Ladies and gentlemen, I've called this meeting to make a quick announcement," Bob said to the assembled staff the next day. "As of eleven am Central Standard Time yesterday, James became the President and CEO of Waterford Industries. I will be leaving tomorrow and leaving you all in James's capable hands. I know I don't have to make the usual speeches about supporting him, because I know you will. Victoria and I will draft up an announcement today that we'll send out to the divisions and the industry press, and Victoria and I will call the various division managers and tell them about James."

"Congrats, James," Mike McKane said.

"Indeed, congrats," Victoria echoed "Are you going to make any changes?"

"Not that I can see," James replied. "I think we've done enough changing for a while, don't you?"

"Do you want to move your office?" Megan asked.

"I think we should do that," Bob said. "Let's set things up for lunch and a celebratory drink tomorrow, then I'll bail out and fly home."

"Yes, Mr Decker," Megan said. On that note, everyone left to go back to their jobs, except Greg Norman.

96

"By the way, James, your secret clearance came through," Greg told him. "I have to give you a security briefing at some time on how to handle documents and information."

"What about now?" James asked.

"Can do," Greg said.

"Megan, what is there that I should be aware of for the calendar?" James asked that afternoon.

"Well, there's the Paris Air Show in late May, early June, there's the Offshore Technology Conference in Houston in early May, there's an AIA meeting in Williamsburg in March and another in Arizona in September," she replied. "Then there's the J&B board meetings, I've got the dates here, I don't know how many they'll want you to go to. As far as the various events go, Berg would take his wife to the Paris show, which is on the odd years, so next year, but not to the Farnborough show, which is on the even years. For the AIA, Williamsburg is all business, no spouses, but Arizona is at the Biltmore, and there are organised events for the spouses."

"AIA?" James asked.

"Aerospace Industries Association," Megan explained.

"Thanks, Megan," James said. "How far ahead do we have to make bookings for hotels and such?"

"That will depend on where you want to stay," she said. "Berg used to stay at the Georges Cinq in Paris, at the Excelsior in Farnborough and the Hilton by the convention hall in Houston. The AIA meetings are both residential, so if we tell them that you'll be there, they'll assign rooms, and we have to pay, of course."

"What should I go to?" he asked.

"That's up to you," she said. "But we are members of the AIA, so you should probably go to those meetings. I'd go to the OTC just to see what is going on in the industry, and I gather that this year the US is returning to the Paris Air Show in force, so I'd do that as well. Mr Decker had asked me to look into reservations for airlines and hotels for Paris. I have the options any time you're ready."

"Let's do that after I've talked to Katrina," he said. "I'll talk to Katrina tonight about Paris and the Arizona Biltmore and see what she wants to do. Could you get from Hank Miller's office the schedule for board meetings, and next time I talk to him, I'll see which ones he wants me to go to. Next week I should probably make the rounds of the divisions before Christmas, so let's look at the calendar."

"Here you go," she said, giving him a calendar for December.

"Let's fly to Tulsa on Monday morning," he thought. "Visit with hoists that day and in the afternoon fly to Pueblo, then on the 18th, Pueblo in the morning and Albuquerque in the afternoon. On the morning of the 19th, hop up to Seattle, visit with Marine, then fly back to Santa Ana that evening, finishing up with industrial and actuation on Thursday."

"He had planned a Christmas party here on the Friday," she said.

"Let's keep that," he said. "We'll close up early for Christmas Eve and be back here on January the 2nd."

"I'll let everyone know," she said.

"I should call the divisions and tell them when I'm going to be there," he said. "Thanks, Megan."

"Lovey, what do you think about going to Paris next May to the Paris Air Show?" James asked Katrina that evening.

"When is it?" she asked.

"Starts the 26th of May and runs until the 5th of June," he replied.

"I could get time off for that," she said. "Even if it's unpaid."

"There's also a big industry meeting at the Arizona Biltmore in the autumn," he added. "Spouses are invited to that one, and I gather there are planned events for spouses if you want to join them."

"Sounds flashy," she said. "When is it?"

"I'll get the actual dates," he promised. "Apparently, we're a member of this association, mixing with the famous names of aerospace. I'm a little apprehensive about that. I don't really see myself in the same league as the boss of Boeing or McDonnell Douglas."

"You'll be fine," she said. "Now, what about taking a trip up to Big Bear this weekend?"

"That sounds like fun," he said. "Bob said to get chains because they could have a chain-up rule partway up the road. I thought we'd get some for your Jeep."

"I'll take care of that tomorrow, one of the chaps in the office knows someone in the wheel and tyre business, and I heard him mention chains one day," she said. "I'll get two sets, so if we have to, we can do both axles."

"Should we stay the night in Big Bear somewhere?" he asked.

"If we can find a room," she said. "I'll call tomorrow morning and see if I can find somewhere."

The celebratory lunch and drinks the next day were quite a short affair as Bob was not drinking; he did not believe in drinking and flying. James thought that most were interested to see if he would change the tone of the company and the office, but he had no intentions of doing that, at least until some situation arose that called for a change. Bob left at one and flew off to Arizona, and James sat in his new office and thought about what he needed to do. As far as he could see, what he needed to do was to continue building the relationships between himself and the division managers. They were the ones who made things happen on a daily basis. What he needed to do was ensure that he could trust them, then focus on markets and strategies to succeed in those markets. He finally called it a day and left at four to fight the traffic on his way home. At least it was just a simple drive up Jamboree, a lot better than sitting in the 55 for an hour.

"I found us a place," Katrina told James when he arrived home. "It's a place called Pine Tree Lodge on the lake that has cabins. The cabin is a little large just for the two of us, but it's all they had."

"When should we leave?" he asked.

"Let's get an early start, say six in the morning," she suggested.

"Early," he commented.

"Early, yes," she said. "It's about eighty miles, so probably close to two hours, freeway all the way to San Bernardino, then up the mountain, which, looking at the map, I would say is a winding road. The lodge told me that we could check in early."

Traffic on the 55, 91, 215, 10 and 210 freeways was quite light, so they made it to the foot of the mountains in under an hour, then things slowed down quite a bit as they wound their way up the mountain.

"There's a sign just ahead that says chains are required," Katrina said. "I see a lay by there, I'll pull over and you can put the chains on."

Just as well I looked at them last night," James commented. "At least I know how to do it. He got out of the Jeep with the chains, laid out and straightened them, then draped them over the back tyres, then got Katrina to slowly inch forward until he could join them up. The last thing he did was use the special tool to tighten the side chains so they would not flop around as they drove.

"All done," he told Katrina as he got back into the Jeep.

"There's a lot of cars coming down," she said. "I wonder why." She drove ahead, and around the next bend was a roadblock manned by a California Highway Patrol Trooper. He turned the car in front of them around because they had no chains fitted, then he looked over their Jeep and waved them through.

"They're serious," James commented as Katrina accelerated away.

"Probably worried that some idiot will slip off the side of the road and go tumbling down the mountain," she said. "I'm glad we got the chains; at least we can go all the way up."

Katrina drove them to the lodge, and they checked in and were shown their cabin. It looked out onto the lake and the hills beyond, now all covered with snow. There was actually quite a lot of snow on the ground, and more was expected that night, another six inches forecasted; no wonder the Highway Patrol was turning people away whose vehicles had not been chained up.

"You know," she said as they unpacked. "We should see if we can't find somewhere up here for Christmas. I know it's short notice, but you never know. Why don't I run over to the lodge and see if they know of anywhere?" She was back in a few minutes with news. "There's a place in the woods, about a mile and a half from the lake, that's available if we go now; the owner will meet us there."

"Let's do that," he said. They drove to the cabin, using the directions given them by the lodge and found the cabin, set among tall pine trees. It was quite isolated; they could see no neighbours around. They saw a woman they presumed to be the owner and pulled up next to her.

"Howdy folks, I'm Liz," she said. "Mary at Pine Tree told me that you might be interested in the cabin over Christmas."

"We are," Katrina replied. "I'm surprised it hasn't been rented out already."

"It was, but a death in the family put paid to that," Liz explained. "Come on in and take a look."

They followed Liz in, and it was a studio cabin, all in one room, except the bathroom, which was separate. It had a porch in the front and a wood shed at the rear with wood for the stove that was there for heat.

"It's lovely," Katrina said. "James, what do you think?"

"I like it," he said.

"When do you want it from, to?" Liz asked. "I can let you have it from Christmas Eve to the 3rd of January."

"Could we take it from Christmas Eve to the second?" Katrina asked.

"Sure," Liz replied.

"That would be super," Katrina said. "We'll do that."

"Why don't you follow me to my house, and you'll know then where to pick up the keys, and we can sort out the money at the same time," Liz suggested. "Where are you folks from?"

"We live in Orange now, we've just moved here from Wisconsin," Katrina replied.

"Okay, but that's not a Wisconsin accent," Liz said.

"No, I'm from Zambia, and James is from England," Katrina elaborated.

"Zambia, where's that, South Africa?" Liz asked.

"Two countries north," Katrina said. "Across the Limpopo and Zambezi rivers, it used to be Northern Rhodesia."

"Right," Liz said. "Bit different to this."

"It is," Katrina agreed. "No snow, ever, in Zambia, much closer to the equator."

"Look, I'll give you the key to the place, so when you come up, you won't have to swing by the house. When you leave, drop the keys in that box there," Liz said. "Remember to bring all your food and drink, the stores we have may not be open when you get here. Oh, something you should know, because your Jeep is four-wheel drive and has snow tires, you don't actually need chains under the California regs."

"I was thinking that I'd leave them on so that I could stop," Katrina said. "Four-wheel drive doesn't really help if there's ice."

"True, too true," Liz agreed, nodding. "But we've got enough snow and it's cold enough that I don't see any thaw and refreeze happening, so we shouldn't get much ice."

"She gave us quite a deal," James commented to Katrina when they had gone back to the other cabin.

"She told me that there was a cancellation policy and the other renters had to forfeit, so she gave us a discount," Katrina explained. "I'll put together a menu for the week we're in the mountains and do the shopping next week. When do you think you could get away on Christmas Eve?"

"I'll try and get away as soon as I can," he said. "I'll bet that traffic on the 91 is going to be a zoo."

"Let's bring the cross-country skis we got in Oak Creek," she suggested. "We might want to go out at least on one day."

"So, what shall we do today?" he asked.

"Take a walk out to the lakefront, have lunch at the lodge, then try out the bed," she suggested.

"I like that plan," he said.

They spent the rest of the day, after lunch, being lazy and making love on the bed, in front of the fire and in the bath. When they went back to the lodge for dinner, Mary commented that she had not seen much of them.

"We had some catching up to do," Katrina said.

"Well, this is as good a place as any to do that," Mary said, grinning. "Are you set for Christmas?"

"We are," Katrina confirmed. "We met with Liz and worked everything out. We'll be driving up on Christmas Eve."

"It'll probably take you a good three to four hours to get up here," Mary said. "Angelinos like to get away for weekends, so traffic is usually bad. If you want my advice, don't come up from San Bernardino; you'll hit a lot of slow traffic. Go up the Cajon to Victorville and come in the backside through Lucerne, it's further in miles, but it's probably quicker. The other option is to take Highway 38 from Redlands and come up that way."

"Thanks, Mary," James said.

"That was fun," James commented to Katrina when they arrived home on Sunday afternoon.

"It was," she agreed. "I'm looking forward to the week after next. Imagine a whole week with nothing to do, nowhere to go, we might even get snowed in. So, this week, what's the plan?"

"I'll fly to Tulsa tomorrow morning, then in the afternoon fly to Pueblo and spend the night there, then I'll hop over to Albuquerque Tuesday afternoon, spend the night there, then on Wednesday fly up to Seattle and come back here that evening, Thursday I'll do the two divisions here," he replied.

"So, only two nights away," she commented.

"Thanks to having the plane to use," he said. "Otherwise, it would probably be all week."

"Let's hope Hank Miller doesn't take it away," she said.

James was up and away early the next morning and drove to the airport and met the pilots there.

"All ready, Mr Martin?" Andrew asked.

"Ready when you are," James replied.

"Flight time to Tulsa, two hours fifteen," Andrew said. "Touch down at eleven fifteen local."

"Thanks, Andrew and tonight?" James asked.

"Hour and seventeen," Andrew replied. "Plus, we pick up the hour coming back to Mountain Time."

James had what he thought was a very good meeting with Ed McIntosh. He and his team were delighted with their projected year-end numbers and saw strong orders for at least the first half of 1985. In Pueblo, he had dinner with Bill and Amanda Evans and was pleased to hear that they had settled in well. At the division meeting the next day, James was gratified to see that the improvements were continuing and that the general tone of the place had changed a lot. There were no loaders sitting on the floor waiting for some decision to be made, and things looked a lot neater and tidier. In the actual meeting, there was banter and laughter, something that had been completely absent before. When James left to fly to Albuquerque, Kathy commented that things were so much better since Bill Evans had taken over; it was now a nice place to work, and she and the others enjoyed coming to work.

In Albuquerque, the report from Phil Johnson was very encouraging, and James even met the DCAS inspector who was fulsome in his praises of the changes made. James imagined that was partly because his job was now much easier; all he had to do was accept the finished product and not get embroiled in long and drawn-out discussions about what was acceptable and what was not. Phil had acquired new machines and had also temperature-controlled the workplace, and that had made the world of difference, as he pointed out to James. If they had a cold morning, then a warm afternoon, some parts could grow by a tenth of an inch or more, which was sometimes the margin of error in the specifications. He had also put in a better paint system, so now they had mirror finishes that pleased the customers. James had dinner that night with Phil and Susan and learned all about their move. Apparently, the moving company had had problems with the van driver with their goods, and he had gone missing for two weeks. When he finally did show up, all was in order, so who knew what he had been up to.

The trip to Seattle was dreary, mainly because the weather was dreary. It was typical of Seattle, overcast skies, light rain, tending to mist and fog, fortunately not thick enough to interfere with landings and takeoffs. The marine operations themselves were doing moderately well; there had been some order cancellations that had left a small hole in the results for the year. Fortunately for James, the improvements at Pueblo and Albuquerque more than made up for the shortfall from Seattle; Oak Creek would be happy, or at least would have little to carp and cavil about. Paul Rose at the marine division was cautious about the outlook for 1985, but for at least the first half, they were booked solid. He felt that the cancellations had to do with a loss of a contract that the customer had had to deal with. That had removed the need for the equipment, and the contract had gone to another company that had contracted with one of the marine division's competitors.

"Let's go home," James said to Andrew when he joined the pilots at Boeing Field.
"Good day?" Andrew asked.
"Not bad," James replied. "What are you doing over the Christmas break?"
"The plane's going in for a routine check, and Greg and I are going skiing in the Sierras," Andrew replied.
"Have fun and try not to break anything," James said.
"I'll try," Andrew laughed. "We'll be on the ground in Santa Ana at four ten."
"Thanks, just in time to hit rush hour traffic," James commented. "Where did you find a place to live?"
"I got an apartment off Harvard in Irvine, and Greg bought a house in Costa Mesa, so both of us are pretty close to the airport," Andrew replied. "If you're ready, we'll go."
They did land at four ten on the dot, and James wondered if they did not deliberately slow their approach so that they would land at the predicted time; they either did that or they were really good at route planning down to the last detail. His drive home up Jamboree was a little slow, but faster than it would have been on the 55. He actually made it home before Katrina did, which was a first.

"You're home already," she commented when she arrived fifteen minutes later.

"We finished fairly quickly in Seattle, so there was no point in hanging around," he said. "I even started on dinner, so get a glass of wine, sit down and relax."

James made his last two visits the next day and was delighted to see that Stuart Winter had taken a leaf out of John Trent's book and had started to implement total quality control and just-in-time methods, and was seeing reductions in scrap and costs already with a longer run program for actuators supplied to one of the major airframe companies. Stuart was so happy with the results that he was making a factory-wide push and had classes running, quality circles going, and teams looking at anything and everything in the processes. The only resistance he was meeting was with some of the old-time quality inspectors who saw their jobs in jeopardy. As things improved, the need for inspectors declined, but to satisfy customers, they were still useful, and Stuart was looking for ways to engage them in the process, rather than have them on the side looking on. John Trent was going from strength to strength and was making improvements all over the place, and he now wanted new machines to cut parts to even tighter tolerances. James approved those that he could and forwarded others to Oak Creek for approval, as a couple of them were beyond his dollar authority level. Back in his own office, he asked Megan to set up a meeting in March where all the division managers would be in Irvine. He felt it would be useful for them all to spend a little time together. He spent Friday going over everything for the past year and writing reports that he would send back to Oak Creek. Katrina had plans for the weekend, mainly around shopping and packing, so that they would be ready to leave as soon as possible on Monday.

Christmas

Christmas Eve, James suggested to everyone that they leave at about noon. He then drove home, and Katrina was ready to leave with her Jeep fuelled, food and drink, and their bags packed and stowed. James changed clothes in record time, grabbed something to eat, and they set off. They cut over the hill to Imperial, then paralleled the 91 as far as Gypsum Canyon, by which time the merging of traffic from the 55 and the 91 was mostly sorted out. The traffic was moving, not very quickly, but it was moving.

"I'll bet this will be at a standstill in another hour or so," James said to Katrina. "I'm glad I closed the office early so that we could get an early start."

"I wonder how long before it thins out a little," she said. "When we get to the 15, we should take it; if we're going through Victorville, we don't need to go to San Bernardino."

"I see the signs ahead," James said. He took the exit that led them to the 15, and traffic sped up, only slowing a little when they crossed the 60 and 10 freeways and had to merge with traffic coming from them. Just past Rancho Cucamonga, the road started to climb, and they merged with the 215 and set off up the Cajon Pass.

"There's a train coming down," Katrina said, pointing to it.

"I'll bet that could be scary if the brakes fail," he said. "I wonder if it's ever happened. I can't believe the amount of traffic we're still seeing."

"Well, this is the main road to Las Vegas, so maybe many of these people are going there," Katrina suggested.

"We're at the top already," James said. "Let's fill up in Victorville before we go to Big Bear. I'd say that we'll be in Victorville by two-thirty, that's not too bad. Where's the turn-off for Lucerne?"

"Looking at the map, it's almost past the town, Highway 18, when you see the signs," she replied.

"Anything else we need?" James asked Katrina as they filled the Jeep.

"Some coffee might be nice, I'll see if they have anything inside," she replied. "For you?"

"That would be nice, thanks," he said. She was back in a trice with the coffees, and they left bound for Lucerne, which turned out to be a small settlement in the desert, strung out along the road. In the background to the south were the San Bernardino Mountains, and to the north, the occasional little hill and lots of desert scrub. They turned off what one would have thought was the main road and started towards the mountains. They passed a huge cement works, then started climbing until they came to a chain-up point.

"So, shall we put the chains on or risk it?" Katrina asked.

"I think put them on, why take a chance," he said. He pulled over and quickly put the chains on, tightened them and then they were off again, climbing even more.

"There's a Highway Patrol car ahead," Katrina commented.

"He's turning those people around," James said. He pulled up to the police checkpoint and was waved through. The road climbed more, getting into an area where the road had been ploughed, but more snow was coming down and accumulating, so ploughing would be needed again at some point. They reached the top, then started down towards the lake.

"This hasn't taken very long," Katrina commented as they drove towards the airport and the turn-off that took them to the cabin. "I'll bet the road up from San Bernardino is a zoo. There's a lot of snow here, and it's really coming down now. Any signs of ice on the road?"

"Not that I can feel," he replied. "Let's slow down a little and see if we stop easily."

"At this rate, we'll be at the cabin by four," she said. "I'm glad you were able to close up early so that we could get away before the big rush."

The side road that actually led to the cabin had been ploughed earlier, so although there was about two feet of snow on the sides, there was only four inches or so on the road itself, but with the snow that was coming down, there would probably be another inch or two on the road before it was finished. James put the Jeep into low range, built up momentum, pushed through the pile of snow that had been thrown up by the ploughs that had dealt with the main road and just kept going, no matter how the snow pushed the Jeep around, until they reached the cabin.

"It's like driving down the road to Mkushi in the rains, only snow, not mud," he said. "Just keep going, don't stop. Fortunately, the Jeep's ground clearance is more than enough for this much snow, so we wouldn't bottom out."

"If you get a fire going in the cabin, I'll unpack," she suggested. "There's someone coming."

They both watched as a truck came up the road, ploughing snow out of the way, further up the sides, so there was now an even bigger pile on each side of the track.

"Howdy folks," a man said as he pulled up to them. "I'm Grant, Liz's husband. You must have made good time to get up here."

"We left early and came through Victorville," James explained.

"No problems with the road here then?" Grant asked.

"None," James confirmed. "It's like driving in deep mud."

"I'll be back when this stops to clear the track again," Grant promised. "Anything you need?"

"No, thank you," James replied. "We're just going to light the stove and unpack."

"Well, enjoy your stay," Grant said. "Watch out for the raccoons, don't leave any food lying around."

"We'll make sure there's nothing lying around," Katrina assured him. "What else might we see up here?"

"Well, let's see, we've got mule deer, gray fox, coyotes, bobcats, mountain lions, and the usual small critters like raccoons and squirrels, plus loads of birds, look out for jays, they'll steal things, we've got bears too, but they're in hibernation right now, otherwise I'd warn you against leaving anything edible in your Jeep," Grant said.

Later that evening, with the stove lit and throwing off heat, it got quite warm in the cabin, warm enough that winter pullovers were not needed. Katrina made some dinner, and they sat and ate it off their laps in front of the stove.

"I wonder what heats the water," Katrina said.

"I saw an electric water heater," James replied. "And it's a big tank, so there'll be plenty of hot water. The only issue with this cabin is that it has a shower and no bath."

"We'll manage," she said. "How cold is it outside?"

"It's still snowing, not too cold," he said.

"Let's get some cocoa and our coats and sit out on the porch and listen to the peace," she suggested.

"I like the way the snow makes everything quiet," he said.

"Here you are," she said a few minutes later, handing him a cup of cocoa. "What can you see or hear?"

"I thought I saw a couple of birds flitting around," he replied. "But no animals yet."

"It's quiet, isn't it?" she commented. "Just a little bit of wind in the trees. This is going to be a wonderful Christmas."

"Do you remember our first Christmas?" he asked.

"That's when you asked me to marry you," she said. "If you hadn't asked, I was going to ask you. This is quite a change from Kitwe."

"I remember when we visited your folks in the Cape that Christmas and we went for a walk up the Gamka and you stripped off completely in the sunshine," he said lovingly as he recalled the day.

"I remember my mum telling me that we were lucky no hikers had come down the *kloof* or botanists looking at the *fynbos*," she said.

"I suppose when you were picking bits of grass out of your hair, it did rather give the game away," he laughed.

"Well, we're not doing that here," she said. "Too bloody cold out here, but the bed does look inviting and it's warm enough inside to do without clothes."

The next morning, when James was out in the woodshed, he saw a couple of mule deer tripping through the snow at the front of the cabin. He went back inside, tapped Katrina lightly and motioned for her to join him at the front door. They watched the deer who saw them, and froze and watched and listened, alert to any threat. Finally, they moved off slowly, intent on whatever their next mission was.

"That was super," she said when they went back inside. "I wonder if anything else came by during the night."

"I'll take a look around after breakfast," he said. "What would you like for breakfast?"

"Porridge," she replied. "I brought some oatmeal and some bananas to have with it. Do you fancy trying some cross-country skiing later?"

"Okay," he said. "At least here we won't get lost; all we'll have to do is turn around and follow our own tracks back."

"It seems like an odd way to spend Christmas Day," she laughed.

"We don't have to be gone long," he said. "Just long enough to build up an appetite."

"An appetite for what?" she asked.

"You, of course, then maybe something to eat," he said.

"Boasting again," she laughed. "We'll see. You're like one of these mule deer bucks in rutting season, but for you, the season is all year."

"That's because you're the most desirable doe around," he said.

"I'm the only one," she remarked. "Just make sure it stays that way."

After breakfast, James got the skis and waxed them, ready for the excursion into the woods. He also looked around the cabin for tracks and found ones that looked like little hands and assumed that those must be raccoon tracks, and even smaller ones that he knew were squirrels. There were also more deer tracks, but nothing else. The snow had stopped and the skies had cleared, and sunlight was streaming through the trees. It was a day for sunglasses as the glare off the snow was fierce. They set off, sinking into the deep snow, but the going was good, but uphill, which meant the trip back to the cabin would be downhill all the way. It was quite hard work, made harder by the fact that they were at an altitude of over 6,000 feet. After an hour going uphill, they stopped, had some tea and biscuits and sat and listened to the quiet and the noises of the forest, the wind in the trees, the birds, the squirrels chattering away, and an occasional far-off sound of human activity, like a plane landing.

"Look, that must be one of the jays that Grant mentioned," Katrina said, pointing to a bird that was looking at them from its perch in a tree.

"Probably wondering if we've anything worth stealing," James said. "I like his little top knot, makes him look most distinguished."

"Ssh," she said, pointing. "More deer over there."

"They've got big ears," James whispered to her. "Like those of a kudu."

"I suppose they must be mule deer," she thought. "Don't mules also have big ears?"

"Those that I've seen," he agreed.

"They're off," she said. "Oh, that's why, there's people over there making a noise, can you see them through the trees?"

"I see them," he said. "Time for us to go."

They put their skis back on and set off back down, a trip of only took twenty minutes.

"That was fun," Katrina said as she stripped off her long socks that were quite wet from pushing through the soft, deep snow. "I'm going to have a shower, are you joining me?"

"If there's room," he said. There was room, if you were cosy with your partner.

"I think the first time we did it in a shower was in Mkushi," she said.

"But there the water was cold; this is better with the hot water. Before that, there was the road past Kamfinsa, and it was pouring with rain, but that was a lovely day. Are you ready?"

"Just feel behind you," he said. She did, found him and guided him into her.

"That's good," she said. "Now make love to me, my big rutting buck."

"Lunch," Katrina said later.

"What are we having?" he asked.

"I brought a chicken I had roasted, baked a couple of potatoes and added some broccoli," she replied. "And I've got a nice Chablis."

"Would you like your Christmas present now or after lunch?" he asked.

"After lunch," she said. "So, Paris in May sounds romantic."

"I'm not sure how much time we'll have and how much time I'll have to spend at the air show," he said.

"I'll amuse myself," she said. "Will you have to do much entertaining in the evenings?"

"I doubt it," he said. "We're one of the smaller companies in the industry and I don't see us making big deals at the show, not like Boeing, McDonnell, Lockheed or Airbus."

"I wonder where we'll be next year," she said. "Life so far with you has been a big adventure, always something new, let's see our first Christmas was in Kitwe, then the next one we took that trip to Kafue, then the third was when we visited my folks in Calitzdorp and yours in England, then we moved to Mkushi for a couple of years, then to the States and we got to go skiing in Durango with John and Roberta. I know we had another Christmas in the States before we went back to Jo'burg and spent that Christmas with my folks, then back here and more Christmases in Wisconsin."

"It's been interesting," he agreed. "Made more so because I've got you to share it with."

"Don't get maudlin on me," she laughed. "Pour me some more wine; neither of us is driving anywhere today."

They spent the next few days skiing, eating and drinking and making love in the evenings, or at odd times of the day as the mood took them, and sitting on the porch watching deer and other animals, and at night listening to the sounds and trying to identify them. They were sure of the fox and the coyote, and debated another sound that they decided must be a bobcat or a cougar. There were no more snowfalls, but there was plenty on the ground, and they saw on their quick trip to the shops one day that the main roads were quite clear now, and they felt that they could remove the chains. The south side of the lake, where the shops were, was much more populated than the north side, and they both felt fortunate to have found a cabin that was as secluded as it was. All too soon New Year came, and they packed up to leave and drive back to Orange. They dropped the keys where Liz had told them, then drove over the pass to Lucerne. That road was now quite clear, and the requirement for chains had been lifted. There was some traffic, and they both guessed that later in the day that it would pick up and slow down. When they reached Victorville, they filled up and then took off down the Cajon Pass. Traffic was already building up, and at each interchange with the various freeways, it slowed down until people sorted themselves out. They were home by eleven in the morning, quite a quick trip, really, of only two and a half hours.

"When's your next trip?" Katrina asked James as they unpacked the Jeep.

"I think later in the month," he said. "I'll have to spend some time in the office for the year-end close."

"I enjoyed our stay in the mountains," she said. "I'm not sure I want to go back to living with snow, but it was fun for the time we spent there."

"Right," he agreed. "Shovelling snow was never my favourite thing to do. If we lived in the snow again, I'd definitely get a snow blower. I did notice that the snow up there wasn't the heavy sticky stuff we got in Wisconsin."

For the next three months, James made his pilgrimages to Oak Creek, made his rounds of his divisions and spent time planning strategies for success. He was invited to the industry meeting in Williamsburg, so packed his bags, said his farewells to Katrina and flew to Newport News then drove out to Williamsburg.

"Mr Martin, welcome to Colonial Williamsburg," the lady at the front desk said. "We have your room here, and you might wish to check in with the event organisers; their desk is over there."

"Thank you," James said. He went to the event desk and introduced himself, and was given a name badge and a packet of information, which included meal times, meeting times and other options available. He looked through the schedule and saw that it was quite full, so prepared himself for a busy couple of days. He then looked through the list of attendees and got to wondering again why he was even there. The heads of Boeing, Northrop, McDonnell Douglas, Raytheon, Grumman, LTV, TRW, Garrett, Rockwell and numerous other personages were there, whereas he was just with a fairly small company that only had a limited involvement in aerospace. He resolved to sit back and watch and try not to be heard, lest he make a fool of himself. As the day progressed, it was apparent that although there were meetings, presentations and reports, there was a good deal of networking between the industry leaders. Many said hello to James and welcomed him to the association, and were very gracious.

On the second day, he was sitting at breakfast when he was joined by a man whose name badge identified him as Tom Ellison, the CEO of Miller Aerospace. James was well acquainted with them and knew that they built planes for the Air Force and Navy, and drones for the Air Force.

"James Martin, right, Waterford?" he asked.

"That's right," James confirmed.

"Are you based in LA?" Ellison asked.

"I am," James confirmed.

"When we get back, come and see me next week, Tuesday at ten," Ellison said, handing James his card.

"Thank you, I will," James said, wondering what this was about. It was hardly likely to be a job offer as he had only recently taken over Waterford.

"Enjoying the sessions?" Ellison asked.

"I feel rather out of place," James admitted. "We're such a small company compared to most here."

"Maybe, but you guys make good gearboxes and actuation systems," Ellison commented.

"We think so," James said. "We've got a line of AMAD and EMAD boxes, plus linear and rotary actuators, and electric motors to drive them that we make ourselves."

"You're new to Waterford. Where were you before?" Ellison asked.

"I'm a transplant from James & Brown," James replied. "I started there as an application engineer sizing mining equipment, then I was sent to Africa to run the South African operation, then moved back here in mergers and acquisitions."

"Interesting background, what's your education?" Ellison asked.

"I'm a mining engineer, started my career as a first-line supervisor in an underground copper mine in Zambia, then I ran a start-up surface mine," James replied.

"That must have been different," Ellison asked.

"It had its challenges," James said. "Border closures, shortages, all that sort of thing. Keeping all the equipment running was a challenge, but we worked it out."

"Ever blow anything up?" Ellison asked.

"Almost every day," James replied. "It was all hard rock mining, so we used a lot of explosives. Tell me, I've seen some things on planes that you build, and I know we supply components, do you have anything particular in mind?"

"We can talk about that next week," Ellison said. "Bring Stuart Winter with you."

"I'll do that," James promised.

"So, I know about you guys from gearboxes and actuation. What else does Waterford do?" Ellison asked.

"We've a line of industrial gearboxes," James started. "Then we have a marine division that makes positioning winches, pipe and cable laying equipment, unrep machinery for the Navy, a hoist division that makes access equipment for building maintenance, an airport service business that makes loaders, and a structures division that makes panels, nacelles, doors, racks and other parts for planes."

"When you come and see me, bring some information about the structures operation," Ellison said.

"Hey, you guys, mind if I join you?" a man said. James took a look at his name tag and recognised the company as being the aerospace division of another major conglomerate. That put paid to any further discussion between James and Tom Ellison.

The man who had joined them was known to Tom Ellison, who made the introductions.

"James, this is Robert Warner. He heads up Locomotive Springs, which builds ballistic missile stages out in the Utah desert. Robert, this is

James Martin. He took over Waterford when they were bought by James & Brown."

"Good to meet you, James," Robert said. "I read about that, bit of a shift for James & Brown, isn't it?"

"Yes and no," James replied. "The industrial gearboxes, marine systems, loaders and hoists are very similar to machines J&B makes; the big shift is with the aerospace companies. Very different go-to-market strategies."

"I can imagine," Robert said. "As you can imagine, our markets are very limited; the government doesn't want us selling rockets or parts of rockets to just anyone."

"Why Locomotive Springs?" James asked.

"It's a small town in Utah, really small, and it's not that far from where the company did its first tests," Robert explained. "The actual springs are now part of a wildlife management area. It's close to the Golden Spike Memorial."

"It's a bit remote for me," Tom said. "I went to the Golden Spike once, bleak as hell out there, but if you like hunting, shooting and fishing, hell of a place to camp out."

"You should come out and see us sometime," Robert said to James. "What did you do before Waterford?"

"I started out as a mining engineer in Zambia, then when the mine I was running closed down, when the copper price plummeted, I joined James & Brown as an application engineer. I've been to Utah, to Bingham Canyon, but nowhere else. J&B sent me to run their South African sub for a while, then I came back here and spent some time in market research, then joined the acquisition team that we had. After we purchased Waterford, I was sent out to learn a bit about the business and took over last year," James replied.

"Interesting," Robert said. "Say, we should head off to the meeting, don't want to be late."

The rest of the meetings that James went to were interesting, and he learned a lot, particularly about the industry in general. He tried as hard as he could to continue to efface himself from the group and be seen but not heard. He felt he had little to contribute to such an august gathering. He did wonder at what point such industry gatherings crossed the line into something that could be interpreted by government regulators as anti-competitive, but felt sure that all those there were clever enough to never get caught in that trap. By the time that James left the meeting, he was actually known by quite a few of the companies that Waterford did business with and some others besides. From his point of view, it had been useful; he had not made a fool of himself, he had not projected himself as someone who knew it all, but as someone prepared to listen to those who had more experience and who dealt with larger companies than Waterford, or even James & Brown would ever be.

"How was Williamsburg?" Katrina asked when James arrived home.
"Interesting," he replied. "We're really a very small fish, so I sat back and listened a lot."
"When's the next meeting?" she asked.
"This autumn at the Biltmore in Phoenix," he said. "That one includes spouses, and I gather from what I heard this week that they arrange tours and things for the spouses."
"I don't suppose any of the spouses are men," she laughed. "That would mean having a woman run one of the companies."
"I don't recall one," James said. "My guess is that it will take some time before that happens, but it would be interesting to see how they handled that."
"So, what do I have to take to wear at this Biltmore thing?" she asked.
"No idea," James said. "When we're in Paris at the Air Show, I'll ask a couple of the blokes I met this week and get some idea."
"What do I take to Paris?" she asked.
"I'd take a nice dress in case we go to a fancy dinner, something casual and comfortable to trot around Paris in," he suggested. "I'll have to take suits and ties."
"Maybe you should get a new suit," she suggested. "That one's getting a little worn."
"Let's go shopping at the weekend," he suggested. "What colour suit?"

"Grey or blue," she suggested. "Don't go with black, you'd look too much like an undertaker, brown's too casual, grey or dark blue."

"So, suit shopping today?" Katrina asked on Saturday. "Where to?"
"Let's try Nordstrom in the South Coast Plaza," he suggested. "I can probably get something that doesn't need any alterations."
"Maybe I should get something for Paris at the same time," she said.
They drove to South Coast Plaza and went first to Nordstrom and the men's department. There were racks of ready-made suits, arranged by colour and then size. James knew where to look for size, so the only decision was colour.
"Grey or blue pinstripe?" he asked.
"I think grey," she said.
"Two-piece or three-piece?" he asked.
"I think waistcoats are not that popular any more," she said. "I think if you got one, it would sit in the wardrobe gathering dust."
"May I help you, Sir?" an assistant asked.
"I need a new suit," James replied.
"Let's see, 40 long," the assistant said. "Try this for size and fit."
James took the proffered suit and went to change. He came back and showed Katrina.
"That looks good," she said. "I doubt that my shopping will be this simple."
"Is there anything else we can get you?" the assistant asked.
"A Navy blue blazer," James said.
"Right over here, Sir," the assistant said. James picked one out and tried it on and was happy with the style and fit, so he had both wrapped up and paid for them. Then they went to the ladies' department and started looking at dresses. That whole process took a lot longer than picking out a suit, but eventually Katrina did find something she liked. After that, lunch was in order, so they went to Moreno's for lunch and were lucky to hit things just right and get a table outside in the courtyard.

The following Tuesday, James collected Stuart Winter, and they drove to Hawthorne to the Miller offices. They waited for a few minutes in the lobby, then were escorted back to Tom Ellison's office.

"James, thank you for coming, and we've never met, but I know of you, Stuart," Tom said. "This is Brent, our security officer."

"Mr Martin, Mr Winter," Brent said. "This meeting may not be recorded. Any notes you take will be available to you after review, and you will not disclose to anyone the nature of this meeting and who else may be involved. For the purposes of publication, this meeting is to discuss an issue that has arisen with certain gearboxes that you supplied for the Marauder program."

"We understand," James replied for both of them.

"Thanks, Brent," Tom said. Brent left, and two others came into the room. "This is George and Mike," Tom said. "You guys, meet James and Stuart from Waterford."

"Is the room secure?" George asked.

"Secure is on," Tom said, flipping a switch on his desk.

"Okay, guys, we need an adaptation of the AMAD that we use in the Marauder, and we also need some fairly small linear actuators for flaps and slats," George said.

"What kind of adaptation?" Stuart asked.

"We need to swap out some of the outputs," Mike explained.

"Same input horsepower and shaft speed?" James asked.

"Same," Mike confirmed.

"And the mounting?" James asked.

"A couple of tweaks," Mike said. "Nothing too dramatic, you should be able to run them through with normal manufacturing."

"What outputs do you want to change?" Stuart asked.

"We'd like the generator shaft to go at 1200 rpm and the hydraulic at 1500 rpm, same shaft size," George replied.

"Stuart, what ratios would we have to change to do that, and would the envelope of the housing change?" James asked.

"Both would, and yes, the housing would have to be bumped out in two places, needs a new casting," Stuart replied.

"Any changes, call it for Marauder B," Tom said. "We'll even come out with a variant that matches that."

"We may have an issue with machining capacity," Stuart said.

"We'll get a new five-axis," James promised. "You tell me what envelope would be most useful to you."

"When can we have some prelim drawings of the box?" George asked.

"Give me a couple of weeks," Stuart said.

"When you're ready, call this number and I'll set up a time for us to meet here," Mike said, showing them a telephone number.

"What about the actuators?" James asked.

"This is the loads we're looking at and the travel we want," George said, showing them a drawing.

"We can do that," Stuart said. "It's almost identical to the ones we do for the Impala program."

"How much would we have to change these to just buy off the line?" Mike asked.

"If you modify the attachments here and here to this, then things would just drop in," Stuart said, making notations on the drawing.

"We'll do that, send us a drawing of the run of manufacturing parts, and we'll make the changes," George said.

"When we're done, we'll send POs from a company by the name of Lincoln Systems for the actuators and Wichita Integration for the AMADs," Tom said.

"Do you have quantities in mind?" James asked.

"I'd say fifty of the AMADs to start and 200 of the actuators, to be delivered five monthly for the AMAD and twenty monthly for the actuators," Tom said. "Beginning on August 1, can you do that?"

"We can," Stuart said.

"Thank you, gentlemen," Tom said. "We'll have a progress meeting in two weeks, same time."

"We'll be here," James promised.

"James, can I talk to you for a minute?" Tom said.

"I'll see you by the car," Stuart said and left.

"Would you meet us at Kirtland Air Force Base on Friday, along with the guy who runs your structures operation?" Tom said.

"I'll be there, at what time?" James asked.

"Ten should be fine," Tom said. "There is no need to mention this to Stuart."

121

"I won't," James said.

"That was interesting," Stuart said as they drove back to Tustin. "Can you really get us a new 5-axis?"

"Just tell me what the envelope is, what tolerance you'd like and who's your preferred supplier," James replied. "I'll take care of the capital request. What's your best estimate of the value of those parts?"

"A mil for the AMADs and another for the actuators," Stuart thought.

"I'm sure they'll want to discuss price soon, so we should be prepared," James said.

"I'll have the numbers by next week," Stuart promised.

"What's our story about the Marauder B?" James asked.

"I think tell anyone who asks that the Marauder box is heating a bit and they want to modify it and see if it helps," Stuart suggested.

"We'll go with that," James agreed.

"We have a secure room," Stuart said. "We should use that for any discussions we have."

"Good idea," James agreed.

"Will you tell J&B anything?" Stuart asked.

"If we get the orders, then it's just two more orders," James replied.

"What did Ellison want?" Stuart asked.

"Just to impress upon me that this doesn't get mentioned to anyone," James prevaricated. "I would have thought that that was clear enough without belabouring the point. I'll start right away preparing Oak Creek for a capital request for a new 5-axis, let me know as soon as you can what the envelope is and what tolerance level you want."

"I'll get that to you this afternoon with a capital request," Stuart promised.

On Thursday afternoon, James flew to Albuquerque and had dinner with Phil Johnson and his wife, Susan. They had both settled in well and were happy with their move to New Mexico. On Friday, James and Phil presented themselves at the gate of Kirtland and were given an escort to a building that was one of many scattered about the base. Tom

Ellison met them and escorted them to a room where Brent, Mike and George were already seated and drinking coffee.

"Morning, James," Mike said.

"Morning," James replied. "This is Phil Johnson, he runs our structures operation here in Albuquerque."

"Brent," Tom said.

"Mr Martin, Mr Johnson, this meeting may not be recorded; any notes you take will be available to you after review, and you will not disclose to anyone the nature of this meeting and who else may be involved. For the purposes of publication, this meeting is to discuss a development program for the Air Force," Brent said.

"Noted," James said, and Phil nodded as well.

"Okay then, George," Tom said.

"We need some panels," George said. "They're quite complex shapes. Here are some drawings of what we're thinking. Can you do that?"

"Made of what?" Phil asked.

"Aluminium," George said.

"We can do that," Phil said. "We have press and machine capacity and capability to do that, there's some challenges here and here, but I think we can manage them. How do you want them finished?"

"Clean finish, no paint," Mike said. "We'll do our own painting. I'm Mike, by the way."

"Bonded or riveted?" Phil asked.

"We're thinking you will probably have to rivet, but if you could bond successfully, that would be interesting," Mike replied.

"When do you need it by?" Phil asked.

"Can you have first articles to us in a month?" George asked.

"We can do that," Phil replied. "We'll give you a riveted and a bonded set, and you can run your own tests."

"We'll give you a PO from Texas Systems," Tom said. "Ship the parts to Houston, and we'll take it from there."

"Are you looking at an order quantity?" James asked.

"If the parts meet our requirements, then fifty ship-sets starting in August, five a month," George replied.

"I don't see an issue with that," Phil said.

"We'll send you an RFP in the normal course of events," Brent said. "Give us prices and delivery, and we'll follow up with a PO."

"Anything else?" Tom asked. There were head shakes of no all around, so the meeting ended. Brent looked over the notes that Phil had made and approved them, after which James and Phil left.

"That was interesting," Phil said as they drove back to the factory. "Has anything like this happened to you before?"

"First time for me," James fibbed. "I gather they don't want us to talk about this."

"I won't," Phil promised. "I'll wait for the RFP and go from there."

"I wouldn't be surprised if we didn't find it already in your mail," James laughed.

"Lunch?" Phil suggested.

"Good idea," James agreed. "Where?"

"There's a place in Old Town, La Placita, good food, been around a while," Phil said. They drove there and got a table, and ordered.

"How are things going?" James asked.

"Good," Phil replied. "I'm enjoying the job, I get to meet customers, as well as run the factory, I'm having fun, plus as you've seen, numbers are better."

"They are, thanks for that," James said. "I'm going to the Paris Air Show in May. Anything you want me to look at?"

"I'll send you some notes," Phil promised. "Do we ever exhibit?"

"We haven't done so far, but there's an American Pavilion and we could take some space in that and display our stuff," James replied. "I'd have to look at what it would cost, the display space, plus shipping parts there and having people on hand to answer questions and make sure nothing gets nicked. I may look at Farnborough next year and see how that goes. If we did do something, it would be from here and Tustin, so a shared space with gearboxes and actuators."

"Makes sense," Phil said. "I'll think about parts we might exhibit and why."

On his way home, James mulled over the two meetings and speculated in his mind about what the program really was. Clearly, it was some kind of secret program, but it was being managed in an interesting way, getting off-the-shelf items where they were available and then piecing them all together. The fact that there would be at least three apparently different companies buying the parts was interesting, too. He thought that he would probably never see what the final article looked like, but that was fine with him; he did not need to know. He knew there were programs for the military that were secret and that there were the so-called black programs that were hidden from all view. Perhaps this was one; it would certainly explain the way it was being handled.

James and Stuart went back to Miller Aerospace and presented the new drawings of the gearbox.

"This looks good," George said. "When can you deliver the first article?"

"Give us two weeks," Stuart said.

"And production quantities?" Mike asked.

"We got our new 5-axis approved, it'll go in next week, and we'll check it out, so if we can get castings by the end of next month," Stuart replied.

"What's the problem with the castings?" George asked.

"I think they're just a little backed up," Stuart said. "We're having issues with all our castings right now, but we've got a team going tomorrow to see what the problem really is, whether they are really backed up, or we're just not head of the queue."

"Nothing we can do about that," Tom said. "This has to be as run-of-the-mill as we can get it to be."

"We have a program that's got a DX rating," James said. "If we push that, we might speed up all our stuff."

"Do that," Tom said. "Okay, actuators?"

"We're getting parts now," Mike said, "They work great, no issues there."

"Good, James, can I see you for a minute?" Tom asked. The others left, Stuart to wait for James by their car and the others presumably to their offices.

"How are things going in Albuquerque?" Tom asked.

"Well," James replied. "We'll have parts for you in two weeks."

"Good, you going to the Paris Air Show?" Tom asked.

"I am," James confirmed. "I've never been, so I'll be interested to see what's there."

"Come by our chalet and I'll buy you lunch," Tom invited.

"Thank you," James said. "Do you have a stand?"

"We do, stand and static display of drones," Tom said.

"I've been wondering about display space in the American Pavilion. Any idea how much all that costs?" James asked.

"Here's who you call," Tom said, handing him a business card.

"Thanks," James said.

"See you in Paris," Tom said.

Paris

James, or more accurately Megan, booked flights for him and Katrina to Paris. There was not much choice, so they went with Air France. Delta had just started flights to Paris, but they were from Atlanta; it was almost as bad with American, United, Pan Am and TWA, so it was more convenient to just use Air France. The company policy was that he could travel first class, and so could Katrina, so that would make the trip of almost eleven hours more comfortable. Megan talked to Paul Sykes, who had found a hotel within walking distance of the Louvre, so that Katrina could wander around that part of Paris and see the sights. Paul also registered them with the Paris Air Show so that they would have access on industry days, not just public days, even Katrina, if she chose to go. Megan gave Paul flight details, and he promised to meet James and Katrina and drive them to their hotel. James also visited a currency exchange place and got French Francs, enough for a day or two and enough so that Katrina could go off on her own and not worry about cash. Before Paris, however, there was the Offshore Technology Conference in Houston that included a display of equipment used for drilling for oil and laying pipelines, everything from blow-out preventers to rope, soap and dope. Waterford usually exhibited, and that year, they had some items that were due to be shipped to customers, but which they had been given permission to display before finally shipping. James flew to Houston and met Paul Rose there.

"Hi, James," Paul said. "Ready for this?"

"As ready as I'll ever be," James said. "I was never a big fan of trade shows. I went to a few with James & Brown and stood around all day answering questions about machines, hard on the back."

"It is that," Paul agreed. "We've got a couple of positioning winches on display, plus some pipe laying equipment. When we're done here, it's being delivered to a lay barge here in Houston."

"What about the academic papers?" James asked.

"I'll see if there's anything that really interests me," Paul said. "But I'm figuring on spending most of my time out in the display hall. I've got Bob Shew, my sales guy and Louis Andrews, my engineer, here with me;

maybe Louis will see something that will help us. How long are you staying?"

"I'm probably not going to be much help to you," James replied. "So, I really just wanted to come to see what all this stuff looked like and if our competition is here, what they look like."

"I'll walk you around tomorrow morning," Paul said. "I've got a list of exhibitors for you and a list of attendees to the conference itself."

"Thanks, Paul," James said.

"We're checked in at the Hyatt," Paul said. "We'll meet Bob and Louis for dinner."

"Sounds good," James said.

"How's Houston?" Katrina asked James when he called her later that evening.

"Hot and humid," he replied. "I'll be home tomorrow night. I don't see any reason for me to stay any longer. I just wanted to see what was here and who."

"Is it all oil stuff?" she asked.

"Judging by the exhibitor list, I'd say yes," he said.

"So, just the Seattle people for you?" she asked.

"Them and maybe in the future the gearbox folks, I can see some opportunities for different industrial gearboxes, particularly bevel drives," he said. "How was your day?"

"Busy," she said. "I've got plenty to do and was making sure that I've got everything done I can before we flit off to Paris."

"How's the company taking that?" he asked.

"It's unpaid leave, so they're not too concerned; all they want me to do is make sure I've got everything done I can before I go," she replied.

"Are you sure you want to work?" he asked. "We can probably manage if you don't."

"I'd rather help out," she said. "I like the idea of me earning as well, and it means that we don't have to just manage, we can do quite well."

"If you're sure," he said.

"I'm sure, lovey," she said. "You should probably get to bed. What are you, two hours ahead?"

"It is," he confirmed.

"So, are you still home tomorrow?" she asked.

"I will be," he said. "I'll spend the day here, then fly back tomorrow evening. Will you pick me up at John Wayne?"

"I'll be there," she promised. "I should let you get some sleep, love you."

"Love you," he echoed.

Paul duly walked James around the exhibit hall the next day and explained what it was they saw. He made a point of stopping at the stands of their customers and even their competitors and introduced James to the people he knew. The variety of hardware was fascinating to James, much of it looked like big stuff that would have fit the shops of James & Brown, but there were also other items, electronic data logging companies, explosive companies that provided charges to fracture the ground immediately around the well holes, companies that provided special vessels for drilling rigs, fire fighting vessels, remote controlled vehicles for investigating undersea conditions, and a whole host of little companies that provided what was known in the business as rope, dope and soap. James had lunch with Paul, Bob and Louis, learning more about the oil industry. Louis had been to a couple of presentations that morning and had some ideas for some new products. He and Bob debated hotly the market size, but even Bob had to agree that there was an opportunity. After lunch, James and Paul went back to their touring and even went back to a couple of stands for a better look, then they took a turn on their own stand and relieved Bob so that he could also take a look around. By five, James had had enough, as had Paul, so they all called it a day, closed up shop and left, James to the airport, and the others to their hotel.

"So, how was the trip?" Katrina asked James when she collected him at the airport.

"Short, interesting and hot and humid," he replied.

"I suppose that's because Houston is near the Gulf of Mexico," she said. "Don't they get hurricanes there?"

"Paul, the chap from Seattle, told me that they do," James confirmed. "He said that for all the dismal weather in Seattle, he prefers it to the heat and humidity of Houston."

"Are we set for Paris?" she asked.

"We've got tickets, we've got a hotel, we just have to pack and go," he said.

"How do we get to LAX?" she asked.

"I thought that we'd leave the car at the office and have Megan take us," he said.

"And coming home?" she asked.

"Same," he said.

"Does Megan mind being a taxi service?" Katrina asked.

"She can use the car," he thought. "That way it's the company car and not hers."

"What's the weather going to be like?" she asked.

"Late May, early June, should be warm, even hot, maybe some rain," he thought. "It'll be warmer than England, just that bit farther south."

"I thought we'd stop at Seranos and get some dinner," she said.

"That's fine," he agreed.

Towards the end of May, they left for Paris, flying from Los Angeles directly to Paris, Charles de Gaulle, a flight of about eleven hours overnight, arriving early in the morning. The flight had been on time, both leaving and arriving and clearing immigration and customs in Paris was quite quick. Paul Sykes was there to meet them as they left the customs check.

"James, welcome to Paris," he said.

"Paul, thanks for meeting us. This is my wife, Katrina, Katrina, this is Paul Sykes, he's our man in Paris and all parts south, covering the aerospace industry in France," James said, making the introductions.

"Your first time in Paris, Katrina?" Paul asked.

"It is," she said. "I haven't travelled much in Europe."

"South African?" Paul asked.

"Born, but lived all my life in Zambia until I met James," she replied.

"I got you a hotel a short walk from the Louvre," Paul said. "If you wanted to come and check out the show and see the air displays, just let me know, you're registered, so I've got a badge for you."

"Where's the hotel?" James asked.

"On the Rue de Rivoli just past the Rue de Castiglione," Paul said. "I asked for a room that looks out over the road to the Jardins des Tuileries."

"And that's an easy walk to things?" Katrina asked.

"It is," Paul confirmed. "Here's a map of central Paris with all the major landmarks. I've put a star where the hotel is."

"What's the weather forecast for the next few days?" James asked.

"Overcast tomorrow, then clearing up, should be good for the show," Paul said. "I was thinking we'd check you in at the hotel, but you probably won't be able to get into your room until this afternoon, so we'd go and get lunch."

"Great idea," James said.

They walked to Paul's car and he drove them into the centre of Paris, navigating the traffic and the congestion that typifies any big city. Paul was right, they would only be able to get into their room at three, so had time to kill. Paul suggested a restaurant on the other side of the river, a short walk away. He had found a parking space for his car and wanted to hang on to it, so did not want to drive. The hotel promised to take care of their suitcases and to deliver them to their room as soon as it was ready, and suggested that they check again at two to see if all was completed. Paul was right, the restaurant was only a short walk away, and it had a nice view of the river and the Louvre.

"How long have you been in Paris?" Katrina asked Paul after they had been seated and served an aperitif.

"Fifteen years now," he replied. "I've no desire to move or live anywhere else, I really like it here."

"James told me that you look after Waterford's interest with the big aerospace companies. What about the other businesses?" she asked.

"The hoist guys have a small sub here that sells hoists and platforms, and they do their own thing, the airport loader stuff, I keep an eye on that and let them know what's going on, the marine stuff tends to be pretty specialised so they go direct to Seattle, but there might be something with the gearboxes," Paul explained. "John Trent has been sending me stuff lately, but there's a lot of competition here from the Brits and the Germans, apart from the French companies."

"Who are the French aircraft companies?" Katrina asked.

"Airbus, Dassault, Aérospatiale for planes and helicopters, and for engines, SNECMA, Hispano Suiza," Paul replied.

"And what does Waterford supply?" she asked.

"Actuation systems, onboard cargo handling equipment and engine gearboxes and some structures," Paul replied. "Enough to keep me busy."

"What about the Brits and the Germans?" she asked.

"There's a lot related to the various Airbus aircraft, and then there are the joint venture military programs like Tornado and Jaguar and some others," he replied.

"This is all a far cry from the copper mines I grew up with," she said.

"What did you do before you met James?" Paul asked.

"My family had a heavy transport business," she replied. "We moved a lot of mining equipment around the country."

"And now?" Paul asked.

"I'm working for a dealer who handles construction machines, like backhoes and cranes," she said.

"Would you like to come out to the show at least for one day?" Paul asked.

"I would," she said. "If I won't be in the way."

"Not at all," James said. "We're not exhibiting, so Paul and I are looking to see what we might do in the future. I'm looking forward to seeing some of the flight displays."

"It can get noisy," Paul said. "But I agree, worth seeing."

"*Madame et messieurs,*" a waiter interrupted. "*Qu'est-ce que vous voulez manger?*"

They placed their orders, or at least Paul did for them. His French seemed to James to be excellent and as far as James could tell not heavily accented with undertones of English, as is often the case with Americans, his own French was adequate, he had managed to get both an O Level and A Level in French while at school, the O and A levels being school exams that were run nationwide and were the bases for university entrance and school leaving.

Lunch was good, and James paid the bill, then they wandered back to the hotel and were told that their room was ready and that their suitcases had been delivered to the room. James suggested to Paul that he not tie up his evening running after them. Paul agreed and said that he would be at the hotel at eight to collect James, and suggested to Katrina that she join them on Friday. Paul saw them to their room, which was an adventure as the lift was tiny and just about fit three people, but with three people left, no room for suitcases. The room was on the top floor and looked out over the gardens opposite and the river beyond. It was not a huge room, but it was well-appointed and would serve their purposes quite adequately. Left to their own devices, Katrina tested the bed and bounced up and down a couple of times, then checked the hot water in the bathroom and was gratified to see that it was hot, not tepid, so she ran a bath and soaked away the travel grime and weariness. Unfortunately, the bath really was not big enough for two, so James had to wait until she was done.

"That feels better," Katrina said after they had both bathed. "I know we just had lunch, but what shall we do about dinner?"
"Do you feel like venturing out?" James asked.
"Why not," she said. "I'm sure we can make ourselves understood, you have enough French, don't you?"
"I'll manage," he said. "I'll ask for suggestions at the front desk."
"Good idea," she agreed. "Paul's interesting, more French than the French, dress, mannerisms, the lot."
"I doubt we'd ever get him out of here," James said. "If we asked him to move, I think he'd leave and go and work for someone else in Paris."
"Does he have a family here?" she asked.
"According to his file, he's divorced, has one daughter who I think still lives here in Paris, not sure what she does," James replied.

133

"Where was he before Paris?" she asked.

"He started out as a field salesman for Waterford in Seattle, then he moved to LA for a couple of years, then they sent him here, so he's worked for the company for twenty years now," James replied. "He became a French citizen, so he went off the expatriate package he was on to more local conditions. He'll probably retire here and stay in Paris."

"Nice for him to have found his niche," she thought.

"Do you wonder if we'll ever find ours?" James asked.

"One day, but not just yet," she said. "There's still so much to explore."

"I do wonder sometimes what's next," he said. "I never thought when I left college that I'd ever go to the States."

"Not even for a holiday?" she asked.

"I wasn't thinking of holidays when I left college," he said. "I was only thinking of the trip to Zambia, first on the boat, then driving up."

"Anyway, what do you think I should wear tonight?" she asked.

"Something that doesn't scream American," he said. "We'd be better off looking like Brits or Germans, less likely to be targets."

"If I yack away at you in Afrikaans, people here would probably decide I was Dutch," she said. "How much do you remember?"

"Bits and pieces," he said.

"So, shall we venture out and try our luck somewhere?" she asked.

"Let's," he agreed.

A quick stop at the front desk elicited four possible places to eat, all within easy walking distance, two of them right on the Rue de Rivoli and the others off on streets that led from Rivoli. James looked at them and decided that it would be easy to walk to all four in a circle so that they could compare menus. It was too early to eat, even for people from the US who typically ate a lot earlier than the French, so they decided that they would walk, look and menus and see the sights for a little while before thinking about eating. They crossed the road and walked through the gardens to the Louvre. There was an area cordoned off, and they learned reading the notices that it would one day be the site of a new glass pyramid. There were images of what it would look like, and it struck both James and Katrina that it would make an interesting contrast to the much older Louvre buildings.

"I'll bet this caused no end of discussion," Katrina commented.

"You can see it can't you, hideous, eyesore, doesn't fit with the style of the existing buildings," James added.

"I'll bet the public hearings were fun," she said.

"I remember when they built the new cathedral in Coventry, right next to the bombed-out ruins of the old one. It was too modern, too much of a departure from what cathedrals were supposed to be, but now it's accepted and even touted as an example of new meets old," he said.

"I'd like to see the Mona Lisa while we're here," she said. "And maybe Rodin's museum."

"Well, we've got plenty of time," he said.

"Let's go and look at some menus," she suggested.

"I think the second place we looked at," Katrina said, after they had completed their circle.

"Sounds good," he agreed. "Let's go back to the room for a while and come back later for dinner."

They went out again after seven and walked to the restaurant they had picked out. It had been open since six, so there were a few early diners, but it was still fairly quiet. The food was good, the service mediocre, and the wine they picked was excellent. They ate, drank, then paid and left for an early night as the nine-hour time difference was catching up to them, and a good night's sleep was called for.

"What do you plan to do tomorrow?" James asked Katrina later.

"I'm going to see the Mona Lisa," she said. "I'll get myself a pastry at that shop we saw just down the road, then sit in the gardens and eat it, then visit the Louvre."

"Do you have enough cash?" he asked.

"I have a couple of hundred francs," she replied. "It should be enough for tomorrow."

"I'm not sure how long a day it will be tomorrow," he said. "My guess is that we'll be done by four or five, then there will be the adventure of getting through the traffic to get back here."

"Will Paul take us to dinner tomorrow?" she asked.

"Probably," he replied. "I'll check with him tomorrow morning before we go and leave a message for you at the front desk."

"Good, then I won't have to get up at sparrow's fart for breakfast with you," she said.

"No need," he agreed. "Get up when you're ready and just enjoy the day."

"If Paul was right and it's going to be overcast, then it's a good day for museums," she thought. "I'll take my little folding umbrella in case."

"At least it's not a long walk from here to the Louvre," he said.

"No," she agreed. "I'm sorry, lovey, I'm tired, I'm dropping off to sleep, I'll see you in the morning, love you."

"Love you," he replied.

James was up with the larks in the morning and left Katrina sleeping while he went downstairs to see about breakfast. The staff were just setting up for breakfast, but did offer him coffee. He sat and drank and looked around, noting several others who had come down early for breakfast. When the dining room was ready, James ate and then went back upstairs to see Katrina.

"I didn't hear you go out," she said.

"I didn't want to wake you," he said. "I'll leave a note for you at the desk when I know when we might be done this afternoon and what the plan is for this evening."

"Have a good day," she said.

"You too," he said. "Love you.

"Love you," she echoed.

James went down to the lobby, using the stairs, which was actually a lot quicker than the ancient lift. He arrived just as Paul was coming in.

"James, ready?" Paul asked.

"I'm ready," James said. "I promised Katrina I'd leave a note telling her when we'd be done this afternoon and what the plan is tonight."

"Use the house phone," Paul suggested. "We'll be back here around six, and I thought we'd have dinner at a place along the Champs Élysées; we can walk there from here, if you're up to that."

"We can do that," James agreed. He called Katrina and passed the message on, and she said that she'd be ready at six.

Paul drove them to Le Bourget and found a place to park. James now understood why he had wanted to leave fairly early, to find a place to park. There were security checks on the way in, and their badges were scrutinised, and they had metal detector wands waved over them.

"They've stepped up security a lot this year," Paul commented. "There'll be another check at the US pavilion."

"I had no idea this was such a big affair," James commented.

"It is, probably the biggest air show in the world, loads of exhibitors, both for static displays of planes and weapons systems and for subsystems and components, and of course the actual flight displays," Paul said. "If you can wangle an invite to some big company's chalet for lunch, then that's the place to see the displays from."

"I don't really know too many people yet," James said. "I met a few at an AIA meeting a couple of months ago, but I've no idea if they'll remember me, and I would have thought that the lunch invitations would go to potential customers."

"Right, but we supply systems that they might want to feature," Paul said.

"What do we do if I get an invitation that is for one only?" James asked.

"Don't worry about it," Paul assured him. "I'll be fine."

"Sure?" James asked.

"I'm sure," Paul said. "So, shall we take a look at the US pavilion and see what kind of stand we might want to put together?"

"Lead on," James said.

They walked the halls and looked at stands and displays, and talked to one of the American Pavilion organisers, who told them who to contact in the future regarding space and pricing. James was more interested in the shorter term to think about what they might do the following year at the Farnborough Airshow. He asked Paul to find out who they had to talk to and to get quotes for space and costs.

"If we did display, what do we show?" James asked Paul.

"Actuation systems and gearboxes, AMAD and EMAD and helicopter transmissions," Pau suggested. "Plus, I'd add some of the on-board cargo handling parts and maybe some structural parts."

"I'll talk to the division managers and see what we can come up with," James thought. "How big would you say that space was over there?"

"I'd say about twenty-five square metres," Paul replied.

"That might be as much as we want to start with," James thought. "I'll get someone in the office to sketch out the space and how much would be actual exhibits and how much open space, then we'd have to decide if there were any privacy booths, if there would even be room for that. Do you suppose Farnborough would be about the same?"

"My recollection of past shows is that some of the stands would be smaller than anything we see here," Paul commented. "More like ten square metres."

"I think if we drew up a layout, we should use the same no matter where we went," James said. "So for Farnborough, we may be constrained by the minimum here."

"I'll get numbers for both, I'll talk to Graham in London and get him to get the Farnborough numbers for me," Paul promised.

"Thanks," James said. "Now, let's go and see if any of our competitors are here and what they have on display."

There were several of their competitors there, and they studied the displays and the products. To Paul, they were all quite familiar, but for James, it was part of his continuing education. The hall started to get busier as more people arrived, so they moved outside to the static displays of actual planes and bits to hang on them.

"All kinds of things here," James said. "Shall we take a look at the French pavilion?"

"This way," Paul said, leading the way to a building festooned with Tricolour flags. "Let's see what the local guys are showing off."

They walked those halls and looked at gearboxes, actuators, seats, galleys, and all manner of systems.

"James, James Martin," a voice called. They looked around and saw a man from the Michelin stand waving to them.

"René," James said. "I didn't know you were now into aeroplane tyres. Paul, this is René Belon. René, this is Paul Sykes. I work for Waterford now, so we're looking at exhibiting."

"Big changes for both of us," René said. "Waterford, gearboxes and actuators, right?"

"That plus some structures and airport ground support equipment and marine machinery and building maintenance hoists," James confirmed. "Paul is based here in Paris. When did you move from earthmoving tyres?"

"1976," René replied. "The company put me into the management training program, and I've had a position in automotive and bicycles, now it's aircraft."

"René was a godsend to us in Zambia," James explained to Paul. "Our big expenses were explosives, fuel, tyres, parts and labour, so René helped us manage our tyre life and cost."

"You must join me for lunch," René said. "One-thirty at the chalet."

"Thank you, René," James said.

"Is Katrina here with you?" René asked.

"She is, taking in the sights today, I think she was planning to go to the Louvre," James replied.

"You must bring her here," René said.

"We were thinking about tomorrow," James said. "How is Marie?"

"Well, ah, Philippe, this is James Martin and Paul Sykes of Waterford. James was a good customer of ours in Zambia," René said to a newcomer who had joined them, forestalling any further reminiscences.

"I regret that I won't be such a good customer now," James said.

"I trust that René has offered our hospitality to you," Philippe said.

"He has been most gracious," James replied. "We should let you get back to talking to real customers, René. It was wonderful to see you again."

"That was interesting," Paul commented to James as they walked on.

"I have to admit I was surprised," James said. "René wasn't the local manager in Zambia; he was a site technician who actually changed tyres for us. Maybe they recognised his abilities and decided to better use him."

"I didn't know they had such a program," Paul said. "Let's have a look at the Airbus display and see if there's anyone there that we deal with."

"Lead on," James said. They walked onto the massive stand that Airbus had. It had models of the various planes that they made and all kinds of literature.

"The real business gets done in the chalet," Paul commented to James. "Deals for planes get signed and orders taken. Potential customers are trooped through the planes they have on the ground, and there's a lot of schmoozing that gets done."

"Well, I don't see us in the market for a plane," James said. "I think all J&B will run to are the Lears."

"It would be interesting to watch the Airbus Chalet, then the Boeing, Lockheed and McDonnell Douglas chalets to see who goes to all of them and where orders finally get placed," Paul said. "Fancy a coffee?"

"That sounds great," James replied.

"I've a friend who works for one of the interior guys, seats, galleys and such, let's go and see him and bum some coffee," Paul suggested.

The friend, Léo Bonet, was on his stand and not occupied when they arrived.

"Léo, this is James Martin. He took over running Waterford a few months back. James, this is Léo Bonet, our daughters went to school together, then college," Paul said.

"Coffee?" Léo asked.

"That's why we came," Paul said. "So, busy?"

"Quite," Léo said. "I expect things to be busier next week, after the public days. We're selling a lot, so everyone is happy."

"What kind of changes do you see in seats?" James asked as Léo busied himself with making the coffee.

"More electronics," Léo said. "People are going to want their own screen in the seat backs, so we're adding capabilities in electronics and communications. Because we'll be adding all that stuff, we have to take a hard look at the seats themselves and see where we can pare down weight. The carriers are already planning the next generation or two of seat configurations. What about Waterford? I didn't see a stand."

"Maybe next time," James said. "Paul and I are looking at what we might do, how big a stand, how many people we would need, what items to display."

"What about Farnborough next year?" Léo asked.

"We'll probably be there," James said.

"Coffee, black, sugar, milk?" Léo asked. "Help yourselves to what you want. Biscotti?"

"Thanks," Paul replied. "How's Florence?"

"Well, enjoying her job with Dassault, she's on their stand if you want to say hello," Léo replied. "And Madeleine?"

"We're having dinner with her tonight at Chez Henri on the Champs Élysées," Paul replied. "She started a new job with Air France as a stewardess; she flies to the US a lot, and to the Caribbean."

"So, will you get cheap flights?" Léo asked.

"There are some benefits," Paul replied. "I haven't used any yet, but we'll see what I can do."

"Thank you for the coffee, Léo," James said.

"Je vous remercie de rien," Léo replied.

"I wonder if there are electronics we should be looking at for gearboxes," James said to Paul as they continued their wanderings.

"What for?" Paul asked.

"Vibration sensors to see if bearings are going bad, temperature sensors for the same thing, something like an electric eye that looks at the oil and picks up turbidity and particles," James thought aloud. "I should talk it over with Stuart."

"We should make our way to the Michelin chalet to meet your friend René," Paul suggested. They walked back to the line of chalets that fronted the airfield itself and offered views of the aerobatic displays.

"James," René said, as they approached the chalet. "Please come in, I have a table here for us and for some people from Air Central Africa, it's a start-up in London that is looking to holiday traffic in Kenya, Tanzania, Zambia and Malawi. They've leased some 757s and are selling holiday packages, flights plus safaris. I'm looking to get the tyre contract."

"How long do tyres last?" James asked.

"If they're recapped, then maybe up to one hundred landings," René said. "It depends on how good the landing is, what the runway surface is like and a few other things. From my point of view, it's good that ACA are planning stops in Cairo, Nairobi, Dar and Lusaka, so eight stops a trip, with twice weekly flights, that's eight changes a year on eight main wheels on three planes."

"That sounds like a lot," James said.

"It's not bad, a short-haul is better from our point of view, two to three landings a day, maybe even more," René commented. "But from the point of view of Michelin, it's not the market that cars and lorries is, even bicycles. Ah, excuse me, there they are."

"Grant, Adam, this is James Martin and Paul Sykes of Waterford Industries, they do gearboxes, actuators, and some structural parts," René said, making the introductions.

"Where are you chaps based?" Grant asked.

"I'm at our headquarters in Los Angeles, and Paul is our man here in Paris," James replied.

"How do you know René?" Grant asked.

"I was a customer of his in Zambia," James explained. "I was running a mine at the time, so bought tyres for earthmoving machines."

"So, what took you to Waterford?" Adam asked.

"I joined James & Brown, who build machines; they gave me a few different assignments, and then we bought Waterford and I was sent out to run it," James replied. "Paul has worked for Waterford for some twenty years, fifteen here in Paris."

"So, should we add Harare and Jo'burg?" Grant asked.

"You might get more traffic," James replied. "South Africa has some nice parks that are affordable, throw a hire car into the package, and they can drive themselves to and through places like Kruger. Zim has

Mana Pools, Bumi Hills, Hwange, and Vic Falls, so I'd look at that, maybe fly into Vic Falls rather than Harare and offer Hwange and Vic Falls as a package."

"Worth looking into," Grant said. "Botswana?"

"I'd add a charter from Jo'burg and fly into Maun," James suggested. "Much better for Okavango and Chobe to fly into Maun, but Maun couldn't take your 57s."

"Which parks have you been to?" Grant asked.

"When we lived in Zambia, Luangwa, Kafue and Chobe and when we lived in South Africa, Kruger," James replied.

"Pity Vincent isn't here," Adam commented to Grant, then, as an aside to James and Paul, said. "Vince is our marketing chap; we're looking to him to put the packages together."

"It strikes me that the safari business is seasonal," James said. "April to November, do you have an alternative for the rest of the year?"

"The Med," Grant said. "Brits like sunshine, so Christmas in the Med is an easy sell, we'll fly to Majorca and Greece."

"We should eat before things get really noisy out there," René suggested. "They'll start soon."

They ate, then repaired to the outdoor space and sat and drank coffee and watched planes. There were lots of displays by fighter jets, which were a big draw; the aerobatics and the noise just grabbed everyone's attention. James did wonder what all the Parisians who lived close to the airport felt about the noise; it was particularly noticeable with the military planes.

"That's a new one for me," James commented to Paul as they saw the Space Shuttle being flown past atop its Boeing 747.

"I wonder what kind of gas mileage it gets," Paul laughed. "At least it's a change from fighter jets."

"These big jets must look good to you, René," Adam said.

"Yes, but they don't land that often," René said. "Better to supply those small commuter planes, always landing and taking off."

"What did you do in South Africa, James?" Adam asked.

"I ran the local sub of James & Brown. We serviced mining equipment and sold and serviced construction machines," James replied.

"What else does Waterford make?" Grant asked.

"Apart from the aircraft parts, we have a line of airport ground support machines, conveyor loaders, container loaders, we make industrial gearboxes, hoists for building maintenance and marine equipment like pipe and cable layers," James replied.

"Who do we talk to about conveyor loaders?" Grant asked.

"Paul will be able to help you," James said.

"Happy to," Paul confirmed. "I can either put you in touch directly with the factory, or I can handle all that for you."

"Could you come and see us in a couple of weeks?" Grant asked.

"Of course, I'll come with Graham Finch, he's our man in the UK, and it may be easier for you to deal through him," Paul said.

"Here's my card," Grant said. "Call me after this is over and we'll set a date, we're easy to find, we're in Hounslow, so Heathrow and a short Tube ride. We set up a ground support services company a couple of years ago. It makes no sense for us to have a dedicated crew on the ground at each airport doing nothing for five days a week, so we will supply contract ground support for others like us who don't have a large enough presence to warrant their own employees. We'd be interested in loaders, GPUs, tugs, container trailers, luggage trailers and a few other things."

"Don't airports do that?" Paul asked.

"In some places, the local airport authority will," Grant agreed. "But not everywhere. Would you and James excuse us? We need to talk business with René."

"Of course," James said. "René, good to see you again; gentlemen, we will be in touch."

"Do you know much about our loaders and other ground support equipment?" James asked Paul when they were well out of earshot. "Sorry to drop you in it."

"No problem," Paul said. "I can bone up on the loaders in the next week or two, get prices and delivery from Pueblo. Gives me a good excuse to go to England, and I can call on Rolls and BAe while I'm at it."

"Thank you," James said. "How long will it take us to drive back?"

"If we go now, thirty to forty minutes, if we leave an hour from now, then well over an hour," Paul replied.

"Shall we leave now, then?" James suggested.

"Good idea," Paul agreed.

"I'll be here at six," Paul said when he dropped James off at his hotel.

"We'll be ready," James promised. He went upstairs to the garret and knocked, and Katrina was there.

"You're back earlier than I expected," she said.

"I'd had enough," he said. "Did you enjoy your day?"

"I did, I got up, got some coffee, then went to that pastry shop down the street and got myself something, then went and ate it in the gardens," she recounted. "Then I went to the Louvre."

"Did you see the Mona Lisa?" he asked.

"I did," she confirmed. "It's small, I was expecting this big painting, but it's actually quite small. I had a late lunch here and have been lazing since."

"Do you remember René, the Michelin man from Zambia?" he asked.

"Yes," she said.

"I saw him today," James told her. "He told me that the company put him into the management training program, and now he's selling tyres to airlines. If you come out with us tomorrow, we'll stop at their stand and say hello."

"Man, that would be nice," she said. "So, what's the plan tonight?"

"Paul meets us here at six and we walk to a place called Chez Henri on the Champs Élysées," he replied. "Apparently, Paul's daughter is going to join us there."

"How old is she?" Katrina asked.

"Not sure," James admitted. "But apparently she works for Air France as a stewardess, and her name is Madeleine."

"I suppose I should think about getting ready. Is this a dress-up thing?" she asked.

"I doubt it," he said. "Wear something comfortable and shoes that you don't mind walking in."

Paul was at the hotel at six; apparently, he had found a place to park near the restaurant and had walked to the hotel to meet them. They walked to Chez Henri and were shown to a table. It seemed to James that well over half the patrons were British or American, and he heard a few discussions about the Air Show and what various people had seen and had been struck by. Madeleine joined them shortly after they had sat down. She was funny, in quiet asides, she took off the Americans who were crucifying the French language. She told them about her new job with Air France; her fluency in French, English, German and Italian had essentially netted her the job. Paul told her about meeting Léo and told her that Florence was now working for Dassault and was at the show. James and Katrina learned that Paul's former wife had moved back to the States and lived in Florida, and that Madeleine saw her when she flew into Miami. She was leaving the next day for Beijing; that flight was Paris, Athens, Karachi and Beijing and back, quite a long trip. She had also signed up for lessons in Mandarin so that she would be better able to manage the China flights. After dinner, James and Katrina took their leave of Paul and Madeleine and walked back to the hotel for a bath and bed.

They were ready the next morning when Paul came to collect them. He gave Katrina her badge that listed her as a representative of Waterford, so she could go to the show on non-public days. People seemed to have gone early, as finding a place to park was more of a challenge. Their badges were scrutinised and they were allowed entry. For the next hour or so, they wandered the halls, James looking at things he had missed the day before. They stopped at the Michelin stand and saw René busy, so waved and left him to it, returning in fifteen minutes.
"Katrina," René said. "Wonderful to see you again."
"Nice to see you, René. How is Marie?" Katrina asked.

"She's coming up from Clermont tonight for the weekend," René replied. "Which hotel is yours?"

"The Mercure on rue de Rivoli," Katrina replied.

"I'll let Marie know, she wants to show you around Paris, I talked to her last night and she announced that she was coming," René said. "Sadly, I have to work, but I will see you for dinner tomorrow night. Would you care for some coffee?"

"That would be very nice," Katrina said. René waved to a young lady who came over and took coffee orders, and she was back quickly with the cups and with some pastries.

They resumed their wanderings, and James stopped at the outdoor display of Miller Aerospace. He was interested to see what their drones actually looked like.

"James," a voice said. He turned and saw Tom Ellison.

"Tom, how are you?" he asked. "Tom, this is my wife, Katrina, and this is Paul Sykes, he's our man in Paris. This is Tom Ellison, the CEO of Miller."

"Mrs Martin, Paul," Tom said. "James and I ran into one another at the AIA meeting this spring. Waterford does provide some systems for us. Do you have plans for lunch?"

"No," James said.

"We have a small chalet, please stop by at about noon, and we'll grab a bite before the displays start," Tom said.

"Thank you," James said. "But we don't want to get in the way of you doing business with potential customers."

"It'll be fine," Tom assured him. "I'm expecting most of our activity next week. Are you here for the whole show?"

"No, I'm just trying to decide if we should display in the future and if we do, how big a stand," James explained. "We'll probably go to Farnborough next year as a test run."

"Good idea," Tom said. "Excuse me, I'm being summoned."

James doubted that anyone from Miller would summon the CEO, but one of the others on the stand had waved to him and had people in tow who were all uniformed, so potential customers.

"You get around," Paul said to James as they wandered off.

"He has that habit," Katrina said. "A great memory for names and faces, even voices and places, we've driven down roads and he's told me that we're about to go around a corner and see a roadside stand and I know we'd only been down that road once before."

"Good talent to have," Paul said. "Shall we look at more before we join Tom Ellison for lunch?"

"Let's do that before it gets too warm," James said. They walked and wandered, pausing to look at things that caught their interest. There was just so much to look at and see. From James's point of view, it was interesting, but he would never be in the market for fighter jets or missile systems.

"I knew that the arms business was big," Katrina said. "But I never really appreciated just how big."

"Each government wants the latest and greatest," Paul said. "Or at least what companies are allowed to sell."

"There are restrictions?" Katrina asked.

"Most governments of countries that make the stuff would like to keep the absolute newest for themselves and sell off older systems to keep the manufacturers afloat," Paul said.

"I suppose that's why Zambia got old stuff from Britain and then went to the Russians," Katrina said. "But even then, I doubt that they got the newest MiG fighters."

"There are countries that will bend rules, particularly when it comes to small arms," Paul said. "But aircraft and tanks are a little different. James, what do we supply Miller?"

"We do some small gearboxes and actuators," James replied. "When I got back from the AIA meeting, I sat down with Stuart and went through what we supply to whom."

Lunch was good, not quite as good as that of Michelin, but good enough and doubly good because they did not have to pay for it. Tom had a Chuck Ramirez join them; he was the marketing manager for

148

Miller and welcomed the break from schmoozing potential buyers, some of whom would not be permitted by the US government to buy any drone systems. After lunch were the flight displays, and they sat outside drinking coffee and watching planes go through their paces. Tom and Chuck excused themselves but told James, Katrina and Paul to stay and watch the show.

"It's all very dramatic," Katrina commented.

"It's meant to be," Paul said. "Put the planes through their paces and try and convince foreign governments or airlines to buy."

"How much business actually gets done?" she asked.

"Quite a lot," Paul said. "You often see during or after the show big announcements that some airline has just placed an order for tens or even hundreds of new planes, great for marketing for the show, the manufacturers and the airlines."

"Will you display, James?" she asked.

"I think we will," he replied. "I'm thinking a small stand in the US pavilion that we can man with a couple of people. It's expensive, both for the space and to have the people here."

"How much longer do you want to stay?" she asked.

"I'm done for the day," James replied. "Paul?"

"I wouldn't mind leaving," Paul replied.

"Let's go then," James suggested. "Would you pick me up on Monday, Paul?"

"Glad to," Paul said. "Hope you have a good time seeing the sights."

More changes

Marie was at their hotel at nine the next day and took on the rôle of tour guide, showing them around Paris. James tagged along behind as Marie and Katrina talked about what had happened to each of them since leaving Zambia. James and Katrina had left when the market for copper had softened and the mining company had shut down the mine he ran, René and Marie had left around the same time, caught in the same circumstances, but René was more fortunate than James, his company had kept him on and just transferred him to France, whereas James had been paid out of his contract and left his own devices. They ate lunch at a small place that Marie knew, and there were no American visitors, and no chat about the air show, just gossip about changes in the government's electoral system. René did join them for dinner and was happy to get away from the demands of the show for a while. He had been busy and expected to get busier after the public days and industry people, and customers returned. Sunday morning, Marie took them on a short boat ride on the river, then had to leave as she needed to get the train back to Clermont-Ferrand, which was the full name of the town where they lived and worked.

On Monday, James and Paul spent some time eyeing various stands and discussing what the Waterford stand might look like. They found the office of the US Department of Commerce, which had sponsored the US Pavilion and got square footage and prices, or at least estimated prices for the 1985 show. Paul promised to get details of the Farnborough show and see what the stand sizes were there. Over lunch, James sketched out a stand and layout. To his credit, Paul did not just agree and say that it looked wonderful, but made suggestions for alterations that he thought would be useful. He and James discussed it for a while and finally agreed on a rough draft of a stand. What might go on the stand, James would discuss with the division managers at the next company meeting. By the end of the day, James was ready to go back to his office and the demands of everyday business. Paul dropped him at the hotel and said that he would be back the next day in plenty of time to get them to Charles de Gaulle for their flight home.

"So what did you like most about Paris?" James asked Katrina on the flight back to Los Angeles.

"So many things," she said. "I liked the Rodin museum, I wasn't that impressed with the Mona Lisa, I liked the view from the Eiffel Tower, and I liked the river trip. I can't say I really liked the air show stuff, noisy planes, men and their toys, so sad that we've dreamed up so many ways to kill each other, you?"

"I liked the city and the people," he replied. "I grew up being told that the French were rude, but that's not true. I knew someone years ago, and they were not rude at all and use a little French, and they're helpful and happy to talk to you."

"Nice to see Marie and René again," she said.

"It was," he agreed. "I was really surprised when René called me. I suppose that was the last place I expected to see him."

"So, what's next for you?" she asked.

"Meetings, both with the division managers and at Oak Creek," he said. "I'll have to give Hank chapter and verse on what I saw and what I think we might do. He'll want some say, maybe even wants to go to the next Paris show, I can't see him wanting to go to Farnborough."

"Where is Farnborough?" she asked.

"West and south of Heathrow," he replied. "It's where the Royal Aircraft Establishment was founded; they do research into aircraft, runways, all kinds of things."

"So if you go, you wouldn't stay in London?" she asked.

"Not the best drive," he said. "Nor is Cores End for that matter, better to find a place more local, but if we go, we'd have to make a booking early, I'm sure that anywhere local fills up quickly, if there's nothing available then I'd stay with the folks."

"If you do that, perhaps I'll come with you," she said.

"Have you made peace with my mother?" he asked.

151

"She's warmed to me a lot in the past few years," Katrina said. "It doesn't seem to bother her anymore that, how did she put it, I'm not completely white."

"I think that trip they took to South Africa and Zambia in 1973 made a huge difference," he said.

"You're right, after that she was sweetness itself," Katrina laughed.

"Megan, could you see if you can find us someone to design a stand for the air shows?" James asked when he was back in his office. "Paul Sykes is going to get information from the Farnborough Air Show people, and this is the Paris information; we should try and get a stand layout that would do for both. This is what Paul and I sketched up while we were at the show."

"I'll see what I can come up with," she said. "Was it a good trip?"

"We may get some business out of it," he replied. "And I met an old friend, but I was never a fan of trade shows. I did my share at James & Brown, and I do recall getting backache from standing around all day."

"Hank Miller called yesterday afternoon, and he wants you to call him," she said.

"I'd better call him and see what he wants," James thought.

"While you do that, I'll get you some tea," she said.

"Thanks, Megan," he said. He called Oak Creek, and Lou Kalan, who guarded Hank's door and telephone, answered.

"Lou, good morning," James said. "I'm returning Hank's call."

"I'll put you right through," she said.

"James, how was Paris?" Hank asked.

"Interesting, tiring, but we may get some business in the short term, but not from gearboxes and actuators, but from conveyor loaders," James replied.

"Will you exhibit?" Hank asked.

"I'm looking into what it would cost," James replied. "If the price tag is not too high, it might be worth it."

"Could you tear yourself away from California and come and see me on Friday?" Hank asked.

"Of course, at what time?" James asked.

"Let's make it eight, then you can be back in California that afternoon," Hank suggested.

"Is there anything I need to bring?" James asked.

"No, we'll talk about the board meeting next week and what we should do for that, but really just to chat and see where things are, plus we need to do a performance review," Hank explained.

James hung up and sat back, and thought about what Hank might really want. He supposed that a performance review was probably overdue; he had not had one for almost two years. He talked to Megan and asked her to make sure that the plane was available the next day for him to fly back to Milwaukee, and to make him a hotel reservation and book a car. Then he spent some time talking to each of the division managers to make sure that he was aware of events, possible new business and problems that had arisen or might arise. He had first-quarter results in hand, but second-quarter results would not be available for a while, particularly as they had only just gone into June, so had a month to go before the quarter even ended.

"I have to go to Oak Creek tomorrow," James told Katrina that night. "I'll be back Friday, Hank Miller wants to talk about something."

"Just as long as it's not another move," she said. "We've only just got here."

"I doubt it's that," he said. "But, you never know. How was your day?"

"Busy," she said. "We just sold several backhoes to a contractor who has a big contract for sewer lines, so we'll be getting them ready to ship in the next few days."

"You had them in the yard?" he asked.

"We did, they've been trying to move them for six months, so this is a really good sale," she said. "When will you leave tomorrow?"

"Around nine, I think," he replied. "That means I won't be in Oak Creek too late. I'll call you from the hotel. I don't know why he wants to see me on Friday; we have a regular board meeting next week."

"Maybe he just wants to pat you on the back," she said.

"Maybe," he said doubtfully. "More likely some special project that he wants looking at."

"Well, you'll find out on Friday," she said.

James duly reported to Hank's office first thing Friday morning.

"James, good, you're here, come in, Lou, coffee for two if you wouldn't mind," Hank said.

"Yes, Mr Miller," she said. She was back quickly with coffee, cups and the milk and sugar to add.

"So, James, how are things going at Waterford?" Hank asked.

"Well enough," James replied. "We have some issues right now with rework at Industrial Power, and we're looking into why, as I told you earlier, we may have the possibility of sales of aircraft loaders to a Brit company that set up as an airport services company. Paul Sykes, our man in Paris, is following up on that."

"No more leadership changes foreseen?" Hank asked.

"Not that I can see," James replied. "I've been working on succession plans so that if I lose one of the division managers to a competitor or something else, I have identified people who can take those slots."

"Good, I see the financials are looking quite good," Hank said.

"Once we turned around the structures and loaders businesses, then things started to look a lot happier," James said.

"Anything about the way you're running things that you think you need to change?" Hank asked.

"I don't think so," James said.

"Nor do I," Hank said. "I'm putting you in for another options grant, and we're also going to push your base up a bit."

"Thank you," James said.

"So, you're probably wondering why I really asked you back here," Hank said.

"It had crossed my mind," James admitted.

"I'm retiring," Hank said. "Next week at the board meeting, we will announce the restructuring of the company into J&B Industries with subsidiaries, James & Brown and Waterford Industries. As I said, I'm retiring and there'll be a new Chairman and CEO of J&B Industries.

The board had a selection committee work on it, and they've made the decision. The guy's name is George Wilcox. Here's his résumé; you can see that it's pretty much all investment banking and consulting, no operations."

"I'll be sorry to see you go," James said, quite truthfully. "I've learned so much in the past few years."

"A word of advice, watch Wilcox, he's a Wall Street guy, lives for the deal, knows next to nothing about machines or mining or even aerospace, so expect more focus on immediate short-term profits and watch out for cost-cutting," Hank said. "Wilcox will be all smiles and full of congratulations for things, but it's an act; I don't think he's to be trusted."

"If the question is not too impertinent, why did the board select him?" James asked, amazed that Hank had shared this with him.

"I hadn't seen it, more fool me, but there's a cabal on the board that has been looking to get their man in place for some time," Hank said, quite bitterly. "As long as we were performing well, there was no reason to make the change, but when I told them six months ago that I was retiring, they went to work, and the final vote was last week."

"You can't rescind your retirement?" James asked.

"If I did, it would be with a hostile board," Hank said. "That wouldn't work well at all. It seems I erred in my picks for good board members."

"So, do I need to start looking?" James asked.

"No," Hank said. "Just be aware that the tone of the company may change, don't be surprised if somewhere down the line you're put up for sale."

"Any guesses as to when?" James asked.

"Not for a few years, he'll want to window dress things," Hank said.

"The change of control agreement I have, will that still be valid?" James asked.

"That will be up to Wilcox," Hank said. "If he's smart, he'll keep it in place, but he may not; the agreements are at the whim of the CEO. He may or may not realise that there's one in place for a while."

"Any advice on what to do?" James asked.

"Just keep doing what you're doing," Hank said. "You're throwing off cash, earnings look good, and there's top and bottom line growth forecast for the next few years. How confident are you in that?"

"High confidence," James said.

"So, you've been salting away reserves to cover unexpected events," Hank laughed. "It's what I would have done."

"I presume, tell no one until after the board meeting?" James asked.

"Of course," Hank confirmed. "Come back next week for the meeting, you'll get to meet Wilcox and be prepared to give a short introduction to Waterford, markets, financial results and outlooks."

"I had that done," James said. "I've brought it all with me."

"Let's take a look," Hank said. James handed him a copy of the slides he planned to use, and Hank went through them, making a few changes as he went.

"I'll make these changes," James said.

"On paper, it looks pretty good," Hank said. "I wonder if Wilcox is smart enough to realise that it only makes sense if the management team is the right one."

"Are you staying in Illinois after you retire?" James asked.

"No, I'm selling up and moving somewhere warmer," Hank laughed. "I've had enough of ice and snow and the commute up from Illinois. I'm going to Arizona to Tucson."

"That's quite a change from Lake Charles," James commented.

"It is," Hank agreed. "But Sylvia and I are looking forward to the desert and being able to play golf more. Before I forget, bring McKane with you next week, and have him on hand in case Wilcox starts delving too deeply into the accounting systems."

"I'll do that," James promised.

"How's Katrina doing?" Hank asked.

"She has a job with a distributor of construction equipment, not ours, I'm afraid; she's busy and her commute is pretty short," James replied.

"It's possible that Wilcox may pull the plane," Hank thought. "But maybe not, he'll get to swan around in the 55, unless he goes bigger and gets a G III or a Challenger, or even a Falcon. Expect snide remarks about California, the guy thinks that the world begins and ends in New York and on Fifth Avenue, particularly."

"Will he move the corporate office?" James asked.

"Don't know," Hank said. "It's an unnecessary expense to do so, but we're dealing with a giant ego here, so who knows what he may do. If he does move the corporate office, my guess is it will be a small office, just J&B Industries, and he'll leave all the operations people for James & Brown here in Oak Creek and your office people in California."

"I don't want to take up your whole day," James said.

"Not to worry," Hank said. "I'm winding down, and I've put off all that I can to let Wilcox deal with it. More coffee?"

"Thank you," James said.

"Lou," Hank called. "Could you get us a refill?"

James finally left at eleven and called the airport to tell the pilots that he was on his way. As soon as he arrived, they left, after a suitable loo break.

"Good meeting?" Greg asked as he came aft to organise lunch.

"He wanted to go over stuff for the board meeting next week," James said. "I'll be going back on Tuesday, with Mike McKane, returning on Wednesday late afternoon, unless the meetings drag on too late that afternoon."

"No problem, Mr Martin, glass of wine?" Greg asked.

"That would be great," James replied. Greg opened a bottle and poured, then went back to the cockpit until the lunch had heated up. James took the information on Wilcox from his briefcase and read it through. Wilcox had a degree in finance, then he had added an MBA, then did a stint with one of the big investment houses, then switched to consulting, hopping between various well-known firms, eventually setting up on his own, specialising in mergers and acquisitions, and with that, divestitures. Hank had been right, nowhere did James read that he had actually run anything, but he was reminded of some comments made to him when he had worked in Zambia, that of being B stream. It had happened that one of the senior mine managers was visiting James at the open pit he ran and he had pointed out that the people in the head office in London came mostly from financial backgrounds and rarely from operations, as he put it the A stream got something like a history tripos from Cambridge or PPE, philosophy, politics and economics, then went to the London office directing the industrial empire, whereas he, and James, had taken mining engineering and gone to work in the mines in the hinterlands. James put away the papers, and Greg came back and served lunch, after which James sat and contemplated life as he watched the ground go by from 42,000 feet.

"So, what did Miller want to talk about?" Katrina asked James over dinner later that evening.

"He's retiring, and he wanted to tell me a little about the new bloke that the board picked," James replied. "I think he's a little miffed that his board went around him and picked one of their cronies."

"Do you know who?" she asked.

"Chap by the name of George Wilcox," James replied. "Hank advised me to watch my back with Wilcox and predicted that Waterford would be sold off in the future, not immediately, but after a period of suitable window dressing."

"Window dressing?" she asked.

"We make the numbers look good, rather like high-grading a mine, then the next owner has to deal with all the low-grade stuff and poor economics," he explained.

"So, when does this all happen?" she asked.

"At next week's board meeting," he said. "I've been asked to go back and take Mike McKane with me."

"It's all go in the big world of corporate doings," she said.

"Hank told me to watch out for cost-cutting, and he said that he wouldn't be surprised if Wilcox didn't move the corporate office to New York," James added.

"What, we'd have to move to New York?" she asked in horror.

"I doubt it," James said. "The company's also being restructured to J&B Industries with the old James & Brown now a separate sub and us as another separate sub."

"I'd rather not move again so soon, and I really don't fancy New York," she said.

"There's nothing certain," he said. "It was just something that Hank thought might happen, but he didn't think it would affect us."

"Well, we'll cross that bridge if and when it comes," she said. "So, what shall we do this weekend?"

"Let's take the train to San Diego, have lunch there, wander around a little, then come home," he suggested.

"Where do we catch the train?" she asked.

"Santa Ana, take the 55 to 17th, then west to Lincoln, then south to the station," he said. "Megan told me that you just go to the station, get your ticket, then when the train comes in, get on and find a seat. Apparently, the train runs along the coast for most of the way."

"Sounds like a plan," she said.

"I wonder where we might get a seat," Katrina said to James as they watched the train pull into the Santa Ana station the next morning.

"It doesn't look too busy," James said as they boarded. "What about here, this side should be the ocean side, and we can still see through the other side."

"*Ja*, looks good," she said. The train only stayed a few minutes and then was on its way again, winding through the built-up areas of Orange County, through Tustin, Irvine and beyond before emerging into the clear along the ocean front at Dana Point.

"Fancy some coffee?" he asked. "I saw they have this thing called Amcafe on the train."

"That would be nice," she said. James made his way forward and found the café, and bought two coffees.

"It's not too bad," he commented as they sampled the coffee.

"Look at all those flowers," she said, pointing out to the landward side of the train.

"It's colourful all right," he said.

"How long is this trip?" she asked.

"I think about an hour and forty minutes," he said. "We should be in San Diego around ten forty-five."

"So, time for a wander, then get some lunch, wander a bit more, then come home," she suggested.

159

"The ocean doesn't look that inviting," he said. "But there's enough surfers out there, so I suppose it can't be too bad."

"That or they're such diehards they don't care," she said.

"I wonder how hard it is to learn how to surf," he mused.

"I'm not sure I want to spend that much time in the ocean," she said. "It's full of things. Things that bite and sting."

"The bush is the same," he said.

"I suppose it's familiarity," she said. "I was brought up taking trips to the bush, so it's comfortable for me."

"It looks like we're leaving the ocean and heading inland," he said. "I suppose not too long now."

"Well, here we are," Katrina remarked as they alit from the train. "Where to?"

"Look, there's a red trolley that goes to Old Town. Why don't we try there?" he suggested.

"Let's," she agreed. They crossed to the trolley line, got tickets and took the next one north to Old Town. They wandered the streets of the old town and found some lunch at a Mexican restaurant.

"I wonder what changes this Wilcox *ou* will make," James said as they ate and drank.

"Apart from what Hank Miller told you, do you know anything else about him?" she asked.

"Not a thing," he replied. "He's not someone that I would have met, he's not from industry, but the world of deals, mergers and the art of using other people's money."

"Will he want to meet your customers?" she asked.

"He might, but I doubt it, unless he thinks they might buy us," he said. "Hank hasn't met any of the customers of Waterford, and I think only the really big ones of James & Brown, so why should Wilcox be any different, particularly if he's a Wall Street person?"

"Well, there's no point dwelling on it," she said. "Take things as they come, and if it gets too bad, then tell them to take their job and shove it."

"You're right," he agreed, an easy thing to say, but not such an easy thing to dismiss completely. It was always unsettling to have someone new come in to run things and have to try and adapt to their ways, or make the unpleasant decision to call it a day and move on. As he thought about that, he also thought about the people he had affected in the same way when he had taken over operations and made changes.

"So, shall we explore a little more, then take the little red train back to catch the train back to Santa Ana," she suggested.

"Kom ons ry," he said.

"So, what did you think of San Diego?" Katrina asked James that night as they sat in the bath together.

"I liked it, more of a typical city than LA," he replied. "LA seems to me to just be a collection of buildings, so a real town centre."

"I suppose with the advent of the car, it just started to sprawl, and it keeps sprawling with one little community running into the next," she said. "So, big board meeting next week?"

"That's what Hank said," James confirmed. "Do you want to come for the ride?"

"Not really," she said. "I'm not sure what I would do in Oak Creek while you were busy."

"Hank already reviewed all the stuff I'm going to present," James said. "But I suppose all that will be overshadowed by the big change at the top."

"It is pretty momentous," she commented. "I would think not that common an event."

"You'd be surprised," he said. "I read somewhere that the average life of a CEO is eighteen months; whether that's true or not, I've no idea, but there are more changes than you'd think."

"I hope you don't get changed out," she said. "One thing to walk out of your own accord, another thing to be chucked out."

"We'll see what happens," he said.

161

On Monday, James met with his staff and went over anything that might come up at the board meeting. There were no huge pressing legal issues beyond the usual nuisance suits that came with the hoist and access business, no human resource issues beyond the mundane, so little to report in the way of concerns. James then went through the numbers for the first quarter with Mike, and they had a discussion about the likely outcome for the second quarter. They were two-thirds of the way through it and had a pretty good idea of how things would finish. Laughing to himself about Hank Miller's comments about reserves, James then talked about what they could do to meet the projected numbers and still be able to hive off some into various reserves for this and that. That was an issue that usually came up with auditors, so there had to be a valid reason for the reserve, banking against future events and downturns was not considered a valid reason, so creativity was involved. James kept his counsel about the impending leadership change at James & Brown, but in all probability, it would not affect them, unless Wilcox thought that he could combine legal departments, accounting and human resources. He then told Mike that he had been asked to take him to Oak Creek for the board meeting, so they went through a more detailed review of the financials, covering items that might raise questions.

James then asked for views about exhibiting at Farnborough and Paris, which led to a lively discussion weighing costs and benefits. The real issue was would the shows provide any more impetus for the airframes to buy their systems or not. They were already quite well known, and the only airframe builders that they currently did not do business with were the Russians, the Chinese, the Indians and a few other minor builders. James was of the view that supplying the Chinese was a recipe for long-term problems, as in his view, all it would do would be to provide the Chinese with something to back engineer and copy. He also doubted if the US government would grant them export licences to ship to either the Russians or the Chinese. The upshot of the meeting was that unless the costs came out well within the budget that they had for publicity and marketing, then the likely benefit could not be justified. James thanked them all and said that he would have the same discussion with the division managers to see if they had differing views. Mike commented that their major concern would be how they would get back-charged for the expenditure.

Early the next morning, James and Mike McKane were at the airport ready to leave for Milwaukee, both having been dropped off by their respective spouses.

"Mr Martin, Mr McKane, we should be on the ground in Milwaukee at one-ten," Greg said as they boarded.

"Thanks, Greg," James said. There was a wait while they waited their turn in line for all the early morning departures from John Wayne, but finally they got to go and took off out over the Pacific, then climbed and turned to head east with a howling gale at their backs.

"Do we have anything on tonight?" Mike asked.

"Dinner with the James & Brown guys, then tomorrow night lunch with the board," James said. "I hope you brought your best bib and tucker."

"I'm prepared," Mike said. "What can you tell me about the board?"

"From the company, there's Hank Miller, Tom Sanders, the CFO and Gene Thompson, the president of James & Brown. Outside, there's Graham Brant, banker, Charles Bristol, insurance, Evan Eastwood, electrical switchgear, Hal Wainwright, money manager, Walter Collier, property management and Peter Burgess, medical equipment," James enumerated.

"Who's the most and least friendly?" Mike asked.

"Hard to say," James admitted. "Brant comes across as sympathetic, but he's a banker, so if the numbers, particularly cash, don't look great, probably would start wanting to delve more into the numbers. Worst, I'd say Wainwright, makes snide remarks about better uses of funds than buying new machine tools. They haven't grasped yet that better tools give tighter tolerances, so less scrap and rework and very little MRB work."

"Are they smart?" Mike asked.

"That's something that I debate often," James said. "I think they're average, but I wouldn't rate any of them as Mensa material, but it would be easy to get arrogant. If I were thrown into banking or money management, I would probably flounder and not look the smartest. They all have to have something going for them to be where they are, so I've learned not to underestimate, even though I'm not that impressed."

"I've read their basic bios in the proxy statement," Mike said. "But it didn't tell me too much about their personalities."

"Would you guys like some breakfast?" Greg interrupted as he came aft.

"That sounds great," James said.

In Milwaukee, James hired a car and they drove to the offices of James & Brown, where Mike went to spend some time with Tom Sanders, and James went off to meet Gene Thompson. He knew him but had not had a lot to do with him. Gene came from the manufacturing side of James & Brown and had moved into the slot of president when Waterford had been purchased and Hank Miller had begun restructuring the management team, to have himself, Tom Sanders, the CFO, Keith Baird, the General Counsel and Ray Pierce, the head of Human Resources as the leadership team of the new company J&B Industries and then have the two new subsidiaries report in through their respective presidents, Gene Thompson and James.

"How's it going, James?" Gene asked when James went to his office.

"Well enough," James replied.

"Not going to steal any more of my guys?" Gene laughed.

"Not that I can see," James replied. "They're doing really well, since we put them in charge of Pueblo and Albuquerque, those divisions have really turned around."

"So, what do you think about Wilcox?" Gene asked.

"I don't know much about him," James said. "Only what Hank told me, have you met him?"

"Only when we interviewed him as part of the hiring process," Gene said. "The selection committee did most of the initial work and interviews, and I only came in at the last minute when he met with the whole board."

"Any impressions?" James asked.

"Wall Street high flyer," Gene said. "Lives for the deal."

"Do you see him making any operational changes?" James asked.

"Can't say," Gene said. "Wouldn't be surprised if he didn't start to push for consolidating factories and, to use the classic asset strip term, rationalising the company."

"So, I could see Pueblo as being a target," James thought.

"Right, consolidate your loader equipment into Pittsburg and our construction machine line, similar manufacturing," Gene said.

"Different markets and different go-to-market," James commented.

"True, but what money man even thought about go to market?" Gene asked.

"What about Tulsa?" James asked.

"That's probably going to be on his target list," Gene agreed. "On the other hand, I can see some argument for moving my marine cranes to Seattle to fit with your marine products."

"What about the smaller gear factories we have in Kenosha and Beloit?" James asked.

"I see them as shutting down and moving the product lines to Santa Ana, leaving me with just mining and construction," Gene said. "Could you handle the expansion?"

"We could," James said.

"Do you have room in Seattle to expand?" Gene asked.

"We could add a fair bit," James replied. "We've got the land and the space, even a slipway for ship or barge construction."

"And again, in Santa Ana?" Gene asked.

"We could add small bits, but any major addition would need more land and buildings," James replied. "Have you thought about setting up mining and construction as two separate entities?"

"J&B Mining and J&B Construction might work," Gene said. "How much extra overhead do you have to carry because you're divided up?"

"I've only got a small office," James replied. "We consolidate financials before sending them here. I've got the legal eagles and a corporate HR to keep pension and health care plans as common as I can, so that we can easily move people between divisions."

"Well, we're probably getting way ahead of ourselves," Gene said. "We've no idea right now what Wilcox might want to do. We'll see you at dinner tonight?"

"We'll be there, Mike McKane, my CFO, is with Tom right now, talking dollars and cents," James replied.

"Okay, well, see you later," Gene said.

They ate dinner that evening at a plush restaurant in Milwaukee. James rather suspected it was something of a farewell dinner, and that was confirmed when Hank told Mike that he was retiring and that his replacement would be named at the board meeting the next day. It was apparent that the others there all knew of Hank's impending retirement. Mike asked the obvious: who was going to be the new chairman of James & Brown, and Hank told him.

"I've heard of him," Mike said. "He made a name for himself with some high-profile deals. Are we up for sale?"

"Not as far as I know," Hank said. "Unless he has a plan already, I think he would be prudent to take time to take stock and see where things are and where they're likely to go."

"So, maybe expect some moves for window dressing?" Mike asked.

"Possibly," Hank admitted. "But I have to say in all that he has told the board during the selection process, all his statements were along the lines of grow the company, possibly by acquisition."

"We would probably benefit from some electronics to integrate with our systems for controls," Mike commented.

"James had made the same observation to me earlier," Hank said. "I have to say that Waterford has lived up to our expectations and that we're happy with the results."

"I'd second that," Tom said. "We're still absorbing the acquisition costs, but operationally, Waterford is fine, not to say that increased earnings and cash wouldn't hurt."

"That's always going to be the case," Keith commented. "As far as Tom's concerned, if we can never have enough cash on hand."

"I hate debt," Tom said. "We borrowed to buy Waterford rather than use all our ready cash, and we've got the debt service to think about, and I'd prefer that Waterford covered that plus, rather than having to burden the core business."

"I recall an economics maxim that applied to mining," James said. "The sell price of the product should be three times the cost to extract, and the investment should be recovered in five years, or don't do it."

"I like that," Tom said. "In our case, it would be good to cover the costs of acquisition in five years, then we look golden."

"Is that possible?" Ray Pierce asked James and Mike.

"We can, if we look at EBITDA," James replied, referring to the commonly used measure of earnings before interest, taxes, depreciation and amortisation. "That supposes our growth targets to be met and the operational improvements that we're looking at to be also met, but if we do that, then yes, five years is doable."

"I don't think we need to go into that at the board meeting tomorrow," Hank said. "Let's just stick to the agenda. James, you and Mike wait until we call you in for the operational review, try and look surprised when you come in and meet Wilcox."

"So, how's Oak Creek?" Katrina asked James later that evening.

"Those in the know about Wilcox are all trying to work out what he'll do and what it'll mean for them," James replied. "The rest are blissfully ignorant. Mike and I had dinner with Hank and his direct reports, and Hank told Mike what was going on, and then told us to try and look surprised when we're brought in and introduced to Wilcox. How was your day?"

"Not boring, but not that exciting," she said. "More of the same, ship machines out, order parts, schedule service calls, oh, I did take over the service and parts departments today, so I suppose that's exciting, they even gave me more money!"

"Good for you," he said. "I was thinking today, how are your folks doing? We haven't heard from them in a while."

"Funny, I had the same thought, so I'm going to call later and get them up in the morning and get the news," she replied.

"I suppose I should also call my folks at some time, maybe this weekend," James said.

"That would be a good idea," she agreed. "You'd better get to bed and get some sleep if you're going to be on your toes tomorrow."

"You're right," he said. "Love you."

"Love you too," she replied.

James and Mike cooled their heels the following morning, waiting for the summons to join the board meeting. They were finally called in at nine-thirty.

"James, Mike, thank you for coming," Hank said. "Let me introduce George Wilcox, who takes over as Chairman of J&B Industries, the new parent company of James & Brown and Waterford Industries, today. George, this is James Martin, who runs Waterford, and this is Mike McKane, his CFO."

"Good to meet you," Wilcox said. "So, tell us all about Waterford and where you think it's likely to go in the next five years."

"I have some materials here," James said, handing the packages to Mike, who quickly went around the room handing them out. "I have some slides that summarise the main points."

"Slide away," Wilcox said. James put up the first slide, talked about the company as a whole, then in subsequent slides went through each division, highlighting the results and the expectations for the balance of the fiscal year and on out.

"So, James, what's your confidence level in the projections?" Graham Brant asked.

"I don't see anything on the horizon to impact things," James said. "The order book is pretty good for the rest of this year, and we're now selling into next year, for the out years we've looked at likely risks and the charts show our best estimates of the future plus some high and low bounds."

"Any way to up the earnings?" Hal Wainwright asked.

"If we continue with our capital program and upgrade manufacturing capabilities, then scrap and rework go down and earnings go up," James replied. "We'd like to get to first pass yield numbers in the high nineties; we're there in some operations, but still have work to do. With high first pass yields, capacity goes up, costs come down, delivery times get shorter, and work in process numbers go down, so a lower asset base."

"So, if you put in better machines, then you throw off more cash?" Wilcox asked.

"Yes," James replied. "It has been common practice before now to buy machines that met the tolerances required, but only met them. We have learned that if we go an order of magnitude better, then all kinds of benefits result."

"Mike, what do you think?" Wilcox asked.

"I used to be of the mindset that said buy an adequate machine and let experienced operators learn how to make good parts, but this way we have tighter groupings of tolerances and, as James said, our first pass yields start to go up and we empty out MRB cages and throw off cash," Mike replied. "Plus, we can sell more, because we can offer better delivery times and be more confident that we'll meet those times."

"What happens to existing contracts?" Evan Eastwood asked.

"Then we generate more in earnings than we had expected," Mike said.

"Didn't I read somewhere that if you change processes, then in the aerospace industry you have to do all kinds of jumping through hoops to re-qualify the product?" Graham asked.

"If we change the process, yes," James confirmed. "We're not changing the process; we might be using better and more capable machines, but the fundamental process has not changed. We never got into the trap of saying that we would mill or turn a part on a particular machine."

"You raided James & Brown for a couple of division managers," Charles Bristol said. "How are they working out?"

"Very well," James said. "If you look at the numbers here, you can see where we've turned those operations around from being lacklustre to performing well."

"Were those guys in your mentoring program, Hank?" Charles asked.

"They were," Hank confirmed. "One of them was with James, my own responsibility."

"So, you'd rate the program successful?" Charles asked.

"Very," Hank said. "We've been able to use all the first group that went through the program to good effect, and we've had no losses, no quits."

"You must tell me about this program sometime, Ray," Wilcox said to Ray Pierce, then he turned to James and Mike and asked. "So, are you guys going to join us for lunch?"

Lunch was served in the boardroom, and Hank was presented with a cut glass decanter and six whiskey glasses and wished bon voyage. At about two, James and Mike left, and they sped out to the airport.

"All done, Mr Martin?" Greg asked.

"We're done, thanks, Greg, let's go home," James replied.

"You might want to read this press release," Greg said, handing James a copy of the announcement that detailed the restructuring and named George Wilcox as the Chairman of the new J&B Industries.

"What's it say?" Mike asked James as they took their seats on the plane.

"Just talks about Wilcox and has a brief bio and says that Hank is off into the sunset," James replied. "It also says that Wilcox, as the head of the new J&B Industries, is looking at opportunities to grow the company through acquisition. I wonder how they'll finance that?"

"Could take on more debt, or issue some more stock," Mike suggested.

"Either way, it may or may not mean anything for us," James said. "It looks to me as if Wilcox is thinking of becoming a conglomerate."

"If that happens, then the only measures we'll have will be ROA and EBIT," Mike said. "If we don't meet whatever expectation he has, then we're gone, to be replaced by the next acquisition."

"Would you guys like a drink?" Greg asked as he came aft when they had levelled out at their cruising altitude of 44,000 feet.

"We would," James said. "I'm not driving home. I called Katrina from the office and told her when we'd be in."

"Very good," Greg said. "This is a nice Chardonnay that you might enjoy."

"Cheers, James," Mike said after Greg had poured them glasses and left to go back to the cockpit.

"Cheers," James echoed. "I'm predicting five years, then Wilcox will start paring off bits of us."

"Which will go first?" Mike asked.

"My bet, loaders or marine, then hoists," James replied. "What's your bet?"

"I was going to say actuators and gearboxes," Mike said. "They'd fetch the highest price, so say sell them off in five to seven years, and use the cash to con people into lending you a bunch of money, then buy something really big."

"I suppose we'll just have to wait and see, you have any plans to quit on me?" James asked.

"No, five to seven years, I'll have enough that it won't matter, and I can tell them to fuck off," Mike said.

"I'm not there yet," James lamented. "So, I'll be stuck looking for another job unless Wilcox turns out to be okay and offers me something worthwhile. But this is all speculation; we've really no idea what's going to happen."

A new regime

James met with his staff the next morning and went through the announcement of the restructuring and the new chairman. He told them that as far as he knew there were no plans to change anything at Waterford, but he could see some items that might affect the old James & Brown business. Then he called all the division managers and went through everything again, answering as many questions as he could and making a note of those he could not. He had just finished that when George Wilcox called.

"James," he said. "I'd like to take a spin through each of your operations, why don't you take a commercial flight to Tulsa and I'll pick you up there on Monday, then we'll do Tulsa and Pueblo on Monday, Albuquerque then whizz up to Seattle on Tuesday then finish up in California later that evening and do the last two there on Wednesday, can you make hotel resers for us in Albuquerque and LA for Monday and Tuesday nights. I'll red-eye the plane back to Milwaukee on Wednesday."

"When would you like to start?" James asked.

"How about Monday coming, meet you in Tulsa at say eight-thirty," Wilcox said.

"I'll be there," James promised.

"Good," Wilcox said. "I saw that you've got a change in control agreement. I'm going to keep that, plus the board approved the next tranche of options, so we've allotted you 50,000 shares, in four tranches of 12,500 over the next four years."

"Thank you," James said, thinking that that was only worth something if the value of the stock actually went up.

"Great, I'm off to Pittsburgh tonight for a spin through there tomorrow, see what these construction machines look like," Wilcox said.

"Megan, can you work out how to get me to Tulsa on a commercial flight?" James asked, after Wilcox had hung up.

"Of course," she said. "When do you want to arrive?"

"Sunday afternoon, evening, not too late," James thought. "I'm going to be meeting Wilcox there; he's flying in Monday morning, and then we're off for the tour. I'd better let everyone know to expect us next week."

"Here's the best way," Megan said a few minutes later. "Santa Ana to Dallas, then on to Tulsa, leave here at noon, Dallas at four-fifteen, leave Dallas at five-thirty, Tulsa at six."

"Sounds reasonable," James said. "Let's do that, plus car and hotel for me in Tulsa, and then two rooms in Albuquerque on Monday, then here one room for Wilcox on Tuesday night, he said that he's red eyeing it back to Milwaukee on Wednesday, that may change, and he might want to stay one more night, visit the office here on Thursday morning, them fly on home."

"What's Mr Wilcox like?" she asked.

"I've only met him once," James said. "He asked a lot of questions, but who wouldn't after taking a new job. I'll have a better idea after I've spent a few days with him. Okay, I should call Edward and warn him that we'll be there on Monday morning. Would you also get Greg to call the other pilots and find out where they're flying into on Monday? I'd look a proper idiot if I went to the wrong airport."

"I'll make sure we know what's planned," she promised.

James then called each of the division managers in order of the visits to let them know he and George Wilcox were coming and to make sure they had information on markets served and projections in those markets, and the latest financial numbers and forecasts. As he had just gone through all that at the board meeting, James suspected that this was a trip to meet the division managers and to have a look at the products and the factories themselves.

"I'm commanded to a tour," James told Katrina that evening.

"When?" she asked.

"I need to leave Sunday lunchtime to go to Tulsa, and then I'll meet Wilcox when he flies in on Monday morning," he replied. "Then I'll be back here Tuesday evening."

"So, a whirlwind tour," she said. "I suppose he's using the company plane?"

"Of course," James replied. "He's probably used to the high life. It does make it easier, getting to all the divisions commercially involves a lot of plane changes."

"So, has he already checked out the James & Brown divisions?" she asked.

"He said he was on his way to Pittsburgh, so he's probably already done mining; now he's going to look at construction machines," James said. "I suppose at some time he'll drive to Kenosha and Beloit and have a look at the smaller gear factories, if he hasn't already done so."

"He's certainly keen," she commented.

"It would seem so," James agreed.

"Are you being too judgmental?" she asked.

"I'm trying hard to keep an open mind," he replied. "But I remember Kasalia Copper Mines and the things they did, so I'm a little leery of any corporate changes in management, and I know what I did at J&B Africa and here at Waterford, only now it could impact me."

James was at the Tulsa International Airport, Atlantic Aviation building at eight on Monday morning, waiting for George Wilcox to arrive. He saw the plane land and watched as it taxied up.

"Morning, James," Wilcox said as he left the plane.

"Good morning, Mr Wilcox," James replied.

"George, the name's George," Wilcox said. "So, out of here at twelve-thirty?"

"That should be enough time," James agreed.

"You guys'll be ready for the off to Pueblo at twelve-thirty?" Wilcox asked of Chuck, one of the pilots.

"Sure thing, Mr Wilcox," Chuck assured him.

"Let's go, then, James," Wilcox said. They walked to the car and James drove them to the factory.

"Tulsa is run by Edward McIntosh," James said as he drove. "Sales of $27,850,000, net before tax of $3,335,000 and 360 people. Products are maintenance hoists, swing stages, scissor lifts and other work platforms. Two million of the revenue comes from the UK and another two from France, the rest is local. Distribution is mixed, direct sales of engineering solutions, some company outlets in high rental markets and distributors in occasional markets."

"What kind of maintenance?" Wilcox asked.

"Painting, window washing, building cladding problems," James replied. "With the scissor lifts, anything that requires you to be above the ground, that's also true for boom lifts, there it could be tree trimming, new construction, demolition, probably uses we haven't thought of yet."

"McIntosh?" Wilcox asked.

"Passionate about the business," James replied. "Always looking for ways to use the products, ways to improve profitability and ways to reduce risk to us by working out how people could hurt themselves and then building solutions into the products."

"Keeper business?" Wilcox asked.

"It's got reasonable earnings numbers, and the asset base is shrinking as we find better and faster ways to build things," James replied. "I see no reason to sell it now."

"Okay," Wilcox said.

"We're here," James said. "Those are some of the scissor and boom lifts in the yard there."

"I like the brand name, HighRise, rings true with the business," Wilcox said.

Edward met them and took them on a tour of the factory, and then introduced his team to George. Edward talked about the markets and growth prospects, which he saw as very good in the US, but slower in France and the UK. He also talked about a new line of boom lifts, which he called spider lifts. They were cunningly designed to fold into themselves to allow them to get through small entry ways into work areas, so no need to dismantle fences and gates just to get the machine there. He saw a strong market there for tree trimmers and for internal building maintenance. George asked about helicopter rescue hoists, and Edward told him that he talked from time to time with Stuart Winter about hoist types and how to design them for use in the air. He felt that the product should be at least marketed through the aerospace side of the company, as he had no experience with it or contacts. George wanted to know what Edward saw in the way of cash for the next few years. Would the operation consume cash or throw it off? Edward explained that with operational improvements, they could grow and stay at least cash neutral, if not throw off some cash. That seemed to please George, and he asked for the charts that showed that over the next five years.

"James," George started when they were on the plane headed for Pueblo. "I want you to come with me to New York in a couple of weeks, I've some meetings set up with some big brokerage houses and with the rating agencies. The brokers will want to hear all about growth opportunities and how big the business could get, and the rating agencies will want to know how liquid the company is and will be, so different messages from the same data."

"Hence the interest in cash demands?" James asked.

"You got it," George said. "Brokers and investors want to hear about high growth rates, rating agencies want to hear a more conservative message with no demands for more cash. So, are the rest of your managers as clued in as McIntosh?"

"They are now," James replied. "We had a couple of weak sisters when I arrived, but they left and we replaced them with guys from J&B."

"I read something about that," George said. "Didn't a couple of them go to jail?"

"They did," James confirmed. "The manager of the Albuquerque plant and his finance chap were running a get-rich-quick scheme. We did an audit and uncovered it and turned the information over to the DOD who prosecuted them for fraud, fortunately we as the company did not have to pay anything over and above the monies that Pratt and his sidekick had skimmed off, I think because we brought it to their attention and showed them what safeguards we had put in place to remedy the situation. Since then, the DOD has had an audit team in twice, and they've been happy with the results."

176

"We were lucky we didn't get slapped with a big fine," George said. "Just as well we self-reported."

"The unlucky one who got caught up in it was the local DCAS inspector, he's the rep that the DOD has to accept parts from suppliers," James added. "He was supposed to have seen this and reported it, how I'm not sure, when I met him, I saw him as capable of reading drawings and accepting parts, but not much beyond that, uncovering a clever fraud scheme would not have been in his area of expertise."

"I guess it comes with the territory," George said. "You're Johny on the spot so you should have known. So, you have a new DCAS guy now?"

"We do," James confirmed. "He tried to make a name for himself by rejecting parts willy nilly, but the customers got tired of being called in for MRB reviews that all turned out to be a waste of time as the parts met specs in all aspects, so he's settled down a lot now and knows to read the specs and drawings before issuing any reject slips, not that we've had any lately."

"So, Pueblo, loaders for aircraft?" George asked.

"They are," James replied. "In many ways, they look very like the scissor lifts that Tulsa makes, but the market and customer base are very different. Apart from the scissor lifts and conveyor loaders, there are all the other ground support pieces, container trailers, baggage carts and tugs. The two divisions now meet regularly to compare notes and engineering developments, but the markets don't overlap at all."

"So, doesn't make sense to combine them into one larger operation?" George asked.

"We could," James agreed. "But we'd have to have two separate sales and marketing arms. I like the idea of smaller operations, keeping the total number of employees below 500 if we can; the larger the workforce, the less flexible and agile it seems to become. The one exception to that we have now is actuators and gearboxes in Tustin, but I'm taking a look at that to see if it makes sense to pull out the electric motor part of the business and set that up as a focused business; if nothing else, we might do that as a focused factory within Tustin."

"So, how do Ford and GM manage with casts of thousands?" George asked.

"I'm sure they do very well," James admitted. "But I'm also sure that changes to the products or manufacturing take a long time to implement."

"How do our customers deal with changes?" George asked.

"Most we can readily manage," James replied. "Aerospace has specific qualification procedures, so fundamental process changes take a lot longer."

"You said something in Oak Creek about that," George recalled.

"That's right," James confirmed. "Adding capability and better machines doesn't involve a process change, so there's no need for a requal. If we were to change something like heat treat, then there would be a requal, but if say we just added a new furnace we'd have to demonstrate that it was capable of meeting the specs for temperatures, temperature gradients and suchlike, we probably wouldn't have to requal the parts, but we'd certainly have to do a lot of work proofing the furnace."

"And the same isn't true of a machine tool?" George asked.

"We'd do some circle, diamond, square tests to see that it held the tolerances advertised, but that would be simple to do," James replied.

"Circle, diamond, square?" George asked.

"It's a standard machining pattern that produces certain parts that are then checked for accuracy," James explained.

"If I'm at an airport and I see these loaders, how do I know which are ours?" George asked.

"Look for the WGS logo," James said. "Waterford Ground Support, you'll probably see FMC and some others; those are not ours."

"I imagine that the loaders come in for a fair amount of abuse," George said.

"They do," James confirmed. "To start with, they're out there in all kinds of weather, hot, cold, wet, dry, and still expected to work on demand."

"Are they easy to maintain?" George asked.

"We're trying to make that so," James replied. "The greatest challenge we have is local makeshift repairs that lead to other problems, so a lot of squabbles about warranties and whether or not actions taken by the user invalidated the warranty."

"We'll be landing in five minutes," Chuck told them over the intercom.

"We'd better buckle up," George said. "How far from the airport to the plant?"

"We could probably walk there," James replied. "It's really close."

"We'll get a car," George said. "I don't fancy a hike."

The visit to Pueblo was almost a repeat of Tulsa. Bill Evans met them and took them on a tour, then introduced his team and went through numbers and projections. George knew a little more about the airline business than the construction business, so asked more questions. He seemed happy with the answers he got and just told Bill to keep up the good work. They left and took the short trip down to Albuquerque and found their hotel for the night, had an early dinner, then turned in.

"How was the day?" Katrina asked James when he called her.

"Busy," he replied. "Yours?"

"Also busy," she said. "Lots of parts and service issues, but nothing insurmountable. What's Wilcox like?"

"Very smooth," James said. "Asks good questions for the most part, he knows less about manufacturing than I did when we first came here, but I'm sure he'll learn quickly enough."

"He must have something else going for him," she commented.

"Numbers, deals, financing," James said. "He looks at everything in terms of what's this business worth to me now, or at least it seems that way to me. I wouldn't be surprised if he didn't start selling off bits in the years to come."

"What would be the first to go?" she asked.

"Probably a toss-up between aircraft loaders and HighRise," he thought.

"That won't make Bill and Amanda very happy," she said.

"It depends," James said. "It would depend on who it was sold to and what they might want to do with Bill; maybe Bill could even buy it himself."

"Would he like that?" Katrina asked.

"He might," James thought. "It would all depend on how much. But I don't see anything happening in the near term, I'm thinking three to five years from now."

"So, tomorrow, Albuquerque, then Seattle, then home?" she asked.

"That's the plan," he confirmed. "I'll probably be home later rather than earlier. I'll drop Wilcox at his hotel and come straight home; we'll have eaten on the plane, so don't wait for me for dinner."

"Okay, then after that?" she asked.

"We'll do the two divisions here, then he changed his plan, he's not going to red-eye back, he's going to stay one more night and visit the office on Thursday," James replied.

"I'm sure the pilots are happy about that," she laughed. "Much better than flying back through the night. I should let you get some sleep. I'll see you tomorrow, love you."

"Love you," he echoed.

George wanted to see the parts that David Pratt had been working on for his fraud with and Phil Johnson took him out into the factory and showed him. There were some members of a government audit team there, but Phil saw no issues, either from an accounting point of view or from the manufacturing side. James saw some of the parts that were destined for Miller Aerospace; they were just there with all the other pieces, a little different in shape and form, but otherwise unremarkable. James glanced at the work order and saw that they were designated as being for Texas Systems. George wanted to know about growth opportunities, and Phil expounded on the commercial and defence markets for aircraft and other systems. James was impressed. Phil had picked it all up very quickly and well, and was conversant with all the current and known future aircraft, helicopter and drone types, both in the US and overseas.

James did raise one issue. For the longer-term contracts, when they built parts, the costs were recorded as inventory, then when the parts shipped, the inventory was relieved. That was all very straightforward and standard practice. However, with the improvements that Phil was making, the latest costs to produce were less than they had been, so when the inventory was relieved, it was with the latest numbers. That left them with an inventory number that was too high, so the excess needed to be written off. All that took a little while to discuss for George to fully understand.

"So, what you're telling me is that there'll be a hit to earnings?" George asked.

"That's right," James confirmed. "The asset base comes down, and this year's earnings come down, but next year's will benefit from the lower costs."

"How much are we talking?" George asked.

"A little under $100,000," James replied. "$98,670 to be exact."

"And this will continue?" George asked.

"It will as long as we make improvements," James said. "But we're also shrinking the time it takes to do these things, so parts don't sit in inventory for very long, so there's much less of an impact."

"What happens to your bonus?" George asked.

"It takes a hit too, because it's based on earnings," James said. "But, it's the right thing to do."

"I guess we need to do it or the auditors will be all over our case," George said. "Does this apply to the other divisions too?"

"Mainly here and Tustin, to a lesser extent Seattle and Santa Ana," James replied.

"But the asset base comes down?" George asked.

"It does," James confirmed. "As we drop the costs to build, then work in process inventories come down."

"Good, good, I like that, we can deal with the hit to earnings, sell it as a good thing because it means we're making improvements," George said. "Do we have to share any of the future benefits with the customers?"

"No, all our contracts are fixed price," James replied. "So, anything we can do to drop the costs is to our benefit; conversely, if we messed up our estimates and it costs us more, then we get nothing from the customer, unless it's a directed change."

"Rather like building a house," George mused. "The contractor is always after you for this or that improvement, which of course means a change and more money for him. Anyway, keep at it, I suppose lower costs and shorter times gives us an edge bidding for new work?"

"It should," James agreed. "A lot depends on how quickly others are making improvements, but I'm confident that we're ahead right now."

"Right, well, thanks, Phil and guys, great job, keep that cash coming," George said. "Shall we, James?"

"That was interesting," George said to James as they flew to Seattle.

"In what way?" James asked.

"The accounting issues, I presume that Tom Sanders knows all about this?" George asked.

"Of course," James replied. "I sat down with him when it first came up and advised him what was happening and why."

"Funny that a CFO wouldn't think to mention that to me sooner," George said. "Well, maybe he thought it was just a routine item."

"He probably had lots of other things to discuss," James said.

"Maybe right," George said. "I'll bring it up with him when I get back. Are we doing any parts that are made from plastics?"

"We have started to get some work that is glass fibres with a resin and some with Kevlar and even one or two with carbon fibres," James replied. "I expect that in the future we'll see more, so we'll need to add a bigger autoclave for curing."

"Are they expensive?" George asked.

"Moderately so," James said. "But necessary, room temperature and ambient pressure cures don't have the strength that higher temperatures do. We'll also need some freezers to keep the pre-pregs in."

"Do you have space?" George asked.

"We do," James replied. "We've got a five-year plan for the factory that shows workflows and layouts and where equipment needs to go."

"Where do we get the string and glue from?" George asked.

"There are suppliers of just fibres, and suppliers of pre-impregnated cloths and tapes; they include Owens Corning, ICI, Hitco, Hexcel, Toray, and a few others," James replied.

"What about the metals?" George asked.

"It depends whether it's titanium, aluminium or something else; there are approved suppliers for whatever we want," James replied.

"Would you gentlemen care for lunch?" Chuck asked as he came aft.

"Thanks, Chuck," George said.

In Seattle, Paul met them at the airport and drove them the short distance to the factory.

"This is very much like the mining machine parts in Oak Creek," George commented as they walked around.

"They do hoists for large machines," Paul said. "And we do winches, the biggest difference is that we have many more feet of rope on our drums."

"Even though it's made of steel, it's still rope?" George asked.

"It is," Paul confirmed. "It's made very much the same way, thin strands spun into larger strands, into even larger strands. Because it's made of strands and not a solid bar, it has flexibility and can be coiled."

"Can you expand here?" George asked.

"We have room," Paul replied. "We could double the business and still have room; the trick is to find that business."

"Is it there?" George asked.

"With more offshore oil drilling, then our markets will grow," Paul replied.

"Have we ever looked at boat building?" George asked.

"No," Paul said. "We've outfitted a couple of barges for people with winches and other equipment, but we don't have the facilities to lay down keels and build boats."

"I suppose the Koreans would do it for half the cost anyway," George commented. "So, let's meet the rest of your guys and talk about things marine."

"So, Chuck, what do we have for dinner?" George asked as they boarded the plane for their flight down to Santa Ana.

"Salmon," Chuck replied. "There's a caterer here that does meals for Alaska and Boeing corporate, so we picked up some for us."

"What do you have to drink?" George asked.

"There's a nice Chateau Ste. Michelle Riesling," Chuck said.

"Let's try it," George said. "So, James, tomorrow?"

"Santa Ana in the morning, industrial gearboxes mainly and a couple of Navy contracts, then in the afternoon, Tustin, actuators and gearboxes for aircraft and helicopters," James replied.

"Why don't Boeing and McDonnell Douglas make their own?" George asked.

"They're focused on the airframe and the wings," James replied. "They can buy the rest, actuators, landing gear, brakes, tyres, electrics and other parts."

"Do they provide the seats?" George asked.

"They don't make them," James replied. "The airlines work with people who do the interiors and specify seats, galleys, toilets, all the bits that you and I see."

"Luggage bins?" George asked.

"They buy them as well," James said.

"So, it's beat on your suppliers to get lower costs," George said, more to himself. "Seen the same thing with Ford, GM and Chrysler. I have to say I prefer the businesses that make finished machines, like our own construction machine line and the mining machines, even your loaders and lifts, making bits for someone else has its good and bad."

"I imagine that in the past, the founders of Waterford saw a need and worked out that they could fill that need," James suggested.

"I'm sure you're right," George said. "So, should I sell this and get a G III, a Challenger or a Falcon?"

"I've no idea what to recommend," James parried. "It would depend on lease or purchase cost and operating costs. The guys up front may have some ideas."

"I'm leaning towards the Falcon 50," George said. "I like the ability to go transatlantic."

"We'll be down in about twenty minutes," Chuck said as he came aft to clear away the dinner trays.

"That was good," George said. "Nice piece of salmon."

"Thank the caterers," Chuck said. "So, back to Milwaukee on Thursday?"

"Right," George said. "Let's say wheels up at eleven, that should give us enough time in the office, right, James?"

"I'm sure it will be fine," James confirmed.

184

"I think Wilcox likes the high life," James told Katrina that evening. "He's talking about a bigger plane already."

"Isn't the Lear big enough?" she asked.

"Apparently not," he said. "We'll see what he does. He does want me to go with him to New York to talk to stockbrokers and rating agencies, I think sell the company to potential investors."

"When?" she asked.

"He said a couple of weeks," James reported.

"Who are the rating agencies?" she asked.

"The best known are Standard & Poor's and Moody's," he replied. "They will rate your company's stocks and bonds based on your ability to pay your debts and live up to expectations."

"Do you know who else is going?" she asked.

"He didn't say," James replied. "I'll wait to hear."

"We heard from Will and Bridget today," she said, referring to James's brother William and his wife, Bridget. "Bridget said that their safari business has really taken off. They took over a camp in the north of Botswana, close to the Chobe River, but in a concession, not a national park, so they can *bundu bash* all they like."

"How many guests can they take?" James asked.

"Eight in four tents," she said. "You fly into Maun, then up to a small strip that's about an hour from the camp, the Pitse Safari Camp."

"That's where we stayed before when we went to Botswana that time and met your cousin Piet Englebrecht and his wife Anna," James said.

"I thought that name sounded familiar," she said.

"That's quite a change from Jo'burg," he said.

"I'll say," she agreed. "So, when can we go?"

"Let's look at holidays that we have and see what we can work out, what's their season?"

"May or June to October, November," she said. "Essentially the dry season."

"I'll check on days off, what about you?" he asked.

"I can probably get time off whenever I want, but paid is going to be a while; American companies don't give much in the way of vacation time," she replied. "So, more factory visits tomorrow?"

"Both the ones here, and I'll probably be out to dinner with Wilcox, unless he's got some other plans," James replied. "Did you call your folks?"

"I did," she said. "They're doing fine, the grape harvests have been good for the past couple of years, so the wine is good and they're selling it all."

"No talk of retirement yet?" he asked.

"Not yet, they said they want to get a few more years of harvests in, then perhaps sell the place and move to Cape Town," she replied.

"I think I'd rather live in Calitzdorp," he said. "Safer than Cape Town."

"I agree," she said. "But as they get older, they'll need better access to doctors and such, so Cape Town might be a necessary evil."

"Well, we'll see what they do," he said.

James collected George from his hotel and drove to the Santa Ana factory.

"This is close to the expressway," George commented.

"It is," James confirmed. "And only a short drive the other side of the 55 to the Tustin plant, the other way is mostly residential, with another bit of commercial and industrial the other side of the Santa Ana River. When Waterford built this factory, it was out in the beet fields; in fact, there was a beet processing plant not too far from here."

"You said the Santa Ana River, there's a river in among all this?" George asked.

"More like a concrete channel down here, but looks more like a river as it runs through Orange and Anaheim," James replied.

"So, not the East River?" George asked, jokingly.

"Not a bit," James agreed. "Okay, here we are."

"That didn't take long," George commented.

"It's an easy drive from the hotel," James agreed. "To where I live is a little more of a challenge, depending on the time of day and the traffic."

"Where do all the employees live?" George asked.

"Scattered," James replied. "Santa Ana, Fountain Valley, Garden Grove, Costa Mesa, Anaheim and a few places a bit further away."

"Anaheim, that's Disneyland, right?" George asked.

"It is, about 15 minutes away, west on Edinger, then north on Harbor, takes you right there," James explained.

"Ever been?" George asked.

"Not yet," James replied.

"Well, I suppose we should get on with this, ready?" George asked.

John Trent gave them the tour, then convened his team, and they talked about results and markets and what opportunities there were for them. George listened, asked a few questions, then seemed happy to leave. James drove them to a local restaurant and they had lunch, then stopped at the Tustin plant. Once again, they did a plant tour, then met with the staff to talk about results, markets and opportunities. George asked a few more questions, but James got the impression that he had had his fill of plant tours and presentations. They finished just before five, and George suggested an early dinner.

"So, what opportunities are there for acquisition?" George asked over dinner.

"That depends on the business," James thought. "For hoists and work platforms, it would probably be a competitor or a logical addition to the line. The same would be true for ground support equipment, perhaps there add portable ground power supplies and air conditioning units and service and maintenance platforms."

"Structures?" George asked.

"We could acquire a competitor, or a company that had more capability with composites, I think that will grow in the future, probably in time replacing some of the metal structures," James thought.

"Marine?" George asked.

"I think add capability with positioning," James replied. "The new Global Positioning Systems could mean that once in place, a barge or rig could hold itself more closely to where it should be. For that, we'd need electronics and control technologies. For industrial gearboxes, I think some electronic capability would be good. Place sensors on the gearboxes and measure vibration, temperature and perhaps even work out how to look at the oil flow for particles."

"Finally, the big aerospace nut?" George asked.

"Again, electronic capabilities to add controls to the actuators and sensors to the gearboxes," James thought. "I'd also add stepper motors to round out our electric motor line."

"Well, hop to it," George said. "Give me an analysis in a few months of what's out there, and your best guess of what we'd have to pay."

"Any limits on size?" James asked.

"No, go as big as you like," George said. "Don't look at buying GE, but something as big as you currently are would be doable. If you find you need help to gather data, just hire someone."

"I may do that," James thought.

"So, what goes on at the office here?" George asked.

"Legal issues, HR programs for health care and pensions, and consolidating financial numbers," James replied.

"Pension plans, defined benefit or what?" George asked.

"Defined contribution," James replied. "Employee contributions plus an employer match."

"Well managed?" George asked.

"It seems to be," James replied. "I've no complaints, and the plan provides for a degree of flexibility where you want your money to go."

"We'll need to switch J&B over to a 401(k)," George said. "Can't go on with a defined benefit plan, just can't keep up with the funding for an ageing workforce and the bill that will hit the plan when we start getting lots of retirements, really true if we have a downturn in the business."

"It looks like Wilcox is thinking about an acquisition binge," James told Katrina that evening. "He wants me to suggest additions to each of the companies we have and take a guess as to how much it would cost."

"Can you do that and run the company?" she asked.

"I think I'll need a research assistant," he said. "Pity the company frowns on spouses working together."

"I'm happy where I am," she said. "I'm not sure us working together would be such a good plan. You can be pretty demanding."

"Me?" he asked in mock horror, but grinning at the same time.

"Yes, you," she said. "I've heard the stories. So, who's going to be the lucky soul that gets to run around and dig up stuff for you?"

"No idea," he admitted. "I'm not even sure what kind of background they should have."

"Just don't run the poor person into the ground," she cautioned.

"I won't," he said.

"Anything more about going to New York?" she asked.

"Not yet," he said. "He'll probably arrange meetings, then let me know where to be when."

"I suppose you can fly to New York easily enough," she thought.

"Possibly not from Santa Ana, but certainly from LAX," he said.

"You know I've no real desire to go to New York," she said. "I know people want to go, but for me it's just a really big city, filled with people, and there's just nothing there that attracts me. I prefer open spaces."

"I agree, it's getting late, I suppose we should have a bath and go to bed," he said. "We both need to be up in the morning."

James collected George in the morning and took him to the office. He made the introductions and then let Jim Beatty talk about legal issues and Victoria Wilson talk about human resources. That discussion focused mainly on the pension and health care plans, their costs and what the liabilities would be in the longer term. As the pension plan was a 401(k), it was much less of an issue than if it had been a classic defined benefit plan, which under the government rules had to be adequately funded, which actually took a fair amount of money each year. George wanted to know how the company managed insurance and payments in cases where they lost. Jim explained that there was a captive insurance company in the Caymans that handled that, and that the funding came typically from the hoist and loader divisions. Unlike many companies that just seemed to want to negotiate settlements, Waterford aggressively defended itself and had been successful in doing so. George called an end to the discussions at ten-thirty, spent a few minutes with James to confirm arrangements for New York, then said that he was ready to leave to fly back to Milwaukee.

James walked him down to the plane and was floored when George asked. "Are you banging that secretary of yours?"

"No," James simply said.

"I'm surprised that you're not. Great legs, nice tits, you should give her a try," George said.

"I doubt that that will ever happen," James said. "Have a good flight back."

"He seems nice enough," Jim commented to James after George had left.

"Looks can be deceiving," James said. "He wants me to look a possible additions to the company. I may need some help with that, any ideas?"

"You might want to talk to Dawn Adams from Santa Ana," Jim suggested. "She's an engineer, but he has an MBA from Wharton, and I think she's pretty smart."

"I wonder if John will let her go," James said. "I can only ask. Fancy some lunch?"

"That would be great. Have you tried that new place over on Jamboree?" Jim asked.

"Which one?" James asked.

"Corner of Jamboree and Michelson," Jim said.

"Let's give it a try," James suggested.

James met with John Trent and got his agreement that he could talk to Dawn. John had been struggling a little with where best to use Dawn because the business and the industry were still very much a bastion of male chauvinism. He did allow that Dawn was a good engineer, but said that customers tended to look to him or someone else if Dawn presented designs or analyses. It did not matter that he always confirmed what Dawn had said; old male prejudices die hard. James met with Victoria Wilson and they concocted a job description and a salary level, then he asked Dawn if she would come and see him and she duly reported to his office and he told her what he was looking for, someone to help him with basic research into companies in the various industries in which they were active, and what it was about those companies that might make them attractive to a buyer. Dawn was quite excited by the idea and accepted the job, and was soon ensconced in one of the spare offices they had. James suggested that she first look at the hoist and access equipment business, and then the ground support business. He would start with marine and structures. A lot of it started with industry publications, as the internet had yet to be introduced, and there was no Google. James also met with Megan and told her that if she ever had any issues with advances from anyone in the company, to let him know.

"Does that include Wilcox?" she asked.

"It does," James confirmed.

"That guy gives me the creeps," she said. "I wouldn't want to be working for him."

Paul Sykes sent over information about the space and rates for the Farnborough Air Show. James then sat down with Megan, and they reviewed the designs and quotes that she had received from the company she had been working with. With the cost of the stand, shipping it and pieces and parts to display and the costs of having people there to man the stand, it all looked very unattractive. James called together the division managers, and he went through all the numbers with them, together with possible benefits. The consensus was that the monies they had in the budget would be better spent on advertising, even to the extent of taking out half-page spreads in Aviation Week for the weeks of the Farnborough and Paris air shows. James did tell everyone that he intended to go to Farnborough the next year and that he would report back what he saw and who he met.

We don't make glass

James had been instructed by George Wilcox to be in New York on the 11th of July, so that meant either a Sunday night red-eye flight or an early morning flight. He was to meet George at the offices of Standard & Poors at ten in the morning, so he asked Megan to book flights and arrange a hotel and a car, he had no real desire to take a red eye flight that would put him in New York very early in the morning, so opted for an early departure out of LAX, returning late on the afternoon of the Tuesday. That gave him a week to gather his thoughts after the 4th of July holiday weekend.

"Anything you fancy doing this weekend?" he asked Katrina the week before the holiday.

"I've booked us a cabin near a place called Big Pines, which is on the Angeles Crest Highway, behind the San Gabriel Mountains," she said.

"I'll try and get away early on Friday," he said. "How long to get there?"

"I'd guess with traffic, a couple of hours at least," she said. "We go the same way as we did before when we went to Big Bear, but halfway up the Cajon Pass, we turn off. I imagine there'll be plenty of people around as I read that Big Pines is a resort that's open all year, skiing in the winter and hiking in the summer."

"I suppose with a city as big as LA, there'll always be people," he lamented.

"Well, we'll make the best of it," she said. "We should take boots for walking as there are tons of trails around."

"At least no chains to worry about," he said.

When Friday came, James closed the office at two-thirty and sent everyone home. He was able to get back the their house in about twenty minutes, which he considered remarkable. Katrina was already home and ready for the off, Jeep packed with clothes and food. Traffic was already building on the 91 freeway, and it took them a while to get to the 15. There was a steady stream of cars going up the Cajon Pass, some of whom turned off where they did, but most of whom carried on, headed towards Bakersfield and possible Las Vegas. A few miles from the turn off from the Cajon Pass, they came to the junction for the Angeles Crest Highway and took it, climbing into the hills and the pine forests.

"This is getting quite pretty," Katrina commented to James.

"I like the trees," he said. "I've always liked pine trees, I like to hear the wind in them and the smell of them."

"Wrightwood," she said. "The road to the cabin is not too far from here, look out for the sign on the left, they told me."

"There," he said, after about ten minutes. They turned off and took the dirt road that wound up into the forest until they came to a ranch house.

"Howdy folks," a woman said as they pulled up. "You the Martins? I'm Rosa, by the way."

"We are," Katrina confirmed.

"Let's get you to your cabin and settled," Rosa said. "Follow me."

Rosa climbed into an ancient Jeep and drove off, with Katrina following. After about ten minutes, she pulled up outside a log cabin.

"You've got hot water any time you want," Rosa said. "There's a gas stove, propane tank is full. If you need anything, just come down to the house. Watch out for bears, raccoons and jays, they'll steal anything you leave accessible."

"We will," Katrina said.

"There's a couple of maps in the cabin for the local area and the trails," Rosa said. "If you go hiking, take water, take food, but be sure that you take water, it's dry up here, and you can dehydrate real quick. If you just want to hike, then that little trail behind the cabin leads you to the wilderness area, and there's a jeep track high up that follows the ridge."

"Thanks for the advice," James said. "Do we have to pay fees for the Angeles National Forest?"

"Depends where you go," Rosa said. "For your Jeep, you'll have to pay in the National Forest. There's a trail map that shows what trails are open; your Jeep should be fine up there. One thing, no fireworks on the Fourth, fire danger is high."

"We weren't planning on any fireworks," James said.

"Okay, folks, enjoy your stay," Rosa said. "If you feel like it, I'm having a barbecue with some neighbours on the Fourth at the ranch house, say around noon, just if you feel like it. When you leave, if I'm not around, just drop the key in the box on the porch."

"Thanks," Katrina said.

When Rosa had gone, James and Katrina unpacked, put perishables in the refrigerator, then made themselves some tea and went out and sat and looked out into the trees.

"She said to watch out for bears," James said. "I've never seen a bear outside a zoo."

"How big are they?" Katrina asked.

"I really don't know," he admitted. "I know that grizzly bears and Kodiak bears can be really big, but the bears that live here, I don't know."

"I'd like to see one," she said. "But not too close."

"I imagine like most things, they'd rather avoid us if they could," he said.

"Still, I'd like to see one," she said. "What shall we do tomorrow?"

"We could try one of the back roads," he suggested.

"We'll do that," she agreed. "Now what are you cooking for dinner?"

They explored the area on foot and in the Jeep, but they never saw their bear. They did see raccoons and jays and quite a few other birds, but never the bear. The closest they got to seeing a bear was tracks on the Blue Ridge trail that they deduced had to be a bear, as they could not imagine them being from anything else; they were certainly not canine or feline, so had to be ursine. Katrina thought that the tracks were quite old, a day or two at least, so if there had been a bear there recently, it was long before they were there. On Sunday, they packed up early and spent a little time with their hosts and met the neighbours before heading back down to Orange.

"I enjoyed that," Katrina said when they arrived home. "But I could have done with fewer people. The views were spectacular, though, I wonder what it would be like on a nice, clear day without the smog."

"Great, I would think," James said. "As for people, it is a holiday weekend, and I suppose many people want to get away from the city and the smog for a while."

"I wonder if there's anywhere within easy driving distance where we could be alone and not meet other people," she pondered.

"Probably not within easy driving distance for a weekend," he thought. "Let's face it, LA is miles bigger than Kitwe or even Milwaukee."

"So, next week it's another big city for you," she said.

"I don't fancy the trip to New York," he said. "I could never work out why people like to live there."

"It's not even as if the weather's nice," she said. "They get snow and ice there as well as hot summer days."

"Well, I'll tell you what I think when I get back," he promised.

James spent the week putting together materials that he could use, whether he was talking to the rating agencies or to investment houses. It was in some ways a lesson on how that same basic data could be presented in different ways to convey different messages. He had second-quarter numbers and was gratified to see that they met forecasts and that there were no unforeseen items or surprises. He put that down to the diligence of his managers rather than particular brilliance on his part. He was surprised that Wilcox did not seem to want to meet before they were in New York, and he wondered if that reflected confidence in him, or if there was not some other motive. On Sunday, he drove to LAX early in the morning and caught his flight to the Kennedy airport, arriving in the late afternoon. The driver that Megan had arranged was there and whisked him to his hotel, in what James thought was record time, but then it was Sunday afternoon, so no rush hour traffic. He ate and then got directions to the Standard & Poor's offices, which were only a short walk.

At a quarter to ten, James was waiting in the foyer of the S&P offices and saw Wilcox come in.

"James, how are things?" he asked.

"Fine, thank you," James replied.

"Ready for the day?" Wilcox asked.

"Ready," James confirmed.

"Okay, let's see if these guys are ready for us," Wilcox suggested. He went to the desk and gave their names and was told that a Mr Henred would be down directly to escort them to their meeting.

"George Wilcox?" a man, who had to be Henred, asked.

"That's us," George replied.

"Let's go up," Henred said. They took the lift up to the tenth floor, and he led them to a conference room. "Coffee?" he asked.

"Thanks," George said. "James?"

"I'll have some," James replied. They drank their coffee, then six others filed in and took seats.

"George," one said. "Welcome back to S&P. We're looking forward to you telling us all about Waterford. It's been a while."

"Thanks for seeing us, Gerard," George said. "This is James Martin, who runs the Waterford businesses. I'm going to hand things over to him, James. This is Gerard Booth, we go way back."

"Thank you, George," James said. "Gentlemen, perhaps I should start by stating that we don't make glass." That raised a laugh around the table.

"So we shouldn't confuse you with the Irish Waterford?" Booth said.

"Not a bit, and so that there's no confusion, J&B Industries shouldn't be confused with J&B Scotch put out by Justerini and Brooks of London," James said. "We make industrial gearboxes, access equipment, marine systems, airport loaders, structural parts for aircraft and gearboxes and actuators for aircraft."

"So, could you take us through the company as a whole, then delve into the different businesses?" Booth asked.

For the next two hours, James talked about the company and its various divisions, then answered questions.

"Anything you want to add, George?" Booth asked.

"No, I think James said it all," George replied.

"It looks like Waterford is in good hands," Booth said. "Tell us a little about yourself, James."

"I started out as a mining engineer for a copper mining company in Zambia," James said. "I worked underground for a while, then they asked me to take over the start-up of a new surface mine. When the price of copper dropped, they mothballed the mine, and I left. I joined James & Brown as an application engineer, then went to Johannesburg to manage the African subsidiary. I came back from that assignment and spent some time in market research, then the acquisitions group, which culminated in the acquisition of Waterford. I moved out to Waterford and took over in December of last year."

"George, we'd like to hear a little about James & Brown," Booth said.

So, it was George's turn to speak, and in James's view, he did credibly well.

"I think you can see that J&B is well set for the future," George said as he finished his pitch. "Both James & Brown and Waterford generate cash, and with the improvements that James is making to the operations, we can expand without heavy demands on cash."

"We see that," Booth said. "Thanks for coming, we'll be in touch."

"Well, that went pretty well," George said as they left the building. "Let's get some lunch before we hit Moodys, there's a place I like just down the way here in Broadway. Good job this morning, by the way, just the right tone."

"I spent some time trying to work out how best to present things," James said.

"You have done something different for the brokerage houses?" George asked.

"I did," James confirmed. "As you said, they will want to see growth, so I've looked at each of the markets and where we think things will go."

"Good, good," George said. "So let's eat. We're having dinner tonight with some guys from Goldrich Faber, and we'll get a preview of what they're looking for."

They ate and talked generalities, as George pointed out, one never knew who might be around to hear their conversation. The afternoon was a repeat of the morning as James made his presentation to a new cast of characters. The Moodys people, though, did not ask anything about the legacy business of James & Brown; they commented that they had heard from Hank Miller not that long ago and doubted whether the mining and construction machine business had markedly changed.

Dinner that evening was at a fashionable place on 46th in the theatre district. They actually ate outside, which was pleasant enough, if a little warm. George knew the Goldrich Faber people well, and they clearly had lots to talk about, so James spent time just watching and listening. It was clear that everything was about the deal, the latest deals they had done, deals that were in the works, deals that were at that time just ideas and remote possibilities and deals that could have been. Clearly, George was very much at home in their company and very much in his element, leading James to wonder just how long it would be before parts of Waterford were offered up for sale. James learned that whichever side of the deal Goldrich Faber was on, they charged fees and did well out of the transactions, apart from any financial position they might take or have in the companies involved. He had seen a little of that when James & Brown had bought Waterford, but as he listened and learned, he realised just how pervasive their reach was and how much influence they had.

When James made his presentation the next day to Goldrich Faber, it was to two who had been with them the evening before and six others. James talked, then answered questions about the markets, the divisions and the competitors.
"Good job there," George said as they left the Goldrich building. "Let's grab a bite, then hit the guys at United Banks."
"Anything I need to add or remove?" James asked.
"Didn't see anything," George said. "This is mainly about letting them see who's running Waterford and building confidence so they'll pitch J&B Industries. Next week I'm coming back out with Gene Thompson

to talk about James & Brown and the mining and construction industries."

"We couldn't do both at the same time?" James asked.

"I suppose we could have," George said. "But I think it's better this way."

"Do you know any of the people we're going to see this afternoon?" James asked.

"Grant Rosenberg," George replied. "He heads up the industrial practice; there's probably going to be someone from aerospace as well, maybe energy for the offshore marine stuff."

United Banks had a cast of thousands, well, perhaps not thousands, but there were twenty of them there, from the practices that George had mentioned and another from the transportation sector that dealt with airlines and airports. James gave the same presentation that he had given Goldrich Faber and then took questions. There were more questions, some of which he thought inane, but he answered them anyway. The United Banks team wanted a life and career history of him, so he obliged, short as it was. He was surprised when one of the bright young men asked him if he had actually worked underground, and if he had not been afraid. James pointed out that it was really not that much different from working in a tall office block; the roof over your head was as safe as the designers or miners made it. George finally called a halt to the questions and suggested that if they needed anything further, he would provide it.

"Those guys can ask questions," James commented to George as they left the building.

"I think half of them are just asking to appear interested to their team leaders," George said.

"Did we make any difference?" James asked.

"Tell you in two weeks," George said. "But Rosenberg was nodding yes, so it bodes well. We'll have to see if they make any recommendations. I'll get a better sense after they've heard from Gene. So, flight back to LA tonight?"

"I was planning on it," James replied.

"At least going west, the clock works for you," George said. "I'm going to Teterboro, so I'll be in touch."

James called Katrina from the Kennedy airport and told her that he should arrive at LAX at nine thirty-five. Then he would have the drive home, so told her to expect him around eleven that evening. He found the driver that Megan had organised for him, and they joined the afternoon traffic getting out of Manhattan. They arrived with little time to spare, so James checked in, then scurried off to find his gate. At least the flight was a non-stop on a Lockheed TriStar, and very comfortable. He was seated next to a man who introduced himself as Walter Bishop. Apparently, he ran one of the competitors that James had in the airport service business, Airport Services Inc., or ASI for short. James introduced himself and disclosed that he ran Waterford and, therefore, Waterford Ground Support.

"Ever thought of selling?" Walter asked.

"No," James replied. "Have you?"

"Not until just now," Walter said. "How big is Ground Support now?"

"About $30 million," James replied.

"How's Morris Whitaker these days?" Walter asked.

"We made a change, the operation is now run by Bill Evans, he moved over from James & Brown," James replied.

"So, you finally dumped Morris," Walter laughed. "That must be why you've been winning more business lately."

"Bill's doing a good job," James allowed.

"Look, come and see me this week, maybe Thursday, I'll buy you dinner and we can talk about cabbages and kings," Walter said. "I'm getting to the point where I'd like to improve my handicap and get in some serious fly fishing."

"You don't have any children who'd like to carry on the business?" James asked.

"We've got one son and all he's interested in is horses," Walter said. "He does pretty well out of them, probably makes twice to three times what I do in a year, so dinner?"

"I can meet you wherever you suggest," James said.

"Okay, let's say six at Five Crowns in Corona del Mar," Walter said. "Very Brit place, you should feel at home there. Ever been fly fishing?"

"No," James replied. "My fishing was generally with a spinner or a float on rivers and dams in Zambia."

"Did you go on safari there?" Walter asked. "That's something else on my list of things to do when I retire."

"I did some camping in the bush," James replied. "But I wasn't there on an organised safari, I worked there for a copper mining company and my wife and I would take trips whenever we could."

"That must have been interesting," Walter said. "How did you land up at Waterford?"

"After the mine I was running shut down, I joined James & Brown, then moved from J&B to Waterford after the acquisition," James explained.

"Maybe I should bring my wife along," Walter thought. "I've been trying to convince her that safaris are safe enough."

"Perhaps we should have my wife join us," James suggested. "She grew up in Zambia, and she's the bush expert."

"Great idea," Walter said. "What kinds of machines did you use on your mine?"

"Underground, it was a lot of drills and some trains and a few scooptrams, in the surface mine it was Cat front-end loaders and trucks, plus the usual dozers and graders," James replied.

"James & Brown, I know from cranes and loaders," Walter said. "Have you had much to do with those lines?"

"I ran J&B Africa in Jo'burg for a couple of years and we sold the line of construction machines and acted as the agent for the larger mining machines," James replied.

"You know, ASI and WGS would make a good combination," Walter said. "We've got some conveyor loaders and scissor lifts, but you have us generally beat there, but we've got the ground power supplies, the honey wagons and the AC units. Still building things in Pueblo?"

"We are," James confirmed.

"I'm thinking ASI should move out of Lynwood and set up shop somewhere like Wichita," Walter said. "More central, with good railroad and freeway access."

"Kansas City might be better," James thought. "Access to the same railways, but better access to both north-south and east-west freeways."

"You're right, and I wouldn't have to compete with Boeing for workers," Walter said. "I'll take a look at Kansas City and see who gives me the better deal, Kansas or Missouri."

James and Katrina found their way to the Five Crowns on Thursday, and it was a replica of an English pub cum restaurant, complete with RAC sign and red telephone kiosk.

"James, glad you could make it, this is my wife, Susan," Walter said as they were shown to their table.

"Nice to meet you, Mrs Bishop," James said. "This is my wife, Katrina. Katrina, this is Susan and Walter Bishop."

"I gather from Walter that you're an expert on Africa, Katrina," Susan said. "I've always wanted to go, and Walter has now promised me that we will."

"I wouldn't say that I'm an expert on Africa," Katrina said. "It's a huge continent and I only really know Zambia quite well and South Africa reasonably well."

"If we wanted to go on a safari, where should we go?" Susan asked.

"It would depend on whether you wanted to do your own driving, or if you preferred to be at a lodge or a camp," Katrina said.

"For a first time, what would you suggest?" Susan asked.

"How much time do you want to spend?" Katrina asked.

"I don't know, three to four weeks," Susan replied.

"It might be an idea to spend a week or so in the Kruger National Park in South Africa, then go on up to Zambia and spend some time in the Luangwa National Park on a walking safari," Katrina suggested. "The walking is not demanding, the camp people move your luggage and you just walk a few miles between camps with a guide and a game scout, who's there to make sure you're safe. In the Kruger, you could also pick one of the private reserves that abut the park, which would mean you'd be driven around from a lodge. If you wanted a really different experience, James's brother and his wife run a bush camp in Botswana."

"I like the sound of that," Susan said. "Any suggestions as to who could set this up?"

"If you give me your address and telephone number, I'll send you some options, and I'll send you the contact information for Will and Bridget and their camp in Botswana," Katrina suggested.

"So, James, thought any more about merging?" Walter asked as Katrina and Susan started talking about what to pack, what to wear and what not to take.

"We're interested," James replied. "How big is ASI?"

"Sales of $25 million, before tax of two, 312 people all told, property is leased and the lease is up in nine months," Walter replied.

"Do you think any of the people would think about moving?" James asked.

"I'm sure some would," Walter replied. "My bet is that the engineers would move, plus some of the management types, hourly on the shop floor, some may think about it, some won't."

"Any patents?" James asked.

"We have some," Walter said.

"Current backlog?" James asked.

"Fifteen million in sales worth," Walter replied. "Total assets on the books $22 million."

"Any notional asking price?" James asked.

"I was thinking of an asset sale at book plus two for patents and goodwill," Walter said. "I can get you audited accounts to review if we come to an agreement that we'll pursue this. We'd want an NDA of course."

"Understandable," James said. "I'd have to look at the terms of the lease and what renewing would entail, versus moving everything."

"Think about it and let me know early next week," Walter said. "I don't have any shareholders or board to get approval from, so if we come to a deal, then we'll have a deal."

"Walter, if you're finished talking business, perhaps we could order," Susan said.

"I think she's had enough of the business and just wants to spend time with Walter and travel," Katrina said to James as they drove home.

"So, she's driving the sale as much as he is?" James asked.

"I think she's the main reason he is selling," Katrina said. "She's tired of taking second place to the business, and now she wants to enjoy the fruits of their labours and the money they can get out of it. Their son has his own life and is so engrossed in his horses that he barely has time for them, and there are no grandchildren."

"I'll talk to Wilcox tomorrow and tell him about our meeting and see what he wants to do," James said.

"What did you think of the Five Crowns?" she asked.

"It was interesting," he said. "Most of the pubs I went to as a teenager weren't that fancy, but I did like the food."

"I was thinking it wasn't like the Green Dragon that you took me to, but then that was just a pub, not a restaurant," she said.

"Who might be a good agent to do their bookings for them if they go to South Africa and Zambia?" James asked.

"Bridget would know," Katrina said. "She might even persuade them to miss Zambia and South Africa and just go to Botswana, but maybe that's throwing them in the deep end a bit, maybe better to do a week in Kruger, then Pitse."

"I'm surprised that you didn't push them towards Pitse right away," he said.

"I was wondering if they would be ready for a true bush experience," she said. "We haven't been to Pitse in a while, so don't know what it's like now or if it would be too wild for them, but I will offer it as an alternative. I'll call Susan in the morning."

"Do it," Wilcox said after James talked to him the next day. "If they've got assets of $22 million, they're only turning it just over once a year, I'm sure you can do better than that, so we could recover cash in two to three years."

"Any thoughts about renewing a lease in Lynwood or moving everything to Pueblo?" James asked.

"Up to you," Wilcox said.

"We've got the space in Pueblo," James said. "I think we'd be better off moving production to Pueblo, so I'll take a look at shutdown costs for Lynwood."

"Who's going to be your acquisition team?" Wilcox asked.

"I'll be part of it," James replied. "And I'll add Bill Evans and Fred Burgess, the manufacturing manager, Bob Nelson, the engineer, plus Mark Brooks, the finance man and Pete Willis from my office for legal issues."

"Sounds good, keep me informed," Wilcox said. "When we're ready to do the deal, I'll have Tom Sanders come out and join you for a day or two. Any idea what the NDA would say?"

"Not yet," James said. "But I would expect it to include the usual do not disclose any information gathered in this process to anyone outside the named parties."

"Make sure your man Willis keeps Keith Baird in the loop," Wilcox said.

"I'll do that," James promised. After he had hung up with Wilcox, he called Bill Evans.

"James, what's up?" Bill asked.

"What do you know about ASI?" James asked.

"We compete a little, but they've got more of the other ground support equipment," Bill replied.

"What do you think about buying them?" James asked.

"Interesting," Bill said. "How much and how do we integrate?"

"How much is up for negotiation, but the offer on the table is book value plus $2 million for goodwill, patents, et cetera," James replied.

"Sales of how much?" Bill asked.

"Twenty-five million," James replied. "I'm leaning towards shutting down their Lynwood operation and moving everything to Pueblo; you may have to add some warehouse and assembly space."

"We would," Bill agreed. "What's the chance of us getting a walk through their place?"

"I'm working on that," James replied. "If you put together a team for the acquisition, who would be on it?"

"Fred, Bob and Mark, plus I'd need one of your legal eagles," Bill replied.

"I was thinking of Pete Willis," James said.

"Good idea," Bill thought. "Doesn't Oak Creek want to have a hand in this?"

"Wilcox told me to keep Tom Sanders and Keith Baird in the loop, and I imagine when it comes to the final handshake, then they'll be there," James said. "I suppose it will depend on whether the transaction is cast as an acquisition by Waterford or J&B."

"Sounds like Wilcox is giving you the chance to shine, or if it all goes south, then you're to blame, not him," Bill said.

"Cynic," James laughed. "But the same thought had crossed my mind, we'll just have to make sure things go well if we do the deal."

"We won't let you down," Bill promised. "So, what's the next step?"

"I need to talk to Walter Bishop of ASI and work things out with him," James replied. "When I've done that, I'll talk to you again."

Walter was pleased that James said that they would proceed, and he suggested that James and his lawyer meet with him and his lawyer to discuss the non-disclosure agreement. What James did not know, and might not discover for a while, if at all, was whether or not Walter had invited others to bid on the business. The discussions that led to the inking of the non-disclosure agreement only took about half an hour. James had been through it before, and Pete Willis knew what to look for, so the alterations and changes were done quickly.

"So, James, when do you want to tour the factory?" Walter asked.

"As soon as I can," James replied. "Could I bring four others from Waterford Ground?"

"Sure thing," Walter agreed.

"Just remember that they'll be bound by the same NDA you've signed," Terry Brown, Walter's lawyer, added.

"I'm sure James knows that," Walter chided. "So, James, when were you thinking?"

"What about Friday?" James asked.

"Friday's good," Walter said. "Who are you bringing?"

"Bill Evans, he runs WGS, his manufacturing man, Fred Burgess, the engineer, Bob Nelson and his finance man, Mark Brooks," James replied.

"Will you come as well?" Walter asked.

"I will," James confirmed.

"Look forward to it," Walter said. "We'll have a packet for you when you come. Join us for lunch?"

"Thank you," James replied.

"There's not much around here in Lynwood, so why don't we go on down to Rosecrans? There's a place there that's pretty good," Walter said.

"We'll follow you, then head on back to our office," James said.

"Bill, can you and your team be here on Friday?" James asked later.

"You bet," Bill replied.

"I'll send the plane for you," James said. "I'll get them to come on up to Pueblo on Thursday afternoon, so you can get an early start on Friday morning, fly into Long Beach here, it's probably the easiest and closest airport to Lynwood. I'll meet you at the Lynwood factory."

"So, any guesses as to who else they're shopping to?" Bill asked.

"Not a clue," James said. "And Walter Bishop is giving nothing away."

"Maybe we'll hear something as we tour the plant," Bill said.

"Maybe, it depends on how chatty they are," James said. "If someone will talk to us, they'll probably talk to anyone. Okay, Bill, I'll see you on Friday, if I don't talk to you beforehand."

James had other divisions to think about, and he also wanted to talk to Dawn Adams to see what she had gathered in her searches.

"I've got reports here," Dawn said when James poked his head into her office.

"Tell me about them," James invited.

"Well, my first recommendation was going to be ASI, but that seems to be well underway. Then for Hoists I've got three possibles, for Marine, two possibles, for structures only one with metals, but four composites, for gearboxes, three and for actuators and systems two," Dawn replied, tapping each pile in turn. "All US except for one of the composites and one for gearboxes, both of them are in the UK."

"Any sense of whether or not they are for sale?" he asked.

"Some," she replied. "I've noted probabilities against each one. Five of them are private concerns, and the rest are small public companies."

"What about market trends?" James asked.

"I've dug through most of the trade literature and come up with ranges for each segment," she replied. "The probables track very closely to the numbers you had before. I've just added probable upper and lower bounds."

"Locations of the US possibles?" he asked.

"Anywhere from Terminal Island to Chicago," she said.

"I wonder if we should just start calling them," James mused.

"It might be an idea to get some of the local press and see if there's anything written about them," she suggested.

"Good idea," he agreed. "It might also be a good idea to ask our chaps if they know the companies and if they know who runs them."

"That I'll leave to you," she said. "Any objection if I make some visits and go and take a look at these possibles?"

"Go ahead," he said. "Some good basic industrial espionage is probably what we need now."

"I'd rather call it intelligence gathering," she said. "Do you have a model to use to analyse the financials of any transaction?"

"I do," James said. "And if we could get the corporate guardians of the computer system to give us some time, we could do runs very quickly."

"Can we input data with the remote terminal we have?" she asked.

"We could, that's how we upload monthly financials now," he replied.

"Is that how you're going to look at ASI?" she asked.

"That and a review by Bill Evans and his team, the financials may not tell us all, and it would be good to have their assessment," he replied. "When we get the package, I'll go through it with you and we'll see what it tells us and what it doesn't."

Things progressed, and Bill and his team arrived and toured the ASI factory. They were shown around by the factory manager, who was very helpful and provided probably more information than he should have. On the tour, James did learn that there had been two other teams through, so obviously, the word was out that ASI was up for sale. Walter gave them a packet of financial data, numbered and marked not to be copied. Quite how that would be enforced was not clear, so James doubted that the data would stay limited to a few for long. Back at the offices of Waterford, James, Dawn, Bill, and Mark pored through the data package and made their own notes.

"Before I run my model on this, would you give me your best estimates of moving costs and construction costs in Pueblo?" James asked Bill.

"We'll do that," Bill said. "We'll put together an outline plan and then Mark and I will put numbers to it, give us a week or so. We probably won't move most of their machines; we've got capacity on our press breaks, we've got welding capacity, so it's the dedicated fixtures and tools we'll need to move, the rest we'll just auction off."

"That'll be fine, Walter wants an indication by the end of the month, so we've got just over two weeks," James said. "If Walter's asking book plus two, what I need to know is how high can we go before it's just not worth it. Who do you think are other likely buyers?"

"I read off the sign-in sheet that someone had left at the door, that CMC and CWI were the other two that had been through," Fred said. "When we left, I noticed that the sign-in sheets had been replaced with new blank ones, so someone screwed up there."

"If either one of those picked up ASI, how much would it impact your competitive position?" James asked.

"CWI not much, they don't have very deep pockets," Bill said. "CMC more of a challenge; they're like us with a much bigger parent behind them. If we could avoid it, I'd rather not have them get any more of a position in the market."

"Okay, well, thanks for coming down, I'll talk to you next week, Bill," James said.

"So, James, where do we stand with this ASI?" Wilcox asked.

"We've done all our analysis and we're ready to make a definitive offer," James replied.

"How much?" Wilcox asked.

"We're thinking of two and a half over book, which would be twenty-four and a half," James said. "There are two others out there bidding, so we plan to offer all cash and engage to remove everything from the site by the end of the current lease term. It's an asset buy, so any hidden liabilities related to hazardous waste are for the seller and the property owner."

"How much expansion in Pueblo?" Wilcox asked.

"We're currently at 140,000 square feet under roof. We need to add another 25,000 square feet, split between warehouse and assembly. We've enough machine shop capacity," James explained. "We'll rent some warehouse space while we build, and we've a plan to move most of the assembly onto the current floor."

"Anything special about the assembly space?" Wilcox asked.

"We don't need fifty-ton overhead cranes," James said. "We can get by with five tons, and we'll probably never approach that; most loads would be much lower, so the building structure is quite light."

"People?" Wilcox asked.

"We'd like to offer jobs and relocation packages to eight engineers, the assembly manager and two salespeople; the rest of the workforce we'll need we'll pick up in Pueblo," James replied.

"Who deals with shutdown costs for their current location?" Wilcox asked.

"Bishop," James said. "I think he's factored that into his thinking and the asking price."

"How much are we going to have to spend in Pueblo?" Wilcox asked.

"Two," James replied.

"So, the total bill is twenty-six five," Wilcox said. "How long to pay that back?"

"Well, the assets are mostly raw materials, work in process and finished goods, with little in the way of fixed assets, just a few machine tools and some equipment, so of the twenty-two, only two won't move in the short term, so two years at the most, we're recovering the costs of the goodwill and patents and new construction, the current assets we'll move most this financial year and the rest in the early part of next year," James replied. "That is without the interest and opportunity costs on the monies we're putting out for what is basically an early current asset buy."

"Okay," Wilcox thought. "I'll send Tom Sanders out with authority to conclude a deal, I'll go up to book plus three if we have to, but nothing higher."

"Fine," James said. "I'll set up a meeting with Bishop for Friday."

"Good, now I want you to get me a plan to transfer all the gearbox work from Beloit and Kenosha this financial year," Wilcox said. "Now's a good time for us to do it."

"I'll take care of that," James said. "How do we handle shutdown costs?"

"We'll make that an extraordinary corporate charge," Wilcox said. "We've reason right now to have some offsetting expenses. Just because we're consolidating Kenosha and Beloit into Santa Ana, don't give up on looking for suitable additions from elsewhere."

"I won't," James promised.

"It's all go with Waterford," Katrina commented when James told her all that was going on.

"It's certainly never boring," he said. "How's your job?"

"Still interesting," she said. "But I was thinking of signing up for a six-month intensive class on computer programming, would that be okay?"

"That would be fine," he said. "We can manage comfortably financially, and if you fancy the idea, then why not? What do they teach?"

"As I understand it, assembler language, COBOL, some query language and maybe some other things," she replied.

"Where's the school?" he asked.

"In Anaheim on College," she replied. "Not a bad drive."

"So, when do you start?" he asked.

"I need to quit first, then sign up, so next month," she said.

"So, should we plan for a holiday before or after your course?" he asked.

"Let's plan for after and maybe go to Botswana to see Will and Bridget," she suggested.

"That sounds like fun," he agreed. "I'll get details from Bridg on their season dates. I suppose we could either fly from here to New York and pick up South African there, or go via Europe."

"What about here to Taipei on Singapore, then on to Jo'burg on South African?" she suggested.

"That sounds interesting," he said. "I'll look into that. Here to New York, then Jo'burg is probably less flying time, but going west might be fun."

Holidays

ASI was purchased, and people, materials and machinery were moved to Pueblo, with the balance of the assets sold off at auction. The small gear factories of James & Brown in Kenosha and Beloit were closed down, and all the production moved to Santa Ana. James's next project was an addition to the hoist and access business and an electronics firm that would add value to both the marine and aerospace businesses. Quite how that would be managed, he was still working out with Stuart McIntosh and Paul Rose, both of whom wanted to absorb the firm into their own business. Those successes had been offset by many bids made on companies and divisions that were not successful, either because the acquisition cost was too high, or they were just outbid, or the terms were too onerous. It seemed that success was rare, driven by just the right set of circumstances. Wilcox moved the corporate office to Fifth Avenue in New York, which both James and Gene Thompson thought was an unnecessary expense, but which Gene was also not unhappy about, as it left him more to his own devices without having George Wilcox looking over his shoulder all the time. It did mean that monthly reviews were now in New York instead of Oak Creek, and that meant more travel for both James and Gene. James did not use the company plane to fly to New York; the expense just was not worth it. He was due some holiday and he had contacted Will and Bridget and booked a trip to Botswana, going through New York to Johannesburg in late October. Katrina had investigated the route through Taipei, but Singapore only flew three times a week and South African only once a week, and the times did not work well, nor did the cost.

"Anything I need to know before we go?" James asked Megan.
"No, I think you've done everything you could," she replied. "There's no real way to contact when you're there?"
"They have a radio, and if it's a dire emergency, call the police station in Maun, that's the number I gave you, and they'll relay a message," James

said. "But I would think that Mike McKane can handle almost anything."

"Well, have a good time," she said.

"I'm sure we will," he said. "Katrina's really looking forward to going back to Africa again."

"Are we all ready?" Katrina asked when James arrived home.

"Ready," he said. "I ordered a car to take us to LAX at nine tomorrow morning, the flight goes at one, so we'll have plenty of time."

"I'm packed and ready to go," she said. "I've been packed and ready for a couple of days. How long do we have to wait in New York?"

"We'll stay overnight," he said. "The Jo'burg flight goes in the early morning, so better to leave LAX today and New York tomorrow and not risk red-eye flights and a possible missed flight."

"From Jo'burg, what are we doing?" she asked.

"A charter from Rand to Maun, clear immigration there, then on up to the strip that serves Pitse," he said.

"Who's in charge while you're away?" she asked.

"Mike McKane," he said. "He can handle any crises that come up."

"They can manage without you for a couple of weeks," she said.

New York was hot and humid, but they were only staying overnight, so did not have to endure the unpleasantness for very long. The flight to Johannesburg was long, but they both managed to sleep for a while, waking as they crossed the border between South West Africa and Botswana. It was hard to imagine at 35,000 feet that there was a bush war going on below between the South Africans and the freedom fighters looking for the independence of what would become Namibia. When they landed in Johannesburg, a ground agent met them and took them to a Southern Sun hotel, promising to pick them up at six the next morning so they could get an early start before it got too hot. The agent was as good as his word, and they were at the Rand airport where their plane was waiting by six-fifteen. It was a little Cessna, four passenger seats and two spots in the front for pilots, but there was only one; two were not necessary for short flights.

"Hi, I'm Dave. I'll be your pilot today. If you'll give me your bags, I'll get them stowed, and we can be on our way."

"Thanks," Katrina said. "How long to Maun?"

"Two and a half hours today, short trip, winds are behind us," Dave said. "So, if you need the loo, now is a good time to go."

"Okay," Katrina said when they both got back to the plane.

"First time to Africa?" Dave asked.

"No, I'm from Zambia," Katrina said. "And James worked there for a while, then we both lived and worked in Jo'burg a couple of years ago."

"You're on your way out to Pitse?" Dave asked.

"My brother runs the camp," James said.

"Okay, I wondered when I saw you were the Martins," Dave said. "Let's just go through the safety briefing, and we'll be off."

The flight to Maun took them over parts of Johannesburg, then over the Magaliesberg, then off over farm lands, then eventually just bush, all looking very dry. The Maun airport was very small, with no fancy terminal buildings, but there was an immigration station, where passports were stamped, then they were off again, headed northeast to the strip that served Pitse. That was a much shorter flight, which was just as well because it was getting quite bumpy as the day heated up. Forty minutes later, they were making high banking turns over the strip, looking to see that there was nothing on the strip in the way of animals that would impede their landing. Seeing nothing, Dave took them down and taxied over to where Bridget was waiting.

"Dave, howzit?" she said.

"Good Bridget, thanks, I got your relatives here safe and sound," he replied.

"Thanks, Dave, Katrina, James, how are you?" she asked.

"All the better for being here," Katrina said. "It's a long way from LA."

"I'll be back in two weeks to pick you up," Dave said. "Enjoy your stay."

"So, how far to the camp?" James asked. "The last time we were here, we drove in from Maun."

"About an hour," Bridget said. "Depends on what we see."

"How are you enjoying this?" James asked.

"We love it," Bridget replied. "It's such a relief not to have to lock every door in the house and worry about who will steal what."

"What about the girls?" Katrina asked.

"They're here with us, we have a nanny to watch them when I can't, but it's a great life for them," Bridget replied. "There's so much for them to learn, Francesca has lessons that come from the school that Beatrice, the nanny, checks on, and in the off-season she goes to school in Gabs, and Alex starts this year as well."

"What will you do for high school?" Katrina asked.

"We've talked to Alex and Vincenzo, and they'll stay with them in Italy and go to school with their two," Bridget said. "That'll be good for them, good schooling, plus another language."

"There's some buffalo over there," James interrupted.

"They hang around this area quite a lot," Bridget said. "It's not that far to the Linyanti, so water's not too far away."

"It's so nice to be in the bush again," Katrina said. "Are you full at the camp?"

"With you," Bridget said. "Four leave in three days, two leave in five days and then after you go we start to pack up for the close of the season. So, how's California?"

"Busy," Katrina replied. "Lots of people everywhere, huge freeways with cars all going sixty to seventy miles an hour. We're lucky, we live in the hills to the east and around us is pretty open; there are even orange and avocado groves not too far away."

"And how's work?" Bridget asked.

"James is really busy, and I quit my job and am going to start a computer programming course when we get home," Katrina replied.

"So, you're a business magnate now, James," Bridget commented.

"Sometimes I feel more like a learner official again, trying to work out what I should be doing," James said. "But it's been interesting so far."

"Okay, here we are," Bridget said as they pulled up to the camp.

"Auntie Katrina," a voice called, and Katrina saw that it was Francesca.

"Francesca, lovely to see you," Katrina said. "Will you take care of us for the next week or so?"

"Of course," she said, confident as only an eight-year-old could be. "We'll have Godfrey with us, he's my favourite guide. This is your tent over here; we stay over there in our own tent."

"Where's Alex?" Katrina asked.

"She's painting a kudu," Francesca said. "As soon as she's done, she'll join us for tea over at the *boma*. Dad's out now with the other guests; they'll be back soon in time for lunch."

"How far are you from Disney Land?" Francesca asked as they sat down for tea.

"Not far," James said. "We can see the fireworks at night."

"One day, we'll go," Francesca announced. "We'll come and stay with you, and then we can go."

"It's a long way to come," James cautioned.

"I know," she said. "Twice as far as London, so hours and hours and hours on the plane."

"Where are the other guests from?" Katrina asked.

"They're all Brits," Francesca replied. "The Bakers, the Wilsons who are together and the Baskervilles."

"Are they nice?" Katrina asked.

"We've had nicer ones, but we've also had worse ones," Francesca said. "We have to stay out of the way, but we're allowed to eat with everyone else."

"What do you do all day?" James asked.

"On weekdays, I have school work from eight to one, then lunch, then some homework, then I'm free in the afternoons," Francesca explained. "If I get all my work done quickly, like today, then I can go and play. Beatrice looks after us, and she also checks all the schoolwork. She's with Alex now; she must be done. Here they are."

"Auntie Katrina, Auntie Katrina," Alessandra called as she came to join them. "This is Beatrice, Mma Beatrice, this is my Auntie Katrina and Uncle James from the States."

"Nice to meet you," Beatrice said. "I understand that you live in Los Angeles?"

"We live in the LA Basin," Katrina confirmed. "We actually live in the City of Orange, which is east of downtown Los Angeles, not too far from Disney Land."

"You girls should go and wash your hands for lunch," Bridget said. "Come, let's give Beatrice a break."

"How is this job?" Katrina asked Beatrice after the others had left.

"They're delightful," Beatrice replied. "It's really nice to be out here in the bush, and I'll get some time off soon when we pack up and go back to Gabs. Francesca said something about your ancestors being from here."

"My great-great-grandmother was San," Katrina explained. "Sadly, she was killed in an incident with some slave traders, as was the rest of the band. The only survivors were my great-grandfather and his father, who was Jan Englebrecht. The band had a camp near the Tsodilo Hills."

"Ah, here comes Will with the guests," Beatrice said.

James and Katrina joined the others at the lunch table and introduced themselves, and confirmed that James was Will's brother. Francesca and Alessandra sat next to Katrina and made the occasional aside to her in Afrikaans, which Bridget frowned upon as the comments were not always complimentary. Beatrice intervened and said something in Setswana, which brought them both back to good behaviour.

"How many languages do you speak, Francesca?" one of the guests, by the name of Rose Walton, asked.

"English and Afrikaans, and I'm learning Setswana," Francesca replied. "I'm not as good as Mma Beatrice, who speaks English, Setswana, Shona, Kalanga and Kgalagadi."

"Goodness, that's a lot," Rose said.

"What do you do in LA?" another guest asked James.

"I run a diverse manufacturing company," James replied.

"Have you always done that?" Rose asked.

"No, I started in the copper mines of Zambia, then joined a company in Wisconsin, worked there for a while, then they sent us to Jo'burg, then back to the US and lately to California with Waterford."

"You make glass, I didn't know Waterford had a place in the US?" Rose asked.

"We don't make glass," James replied. "We're Waterford Industries, and it's mainly gearboxes and access equipment."

"I know you chaps," another guest said. "You have HighRise, I've been interested in you for a while. Let me know if you ever want to sell. I'm John Peel, no relation to the famous Lake District chap. I'll give you my contact information before we leave."

"Thank you," James said.

"So, I presume you've been out in the bush before?" Rose asked.

"I grew up in Zambia," Katrina said. "So we would camp out in the bush a lot, then when James came out to work, we took trips when we could."

"Have you ever been to Botswana before?" Rose asked.

"We have," Katrina confirmed. "In fact, we've been to this camp before, back in the seventies when it was run by Piet and Anna Englebrecht. It turned out that Piet is a distant relative of mine."

"Those are the folks we bought the business from," Will added.

"They certainly picked a beautiful spot," Rose said.

"So, preferences for this afternoon?" Bridget asked.

"Could we take a walk?" John asked.

"Of course," Bridget said. "Who else for the walk?"

"We'll go," added three others, and the other two opted for a drive. Katrina was co-opted to take the drive along with Godfrey the guide, so that Bridget could take care of dinner. Godfrey was quite capable of taking the drive himself, but for some reason, the guests seemed to think they might not get as good an experience with a Botswana guide, something that Bridget and Katrina thought was rubbish. Godfrey and Katrina discovered that they could communicate in a pigeon language, Godfrey using Fanagalo, the South Africa version and Katrina in ChiKabanga, the Zambian version, but which were both so similar that there was no problem understanding one another. The languages had been developed for use in the mines and had been derived from a simplified version of Zulu with additional words from other languages thrown in for good measure. Godfrey and Katrina compared notes about what they were seeing, and Katrina relayed things to the guests.

After tea that afternoon, James borrowed a spare Land Rover that Will and Bridget had and took Francesca, Alessandra and Beatrice for a drive. James remembered the various tracks that had not changed through the years and took them to a waterhole where Piet and Anna had taken them before. They just sat and watched what came with Beatrice identifying birds for them. They also learned a little more about Beatrice, she had gone to the University of Botswana and had a degree in English and she had been wondering what to do for a job when she had been introduced to Will and Bridget and had jumped at the chance to have a nanny cum tutor job, with the added benefit, from her point of view at least, of being out in the bush. She was well paid, and the girls got on well with her and were learning at a prodigious rate. That is what one-on-one tutoring did.

After dinner that night, Katrina and James retired early; the ten-hour time difference would take a few days to become accustomed to. They were up with the dawn in time to see the others grab a quick breakfast, then leave for a walk with Will and Godfrey.

"What do you two have planned for the morning?" Bridget asked.

"I think just sit in the deck here and look out over the river and see what we can see," Katrina replied.

"There's plenty to see," Bridget said. "Has it changed much since you were here before?"

"Obviously, you've put up new tents and added a few things that make it comfortable," James said. "But the surrounds stay the same, and the amount of game seems to be the same as it was before."

"How's it going, Bridg?" Katrina asked. "Can you make a living doing this?"

"We can," Bridget replied. "We were lucky, early on we had some booking agents come out and they wrote up really good reviews, so bookings have been steady, we're already more than three-quarters sold out for next season. We might even extend the season by a week or two each end."

"How long will Beatrice stay with you?" Katrina asked.

"We'd be happy to keep her on until the girls go away to school in Italy, but it remains to be seen if that's something she wants to do," Bridget said. "I'm also teaching her the business, so she can manage bookings for us and supervise the cooking, so that I can guide groups as well as Will, and she's teaching herself botany while she's here."

"It's a different business," Katrina commented. "Not like James's gear factories."

"This appeals to us," Bridget said. "We'll see how it goes. I like it better than making explosives, and Will prefers it to the paint factory."

"Probably less risk here too, not like Jo'burg," James added.

"It was getting to be annoying having to lock everything up all the time," Bridget said. "Still, it gave us a good start. Let me go and see how the girls are doing. I'll be back and we'll have coffee."

The days passed, and the guests left until it was just James and Katrina.

"So, James, any preferences today?" Will asked.

"No, just sit and enjoy the view and the hippo and antelope that we can see," James replied. "Maybe later take a walk."

"Now that the guests have gone, we'll take the girls with us," Will said. "You may land up carrying Alex. So, how do you like the new job?"

"It's got its challenges," James said. "I've learned a lot, and there's more to learn. We're doing fairly well right now, but that's because I've got good division managers."

"Are you buying or selling?" Will asked.

"At the moment we're looking at companies or divisions to buy," James said. "But that may change in the future, who knows, it depends on what analysts and investment bankers tell the chairman and the board, they may couch things in terms of being good for the stockholders, but in my view, what it means is that it's good for them."

"So, what about selling your HighRise to John Peel?" Will asked.

"I suppose if he offered enough, Wilcox, he's the chairman, would look at an offer," James replied.

Their walk was an adventure with Godfrey guiding and pointing out things along the way, things as small as a praying mantis to as large as an eland, things as varied as tracks and sign, actually a euphemism for dung, to spiders' webs. James did land up carrying Alessandra, who announced that she wanted to be carried back to the camp. They stopped on the way back for a sundowner and watched the sun sink below the horizon, and then used torches to light the way back to the camp, with Godfrey identifying the night noises as they went.

"That was lovely," Katrina said when they arrived back at the camp.

"It was fun," Bridget agreed. "Girls, why don't you go and wash your hands, and I'll get dinner ready."

"Do you need help?" James asked.

"No, it's all ready, all I have to do is throw it on the fire, and it will be done," Bridget replied. "We're having warthog tonight."

Dinner was eaten, wine was drunk, dishes were cleaned, and then everyone turned in for the night.

"You're leaving today?" Francesca asked James and Katrina.

"We are," James confirmed. "I have to go back to work, and your Auntie Katrina is going to start classes in computer programming."

"When will you come back?" Frances asked.

"As soon as we can," Katrina promised. "Perhaps we'll come for Christmas and stay with you in Gabs."

"That would be only *lekker*," Frances said, mixing her languages. "Mum, Auntie Katrina said that they'll come and see us at Christmas."

"Perhaps not this year," Katrina hedged. "It's a bit soon after this visit. We'll see how things go next year."

"If you're packed and ready, we'll run you down to the strip," Bridget said. "We'll all come with you to see you off."

They drove to the strip and waited a few minutes, then saw the plane circling, then land.

"Howzit Dave?" Will said as the pilot got out of the plane.

"Howzit Will, so James, Katrina, how was it?" Dave asked.

"Wonderful," Katrina replied. "I've missed the bush."

"Auntie Katrina, you will come back?" Alessandra asked.

222

"We will, promise," Katrina said. "Will, Bridget, thanks for a lovely time, we will come back, not sure when, but we will come back."

"Let's get you boarded, and we can be off," Dave said. Goodbyes were said, hugs and kissed were shared all around, and then James and Katrina climbed aboard, followed by Dave, who went through the safety briefing again. Then they waved goodbye, and he started up and taxied out to the strip, and they were off on the first leg of their marathon trip home.

"That was fun," Katrina said as they arrived home. "I'm glad we have a couple of days before you go back to work and I start computer school."

"That ten hours does mess things up," James agreed.

"I wonder what this computer school will be like," she said.

"I'd say busy, it's six months, so I'd think pretty intense," he thought.

"I wonder how different the languages are to BASIC," she said. They used BASIC as the language to program the Radio Shack desktop computer they had. It was limited in what it could do, but It was a useful way to get introduced to programming. James had done some at university, using FORTRAN, and had become reasonably adept at using the punched card machine to create the instruction set for the computer. His biggest gripe was that programs were often rejected for things like syntax errors, even describing them, but the computer was not able to fix those errors. He knew that at Waterford they used COBOL, a common business language, for their accounting and financial reports, but was not that familiar with COBOL himself.

"I was thinking of getting an IBM PC," James said. "Does the school include PC DOS?"

"I'll find out, but I doubt it," she said. "We'll probably have to teach ourselves that."

"I'll check at the computer shop and see if they have books or classes," he said. "I'd really like an Apple, but I see problems for them, they've brought in some *ouk* from Pepsi to run the company, and I think he's going to miss the point, maybe I'm wrong, we'll see what happens in the next year or two."

"How was your trip?" Megan asked James on Monday when he went back to his office.

"Just great," he replied. "Long trip to get there and back, but worth it. Anything happened that I should know about?"

"No," she said. "It's been quiet. You're due in New York for a board meeting on Friday. I talked to Madeleine in New York, and she gave me the schedule, so I made resers for you to fly to JFK on Thursday to be there in time for a dinner with the board."

"Thanks, Megan," he said. "I'd better go and see Mike and catch up on things, then call everyone and get the latest."

James talked to Mike McKane, then called his division managers and quickly brought himself up to date with events, new orders, prospects, financial performance and anything else that they thought he should know. Things were going moderately well, and it looked as if they would meet their year-end targets, which should make Wilcox happy, but James cynically thought that Wilcox would be asking why they could not exceed their forecasts, anything to boost the year-end results and push the stock price up. James then called Wilcox and got him as he was returning from a late lunch.

"James, glad you're back, what's the chances of an extra mil or two in the year-end earnings?" he asked.

"I'll take a look, but I'm not that hopeful," James replied. "We'll have to see what November brings."

"It would be really good if you could come up with something extra, James & Brown is probably going to miss their target by a little, maybe as much as a mil," Wilcox said.

"I'll take a look," James repeated. "Anything special that you want for the board meeting?"

"Just where we are on the acquisition front," Wilcox said. "Who our next targets should be and why."

"I'll have the information with me," James promised.

"Good, dinner Thursday evening with the board," Wilcox said. "I'll leave details at your hotel."

"Fine," James said. "I did meet someone on my trip who told me that if we ever want to sell HighRise, he'd be interested."

"Who is he?" Wilcox asked.

"Name's John Peel, I looked him up and he owns a large Brit building supply company, revenues of about 200 million, earnings after tax of 25, Sterling not Dollars, so he must be doing something right," James replied.

"We'll keep him in mind," Wilcox said. "Okay, James, keep at it, see you Thursday evening for dinner."

James went back to talk to Mike McKane again to discuss Wilcox's request. They mulled it over for a while and concluded that it might be possible to find another million in earnings, if certain things went well and they adjusted reserves that they had set up. Reversing the reserves would take some explanation, so that was something they would have to decide upon before they committed to the extra earnings. James then called Gene Thompson at James & Brown.

"James, what's up?" Gene asked.

"I've been talking to Wilcox, and he told me that you'll miss his targets for the year-end," James replied.

"We might," Gene said. "But if we do it won't be by much."

"Wilcox said that you'd be shy a million of your forecast," James said.

"Only if everything goes south," Gene said. "My best guess right now is a hundred thousand short."

"That's a long way from a million, anyway, he wanted to know if I could pull a rabbit out of the hat and come up with a million or two," James said.

"Can you?" Gene asked.

"If we reverse some reserves and things go really well between now and the end of the year, we might be able to come up with a million," James replied. "Why the big push?"

"He wants to float some more stock, and he wants to show his backers that we're a good bet," Gene explained. "Sorry, James, have to go, got a major customer waiting, could be a really big order. See you Thursday."

Dawn was next on James's list. He was interested to see what she had uncovered about the various companies and divisions they had identified as possible acquisition candidates.

"James, how was your trip?" she asked.

"Great," he replied. "Can't wait to go again."

"I'd like to go to Africa one day," she said. "I'm trying to persuade my husband that Michigan is nice, but wouldn't it be nice to do something a little different for once?"

"Why Michigan?" he asked.

"That's where his family lives, I'm working to try and wean him away from them; they don't approve of me," she said. "Too independent. I don't like it when he gets together with his brothers; they behave like adolescents at college. Anyway, you probably want to know what I've dug up."

"That would be useful," James agreed. "I'm supposed to give the board a review of where we are on Friday."

They reviewed all the data that Dawn had gathered, looking for background information that would give them some sense of whether or not the owners would consider selling and how the companies were viewed in their locales. Industry publications, like Aviation Week, were also a useful source, both from the aspect of contracts and products and for management appointments. James had also asked the various division managers for input as to who they would like to acquire, if it was possible and more importantly, why and how they would integrate any acquisition into the company. Much of what James had read showed that acquisitions had an abysmal record of success, driven largely by what happened after the actual acquisition, often because no matter what trite words were said about valuing employees, events proved otherwise. The electronics company that he had been looking at turned out to be a disaster waiting to happen, the owner had played fast and loose with his accounting and was on his way to prison for fraud and the company had gone into bankruptcy and as far as James could see there was no way to salvage anything, not even the intellectual property, the best they might be able to manage was offer employment to some of the engineers who designed the various systems. He had told both Paul Rose and Stuart McIntosh to see if they might be interested in any of the people who were all now looking for work. With the hoist company, they had made an offer and were awaiting the response of the owners. Between them, James and Dawn identified three more possible candidates for acquisition, another electrical company and two small structures companies, one of which had expertise with composites. They were not ready to approach the companies, but James was confident that they would be in a position to do so before the end of the year.

On Thursday, James drove himself to LAX and parked, avoiding the construction that seemed to be never-ending, some of it probably driven by the Olympic Games scheduled for the following year. He flew American Airlines, adding to the travel award points he had already earned under their AAdvantage program. When he landed in New York, the weather had taken a turn for the worse, and instead of being hot and humid, it was cold, windy and downright wintry. He saw the driver Megan had organised for him holding up a sign that read, Martin. James did wonder how many times that wrong Martin had been picked up and driven somewhere unexpected. This driver did at least confirm his full name and destination, and he also told James that he would have to wait for about ten minutes for Gene Thompson to arrive. Megan must have coordinated things with Lou in Oak Creek.

"James, how's things?" Gene asked as they were driven to the hotel.

"Well enough," James replied. "I didn't plan for it being this cold."

"This California living is making you soft," Gene laughed. "So, Lou told me that you were in Africa last week."

"Katrina and I went to a bush camp in northern Botswana," James said. "My brother runs it, so it was a family visit at the same time. How's J&B Africa doing?"

"Good," Gene said. "Your man Leon is doing a bang-up job, sales of construction machines are up, parts sales are doing well as we build up the mining machine population, and their service business has grown. I did wonder when you recommended the accountant, but as I said, he's great, exceeded my expectations."

"Anything you know that I should know about the meeting tomorrow?" James asked.

"Nothing that I know of," Gene said. "After the bastards decided to take me off the board, I'm often as much in the dark as you are. Now, it's just Wilcox and Sanders from the company, plus a shitload of cronies."

"Looks like we're here," James said as they pulled up outside the Parker Meridien. "Ever stayed here before?"

"No, first time for me, I think Wilcox likes the high life and he's put the out-of-town directors here as well," Gene said. "I suppose we'd better get checked in and find out where dinner is tonight."

The rooms in the Meridien were elegant, reflecting the style that French ownership brought. Dinner that night was in a private room. As he went down to the private room for dinner, he reflected on the board members. They had changed since Wilcox had taken over; gone were Evan Eastwood, Walter Collier and Peter Burgess, to be replaced by Alan White, an investment banker, Ray Thomas, a hedge fund manager, Malcolm Baker, an advertising company executive, and George Maxwell, a capital fund manager. Both James and Gene had concerns about the board makeup, which was heavily skewed to the financial markets, with no industrial representation. They both wondered if that portended anything. When James arrived at the room, there was a seating chart that Madeleine was supervising. James wondered about the relationship between Wilcox and Madeleine. She clearly managed day-to-day things in the New York office and acted as the ultimate gatekeeper for Wilcox, and the darker side of him wondered if there was anything more. Given that George had once asked him if he was banging Megan, he would not have been surprised to learn that George and Madeleine were sleeping together.

"So, James, how are things in sunny California?" Charles Bristol asked as they sat down for dinner.

"Going well," James replied.

"Ready for the Olympics?" Charles asked.

"The city has been suggesting that companies shut down for the period to ease traffic congestion," James said. "There's all kinds of construction still going on."

"Got any tickets?" Graham Brant asked.

228

"They haven't gone on sale yet," James said. "I'll see if there's anything that I'd really like to see that I can afford."

"Will any of the events affect our factories?" Wilcox asked.

"I don't think so," James said. "The 91 will be shut down for a while for a cycling event, which will cause delays on that day, and we've got wrestling in Anaheim and swimming in Irvine, but I don't see any real impact on us. Most of the events with be at the LA Coliseum and Long Beach."

"James, George told us you'd just got back from Africa, how was that?" Ray asked.

"We went to a bush camp in Botswana," James said. "It's very remote, no phone service, about an hour's drive from the closest airstrip, which is about three hours from Jo'burg in a light plane."

"When you say camp, do you mean tents?" Ray asked.

"That's right," James confirmed.

"Weren't you bothered by lions and such?" Ray asked.

"When we lived in Zambia, we camped out in the bush quite a bit. It never bothered us, we don't bother the lions and they don't bother us," James said.

"Rather you than me," Ray said. Dinner was served, and conversation ranged from the state of the markets to the election in the following year, the consensus on that being that it would be a victory for Reagan. James got no hints on what the board might like to hear in the meeting, so went back to his room and did one quick last review of the materials he had brought. He called Katrina and told her what the hotel was like and about the dinner, then retired for the night.

"Ready for today?" Gene asked James when he joined him at the breakfast table.

"As ready as I'll ever be," James said. "You?"

"We're doing okay, but the bloom is off the mining markets, so we'll have to see what the next couple of years bring," Gene said. "We've got some good activity in Australia and South Africa, but those markets are just not as big as the US. Don't you wonder if there's something going on between Wilcox and Madeleine?"

"I've wondered," James admitted. "But it struck me that we're all likely to think the worst, so I decided that it's none of my business."

"Probably right," Gene said. "We should get up to the room, wouldn't do to be late."

"Mr Thompson, Mr Martin," Madeleine said when they arrived at the meeting room. "George has a comp committee meeting right now, and they should be finished soon. May I get you coffee, tea?"

"I'm good, thanks," Gene said.

"I've had my ration for the morning," James said.

"If you'll just wait here, I expect the others shortly, and as I said, I expect the committee meeting to end soon," Madeleine said. Others arrived, and she greeted them and served coffee to those who asked for it, then George Wilcox arrived with the three directors who comprised the compensation committee.

"Good morning, everyone," George said. "Let's get things started, shall we?" He then went through the agenda, with Madeleine behind him, taking notes. He reviewed the overall position of the company, then asked first Gene then James to review their respective parts. That all took until eleven, then they took a quick break and got back to it, and George asked Gene and then James to review potential acquisition candidates. Then it was question time, which went on until after one, until George finally called a halt to the meeting and suggested that they have lunch before leaving.

"So, learn anything?" Gene asked as he and James were whisked back to JFK.

"There's something in the wind, not associated with either James & Brown or Waterford," James thought.

"I agree," Gene said. "I think Wilcox is looking at a third leg in a different industry, and my best guess is something property-related."

"What, as a property developer?" James asked.

"That's my guess," Gene confirmed. "Look for shopping malls and hotels."

"That's quite a shift from mining and aerospace," James commented.

"Damn right," Gene said. "I hope he knows what he's doing."

"Is that why he's pushing for more earnings?" James asked.

"I guess so," Gene said. "He wants to exceed the forecast that the analysts have issued for us."

"What about 1984?" James asked.

"If he can get his third leg by the end of the second quarter, the heat will be off and he'll be spending all his time schmoozing banks, looking for someone to lend him the money to build something somewhere," Gene said. "Don't be surprised if he doesn't start piecemealing your business, looking for lumps of cash."

"I may have given him an idea already," James bemoaned. "I met a chap from the UK who is interested in HighRise."

"Just keep your eyes and ears open," Gene cautioned. "Here we are, when's your flight?"

"At five," James replied.

"Okay, James, call me if you hear anything," Gene said as they went their separate ways.

"How was the big meeting in New York?" Katrina asked when James finally arrived home.

"Fine, I think, Gene Thompson and I both think that Wilcox is looking to buy something not related to any of the current business," he replied.

"What will that mean for us?" she asked.

"No idea," he admitted. "We'll have to wait and see."

"So, what's next?" she asked.

"The AIA meeting at the Biltmore in Phoenix next week," he said.

"That's right," she said. "My classes start right after we get back from that. Have you ever been to the Biltmore?"

"No," he said. "When I did visit mines in Arizona, it was either to the Tucson area for copper, or up on the Navajo Reservation for coal."

"What do I wear?" she asked.

"I'd guess that something casual for the daytime, then a dress for the dinners," he suggested. "At the last meeting I went to, it was suits and ties for the men, so I'd better go prepared."

"How do we get to Phoenix?" she asked.

"We could fly, or we could drive," he said. "It's probably under an hour by plane, or five and a half hours by car."

"You know, it might be interesting to drive," she thought. "We could leave around lunch time the day before and get there in the early evening. Is there a time difference?"

"One hour," he said. "So, if we left a lunch time, we'd be there by six-thirty."

"Let's do that, but let's leave around ten and get some lunch on the way," she said. "I did go to the AAA office in Anaheim Hills and get maps of California and Arizona and guidebooks as well. I'll find us a place to have lunch."

Biltmore

The drive across the California desert was interesting, long flat straight stretches of road, with sparse scrub on either side and in the distance, ranges of hills. They stopped for a late lunch in Blythe, the last town before crossing the Colorado and going into Arizona. Katrina had picked out a restaurant in Blythe, a small Southwestern place on Hobsonway, Hobson's choice, she had joked to James. After lunch, it was back to the freeway, which climbed up away from the Colorado to go through a line of hills. They went through one or two more lines of hills, but again, the road was generally long, flat, straight sections. When they got to Phoenix, there was some traffic to negotiate, but they soon found their way to the Biltmore.

"This is an interesting-looking place," Katrina said to James. "Very different for a hotel."

"It is," he agreed. "Let's check in, then take a wander around before we have dinner."

"Mr Martin, welcome to the Biltmore," the person at the desk said. "You are here for the AIA meeting, their check-in desk is right over there, let me get you checked into your room first and give you your keys."

"Thank you," James said. He handed over his credit card, and formalities were quickly taken care of; then he went to the AIA desk.

"Mr Martin," one of the ladies said. "This is your packet with meetings and events over the next few days. There is also a list of events and visits for spouses, so Mrs Martin, please look them over and let us know what you may have an interest in. You will be on your own for dinner tonight and breakfast tomorrow morning; the meeting officially starts tomorrow at lunchtime."

"Thank you," James said. He and Katrina went off and found their room, then took a wander around the hotel and its grounds.

"I like the desert look," Katrina said. "Complete with cactus, and there are even hills in the background. I wonder if there's gold in them thar hills?"

"I don't think those," he said. "But not too far away is the supposed Lost Dutchman mine in the Superstition Mountains."

"How about a drink, then dinner?" she suggested.

"Good idea," he agreed.

They sat down for dinner, and James was hailed by a man he had met at the previous AIA meeting, Robert Warner of Locomotive Springs Technologies, LST for short.

"James, nice to see you again. This is my wife, Betty," Robert said.

"Nice to see you," James echoed. "This is my wife, Katrina."

"Katrina, you look lovely," Betty said. "From his accent, James must be from England. Are you from there as well?"

"No, James and I met in Zambia, where I lived," Katrina said.

"Oh, were you there as missionaries, you and James?" Betty asked.

"No, my family had a heavy transport business, and James worked on one of the copper mines," Katrina explained. "Would you care to join us?"

"That would be lovely," Betty said. "You can tell me all about Africa."

"I only really know Zambia and parts of South Africa," Katrina said. "There's so much more to the continent that I've never seen."

"You've lived in South Africa?" Betty asked.

"We lived there for two years while James ran J&B Africa," Katrina replied. "J&B Africa was the South African sub of James & Brown, the company that bought Waterford Industries."

"Did your parents go out from England?" Betty asked.

"No," Katrina said. "A long time ago, my ancestors left Holland and moved to South Africa, and we've been there ever since."

"Why did they leave Holland?" Betty asked.

"I suppose back in the late 1600s, there were opportunities to be had in South Africa," Katrina replied. "My family has been in South Africa for just about 300 years."

"Is this your first visit to the Biltmore?" Betty asked.

"It is," Katrina said. "It's my first trip to Arizona; James has been before, but his trips were to copper mines near Tucson or coal mines in the north."

"Do you have a family of your own?" Betty asked.

"We don't have any children," Katrina replied.

"Perhaps one day," Betty said.

"I doubt it," Katrina said. "Neither of us really wants any children; we have three nieces and a nephew, and we enjoy them."

"Oh, where do they live?" Betty asked.

"Two live in Botswana and two in Italy," Katrina said.

"You are a far-flung family," Betty said. "Where do your parents live?"

"Calitzdorp, it's a small town in the Cape Province," Katrina replied, then to forestall the obvious next question, she added that James's parents lived about thirty miles west of London.

"We should order and let these two eat," Robert interrupted.

Dinner was eaten, further conversation was had, and James and Katrina learned a little about Robert and Betty and their offspring, probably more than either of them really wanted to know. James was reminded of an item in *The Flame Trees of Thika*, where their hostess for their first night out of Nairobi was described as a gushing woman and therefore condemned. Betty was nice enough, but James and Katrina agreed that she was not someone they would go on holiday with; she would be hard to take, for them at least. Robert was more down-to-earth but clearly held Betty in great affection, gushing woman or not.

"I wonder what she's going to sign up for," Katrina said to James when they went to bed that night.

"You could always ask," James said.

"Not a chance," she said. "If I asked and then avoided that outing, she might think it was deliberate, she might put the question back to me, then sign up for whatever I do. Better to leave it to chance."

"Well, I doubt that it would be just the two of you," James said. "So, you'll have others as buffers, and she probably knows some of the others; we're the newcomers."

"Well, we'll see what happens tomorrow," she said.

While they were eating breakfast the next morning, James saw Tom Ellison and nodded to him. He came over to their table and said his good mornings.

"Tom, this is my wife, Katrina," James said. "I met Tom this spring in Williamsburg," he explained to her.

"Nice to meet you, Katrina. James, come and see me when we get back to LA," Tom said. "If you'll excuse me, I've got a breakfast meeting."

"What does he do?" Katrina asked James after Tom had gone.

"He runs a company called Miller Aerospace," James replied. "They make planes for the military, we supply some bits to them."

"So, what does he want?" Katrina wondered. "To thank you, to give you more orders, or complain?"

"No idea," James said. "I'll find out next week. So, what do you have planned for the day?"

"I signed up for the desert tour," she said. "It's a trip out into the desert with a guide; it leaves at nine, so soon."

"So, you'll get lunch out somewhere," he said. "What will you wear?"

"I was thinking of shorts and a shirt," she said. "But, that might shock these *ou tannies*, so I'll go with trousers and a shirt, a hat on my head and *takkies* on my feet."

"Enjoy the day," he said. "I'll see you when you get back."

When the meeting started, James tried to sit back and not be noticed; he was still unsure how the august leaders of industry would accept him. There were general statements, then committee reports, then lunch and then more reports and discussion. It was interesting, and James wondered if he would ever be able to contribute, or if he was there just to make up the numbers. Things finished at four, and they were on their own until dinner time. Dinner was to be served in one of the banquet rooms, and they were actually spared a speaker, so it was truly a social occasion, which was probably best as the spouses would also be at the dinner. He went back to their room and dropped his briefcase, and was just thinking about what to do next when Katrina came back.

"Good day?" he asked her.

"Baie goed," she replied. "We drove in groups of three in Jeeps, Jeeps like mine. My ladies were me, of course, Charmaine, and Geraldine, no idea who they're connected with. We saw cacti by the hundreds, wild donkeys, a couple of coyotes, road runners, eagles, tortoise, gila monsters, cactus wrens, vultures and even a rattlesnake. Our driver was Javier, who was a better naturalist than Jeep driver."

"Were the *tannies* as bad as you thought they could be?" he asked.

"They weren't as old as all that," she said. "I'd say one barely out of her twenties, and the other in her mid-forties, both dressed in fancy tailored shirts and slacks with expensive-looking handbags."

"Did your guide, Javier, know his stuff?" James asked.

"When it came to flora and fauna, he knew his stuff, good guide too, saw things and pointed them out, anyway, what about your day?" she asked, changing the subject.

"Meetings and more meetings," he said. "What are you going to wear to dinner tonight?"

"I was thinking of that simple black dress that I bought, the one that has the lace jacket with it," she said.

"You look great in that," he said.

"I even brought some fancy shoes," she said. "So, I'm grubby from the desert, why don't we have a bath, then go and get a drink before dinner?"

Bathing started with just washing and cleaning, but quickly led to other things, which were continued on the bed. Fortunately, James had set an alarm to remind them when it was time to get dressed and go down for dinner, otherwise they might have dozed off to sleep, sated as they were.

"We're being waved to," Katrina said to James as they entered the banquet room. "That's Charmaine, one of the ladies on my tour."

"You're right, she's not that old, I'd guess late twenties, early thirties, can't say that about him though, he's got to be sixty if he's a day," James commented. "We should go and say hello at least."

"Katrina, come, come and sit with us," Charmaine said. "David, this is Katrina, who was with us on the desert tour."

"Thank you, we will," Katrina said. "This is my husband, James."

"Right, you're James Martin of Waterford," David said. "You've been very quiet in the meetings."

"I'm not sure I have anything to contribute," James said. "Waterford seems such a small company compared to everyone else."

"There's Geraldine and Vincent," Charmaine said.

"David, Charmaine," Geraldine said when she and Vincent joined them. "Vince, this is Katrina and her husband."

"James Martin, right, Waterford," Vincent said. "I gather from Gerry that you gals had an interesting tour in the desert today."

"Our guide knew his animals, birds and plants," Charmaine said. "But it took Katrina to get us out of the sand."

"You didn't say anything about sand," James said to Katrina.

"Let me tell you," Geraldine said. "We were tail-end Charlie in this line of Jeeps on the tour, and things went well until we got to this soft spot and our Jeep bogged down in the soft sand. Well, the others disappeared, and Javier tried and tried to get us out, but all he seemed to do was dig us in more. Finally, he said he would walk out and get help, but Katrina asked if she could try. She asked him if there was a pressure gauge in the glove compartment, she got that and got out and let air out of all our tyres, then she just drove us out, just like that."

"How did you pump up the tyres?" James asked.

"We stopped at the first gas station we saw on the way back and she used their air pump to pump the tyres back up," Geraldine replied.

"Katrina used to live in Africa and said that she had learned how to do that there," Charmaine added. "I'm surprised she didn't tell you, James, about her rescuing us."

"All she said was that Javier was a better guide than driver," James said.

"What did you do in Africa, Katrina?" David asked.

"My folks had a heavy haulage business in Zambia," she said. "We moved mining equipment mainly, but we did move a sugar mill once and some other big industrial pieces."

"So, how did you and James meet?" Vincent asked.

"James came out to Zambia to work on one of our copper mines," Katrina explained. "We left Zambia when the one mine we were on was shut down, when the copper prices dropped."

"Is that when you came to the States, James?" David asked.

"It was," James confirmed. "I joined James & Brown, who make mining and construction machines. I travelled the US visiting mines all over, making recommendations for machine sizes, then J&B sent us back to South Africa for a while to run their sub there. After that, we came back here, and I was part of the acquisition team for Waterford, then I was moved to Waterford."

"I heard that one of your guys was had for fraud," Vincent said.

"The chap who ran our structures operation in Albuquerque was running a get-rich-quick scheme," James explained. "When I came on board, things didn't look right, and when the division manager and his finance man both quit when we started asking awkward questions, we investigated, then turned things over to DOD and the Justice Department. Both are doing time now, and I think we were lucky not to have penalties assessed against the company as well."

"I'll say," Vincent agreed. "So, what do you ladies have planned for tomorrow morning?"

"There's a trip to the Heard Museum," Charmaine said. "We signed up for that, then in the afternoon we're taking you two on on the golf course. James, Katrina, do you play golf?"

"We don't," James replied.

"You should take it up," Geraldine said. "It gets you out and about."

"Would you mind if we joined you?" a man said.

"Please do, Howard," David said. "My wife Charmaine, this is Vincent's wife Geraldine, and this is James Martin and his wife, Katrina."

"Pleased to meet you all, I'm Howard Jones, and this is my wife, Anne," Howard said, making his introductions. James recognised Howard from the meeting earlier; he would have put him in his mid-fifties and his wife in the same age bracket.

"Excuse me, ladies and gentlemen," a waitress said. "If you would follow me." She led them to the buffet line, which was extensive and featured all manner of fish, meat and vegetables. James and Katrina made their way past all the various dishes, taking what they fancied, trying not to overload their plates. When they returned to their table, it had been neatened up, with serviettes refolded, water poured, and wine glasses refilled. The meal was excellent, doing justice to the chefs and cooks of the hotel. After dinner, Geraldine and Charmaine invited Katrina and James to join them in the bar for a nightcap.

"I've always wanted to go on Safari in Africa," Geraldine said when they were comfortably ensconced in deep plush armchairs. "So, should we go to Kenya, Tanzania or where?"

"I suppose it depends what you're looking for," Katrina said. "Kenya and Tanzania share the Serengeti plain, which usually means relatively easy game viewing, but private safaris there end at the outside of your car. I went to a private reserve in South Africa that abuts the Kruger National Park, and that was really good, but you don't have vast herds of wildebeest and zebra there, just small groups. James and I were in Botswana recently at a tented bush camp, which is another experience, that plus the walking they do."

"When you say tented, you mean in an actual tent?" Charmaine asked.

"That's right," Katrina confirmed. "The camp we went to can take eight guests in four tents, and they'll do whatever you want."

"That sounds like fun," David said.

"You have to remember that when you're there, there's no telephone, so if there's an emergency, they have to radio in to get help," Katrina said.

"I suppose that also means no calls in?" Vincent asked.

"That's right," Katrina confirmed.

"Can you give us details?" Geraldine asked.

"Be happy to," Katrina said. "But so that you know, it's James's brother who runs the camp, so we wouldn't want you to think that we're pushing that experience rather than Kenya."

"Appreciate that," David said. "Where is this camp?"

"It's in the north of Botswana, on the river that is the border with South West Africa, about three hours all told by light plane from Jo'burg," James replied.

"Are there lions there?" Charmaine asked.

"Lions, leopards, elephants, buffalo, lots of antelopes, but no rhino, they've been poached out," Katrina replied. "To see rhino, you'd have to go to Kenya or Tanzania or South Africa; the reserve that abuts Kruger had both black and white."

"We could do a week in each," Vincent suggested. "Fly into Jo'burg, do South Africa, then hop on up to Botswana. How do you get to Jo'burg?"

"You can go from JFK to Jo'burg nonstop on South African," James replied. "Or you can go via Europe and pick up almost any of the carriers there, BA, Air France, KLM, Lufthansa and a few others."

"No US carriers?" David asked.

"None," James replied. "The other option is via Asia, but that's not easy as flights don't connect, so there can be a day or two layover."

"Sounds like South African is the way to go," David said. "And to Kenya?"

"As far as I know, you have to go via Europe," James said. "There's nothing from here that gets you even close."

"Katrina, could you send us details of the place in South Africa and the one in Botswana?" Geraldine asked.

"I'll do that," Katrina promised.

"Are you based in Wisconsin?" David asked.

"No, the Waterford office is in Orange County, not that far from the Santa Ana airport," James replied.

"So, come up and see me when we get back," David invited. "We should talk."

"Business tomorrow morning," Charmaine said.

"If you'll excuse us, we're going to call it a night," Katrina said. "I'll see you on the Heard trip tomorrow."

"Who are David and Vincent?" Katrina asked when they were in bed later.

"David North is the boss of Amalgamated Controls, they make electrical and electronic systems for planes, and Vincent Manning is the boss of Burbank Rotocraft, they build helicopters, and we supply them with some gearboxes," James explained. "ACL is in San Diego, and Rotocraft, believe it or not, in Burbank. Howard is the boss of Grant Williams, they're a big aerospace company with a lot of divisions, including some structures factories that compete with our place in Albuquerque. Grant Williams is based in Houston."

"So, is Charmaine one of the trophy wives you hear about?" Katrina asked.

"It would seem so," James said. "What did you learn on your desert trip?"

"She was his tennis instructor, no idea whether he dumped another wife for her, or if there even was another," she replied.

"Certainly looks like she could be a trophy wife," he said.

"Don't you go getting any ideas about trophy wives," she cautioned.

"I doubt that will ever happen," he said.

"Well, just don't," she repeated. "So, while everyone else is playing golf tomorrow, what shall we do?"

"Nothing," he said. "Let's just find a quiet spot to sit and just enjoy the afternoon."

"I like that," she said. "Meanwhile, there's something we could be doing now, and I'm surprised you haven't mentioned it."

"Just roll over towards me and we'll see," he said.

At the coffee break mid-morning the next day, Vincent pulled James aside and told him that he had a project for him and to be in his Burbank office the next Wednesday at ten. He would not elaborate any further. James had seen Vincent closeted with a couple of others earlier, so wondered if it had anything to do with that. By lunch time, he was ready for a break from meetings, so was delighted when proceedings were brought to a close. Golf tee times were read out, then people left to get lunch, play golf or do whatever else they may have planned for the day. He went back to their room, and Katrina returned about five minutes later.

"Good morning?" he asked.

"Fascinating," she replied. "Bobby would have been able to tell me so much. Much of the art was Navajo, Hopi and Comanche, whereas Bobby was Lakota, but I'm sure that much of the symbolism would translate. I think Bobby would have had an issue with the name of American Indian Art; she would have pointed out that Indians live in India and that Native Americans came from many different peoples."

"When you think about it, even Native Americans is flawed," James said. "Before Vespucci, the land probably had very different names to the people that lived here."

"I'm glad we knew Bobby," Katrina said. "She opened my eyes to a lot that went on with the Americans, both in the early days on the East Coast, then with the expansion west. Rather like comparing *Oom* Jan's life with the San to his life with the Cape Dutch."

"So, philosophy aside, shall we find some lunch, then find a spot to loll in the shade?" he suggested.

"Let me just change first," she said. "Judgmental *tannies* or no, I'm wearing shorts this afternoon, you should too, did you bring any?"

"I did," he confirmed.

"You know," Katrina said when they were seated in the gardens later. "We could think about taking a quick trip to the Grand Canyon on the way home."

"Great idea," he agreed. "If we left here at sparrow's fart on Saturday, we could get to the Grand Canyon before ten, see the sights, then we could stay overnight in Kingman and drive home from there on Sunday."

"I like that idea," she said.

"Excuse me, Madam, Sir, may I get you anything?" a waiter said.

"Would it be possible to get some tea?" Katrina asked.

"Tea, of course, Madam, lemon or milk with the tea?" he asked.

"Milk, please," Katrina replied. The waiter went off and was back in a few minutes with a tray laden with cups and saucers, teapot, strainer, milk jug, sugar basin and a hot water jug, and a plate of biscuits.

"Is there anything else?" the waiter asked.

"No, thank you, this is super," she said, at which point the waiter left.

"James, shall I pour for you?" she asked. "Look, they actually used loose tea, no tea bags here."

"Please," he said.

"So, has it been interesting?" she asked.

"It has," he said. "I still feel a little out of place with the titans of the aerospace industry, but they all seem nice enough, not condescending at all, even though I sometimes think I'm just here to make up the numbers."

"So, meetings tomorrow, then you're done?" she asked.

"We wrap up at noon tomorrow," he said. "Why don't we leave right after the meetings end, grab some lunch on the way and see if we can find a place to stay tomorrow night?"

"Let's finish our tea, then go and see the concierge and see what they can find us," she suggested.

The concierge was most helpful and found them a room in the Grand Canyon Village. It seemed to James quite pricey, but beggars cannot be choosers, so they took it. That done, they went to the front desk and changed their departure. Dinner was next, so they went back to their room to bathe and change, then joined the others in the banquet room. That evening, there was a speaker talking about Arizona and its history, before and after statehood. His talk was fascinating and included things that neither James nor Katrina knew. He also touched on the history of the Biltmore and reminded everyone that, contrary to popular legend, the hotel was not designed by Frank Lloyd Wright, but one of his pupils. There apparently had also been some controversy about payments for use of a patent that the designers thought Wright owned, but which he did not.

The meeting the next day actually finished a little early, so James skipped lunch, and he and Katrina left for the Grand Canyon. The drive north took them through the suburbs of Phoenix, then the road started to climb steadily, which it did until they reached Flagstaff. They ate a late lunch in Flagstaff, then started out for the Grand Canyon. Their route skirted the ski resort just north of Flagstaff and made its way through the hills and pine trees until dropping them down a little onto flatter lands that were covered with scrub grasses and small trees, and bushes. They were in the Grand Canyon Village by three-thirty and looked for their hotel.

"The place is called the El Tovar Lodge," Katrina read out from the sheet the concierge had given them. "Take the next right, then left."

"I see a sign that says Lodges," he said.

"Okay, follow this road, then left, and then you should see the entrance to the Lodge on your right," she said, reading from the map that the park service people had given them. "There," she said.

"Impressive looking place," he said. "I like the log construction, very rustic. Let's get checked in, then find out where we park, and then take a look over the edge."

"Good afternoon," the desk clerk said.

"Good afternoon," James echoed. "We have a reservation, the name is Martin."

"Ah, yes, Mr and Mrs Martin, the Biltmore told us you were coming," the clerk said. "We have a room for you on the second floor, and we also made a dinner reservation for you at seven at the request of Penelope at the Biltmore. Is that acceptable?"

"That would be fine," James said.

"Your keys," the clerk said, handing them over to James. "Your room is up the stairs and to the right."

"Thank you," James said. He picked up their bags, and Katrina led the way to the stairs and the room.

"This is nice," she said. "Let's go and move the car, then take a walk out to the rim."

"Wow, look at that," Katrina said a few minutes later when they were on the rim of the canyon.

"It's huge," James said. "Makes the Blyde River Canyon look quite small."

"How far down is it?" she asked.

"According to the brochure that the National Park people gave us at the gate, 5,000 feet, give or take, six thousand if you take it from the North Rim," he read off.

"That's a long way down," she said. "Let's walk along the rim a little."

"It seems never-ending," he said as they gazed down into the abyss and across to the North Rim.

"Imagine how much water must have come down here to erode all this," she said.

"It's very different from flying over," he commented. "You don't get a sense of just how big it is from 40,000 feet."

"Let's go to this Yavapai Point, the map says that it's only about a mile and a half," she said. They walked along the rim to the point and looked out and down. "It really is big," she said.

"You can actually see the river from here," he said.

"Where, I don't see it?" she asked.

"You see the trail down there, follow it to that point and look just to the right of that and down a bit," he said.

"Oh, I see it," she said. "I wonder what it looks like, looking up from the river."

"I suppose that would depend on how steep the canyon walls are where you are," he said. "If they're close, all I suppose you'd see are the canyon walls. Even fancied a white water trip down the canyon?"

"I'm not sure," she said. "I did read something about raft trips on the Zambezi, just day trips, that might be a good idea first to see if we like it. I would imagine that a trip down the Colorado would be a few days, camping out on the way."

"There's people down on that trail," he said, pointing.

"You're right, coming back up, that's going to be quite a climb," she said. "I saw something in the lodge about mule rides down the canyon, staying at a place at the bottom and coming back the next day."

"A long time on the back of a mule," he thought. "I suppose mules have more stamina than horses, for them it must be really hard work, not just climbing down and up, but lugging a tourist along with them. I wonder if there's a weight limit for those who take the ride."

"I'm sure there is," she said. "You wouldn't want to saddle some poor mules with a fifteen stone chap, no pun intended there."

"Good one though," he laughed.

"Let's walk back the other way and take a look," she suggested.

"Now we know," Katrina said, pointing to a large scale that was used to weigh visitors wanting to take the down the canyon mule ride. "200 pounds, what's that, just over fourteen stone."

"Makes sense," James said. "It's got to be a tough climb back up anyway, and with the extra load of a visitor, hard work for the mules."

"Shall we at least take a look at the trail before dinner?" she suggested.

"I wonder how many twists and turns before you get to the bottom," he said as they walked a little way down the trail.

"I'm sure someone has counted them," she said. "Let's go back up and get a drink before dinner."

"So, what do you fancy?" he asked when they were back at the lodge.

"I think a beer," she said.

"I'll get us one," he said. He was back quickly with the beer, and they sat looking out of the window at the view.

"I'm glad we decided to make this trip," she said. "So, tomorrow, drive along the rim to the east, then back and then off to Kingman to start home?"

"Sounds good," he agreed.

They stopped at a dozen places along the way between the Grand Canyon Village and the eastern gate. Each vista had its own magic, and surprisingly, they did not get tired of views of red rocks, eroded peaks, and cliffs. It was not too busy, but they could both imagine that in the summer months that traffic would be heavy and there would be people everywhere. They climbed the Desert View Watchtower and marvelled at the view below. From the viewpoint below the tower, they could see much more of the river than at other points along the way, and it struck both of them as huge, even from the height they were seeing it from. By three, they were on their way to Kingman, first to Williams, then the freeway that followed much of the route of the famed Route 66. Kingman had little to offer in the way of sights or vistas, but did boast a Best Western, not quite the Biltmore or the El Tovar Lodge, but perfectly adequate for travellers. The next day, they decided not to stop in Barstow for lunch, but to press on farther to Victorville, the home of the Roy Rogers ranch. From Victorville, it was just over an hour home, slowed only by the typical traffic buildup on a Sunday afternoon as people returned from the desert, from Las Vegas or the mountains.

"It's good to be home," James commented to Katrina as they unpacked the car.

"Now work starts," she said. "Tomorrow I start my computer class."

"That will be interesting," he said. "I'm sure you'll whizz through it."

"I'll find out," she said. "So, what shall we have for dinner?"

"Something light," he said. "It seems that I've done nothing else but eat for the past few days."

"How was the Biltmore?" Megan asked James when he arrived at the office.

"Very posh," he said. "Lots of meetings, and I'm sure there were others less official on the gold course. I need to call Tom Ellison, then David North of Amalgamated Controls and Vincent Manning of Burbank Rotocraft. I'm supposed to be seeing Vincent on Wednesday at ten, and the others also both want meetings. Anything that I missed while I was in Arizona?"

"The only thing of note was a couple of calls from George Wilcox; he wants you to call him back," she replied.

"I suppose I'd better do that first, then I'll call the others. Would you mind getting me some tea?" he asked.

"Of course," she said.

"James," George said when James called him. "How's things?"

"Going well," James replied.

"Need you in New York next week," George said. "Need you to talk to some investors about Waterford, they want to know what programs we're working on for DOD."

"I have a list by division," James said. "I could send it to you."

"Don't bother, it sounds better coming from you," George said. "What can you tell me about the Biltmore?"

"A lot of meetings where I felt almost like an interloper," James replied. "Sitting at the same table as the heads of Boeing, MacDac, Lockheed, and others makes you feel quite small and insignificant."

"We're big enough, not quite their size, I grant you," George said. "But, we'll get there. Anything I should know?"

"I don't think there was anything of note," James replied. "I'll send you a report. I do have a couple of meetings that came out of the sessions; if anything comes of them, I'll let you know."

"Do you know anything about a program called Mongol?" George asked.

"Rumours, that's all," James replied. "It's supposed to be some kind of super-fast plane."

"So, we're not involved?" George asked.

"Not that I'm aware of," James replied, quite truthfully.

"Any suspicions?" George asked.

"None," James stated. "Have you heard something?"

"Guy I know on the Street told me that ConsAir had something going with Mongol and that we were a big part of it," George said.

"He's wrong," James said. "We've got nothing big going with ConsAir, unless you count flap and slat drives for their 350-seat plane. You'd hardly count that as a super fast plane, it's not the Concorde, it's a regular, pretty big passenger plane, rivals the L-1011, the DC-10 and the 747."

"Can the market sustain that many?" George asked.

"I wouldn't have thought so," James replied. "But as far as I know, all sales of the ConsAir 350 are going offshore."

"I heard that ConsAir slipped a few mil to some government guys in a couple of countries to get the orders," George said.

"I've heard the stories," James said. "We just sell ConsAir parts and have nothing to do with their plane sales. I steer clear of any discussion that's not strictly price and delivery of the flap and slat drives."

"Could it be repurposed as a bomber?" George asked.

"As a subsonic, I suppose it could," James said. "If you go back to the first and second world wars, then the crossover between bomber and passenger plane happened quite a bit."

"But not supersonic?" George asked.

"Wrong shape," James replied. "If you look at Concorde and the Valkyrie, they're completely different to any of the big passenger jets."

"The Valkyrie, what's that?" George asked.

"A Mach 3 bomber from the sixties," James explained. "Eisenhower didn't like it, Kennedy did until I think even he had to agree that it was going to be obsoleted by new ground-to-air missiles, plus it cost a bundle."

"Mach 3, that's fast?" George asked.

"Three times the speed of sound," James explained. "Typical passenger jets fly at Mach 0.8 or thereabouts."

"What does the Concorde do?" George asked.

"Mach 2 or thereabouts," James replied.

"What will our Lear do?" George asked.

"As I recall, Mach 0.81 is the rated max," James replied.

"Why can't we go faster?" George asked.

"The design is wrong for supersonic speeds, plus at that speed you're using fuel at a pretty high rate," James said.

"What's the fastest thing out there flying today?" George asked.

"Probably the SR-71," James said. "It's a reconnaissance plane, capable of flying really high and fast, I think above 70,000 feet at Mach 3."

"Spy plane?" George asked.

"That, plus it's now being used by NASA for research," James said.

"Okay, thanks for the info, see you next week, Wednesday in New York," George said.

"Megan, I'm summoned to New York on Wednesday next week. Would you make me a reservation on Tuesday morning to fly east?" James asked.

"Of course," she said. "Any airline preferences?"

"The one I have the most miles on," James laughed. "Might as well get something out of these jaunts across the country. Now, I should call Tom Ellison."

"James," Tom said when he answered his telephone. "What are you doing on Thursday of this week?"

"Nothing scheduled," James replied.

"Good, meet me at the Long Beach airport at the Atlantic FBO at seven in the morning," Tom said.

"I'll be there," James promised.

250

"Wear something casual, jeans, boots, no need for ties, bring binoculars if you have them," Tom said. "We'll be gone most of the day, should have you back in Long Beach between four and five, not the best for traffic, I know, but thems the breaks. Must go, see you Thursday."

"Thanks for the tea, Megan," James said when she brought it through. "I'll be gone all day Thursday, not sure where, but I have to meet Tom Ellison at the Long Beach airport at seven and won't be back until closing time."

"Very mysterious," she laughed.

"Very," he agreed. "Okay, so that's Vincent Manning on Wednesday in Burbank, Tom on Thursday, who's next? Let's try David North and see what he wants to talk about."

"It looks like you'll be gallivanting all over LA this week," she said.

"Sitting in traffic more like," he said. "How do I get to Burbank?"

"There's no easy way," she said. "The most direct is the 5, but that takes you through downtown LA, might be longer, but quicker to take the 57 to the 210, then across the foothills to the 134, then cut over to the 5."

"So, allow myself ample time," he thought.

"Ample," she agreed. "What about North? Where does he hang out?"

"San Diego," James replied. "So, if I go there, Wednesday and Thursday are out. I'd better get that set up quickly or the week will be totally gone."

James did have the rest of Monday free and all Tuesday, so was able to attend to regular business and talk to all the division managers as well as spend time with the staff in the office. He did get an appointment with David North on Friday at ten in San Diego. At home later, Katrina was agog to tell him all about the course she had started. It included the basics of computers, then delved into programming, starting with basic query languages, then going into the mysteries of COBOL then assembler languages. COBOL because it was the preferred language used for business applications. On top of that, Katrina was also going to teach herself the IBM DOS, BASIC and Apple DOS, languages that were being touted for home computer use. She had also bought an IBM personal computer and an Apple II computer to experiment with, and she allowed and encouraged James to do the same. She had homework to do, so James got dinner ready while she studied.

On Wednesday, James presented himself at the Atlantic FBO in Long Beach and joined the group that was there being corralled by Tom Ellison. He recognised two of the others as being presidents of other companies that supplied components for aircraft; the other six he did not know. Tom did not make any introductions and only told them what they were going to see when they were in the air on a DeHavilland Twin Otter headed for the desert beyond the San Gabriel Mountains.

"We're going to a demo flight today of our new stealth drone that you've all been part of," he told them as they flew north. "What we've managed to achieve is a radar cross section about the size of a hummingbird, and we've got the noise down to where it's almost on top of you before you hear it, so at night it would be great, even in the daylight it's hard to spot."

"What's the range?" a man asked.

"Can't give you any operational details," Tom said. "Just safe to say, enough that you wouldn't have to operate too close to a front line. For the purposes of this demo, keep to yourselves any details you have of performance for your contribution, that way none of you knows the whole scoop, safer that way. This is a black program, and I don't want to hear of any leaks. We're flying into Edwards, and our demo flights will be out over the desert."

They flew over the mountains and into Edwards Air Force Base, where Tom handed out caps with the logo of Miller Aerospace. That identified them all as belonging to his group. An Air Force colonel met them and escorted them to a bus, and they were driven out to a vantage point in the desert.

"The drone will be here shortly," the colonel said. "I'll leave you to try and work out where it's coming from."

James joined the others in scanning the horizon for any sign of the drone and occasionally glancing at the mobile radar screen that had been set up and that was actively searching for the drone. James saw the odd blip on the screen and guessed that some were actually birds. He wondered if the drone operators altered the flight pattern to try and mimic that of birds so as to confuse the seekers. He saw what he thought must be the drone when it was almost on top of them, as Tom had predicted. At night, with no navigation lights, it would have been impossible to see, and it made only the minimum of noise.

"Good test," Tom said.

"Excellent," the colonel echoed. "Anyone spot it until it was right overhead?"

"No," was the collective response.

"Good job, Tom," the colonel said. "There's a couple more flights coming up, so stay tuned and stay alert and tell me if you spot one."

James picked up a pair of binoculars that were on the viewing stand and scanned the horizon. He had no idea whether the drones would come in low or high, and he had noted from the first flight that the underside was painted blue to meld into the sky.

"There," one of the others said, pointing.

"Sorry, that's a turkey vulture," the colonel said.

"Damn, I thought I had it," the man said. James never got his name and did not ask. Those he knew, he knew, but he thought it politic not to ask unless Tom made introductions. The drone actually came in high and loitered above them, doing three full circles around them before they spotted it, and while they were focused on that one, another came in low and flew right over their heads.

"Got good pics from that one," the colonel laughed. "You're all staring up at the sky, and we caught you unawares."

"Okay, time for lunch," Tom said. "The colonel has kindly set things up for us to eat on base. No chit-chat over lunch about what you saw today, talk about the weather, about baseball, anything but why we're here."

Lunch was interesting, a gaggle of men busy dissembling as best they could, which James was sure was a common event. On the flight back to Long Beach, Tom did name everyone and the company they represented. He also repeated his instructions about talking out of turn and made it clear that any leaks would have serious repercussions. James had no intention of revealing anything, unless he was directed to do so by Tom. After they landed and went their separate ways, James drove home, amazed by what he had seen. For something that big to be so hard to spot was a feat of engineering, and he was proud of the contribution that Waterford had made.

"Good day?" Katrina asked when she got home.

"Interesting," he replied. "What about you?"

"We got into how computers actually work," she said. "All ons and offs, so ones and zeros, the trick is to create programs that can eventually all break down to simple questions."

"Do you think it will be interesting?" he asked.

"Definitely," she said. "I'm looking forward to creating something that actually does something, a much more sophisticated program than the ones I've created for the PC and the Mac."

"We've decided to go with the Mac computers at work," he said. "Easy to work with and very intuitive."

"That's true," she agreed. "But the PC will probably have a bigger market share. What I'm working on is mainly on big machines, mainframes that take whole rooms."

"So, I started dinner," he said. "If you'd set the table, I'll finish making it."

New York

James flew on an early morning American Airlines flight to New York, arriving in the late afternoon, just in time to be part of the madhouse that is New York traffic. He took a taxi to the hotel and found a message there to join George Wilcox for dinner at seven. He had time for a quick shower to wash off the travel grime, then went down to meet George. He saw him in a corner, seated with Gene Thompson and another man.

"James," George said. "This is Chris Cohen, he's with Rosenberg and Davies, big investment bankers here in town."

"Good to meet you, James," Chris said.

"Nice to meet you," James said, wondering what this was about.

"Chris is helping me with a rights issue," George explained. "I'm looking to raise capital for acquisitions, and we need to know where the cash comes from right now. That's where you and Gene come in."

"All the cash flow information is in the monthly financials," James said.

"True, but what Chris wants to know are new and exciting programs and opportunities that might crop up in the next year or so," George said.

"The market for new mining machines is softening in the US," Gene said. "Look to Australia, South Africa and Brazil to be the hot markets for the next couple of years."

"James?" Chris asked.

"We're firmly in place with some major commercial programs and quite a few DOD ones," James replied.

"What about Mongol?" Chris asked.

"I've only heard rumours," James said. "It's definitely not the new ConsAir 350 seat plane, that's competition for the 747, L-1011 and DC-10, nothing mysterious about it."

"It's not a cover for something secret?" Chris asked.

"That would seem unlikely," James said. "The flap and slat drives we provide are standard for sub-sonic planes, plus we've just landed a big order for the on-board cargo handling systems."

"What secret programs are you working on?" Chris asked.

"If we were working on any, I would not be at liberty to discuss them," James replied.

"I heard that you're working on some super secret program," Chris pressed.

"As I said, if we were, I would not be at liberty to discuss anything," James repeated. "If we had any classified programs, my revealing that or them would be a criminal offence and I've no desire to go to prison."

"Yes, but you must have some," Chris said.

"I can neither admit nor deny," James said.

"So, you have," Chris said, pouncing on what he thought was an opening.

"I cannot comment," James said.

"Hey, Chris," Gene said. "He's just told you that he can't talk about it, and if he does and they really do have something, then he commits a crime."

"I don't know why it's so hard to just list what you have," Chris complained.

"Well, we do make parts for a number of military planes," James said. He then reeled off a whole list of model numbers, which he followed with a list of commercial planes.

"What about business that is not aircraft-related?" Chris asked.

"We've got the access business, marine equipment and airport loaders and such," James replied.

"What generates the most cash?" Chris asked.

"The access business," James replied. "It's not like the long-term contracts that typify the aircraft business; it's short-term rentals and purchases, so although it can be a liability-driven business, it does throw off ready cash quickly."

"What about the mining and construction machines, Gene?" Chris asked.

"The mining machine contracts are structured so that payments are made through the process, which means cash coming in early, but it is offset with the need for cash as the manufacturing progresses," Gene replied. "The construction machines are sold through a dealer network and are typically met from inventory and have a 90 to 180 day pay."

"And if you had to raise lots of cash quickly, what would you do?" Chris asked.

James looked at Gene, and Gene nodded. "Apart from borrowing, the other way we could do it is sell a division," James replied.

"Which one would likely yield the most cash?" Chris asked.

"In the short term, or the long term?" James asked. "Selling mining or aerospace would take time, so although they would give you the most, it would take a while."

"If we sold access, say, what would you expect to get?" Chris asked.

"If we look at ten times earnings, then somewhere around $50 million," James replied. "We have the original HighRise, and we added Reach for the Sky to that."

"And marine?" Chris asked.

"Closer to $90 million," James replied. "Again, we had the original marine business, and we added Deep Ocean Systems to that."

"What about the basic gearbox business?" Chris asked.

"We combined what had been in Beloit and Kenosha with Santa Ana, and that has us at sales of $75 million with before tax of $8.5, so ten times earnings, $85 million give or take."

"What about the airport ground support stuff?" Chris asked.

"Since we acquired ASI, then ten times earnings would be $60 million," James replied.

"There's your answer then, George," Chris said. "Market the hell out of this aircraft ground support stuff, the access business, gearbox and marine stuff, get a bidding war going and raise $285 mil."

"So, James, what about it?" George asked.

"If that's what you want to do," James said. "I think the company is better served with all the divisions, but if you want to sell off pieces to raise cash, then it's possible, it will still take some time, though, it's not going to happen in a month."

"What would you get if you sold off construction machines?" Chris asked.

"Again, if you take ten times earnings, $95 to $100 million," Gene replied.

"So, which is easier to sell?" Chris asked.

"There's already consolidation going on in the construction machine market," Gene said. "That may or may not make it easier."

"I'll think about it," George said. "What about borrowing, Chris?"

"We could think in terms of $100 to $120, five basis points over LIBOR," Chris replied.

"And if we float more stock?" George asked.

"You'd have to come up with some good arguments as to why a new rights issue would be good. Are any of the existing businesses looking at major growth?" Chris asked.

"Gene?" George asked.

"Major growth, no," Gene replied.

"James?" George asked.

"Nothing on the horizon that indicates major growth," James replied.

"So, new shares is an unlikely mechanism," Chris mused. "My advice, borrow and see if you can sell off some smaller bits, take your time and get the most for them you can and then pay down the debt."

Discussion was halted as a waiter came to their table for dinner orders. They ate, talking about more mundane matters, then split up and went their separate ways. Gene did nod to James and motioned to the bar.

"So, what do you think?" Gene asked James as they sat down over a late drink.

"George has talked in the past about property development, maybe he's got something he wants to do," James replied.

"I can see us being broken up and sold off in bits," Gene said.

"I agree," James said. "The question for us will be which bits get sold to who, and how long that will all take, and how much it will degrade the business while all that's going on."

"My guess is that George will do this in semi-secret," Gene said. "Don't tell the peasants what you're up to."

"That's going to be hard if potential buyers want plant tours and to meet the management," James said. "But I suppose we could gather up documents, stick them all in a data room somewhere and get bids, with non-refundable deposits before plant tours."

"That sounds like all kinds of fun," Gene said. "I think he'll go after your business first, smaller units, in different markets, sell off access, then marine, then airport equipment, then the gearbox business and finally the bigger aerospace chunk."

"You know, if George sells off bits of us, I wouldn't put it past him to want to pay us less because he'll argue that we have less to manage," James said.

"I hadn't thought of that," Gene said. "You're right, I can see him doing that."

"Well, we'll see what this big meeting tomorrow is all about," James said. "I'm off to call Katrina, then turn in."

The meeting with the bankers at Rosenberg and Davies was held in an office that overlooked the Upper Bay with a great view of the Statue of Liberty. James shuddered to think what the monthly rent would be, but he was sure that their fees were extortionate enough to cover that and more. George introduced Gene and James, then handed the meeting over to them to discuss their respective businesses and what current and future markets looked like. James noted that Chris stayed quiet for most of the meeting, which left him wondering where in the hierarchy of the bank he actually stood. George then excused Gene and James and had his own meeting.

"I wonder what he's really up to?" Gene asked as they sat in an ante-room and drank coffee.

"Probably engaging their services to sell us off piecemeal," James suggested.

"Can't imagine these guys are cheap," Gene said. "Everything about this place screams expensive. Great view though of the Statue of Liberty."

"Looks like they finished with the private session," James said.

After lunch, Gene and James left to go back to the airport to catch their flights back to Milwaukee and Los Angeles.

"Stay in touch, James," Gene said as they split up to go to different terminals. "We need to compare notes regularly to find out what's going on."

"I'll do that," James promised. He went to the American gate and waited until the flight boarded, then joined the throng. The one thing that James did like about George was that he insisted that they fly first class, especially on the long cross-country routes. He took his seat and sat back and considered the morning, and tried to imagine what the next move would be. He guessed that it would be a presentation to the board to get approval to proceed with selling off bits of the company. Even George would not do that off his own bat; he would want someone else to take the blame with him if it all went wrong. Perhaps that was a very cynical way of looking at things, but James had become leery of corporate politics and machinations. His view of George was that he would accept all the accolades when things went right and attempt to divert blame when things went wrong.

"Good trip to New York?" Katrina asked him when he arrived home.

"That remains to be seen," he said. "I think George is going to start selling off bits of the company to pursue his own agenda."

"What does that mean for us?" she asked.

"No idea now," he admitted. "I suppose it will all depend if George goes ahead and starts selling, and then which bits when."

"Do we need to look for another job?" she asked.

"Not in the short to medium term," he replied. "But, I think in the longer term that may become necessary. Meanwhile, I've got plenty to do with what we have. So, how was your day?"

"We got introduced to query languages," she said. "Simple enough, just writing routines to get information."

"Still interesting and fun?" he asked.

"Oh yes," she said. "It's stretching my mind a little and teaching me new things. Let's go out to dinner tonight."

"What about the Mexican place on Chapman?" he asked.

"Moreno's, that's good," she agreed. "Are you driving, or shall I?"

"I'll drive," he said.

James spent the next week or two just waiting for George to tell him what he had decided to do. He finally got the call after Thanksgiving.

"James, the board has elected to retain the services of Rosenberg and Davies to see what can be done to maximise the return to the shareholders," he said.

"I see," James said. "What do you want me to do?"

"Start putting together all the materials we'll need for an offering memorandum," George said. "Do it for the Pueblo, Tulsa, Santa Ana and Seattle operations to start with."

"It's going to be a lot of paper," James said.

"Rent a room, a building, whatever, just somewhere it can be reviewed without too many people being involved," George said.

"Can I get help from anyone here?" James asked. "I've got someone working on markets and opportunities already, Dawn Adams. I'd like to have her help, also, my secretary, Megan Grant, will need to be in on it"

"Okay, also get your head legal eagle on board," George suggested. "Plus your chief accountant and your HR head, Victoria. That should be enough. I'm sending Keith Baird out with some non-disclosure agreements for you all to sign."

"When do you want this done by?" James asked.

"Tomorrow would be good, but let's say by the end of January, Christmas gets in the way of stuff. Rosenberg and Davies have said that after they've reviewed all the data you're going to collect, it'll take them a month to put together the materials they'll need," George replied.

"When is Keith Baird coming out?" James asked.

"He'll be flying out on the company plane tomorrow," George said. "He can fly, get you all to execute the agreements, then fly back, same day."

"We'll be ready for him," James promised.

"I'll be out over the Christmas break," George said. "Off to the Caribbean."

"Have a good time," James said.

"Oh, I will," George said. "My wife is off to Switzerland with a couple of her girlfriends, so I'm free as a bird. Fancy a trip to see what we can find?"

"I'm booked for Christmas," James said. "And that's not something I would do."

"Well, your loss, I'm planning on banging everything in a skirt I can see," George boasted.

After George had hung up, James shook his head and hoped that he never tried anything at their offices, or even said anything. He then asked Megan to get Dawn Adams, Victoria Wilson, Jim Beatty and Mike MacKane for him. She was duly back with the three.

"Please stay, Megan," James said. "Tomorrow, Keith Baird is coming out with some documents for us to review and sign. I can't go into details now, but if you'd all be here by ten, I'd appreciate it."

"Very mysterious," Jim said. "Does this have something to do with the flying trip to New York?"

"You'll find out," James said. "Sorry, I can't be more open, but George issued edicts."

"Okay, we'll wait," Jim said.

"It's official," James told Katrina that evening. "I'm supposed to start gathering all the materials we need to put together what's called an offering memorandum, basically a sales brochure for bits of the company."

"So, does that mean you'll be busy over Christmas?" she asked.

"No, I'm taking the time off," he said. "I've got more put together than I told Wilcox, so we've not got that much more to do. So, any plans for Christmas?"

"I thought we'd go back to the mountains, to that place we went to last Christmas," she said.

"I like that idea," he said. "When do your classes end for the Christmas break?"

"The Friday before," she said.

"Okay, I'll take off from then too," he said. "We can drive up on Friday afternoon. You know George is a sleazy character, he told me that he's off to the Caribbean for Christmas, without his wife and that he was planning to bang everything in a skirt he could see. He even asked me if I wanted to go with him. I told him that I was booked for Christmas."

"Has he ever done anything or said anything at your offices?" she asked.

"No, he hasn't," James said. "But Megan once told me that she thinks he's creepy. I have to say, the more I get to know him, the more I agree with her. It's a good job he doesn't like to travel out here and that he stays in New York with his banker friends."

"Well, as long as he stays away, maybe he's smart enough to keep his activities separate from the company," she said. "I'll call and book the cabin tomorrow."

Keith Baird arrived and sat down with James and his team, and went through what was expected and the board decision that had triggered it. No one bought that story; they all knew that it was George, and the board had just gone along with what he wanted to do. Keith handed out the non-disclosure agreements, and they all read them, then looked to Jim for a lead.

"Looks harmless enough," Jim said. "Standard legal wording for an NDA, but what do we get for our silence? The NDA only has value in court if there's a quid pro quo."

"This is an addendum for each of you that lays out a series of bonuses if and when each part of the company is sold," Keith said. He had copies for each, and James noted that they were marked by name, so assumed that the amounts differed. "This will require a signature as well. I am authorised to tell you that you have a free hand in setting up a data room and putting in place a recording system to track who goes in and what they actually look at and what, if any, additional documents may be requested. Set up a separate account for all the expenses and back-bill it to corporate."

"We'll take care of that," James said. "At some point in the process of selling off any division, we're going to have to bring in the manager of that division. How do we handle that?"

"When, if, no when, it comes to that, we'll get an NDA for them as well and make them privy to the transaction," Keith said. "We'll also make it worth their while to present their operation in the best light."

"Is there anything else we should know?" James asked.

"It isn't anticipated that this will be a quick process," Keith said. "If we sell anything, we want it to be for the best price we can get."

"And if the managements of the various divisions want to make an offer, then will it be entertained?" James asked.

"We can do that," Keith said. "But the winning bids will be the ones with the least restrictions, and J&B Industries won't carry any paper."

"When do the bankers arrive?" James asked.

"At the end of January," Keith said. "Give them access to the data room so that they can put together their pieces, and then they'll let us know how they want to proceed. Okay, that's it for me. If I could just get my copies of the executed NDAs, I'll let you get on."

"I'll see you down to the plane," James said.

"George gave me a message for you," Keith said as they walked out to the plane. "He said that he's looking for the first two divestitures next year, then the other two industrials the year after that, then a break of a year or two to consolidate the aerospace stuff, then start positioning it for sale."

"What, window dress it?" James asked.

"Your words, not mine," Keith said. "But you get the idea. I'll be in touch mid-January to see when you'll be ready."

"We'll be ready," James said. "Good flight back to New York."

"So, that was interesting," Jim said when James rejoined them

"But, not unexpected," James said. "Rosenberg and Davies have probably shown Wilcox how to make a killing by selling off the company piecemeal."

"A pity that Hank Miller retired," Mike said. "What the hell was the board thinking when they brought in Wilcox?"

"I'm sure he can be very persuasive," James said. "So, Megan, Dawn, would you find us space and set up some kind of document control system?"

"We'll take care of it," Dawn promised. "Do we need to hire someone to act as gatekeeper?"

"I think that would make sense," James said. "We should also be there, either you or me, as long as they're there. We'll need a system to record who comes and goes, what they look at and what else they ask for. They cannot take copies unless we get specific instructions about that, or take anything away with them; they can make notes, of course, which I would expect them to do. I want to see some kind of NDA from them that tells us what we can show them and what we can't, I'll talk to New York about that. We'll need meeting space as well, because if we ever get to bring in buyers, we'll have to be there. Mike, we'll need financials going back five years, and we'll use the current business plans for the future. Dawn and I have the market information for each division, so Dawn, if you'll gather that up and put it into a format that we can show the bankers. I've no idea how much they will skew the numbers to show improving revenues and earnings, but I'm sure they'll find a way. They'll probably also have their own people look at the markets we're in and make their own projections."

"How do we keep this quiet?" Jim asked.

"That's going to be difficult," James agreed. "But any questions from our people, we just tell them that we're providing information to New York per their request. Queries from outside the company, just refer them to New York."

"Is the same thing happening to James & Brown?" Mike asked.

"I would think so. Gene was in the same meeting I was, and they asked all about the mining and construction divisions. If anything goes quickly, it'll be construction as that market is consolidating anyway," James replied. "Okay, any questions, just come and see me and I'll see what I can do or find out."

The weeks before Christmas were filled with document gathering and copying. Dawn and Megan found space that was close enough, but far enough away so that visitors would not be noted by the office staff at Waterford. By the time the Friday before Christmas came, James was happy to take a break and leave things for a while. When he arrived home, Katrina had the Jeep packed and was ready to go; all James had to do was change clothes.

"Ready?" Katrina asked as James went downstairs.

"Let's go," he said. "Do you want to drive?"

"Why not," she said. "We'll swap at Victorville."

"So, computer programming is still interesting?" he asked.

"COBOL now, so all very structured with main lines, subroutines and all kinds of rules about how things are actually written," she said. "I can probably do any business thing you want."

"When you're finished with the classes, then what?" he asked.

"I'll see," she said. "I could always get a job as a programmer, but I wonder if that's what I really want to do. I did hear about this zoo just off the 5 that's looking for docents. They're the ones that escort you around if you want, have displays and things to show people stuff and even go out to schools and talk to them about animals."

"That sounds interesting," he said. "Whatever you want to do."

"Okay," she said. "Traffic's already building, look at it, at this rate it'll take us two hours just to get to Victorville."

"Should we fill up?" James asked as they left the freeway and drove into Victorville.

"We should," she agreed. "Cheaper here than in Big Bear. I'll get us some coffee while you fill us up."

"It didn't take that much," he said when Katrina came back with the coffee and some fig newtons.

"Good," she said. "Let's go and see if there's any snow at Big Bear."

They drove on and came to the place where the Highway Patrol had placed a man to enforce the chain-up rule. James pulled over and quickly put their chains on, and they were waved through.

"It's snowed here," Katrina said as they drove up and over the pass that led to Big Bear. "Looks like a lot too."

"At least the road's been ploughed," he said. "I wonder how much they got."

They found out when they collected the key to the cabin. The three days prior to their arrival had seen a total of over twenty-six inches of snow, so there was literally snow everywhere. The track to the cabin had been ploughed, which was as well, as James was not sure if the Jeep could handle that much snow.

"This is beautiful," Katrina said as they unpacked the Jeep. "We're going to have a white Christmas. Liz said that to expect a little more snow on Boxing Day, but otherwise, it promises to be sunny, cold, but sunny."

"I didn't see any deer prints around the cabin, so it doesn't look like there's been any around for the past few days," he said.

"We'll see what tomorrow brings," she said. "So, wrap up warm and let's have a drink on the porch and enjoy the quiet."

"It is peaceful, isn't it?" he said as they sipped on cocoa laced with rum and listened to the sounds of the wind in the trees and the birds.

"Did you know there's actually a word for the wind in the trees?" she asked.

"I didn't," he said. "What is it?"

"Psithurism," she said. "Actually, there's two words, that one and sough, sough being old English and psithurism being one of those scientific words that was invented and very few people use."

"Where did you pick that up?" he asked.

"Margaret, one of the girls in my computer school, she's really into language and comes out with all kinds of obscure words," Katrina said. "She's invited us to dinner with her partner when we get back from this trip."

"Is she a good programmer?" he asked.

"I think so," Katrina said. "She and I work well together. It's mostly men in the class, only six of us women, but we're at least as good as any of them, if not better."

"Did you bring the mail?" he asked.

"Oh, I almost forgot," she said. "It's in my bag and there's a letter from your folks, they want to come and visit at Easter."

"Did they say for how long?" he asked.

"Two weeks," she said. "They've already booked tickets and fly from Heathrow to LAX; one of us should probably meet them."

"I'll go," he said. "When does the plane get in?"

"About four in the afternoon," she replied.

"Great, right in the middle of rush hour, or are they coming on the weekend?" he asked.

"Saturday," she said.

"I suppose we should be thankful for small mercies," he said.

"Have another cup of cocoa with a bigger belt in it," she laughed.

It was a white Christmas; that much snow just did not melt and disappear overnight, or even over the few days it was before Christmas Day. Fortunately, they had brought enough food and drink for their stay, so had no need to go into the town of Big Bear and fight the holiday traffic that would be pouring into the resort. The break away from work was a blessing, and James just hoped there would be no crises that actually required his attention, that would include a death at one of the factories, or the place burning down or a major aircraft crash that could be shown to link to their components. The company was doing well, each of the divisions was standing well on its own two feet and earning money and generating cash. There were always little things that came up, things that some in the divisions liked to call one-time events, which in and of themselves might be true, but which were part and parcel of running a business. To him, it was a shame that George had his own personal ambitions and that they did not include keeping the business as it was. He was happy that Katrina was busy and learning new things, not that she needed to work to earn for them; he earned enough for them both to live comfortably, but he knew she was happier doing something than just staying at home.

"Penny for your thought?" she asked him on Boxing Day morning as he sat outside with some tea and watched the birds.
"I was just wool gathering and thinking how lucky we've been," he said. "When we left Zambia, I never thought we'd end up here."
"I didn't either," she said. "Going to Oak Creek was for me a huge step. When I was growing up, the US was this place that had everything, and if I was very lucky, I might see once in my life."
"Right," he said. "The US was the place I'd heard about where you could get a Greyhound bus ticket and tour the country on a budget, but that getting visas to work here was difficult. But, then until I got my degree, Africa and Zambia were somewhere to holiday, maybe go on a safari if I was rich enough."

"It's interesting how much things have changed," she said. "If you think about it, to make a phone call overseas, you used to have to book the call and go through half a dozen operators; now you can just dial and it's done."

"The next big thing will be internet calls," he said. "You see, it won't be long and there'll be ways to use the internet to call, maybe even video calls."

"That would be nice," she said. "I wonder how soon before that happens."

"Anyway, what would you like to do today?" he asked.

"We brought our skis with us, let's take a trip into the woods," she suggested.

In the forest, it was quiet; the snow did that, it blanketed everything, dampening down noise, so that the only real sounds were the birds and the wind in the trees, and the shushing sounds that the skis made. The sun shone, so although it was still cold, it did not feel that cold, not the damp, bone-chilling cold that they had lived with in Wisconsin. The trees also cut out the wind, so that at ground level it was quite still, even though they could hear the wind blowing in the tops of the trees. The day was delightful, and best of all, there were no crowds of people; in fact, they only saw two others, who, like themselves, were on skis, making their own trail through the forest.

"Time for a break," Katrina said to James. "Did you bring coffee?"

"I did, and Christmas cake," he said. "My cake turned out pretty well."

"Not bad," she agreed. "I wonder if it's true that people are either bakers or cooks?"

"I wonder," he said. "I think I'd be more of a cook, but baking once in a while is fun too."

"We should invite Gran to come and see us," Katrina suggested.

"You think she'd come?" he asked.

"I think so," she said. "Has she ever been on a plane?"

"I don't think so," he said. "My folks could put her on the plane at Heathrow, and she could fly to LAX, and we could meet her there. I'll write and ask her if she'd like to come."

"Rather her than your Mom," Katrina laughed.

"Wouldn't it be better if there were someone to come with her?" he asked. "We're both out all day at work, so she'd be on her own."

"Tell her to bring a friend," Katrina suggested.

"I'll do that," he said. "If my folks come at Easter, then maybe Gran could come after that, the weather'll be nice enough, we could take a week or so and take them on a trip."

"Let's make a plan," she said. "Ready to go back to the cabin?"

"After you," he said.

Their break in the mountains was soul-restoring; it was interesting how wild places did that, but all too soon it was time to go back down the mountain, into the smoggy air of the Los Angeles basin and back to work.

"How was your Christmas?" Megan asked James when she came into the office.

"It was really nice," James replied. "Quiet, lots of snow, very few people, at least we didn't see many. How was your Christmas?"

"Busy," she said. "I spent it with my folks, and they were trying to set me up with this guy, he's a total jerk, but they think because he's got money, then I should be grateful."

"Sorry to hear that," he said.

"I'll manage," she said. "It's mainly Mom, Dad just keeps quiet and stays on the sidelines."

"I made coffee," James said. "Like some?"

"Thanks," she said. "Are we really going to be sold off and shut down?"

"I've no idea what Wilcox is really up to," James admitted. "But I do think he's looking at something to buy, and I'm pretty sure it's not in aerospace or machinery. I'm surprised that they're taking the approach they seem to be, I would have thought that if they wanted to sell and get lots of money, then they would have done it all at once, this hiving off small bits at a time doesn't make sense to me, unless he's looking at boosting earnings to get a bonus or push up the stock price."

"If we are sold off, do you know what you'd do?" she asked.

"Not really," he admitted. "I'd have to find another job, I can't retire on what we have now. Have you any ideas about what you'd do?"

"I do some modelling on the side for fashion ads," she replied. "I do everything for Norwest, it pays pretty well, and I get to keep the clothes. If this office closed down, then I'd do more, probably make more money, but I like this job, I like you, I like working here, the people are fun to work with."

"I wouldn't let Wilcox know that you model," James said. "The guy to me is a sleaze, and I wouldn't put anything past him to try it on with you."

"I keep my distance," she said. "I read him like you do, a total sleaze and watch him carefully when he's here, not that that's very often. How did you meet Katrina?"

"At a boat club in Kitwe," he replied, remembering the day. "I had met her folks, and one day she was there, and I was smitten. We started going out, and it wasn't long before we got married. It's funny, when I called my folks to tell them that I was engaged, all my mum wanted to know was, was Katrina black."

"What did you tell her?" Megan asked.

"That Katrina was Afrikaans, not African," he said. "Her family is Afrikaans speaking and has been in Africa for 300 years or so, and one of her great-great-grandfathers was actually San, the people we often call Bushmen, at least I think it was great great, there might be another great in there, I'd have to draw out the tree to see."

"My family moved here from northern Italy last century, so we weren't part of the big Italian immigration that came mostly from the south," she said. "We've still got family there, but we only see each other every few years; we're not that close. I suppose I should get back and sort out all the mail we got over Christmas."

"Thanks, Megan," James said. He then went through all the telephone messages that he had, sorting them into call back soon, call back later, and call back if the mood suited him. One caught his attention, it was from Chuck Harris at ConsAir, so that one he responded to right away.

"James, thanks for calling back. Can you come and see me tomorrow at nine?" Chuck said.

"I'll be there," James said, wondering what the president of ConsAir wanted to talk to him about.

James drove to Hawthorne to the ConsAir headquarters. He announced himself and was asked to wait. He did not have to wait long before a secretary came to collect him.

"Mr Martin is here," she told Chuck Harris.

"Thanks, Jill. James, come in," Chuck said. "We met in passing at the AIA meetings."

"We did," James confirmed.

"You're probably wondering what this is about," Chuck said. "Well, nothing bad, I've been told that your deliveries are on time, no rejects or any questions, so all's good there. I have another project. Heard anything about Mongol?"

"Rumours, that's all," James said.

"Well, the rumours are all wrong, which is fine with me. We're actually working on a major upgrade for the B-52; we've got the B-1, and they're working on low observables for another bomber, but the Air Force wants to seriously update the B-52 and keep it in the fleet for years yet. So, we're doing all the avionics and such, we've already contracted for engines, what we need from you are flap and slat actuators, rudder actuators, plus the PDUs that go with them, and some new stores racks, we're looking at one hundred ship sets, plus another ten ship sets for test and evaluation," Chuck said. "It's an order of about $150 million, give or take, over ten years. I'd like a commitment from you that you'll do this. I don't want to do all the RFP stuff, leaks happen that way, this is a black program, we're not letting anyone know it exists."

"What about the designs?" James asked.

"We'll take the parts you're doing right now for the 350, so no major mods, the only design is the stores rack, you should second some of your guys here to work on that," Chuck said.

"If we make all these parts, what do we pass them off as?" James asked.

"It's a foreign order, say the Brits or the Frogs, maybe even Airbus, building the 350 for us," Chuck suggested.

"We'll do that," James said. "I'll look at capacity at Tustin. I may need to add some machining and heat treat capacity, but that will just be in addition to what we have, and I don't expect it will be much. When do you want the first parts for evaluation?"

"We've already taken some of the 350 parts, so we'll be replacing those," Chuck said. "What we'll do is up the order quantities for the 350, indicating that deliveries will be split and have part of the order go to our assembly plant in Kansas and part to LAX, so three ship sets a month to Kansas and one to LAX."

"The stores racks will come from Albuquerque," James said. "How similar to the ones we already make would they be?"

"Similar, but different attach points, and most are internal to the plane, so not as robust as the ones you make now," Chuck said. "We'll just give you an order for stores racks to be delivered to Tinker. We'll pick them up from there, again, one ship set a month, and there'll be one hundred parts per ship set, so maybe one-third of the value of the order will go there."

"We have the capacity at Albuquerque," James said. "The order for those parts, who will it be from?"

"A shell company under the name of Integrated Logistics," Chuck said. "Get your engineers here next week and we'll start right away, have them fly into LAX and we'll pick them up from there."

"I'll do that," James said.

"Good, thanks for stopping by, James. Let me know who the guys from Albuquerque will be as soon as you can and what flight they'll be on," Chuck said. "Jill will see you out."

James drove back to Tustin and sat down with Stuart and told him that the ConsAir 350 quantities would be going up by a ship set a month and that the deliveries would be split. That raised Stuart's eyebrows a little, but James just shook his head, and Stuart nodded in understanding. Whatever this was all about, he had no need to know.

"Do you have the capacity?" James asked.

"We do," Stuart said. "We've made so many improvements that we're finding extra capacity just about everywhere. The only place we've yet to really figure out is deburr. This is great, it'll add $10 mil a year to the top line and one of that, maybe more, will drop right through."

"Thanks, Stuart," James said. "Oh, and one other thing, don't make any special note of this in your monthly report, New York doesn't need to know, all they'd do is ask questions that we can't answer. Just take a look at your forecast for the year and at the end of the first quarter, move things up a bit if things are going well."

"Sure thing," Stuart said. "You can bring me this kind of news any time you like."

James left and went back to his office, and asked Megan if she could get the plane for that afternoon to take him to Albuquerque, then he called Phil and told him that he was coming. He then called Katrina to tell her that he might be a little late coming home. Megan told him that the plane would be ready in half an hour and that she had lunch for him on the plane. The flight to Albuquerque only took an hour a twenty minutes, plus there was the time change, so it was two-thirty when James arrived. Phil collected him at the airport and they drove to the factory.

"So, what's up?" Phil asked when they were safely behind closed doors.

"We have an order forthcoming for stores' racks, but you need to send a couple of engineers to LA for a few weeks to firm up the design," James explained. "The order's worth five mil a year to your top line. You'll get an order from Integrated Logistics, and the parts get delivered to Tinker Air Force Base at the rate of 100 parts per month, for the next ten years."

"Wow," Phil said. "Anything else you can tell me?"

"Sorry, no," James said. "I'll need to know the names of the engineers, they'll need to have secret clearances and they'll fly to LA on Monday and be met there."

"What and taken to an undisclosed location?" Phil joked,

"That's about right," James said.

"Bill Black and Harry Windsor," Phil said. "I'll tell them after you've gone and I'll let you know the flight as soon as we've made resers."

"Thanks, Phil," James said.

"No, thank you," Phil said. "You can come with that kind of news any day. Want me to run you back to the airport?"

"Please," James said. "Oh, by the way, don't make any special mention about this in your monthly report; it's just another order, and for your forecast for the year, make an adjustment after the first quarter if things are going well and nothing drops out."

"I get it," Phil said. "Too many stupid questions from the dicks in New York."

"They don't need to know," James said.

James was actually back at his office by five, just was the luxury and convenience of a company plane at one's beck and call. Things were looking up; the orders from ConsAir, plus those from Amalgamated Controls and Burbank Rotorcraft, just added almost $20 million to the revenue numbers at Tustin, which would translate to at least $2 million, probably closer to $3 million, at the bottom line. It was a good way to start off a new year. The data room was coming along nicely. They had racks of files with documents from each division, plus a system in place to record who came and went and what files they pulled, rather like the registry system that John Le Carré described in his recent novel, Smiley's People. They even had a camera installed to record who came and went, so that they would have a photographic record as well. The office in New York had provided them with a copy of the non-disclosure agreement they had signed and permission to copy certain documents. They had hired a person to help Dawn, and Hermione Pitts was already on board and had helped with the data centre, so she was familiar with the documents and the recording system. So, all was ready for the bankers.

Investment Bankers

"You ready for Rosenberg and Davies?" George Wilcox asked James towards the end of January.

"We are, you have the address?" James asked.

"Got that," George said. "Expect them to be there at ten on Monday, probably be a cast of thousands, just keep track of them and don't let anything out that's not listed in the NDA. I know these guys, they've always got some angle. Things seem to be going well at your end. Maybe this is a good time to sell some things and raise a bunch of money."

"Things are going quite well," James agreed. "The companies we acquired got integrated well, and we actually picked up some good talent apart from the products and markets."

"Just to keep you in the loop, we're probably going to put the construction machine business on the market first; that whole industry is consolidating," George said. "Rosenberg thinks we can put together a compelling argument for consolidating our construction with two others and make a halfway decent company that has a market presence, the elephants are still Cat and their ilk, but with the right combination, we can give them a run for their money."

"When does that happen?" James asked.

"We've been in discussions since Thanksgiving," George said. "Expect something in the next ninety days, then we'll look at your airport access stuff."

"When do I tell them?" James asked.

"When you have to," George said. "We're going to make some quiet approaches and test interest. If it's strong enough and we have a few potential bidders, we might go public then, but otherwise tell them when there's enough out there that it gets hard to deny."

"Okay," James said, thinking that that was going to be an almost impossible thing to manage.

James called Gene Thompson to commiserate.

"Hey, James, you've talked to the dickhead?" Gene asked.

"He told me that Construction is on the blocks first," James said.

"Right," Gene confirmed. "I guess if that goes at all well, then you're next, then it wouldn't surprise me to find Mining is up for grabs as well. I might put something together myself for that."

"How much would Wilcox want?" James asked.

"My guess is something in the order of $250 million," Gene thought. "It would need an equity partner and a shitload of borrowing."

"I've always been leery of equity partners," James said. "They strike me as being avaricious in the extreme, and they'll let you do all the work and then take all the money."

"I know," Gene said. "It's something I'd have to watch really carefully. Are you going to New York for the next board meeting?"

"Nothing's been said yet," James said. "I'll make sure I don't schedule anything else the same day."

"Well, I've been summoned, my guess is to talk about selling off Construction," Gene said.

"Good luck," James said.

"It's started," James told Katrina when he got home. "The Construction business is on the block."

"What's next?" she asked.

"Pueblo," he replied. "At some point, I think I should just go there and sit down with Bill and talk about life."

"Would he be interested in buying?" she asked.

"Maybe," James said. "He likes the business, they like living there, he'd have to find an equity partner to ante up some cash, then borrow the rest."

"You know who might be a good equity partner, Jan Hofmeyr," she suggested. Hofmeyr was the chairman of the company that had been the distributor for James & Brown construction equipment in South Africa. They had had some cash flow issues, and James & Brown had taken back all the machines. But since then, CMI, the company that Hofmeyr ran, had gone from strength to strength and was always looking for new opportunities. Katrina had worked for CMI as a financial analyst and knew the company well.

"I wonder if they might be interested in a US venture," James mused.

"Only one way to find out," she said. "Do you want to call him, or shall I?"

"I'll do it," he said. "What's the time there?"

"Four in the morning, so a little early, try around six in the morning, that'll get him late afternoon," she suggested.

"I wonder if they have any money that they can use outside South Africa," James said. "I suppose the only way to find that out is ask. You know he might be interested in the access business as well, and there's always that chap Peel we met in Botswana."

"What do you feel about selling bits off?" she asked.

"I'd rather we didn't," James said. "But if that's what the company really wants to do, then I'll do the best I can, and if we succeed, we do get some money out of it."

"You've no interest in buying one of the companies yourself?" she asked.

"I've toyed with the idea," he said. "There are pros and cons, I'm not sure it's something we really want to do, what do you think?"

"I think I see little enough of you now," she said. "If you actually owned the business, I'd never see you; you'd be too worried about it. I remember what Susan Harris had to say, we might land up with a load of money at the end, but what about the time between."

"You're right," he said. "When is enough enough?"

"That's something we'll have to think about in the years to come," she said. "For now, we're doing pretty well and we're building up some savings."

"Anyway, what shall we do for dinner?" he asked.

"Orange County Mining Company," she suggested.

Early the next morning, James called Jan Hofmeyr, who actually answered his own telephone.

"*Middag*, afternoon," he said. "Who am I talking to?"

"Jan, this is James Martin," James replied.

"James, how are you, man? I heard a rumour that you'd gone off to LA to run some business," Jan said.

"That's true," James said. "The company is called Waterford Industries, nothing to do with glass. It's aerospace, gearboxes, access equipment, and airport ground support stuff."

"Sounds interesting," Jan said. "So, what's up?"

"I was wondering if you might have an interest in the airport ground support equipment," James said. "It makes scissor loaders for containers, conveyor loaders, tugs, container carts, honey wagons, mobile stairs and ground power units."

"Interesting," Jan said. "How big?"

"Sales of between $55 and $60 million, six before tax," James replied. "The division is in Pueblo, Colorado."

"Why are you interested in selling?" Jan asked.

"I'm not particularly," James said, honestly. "But the CEO and the board have embarked on a program to sell off stuff, and this is probably the first that will go in my portfolio."

"Can I get a look?" Jan asked.

"Of course," James said. "Doesn't one of your companies provide some ground support at Jan Smuts?"

"We do, JetAirBridge, we represent them in South Africa and do all the installation and maintenance. Wait a minute, you must be talking about Waterford Ground Support, we might be in the market for a couple, good excuse to come over and take a look," Jan said. "I'll make a plan and let you know, what's your number there?"

James gave Jan his office number and home number and said that he would be looking forward to hearing from him.

The cast of thousands actually turned out to be only four, and James, Dawn and Hermione got them situated and then asked them what they wanted to see first. They asked for all the information on the airport ground support operation first, so Dawn retrieved the files and marked them as being out and to whom, and Hermione logged the request into the computer system. The Rosenberg and Davies people made remarks about that, but James told them that those were the rules and that their

279

company had agreed to those rules. They had questions about the information, and James and Dawn answered those that they could and noted the few that they could not and promised to get answers. The Gang of Four, as Dawn labelled them, pored through the documents, made copious notes, argued among themselves, drank endless cups of coffee and finally left for the day at five. James and Dawn spent a few minutes making sure all was back where it should be and updating the log, then left themselves.

"Thanks, Dawn and Hermione," James said as they locked up.

"They're interesting," Dawn said. "They're actually smarter than I thought they would be; they've asked good questions."

"They'll probably try and recruit you," James said.

"If everything really does get sold off, I might think about it, but I'd keep my options open," she said.

"I'll see you tomorrow," James said. "I'll have to leave you two in the morning, I've got meetings I should have. If anything comes up that you can't handle, call me and I'll come over."

"I'm sure we'll be fine," Hermione said. "I think we've got the measure of these four. Alan is the one to watch; he's slippery, I think, given half a chance, he'd be dropping pages into his briefcase, which is why I insisted that all briefcases be left at the door."

"I don't think they were thrilled by that," James laughed. "They may think we don't trust them."

"I don't," Hermione said. "My brother works for one of these outfits, and he's told me a lot about the way they operate."

"I'd be surprised if something doesn't go missing," James said. "We'll just do the best we can."

"So, when do I get to meet the bevvy of beauties you have working for you?" Katrina asked. "I've met Megan, but not Dawn and Hermione."

"Any time you'd like," he said.

"See if they'd like to come to a braai on Saturday, bring a partner if they have one," she suggested.

"I'll do that," he said. "Four in the afternoon?"

"Sounds good," she said. "Now what about these bankers?"

"Four of them," he said. "All very keen, all taking masses of notes and asking questions, some of which are pretty good."

"And, what's next?" she asked.

"They go away and put together the offering memorandum, which is basically the sales brochure for the business. It would be interesting to see what that looks like for the Construction business," he said. "If we could see that, then we'd have some idea what to expect for us."

"It's all very unsettling," she said.

"It is," he agreed. "But then we've weathered stuff before."

"There was a letter from Gran today," she said. "She says that she'd love to come in June for a month and bring her friend Annabelle with her."

"I remember her," James said. "Lady Annabelle Watson, widow of Sir Henry Watson, who was a big wheel in the City."

"Do we have to call her Lady Annabelle?" Katrina asked.

"I doubt it," he said. "When I met her, she was very down to earth, not at all snooty."

"What's she like?" Katrina asked.

"Big into exercise and yoga," he said. "Really looked after herself."

"She must be getting on now," Katrina remarked.

"I would guess a contemporary of Gran, so yes, nineties," he said.

"Well, the two tannies will keep each other company," Katrina said.

"Did she have flights yet?" he asked.

"I think they're waiting for us to do that," Katrina said.

"I'll take care of it tomorrow," he said. "It's not too far out to make bookings."

The sessions with the bankers continued for the rest of the week, moving from ground support to access, then marine, until finally they said that they were done, for now, and left to create their memoranda. Things had gone well, the registry system had functioned well, no files had been misplaced or purloined, and all additional questions and requests had been logged and answered. James was delighted with the work of Dawn and Hermione and wondered how he could keep Hermione on in some role after the data room closed down. Jan Hofmeyr had a date set to visit Pueblo, and James set his schedule to be there. James also made the bookings for his grandmother and Annabelle, flying directly from London to Los Angeles, a long flight, but with no changes, it meant a simple trip. His parents had committed to getting the ladies to Heathrow, and he would meet them at LAX. Megan, Dawn and Hermione all accepted the invitation to the *braai*, and all said that it would be just them, so James was cooking for five. Gene sent him a copy of the offering memorandum for the Construction division of James and Brown, and it made interesting reading. He shared it with the others on the divestiture team, and they speculated on what would be said in the memoranda for their divisions.

Megan was the first to arrive on Saturday.

"Mrs Martin, so nice to see you again," she said.

"Please, call me Katrina. I saw at the AIA meeting that the spouses were essentially identified as adjuncts to the men and not as their own persons," Katrina said.

Dawn and Megan arrived together, and Katrina met them at the door.

"Hi, I'm Katrina," she said, forestalling any reference to Mrs Martin.

"I'm Dawn, and this is Hermione," Dawn said, introducing them.

"Please come in," Katrina said. "James is doing the male thing by getting the braai going."

"We guessed that *braai* must be barbecue," Hermione said.

"Very traditional with us," Katrina said. "Our only real break with the tradition is that we add green vegetables, as a typical braai is mostly meat."

"Megan told us that you're from Zambia," Hermione said. "I'd love to go one day. Can I go on safari there, or do I have to go to Kenya for that?"

"Kenya and Zambia would be different experiences," Katrina said. "The typical image of Kenya safaris is wide open plains and lots of animals, Zambia is more scrub, and sometimes you have to look for the animals, but there would be fewer people, fewer cars, and it could be just you watching a leopard and not a ring of ten safari trucks."

"Dawn, Hermione, what can I get you to drink?" James asked as they joined him on the patio.

"A beer would be great, thanks," Dawn said.

"Same for me," Hermione echoed.

"James was telling me that you've had a busy week," Katrina said.

"It was," Dawn said. "Lots of paper and note-taking and some questions to research, but we managed."

"James told me that you're new to the company, Hermione. What did you do before?" Katrina asked.

"I worked for a chain of clothing stores in their acquisitions department," Hermione replied. "We were always on the lookout for things to buy and even sell if the brand did not do well. I knew Megan from there; she models all the fashions for the NorWest catalogue."

"What made you leave them and join Waterford?" Katrina asked.

"The cheap clothes and everything were nice, but this sounded like a challenge, and Megan told me that the people in the office were all very nice and fun to work with," Hermione explained. "It's been different, but fun, and I'm enjoying it."

"Even though you know at the end of it all, there may be no job?" Katrina asked.

"I don't think I'll have any difficulty finding a job; the guys this week already have been asking me if I want to go and work for them," Hermione said.

"We'll have to move inside," James said. "It's raining."

"Can you finish the *braai* out here?" Katrina asked.

"No problem," James said. "I'll just get a hat and a jacket and I'll be fine."

Food was served, beer was drunk, and conversation continued. Katrina concluded that the three were very nice, fun to have around and that none of them had designs on James. Not that she did not trust him, she did absolutely, but she did not want him to be in an awkward situation of having to fend off advances.

"I think it best if you all just stay the night," she said later in the evening. "We've all had a little too much to drink to be driving."

"Are you sure that won't be an inconvenience?" Megan asked.

"Not at all," Katrina said. "Is anyone expecting any of you?"

"No," they chorused.

"So, two will have to share a room," Katrina said.

"We'll do that," Dawn said of her and Hermione.

"James, if you'll just go up and make the beds and get some towels out," Katrina instructed.

"Are you sure this is not an inconvenience?" Dawn asked.

"Not at all," Katrina said. "When we lived on the mine in Mkushi, we put up an army of geologists one night, they ate us out of house and home and drank all our beer, but we managed."

"We heard that James worked underground in a mine, didn't that worry you?" Megan asked.

"It was, was it was," Katrina replied. "I grew up in the mining town, and that's what a lot of people did, so for us it was normal, we didn't worry unless the siren went off at an odd time, which told us that there had been an accident. James told me it was in many ways just like working in a building; there was a roof and walls, the only issue was how safe the roof was, and that was part of his job, to make sure it was safe. But, I have to say, when we moved to Mkushi and he ran the open pit, I was happier."

"What did you do in Zambia?" Dawn asked.

"My family ran a heavy transport business, so we would move mining equipment and other big things around," Katrina replied. "Then in Mkushi I sold industrial minerals, then when we went back to South Africa I got a degree in finance and worked as an analyst for a big company there, here I worked for a distributor of construction machines until I decided to take a course in computer programming, which I'm still doing."

"So, you've done all sorts," Hermione said. "Has it been difficult getting jobs? I've found that because I'm not a man, I have to prove myself more."

"I've seen some of that," Katrina said. "But with the family company, I had no brothers, so it was just Dad and me, and I did fine, I could drive all the heavy trucks and most of the equipment we loaded."

"Cool," Hermione said.

"When you worked for the clothing shops, did they give you discounts?" Katrina asked Hermione.

"They did," she replied. "So, I've got a pretty extensive wardrobe and know where to shop for the best buys. You know what we should do is have a girls' day, and Megan and I will bring clothes to try."

"Sounds like fun," Katrina said. "We'll send James off on an errand somewhere. Keep him out of the way."

"Keep me out of the way of what?" James asked as he rejoined them.

"We're going to have a girls' day and look at clothes," Katrina replied. "We wouldn't want to bore you."

"I doubt that I'd be bored," he said.

"We'll see, you can stay, but we won't be offended if you take off and go for a walk or something," she said.

When James and Katrina awoke the next morning, it was to the aroma of things from the kitchen. Breakfast had been prepared, and tea and coffee were made, and even the table on the patio was set.

"Morning all," James said. "Did you all sleep well?"

"We did," Dawn said. "I hope you don't mind that we raided your pantry and fridge."

"Not at all," he said. "What are we having?"

"Breakfast burritos with blueberry muffins and a fruit plate," Dawn said.

"I won't need lunch after that," Katrina said. "This looks super."

"Thank Hermione, she's the cook, we're just the gofers in the kitchen," Megan said.

"If and when these sales go through, I'm going to take a break and take a trip to Africa," Hermione said between mouthfuls. "Where should I go?"

"If you want a truly African experience, then James's brother and his wife run a tented camp in Botswana," Katrina said. "If you want, I'll get you details."

"Let's do it," Hermione said to the others.

"Let's," Megan said. "Dawn?"

"I'm in," she said. "So, James, when is this likely to happen?"

"I'm not sure," he admitted. "Wilcox told me that he wants the first three done this year and then a break for the aerospace, so next year, June to October is what you should plan for your trip."

"Will we get enough from the sales bonuses?" Dawn asked.

"I would think so," he said.

"So, Katrina, next Saturday for a girls' day?" Hermione asked.

"Sounds like a plan," Katrina replied. "Looking forward to it. Can I invite one of the girls from my computer class?"

"Please do," Hermione said. "What size are you?"

"I'm usually a six or an eight depending on the brand," Katrina replied.

"About the same as me," Hermione said. "What about your friend?"

"I'd guess an eight or a ten," Katrina said. "She's a little fuller than me, but not much, about the same height."

"Shoe size?" Hermione asked.

"US eight," Katrina said.

"Okay, we'll see what we can come up with," Hermione said.

Jan Hofmeyr called James at home that afternoon, after the ladies had gone, and told him that he was in the US in Denver and was looking forward to their meeting. James told him that he would be in Pueblo the next day. As the bankers had left, he decided to take Dawn and Hermione with him. They would fly up early in the morning, Dawn and Hermione could take plant tours while James met with Bill Evans and the Hofmeyr, then come back later that day.

"James, good to see you," Bill said when James arrived.

"Good to see you, Bill. This is Dawn Adams and Hermione Pitts, they're both in my office looking at markets and opportunities, and I thought it would be good if they could actually see the place," James said. "If you've got a few minutes?"

"Of course, ladies, I'll get Mark Brooks, he's my numbers guy, to show you around," Bill said.

"How are things, Bill?" James asked when they were alone.

"Here's fine, but I've been hearing all kinds of rumours about the Construction Division, up for sale," Bill said.

"That's true enough," James said. "Wilcox is breaking us up, they say returning value to the shareholders, but in my mind, he's got another plan and we're not part of it."

"So, when do we get the chop?" Bill asked.

"I'm not sure," James said. "Wilcox wanted to do Construction first, then our three non-aerospace divisions. Tell me, if you had the chance, would you buy this place?"

"Damn straight," Bill said. "It's a good business and we're making it better by the day, but I'd need an equity partner and I've no idea who I might get that I would trust not to screw me."

"That's one of the reasons Jan Hofmeyr is here," James said. "I asked him if he had an interest in the business, and he said yes. So, he's still looking to buy some loaders, but he's also interested in the business, and he would need someone good here to run it, can't do that from Jo'burg."

"Are you going out on a limb telling me this?" Bill asked.

"I am," James said. "I've read the NDA a few times and there's a clause in it that I can use to skip around the restrictions, but it would still be better not to let Wilcox know that we've talked."

"So, what do you want to do?" Bill asked.

"I'll make the introduction to Hofmeyr; what you talk about after that is none of my business," James said. "I expect an offering memorandum from Rosenberg and Davies to be out in about a month. How long that will stay under wraps, I don't know, but at some point, we're going to have to come clean about selling the company."

"What does Hofmeyr do?" Bill asked.

"He runs a conglomerate, CMI. They have all kinds of industrial products; they used to be the distributor for James & Brown in South Africa," James replied. "Jan is the chairman and has done an amazing job of pulling them out of the doldrums and turning it into a very successful company. Katrina worked for him as an analyst when we lived there. He won't want to invest if he doesn't trust the guy here, so make your own deal with him and hope that his bid, when it comes, is successful."

"Thanks, James," Bill said. "Don't worry, nothing will leak out of here. I won't tell my guys until we're either directed by you, or it's so bloody obvious that we have no choice."

"Jan will be here after lunch, you might want to do the loader business, then have dinner later and talk about the company," James suggested.

"Will do, so do you and your two analysts fancy lunch?" Bill asked.

"I could certainly eat," James said.

"So, what do you think of Waterford Ground Support?" James asked Dawn and Hermione as they flew back to Orange County.

"It's better in real life than on paper," Dawn said. "The place looks well run to me, very organised, not a lot of junk lying around, no secret cabals plotting in the corners, seems a pity to sell it."

"That was my thought," James said. "But the die is cast and we've no control over it."

"Would it be possible to see the other operations?" Hermione asked.

"We can arrange that," James said. "I've got regular monthly reviews coming up next week, just tag along. I'll get Megan to fix hotels."

"I have to say that I like this flying in the company plane," Dawn said. "When I was with Waterford Power, I got to see the place in Seattle, but I had to go commercial, which wasn't too bad, but this is nice."

"It makes getting to Tulsa, Pueblo and Albuquerque a lot easier," James said. "I'm surprised, though, that Wilcox hasn't taken it away and sold it off."

"Isn't there another plane?" Dawn asked.

"We had a Lear 55, but Wilcox wanted bigger and better, so he went with a Gulfstream, a little bigger and flashier than the Lear," James said.

"Ever been on it?" Hermione asked.

"Not yet," James said.

"Ten minutes to landing," Chuck said over the intercom. "Please buckle up and put away tray tables."

When James stopped at the office, there was a message to call George Wilcox, so he did and learned that the offering memoranda's first drafts were ready, and could James be in New York on the following Friday to go through them with the bankers. That fit with James's schedule, he could do his monthly reviews on Monday, Tuesday and Wednesday, then take off for New York on Thursday, so he asked Megan to set things up.

When the clothes session started, James took himself out onto the patio to give them some privacy. Megan and Hermione had arrived with boxes of stuff, and it was not long before they were all trying things on and critiquing the looks. There was a lot of conversation, and James heard snippets which told him that it was not just about fashion but also why none of the three was currently attached. It seemed they had all had relationships that had ended in the past three months for one reason or another, and none of them was in a hurry to start anew. Katrina came out a couple of times to show him dresses, skirts and jackets, and he was asked for his opinion. He thought that everything she showed him was really nice, and he meant it; he was not just saying it. Megan and Hermione really did have a sense of style, and they were passing that on to Dawn and Katrina. He did wonder what it was all going to cost them, but reasoned that it was all worth it. Dinner was prepared by Hermione, who put together a delightful salmon dish followed by a lemon tart. They did stay the night again, but this time had come prepared.

James was in New York on Thursday afternoon, in time for dinner with George Wilcox and Chris Cohen from Rosenberg and Davies. His monthly reviews had gone well, with Dawn and Hermione asking all the questions.

"So, James, ready to read and edit?" George asked as they sat down for dinner.

"I doubt that there'll be much editing to do," James replied. "I'm sure that Chris's company does a good job."

"That's as maybe," Chris said. "But we want to be sure our spin doesn't stretch the bounds of credibility."

"How is the sale of J&B Construction going?" James asked.

"Got three live ones," George said. "Trying to prod them into a bidding war. It's a tough sell because the market's consolidating everywhere, and we're not the only ones with something to sell. But, we've shown how some combinations can work."

"I've looked at the numbers for your loader business, James; they're looking pretty good," Chris said.

"We, or rather Bill Evans and his team, have worked hard," James said.

"How much of the growth was due to the addition of ASI?" Chris asked.

"About $25 million," James replied.

"So the combination really helped?" Chris asked.

"It did," James confirmed. "We made improvements to our original business and then had the capacity to add ASI without too much in the way of buildings, tools or materiel."

"We can sell that idea for J&B Construction," Chris said to George. "It makes the package attractive, we have to pick the right candidates and show them which facilities to consolidate, which to streamline and which to shut down."

"I've got Gene looking at that," George said.

"How soon are you thinking of testing the waters for the loader business?" James asked.

"After Easter," George said. "We'll have good first-quarter numbers by then, and a view of the second quarter. I presume your numbers are still looking good for the first quarter?"

"They are," James confirmed. "We see nothing on the horizon to change anything materially."

"I'm interested to see what you think of our memorandum," Chris said. "We think it's pretty good and makes the loader business look like a buy."

"You still want to sell?" James asked George.

"We do," he confirmed. "We need cash for the third leg of the business. We'll have a strong position in mining, one in aerospace, and I'm looking at something unrelated that gives us a hedge against downturns in either of those sectors."

"So, James, nine in the morning at our offices," Chris said.

"I'll be there," James promised.

James went through the documents and made comments, mainly about the forward-looking projections. Rosenberg and Davies painted a rosy picture of the future using all the best-case scenarios that James and his team had come up with. He had a few edits on the descriptions of the various businesses, and those were accepted. His comments about the forward-looking projections were noted and politely put aside, and it was pointed out that there was the usual caveat in the language that cautioned against total reliance on those numbers. All in all, they had done a good job and James was, if not happy with them, at least prepared to accept them.

"So, James, what do you think?" George asked when he joined the group.

"It will serve," James replied. "I've got the usual operations caution about the future, things can change, markets can change, disrupting technologies can happen, so I've tended to err on the conservative side of forecasts."

"I get that," George said. "But, we're selling here, so we want to put the best face on things."

"What do we do about environmental issues?" James asked.

"I want to sell these businesses absolutely, the buyers take everything, warts and all, but you're right, we'll need to do baseline surveys to make sure there's nothing buried out there so that in the reps and warranties we can legitimately say that to our best knowledge and belief, there's nothing there. If there is, we may have a problem, not only with a sale, but also with the EPA and the states," George replied. "But, we won't do the baselines until word is actually on the street, do it too early and it'll flag that something's up."

"You could always appoint a new VP of environmental, and then they could ask for baselines at all the businesses, just to know where we are and check on our practices for waste disposal," James suggested.

"I'll think about that," George said. "I could lay the blame on Hank Miller and cast myself as the new broom wanting to be sure everything is legit and above board."

"Do patents go with the businesses or stay with Waterford?" James asked.

"Good point," George said. "My thinking is that we retain ownership, but licence the buyers for general use for one dollar a year."

"And if they sell?" James asked.

"Then it could get messy. Maybe they can buy the patents from us and sell them with the business; it'll be a pass-through for them," George said.

"When do we announce?" James asked.

"If word isn't out by then, July one," George said. "You'll have a sense of the second quarter by them even if you don't have final numbers."

"We're already hearing rumours about Construction being on the blocks," James said.

"Can't help that in an industry that's consolidating all over the place," George said. "When the first buyer wants plant tours, then we'll announce that."

"Do we need to think about retention bonuses for the division managers?" James asked.

"Probably should," George said. "Find a way to take that out of the sell price. retention up to the day of close, after that it'll be up to the buyer what they want to do."

"And if any of the managers want to make an offer themselves?" James asked.

"They can do that, but as I said before, we're not carrying paper, so the cleanest deal for the most gets it," George said.

"I don't see any issues with non-competes after the sales," James said. "We don't have any overlap in markets between the divisions."

"You've thought about this," Chris said.

"A lot," James said. "I may not agree with the sales, but as long as I'm in this job, I'll do what the board wants to the best of my ability."

"If you quit on me, then all the sales bonuses go out of the window," George said.

"I understand that," James said.

"You'd have to get a pretty good offer to walk now," Chris commented.

"I realise that," James said.

"Okay, well, hop on back to LA and make sure things go well," George said.

James left, pissed off at the dismissal by George. If he had had enough in the back to last him six months, he might have quit then and there, but he still needed the job. So, he promised himself that he would talk to Katrina when he got home and make a plan to be sure they had enough in the future.

"So, what shall we call it, fuck you money?" Katrina asked when he discussed it with her.

"I like that," he said. "We need to look at what our expenses are and see how much we would need and how long it would take to build that up. Plus, this would be separate from retirement savings."

"I agree," she said. "Stick it out with Waterford until it all gets sold off, then find something else. Meanwhile, do what Dickhead asks you and try and ignore him if you can."

"The corporate world is not always that nice, is it?" he commented.

"We saw some of that in Zambia when that chappy came out from London to tell you all to improve things," she recalled.

"Right, Colin, Beauchamp," James said. "Told us to get our act together and, in a roundabout way, told us to high grade the mine to make earnings look better that year."

"I wonder if he's still with Kasalia in London," Katrina said.

"I would think so," James said. "He wasn't that old. I wonder where John Wells is these days."

"Probably head of something in London," Katrina said.

"I do wonder sometimes where everyone is these days," James said. "It's amazing how quickly you can lose touch with people."

"It is," she agreed. "So, what do we need to do for your folks coming for a visit?"

"Maybe I'll take a few days off and we can drive to the Grand Canyon," he suggested. "Maybe even take a helicopter tour."

"Let's do that," she said. "You tell me the days and I'll make bookings."

There were some follow-up questions from Rosenberg and Davies, and another visit from the Gang of Four to Irvine. They wanted to talk about people, so James got Victoria Wilson to join him, and they sat down with the bankers and talked about organisation charts and who might replace whom in case someone left. They also went through the various agreements they had with those unions that represented the workers at some of the sites. None of that went into the offering memoranda, but Rosenberg and Davies wanted to be prepared. George Wilcox did not hire someone to look after environmental affairs, but he did give the task to Keith Baird, reasoning, James supposed, that any issue that did arise would be a legal issue. Baird made no move to review any practices or procedures, but James felt that he should be prepared and sat down with each of the division heads and talked about waste streams and disposal. They did agree on some changes and started looking at the waste streams to see what could be eliminated, what could be reduced, what could be sold and what they would just have to accept as part of doing business. For that, he asked for a list of approved sites where waste, hazardous and non-hazardous could go to.

First sale

It was announced the week before Easter that J&B Construction was being sold to a group of investors from Chicago. James called Gene to get the scoop.

"They're pulling together five of the smaller companies, us plus four others, to try and take on Cat," Gene said. "The sell price was $120 million, for all the assets, materials, buildings, patents, land, we're on the hook for anything untoward that's buried, but if there's anything there, it's ancient, well before my time, but who knows, the place has been there long enough that there could be anything. I suggested to the dickhead that he set aside $10 mil in case."

"Did he agree?" James asked.

"I don't think he wanted to, but Keith Baird agreed with me, and we set up a reserve in the parent just for that," Gene said.

"I thought Wilcox wanted to hang on to the patents and just give licences?" James asked.

"That's what he proposed," Gene confirmed. "But they pushed back and said that they had to be part of the deal."

"What facilities get shut down?" James asked.

"The initial plan is for Green Bay to be shut down and all that is not crane moved to Pittsburgh, all the crane stuff, even from Pittsburgh, goes to Manitowoc, the Minnesota and Iowa factories get shut down, and everything consolidated into Pittsburgh," Gene explained.

"Is there enough space in Pittsburgh?" James asked.

"I doubt it," Gene said. "Maybe they're also going to rationalise the lines as well."

"What about the UK operation?" James asked.

"Interesting," Gene said. "The Chicago investors didn't want that, so the Brits have found their own buyer and have a free licence to continue to build and sell under the J&B UK name. Oh, by the way, the new company is going to be called Loop, just Loop, Loop Inc, I think, and they've got some logo already with what looks like an infinity loop."

"What about J&B Africa, Australia, Canada and Brazil?" James asked.

"They're staying as subs of J&B Mining, and will be distributors of both J&B UK and Loop," Gene explained.

"Isn't that rather messy?" James asked.

"I think so," Gene agreed. "But I wasn't the deal maker, I said my piece, and George did what he wanted to do. Where do you stand?"

"I haven't been told about any interest yet," James replied. "But I'm hearing rumours."

"I haven't heard anything," Gene said. "And the dickhead doesn't tell me squat about you guys."

"Well, when I hear something, I'll let you know," James promised.

James went to LAX to collect his parents. Their flight from London had been long and tedious, but Air New Zealand did a good job and had made it as comfortable as they could. They had picked Air New Zealand because it offered the best price, and they even offered free New Zealand wines to all and sundry, not just the First Class passengers.

"How are you both?" James asked.

"Glad to be here," his dad replied. "It's a long flight."

"Imagine going on to Auckland," James said.

"God forbid," his dad said. "How's Katrina?"

"She's well, doing well with her computer programming," James replied.

"How long is the drive to your house?" his mother asked.

"About forty-five minutes to an hour," James replied. "We'll pick up the 405, then take off onto the 22 and then up the 55 to Katella, then we'll go out to the house."

"What was all that?" his dad asked.

"The freeways," James explained. "It's just numbers here, so the 405 would be like the M1 or the M6."

"How long did it take to learn all that?" his dad asked.

"Not too long, plus I've got a Thomas Guide in the car, it's got maps of LA and Orange Counties with all the streets marked," James said.

"This Thomas Guide is like an A to Z?" his dad asked.

"It is, but easier to use because it can be folded to show the page you want," James replied. The traffic on the 405 was not too bad, certainly less than it would have been on a weekday. There was less on the 22, and they were not on the 55 for very long, exiting for Katella after a forty-minute drive. Then it was through Orange and Villa Park and back into Orange, and then home.

"Nice trip?" Katrina asked them as they went into the house.
"Long," Mrs Martin said. "But the Kiwis looked after us nicely and we had a seat up by the door that gave us more legroom."
"Are you hungry, thirsty?" Katrina asked.
"I'm dying for a cup of tea," Mrs Martin said.
"I'll make some and bring it out to you on the patio," Katrina suggested.
"This is very nice," Mrs Martin said as she sipped tea later and looked around. "I like what you've done with the garden."
"It's easy to take care of," James said. "No flower beds to weed, just grass to mow and bushes to keep trimmed."
"What kind of tree is that?" his dad asked.
"A jacaranda," James said. "You might remember those from South Africa and Zambia, the ones with the purple flowers."
"Oh yes, I remember those," his dad said.
"And that bushy-looking hedge at the back?" Mrs Martin asked.
"It's called Mexican Honeysuckle here," James said. "It does attract hummingbirds; there's one over there."
"Oh, I see," his mother said. "Aren't they pretty?"
"They're amazing," Katrina said. "The way they just hover by the flowers is fascinating to watch."
"So, how's the business, James?" his dad asked.
"Doing nicely, Dad," James replied.
"And the computer stuff, Katrina," Mr Martin asked.
"It's got my brain working," she replied. "I'm not finding it very difficult, but I do have to study and concentrate."
"I'm thinking of getting a computer," Mr Martin said. "What should I get?"
"It depends on what you want to do with it," Katrina hedged.
"I just want to get comfortable and learn a bit," Mr Martin said.

"I'd get an Apple then," Katrina said. "Easier to learn than the DOS machines, it's a little pricier, but I think you'll be happy. We've got one you can take a look at."

"I'll do that," he said.

"Anything you'd really like to do tomorrow?" James asked.

"Maybe just a drive around the neighbourhood, so that we can get familiar with the area," his dad replied.

"How do you feel about taking my Jeep?" Katrina asked.

"Let me drive it around the houses a bit here and see how I do," James's dad suggested. "I imagine it's like driving in France."

"A little less chaotic, but faster," James said. "You just have to be on your toes in the rush hour, there's just so much traffic. There is one thing to keep in mind, here: if you're turning right at traffic lights that are red, you can go unless it specifically says no right turn on red. I got hooted at a few times because I didn't turn when I could. You have to stop and give way to through traffic, of course, but it's not a bad idea."

"What will you do for another car, Katrina?" Mrs Martin asked.

"One of the other girls in my class lives on the other side of the hill, so just drives past every day, and she'll pick me up," Katrina replied.

"Can we visit your factories, James?" his dad asked.

"I'll arrange for you to see the two here," James said. "The others are a little far away."

"Would you like some dinner before you go to bed?" Katrina asked.

"Just something light, Dear," Mrs Martin replied. "And then I think bath and bed would be a good idea, the jet lag is catching up with me."

On Sunday, they took a drive around, and Katrina even turned the Jeep over to James's dad, who took to it right away and announced that he would have no problems navigating the roads around the area and that he might even venture onto the freeways. James showed him the Thomas guide and pointed out what page they were on.

"This is simple enough," his dad said. "Elizabeth, you'll have to navigate."

"Let me see," she said. "Oh, I see, simple enough."

"What I do when I want to go somewhere is work out the route, then write it down," Katrina said. "So then I know which turns to make without having to look at the map each time."

"That's a good idea," Mrs Martin said.

"So why don't we think about Tuesday and Wednesday for factory visits?" James suggested. "Come to the office and I'll take you from there. If you plan to arrive at about nine-thirty, then we'll have time for a visit and lunch, and you can be on your way back here before the mad rush starts. The easiest way is down Jamboree, I've got directions here."

"Let's see," his mother said. She studied the street names, then the Thomas Guide and announced that she could navigate their way there.

James talked to Stuart Wilson and John Trent and set up factory visits, then he turned his attention to messages from George Wilcox. The bankers had two tentative enquiries and, surprising James, George asked if the management had any interest. James said that he would find out, but pointed out that that meant telling at least Bill Evans what was going on.

"Do it, James," George said. "Hop on up there later this week and sit down with them. You know what our expectation is, so sound them out."

"Does this mean that the initial interest from other potential buyers is coming in lower than you'd like?" James asked.

"Not saying," George replied, which meant to James that they were low.

"I'll talk to Bill," James promised. "He may already suspect something because he has a lot of ties to J&B Construction and knows what's going on there. Who are the other interested parties?"

"Don't give this information to Evans, but LHDLoaders and RampQuip," George replied.

"I know both of them," James said. "Both are quite small and are probably trying to work out where they'll get financing from, my guess is that they'll go to an equity partner who will also set up loans and none of that will be cheap and they'll be stuck with an equity partner who'll be looking to strip out what they can and flip the business in under five years."

"Very cynical," George laughed. "But probably true, equity fund managers don't get rich by being nice guys. Will Evans need an equity partner?"

"He may," James said, skipping around the question. "I'm sure he'll be looking at financing as well."

"Tell him to think about it and make an offer, take a copy of the offer memo and the NDA and give them to him and have him respond to Rosenberg and Davies," George instructed.

"At some point, Bill will have to tell this staff what's going on," James said. "Particularly if the other possible buyers want to visit."

"As soon as one of them asks, I'll let you know and we'll send out a release to Evans that will give him something to share with everyone," George said.

James took his parents to Tustin and Santa Ana, then flew to Pueblo to talk to Bill Evans.

"Bill, this is the offering memorandum," James said. "You'll need to sign for it, and you'll note that there's an NDA as part of it, and by signing, you'll agree to the NDA."

"The guys in Pittsburgh told me all about this," Bill said. "So, what's up?"

"If you want to make an offer, talk to the bankers and tell them how much and whatever other terms you want," James said. "Wilcox told me to ask if you have an interest, so now I've asked, you still have an interest?"

"I do," Bill said. "Jan Hofmeyr will be here this weekend for some skiing, so I'll talk to him and we'll dream something up. Do you know if there have been any other offers?"

"Wilcox told me not to say," James said.

"So, there have been, but they're not stellar," Bill said. "Let's see, based on odd queries we've been getting, my guess is LHDLoaders, RampQuip and BagHandlers."

"I've heard nothing about BagHandlers," James said. "Who are they?"

"New to the business," Bill said. "Couple of guys trying to piece a business together by picking up companies on their way out. They've got some money but not much."

"If you offer somewhere around ten times earnings, can you manage the debt load?" James asked.

"We've figured out what kind of equity we'd need to not load us up with too much debt that we'd have a hard time with cash," Bill said. "Jan is amenable and has lenders lined up as well. In fact, we've even looked at RampQuip to see what it would take to pick them up as well and consolidate them into us."

"What will that do to market concentration?" James asked.

"There's still LHD, FMC, Lantis and a couple of others out there," Bill said. "So, if there's an FTC or a DOJ review, I don't see problems; we'd still have under 25% of the market."

"If you picked up RampQuip, do you have enough space for their products as well?" James asked.

"We've really gone to town on the Just in Time philosophy and machines are zipping through the factory, so we've landed up with a fair amount of extra space that we don't need for WIP," Bill said. "By pulling down work in progress and by stripping out a fair amount of raw materials and getting deliveries faster, we've got space there too."

"What if there's something that's vital but hard to come by?" James asked.

"We've protected ourselves there," Bill said. "It cost us a little, but not that much when you look at the whole."

"What does Amanda think?" James asked.

"She's excited, says that if we buy, she's quitting the zoo and coming to work at this zoo to keep an eye on things," Bill said.

"If ever you fancy a trip to South Africa and a game park, Jan has a cottage in a private reserve," James told him.

"He mentioned that," Bill said. "I'll see how things go for the first year, if we get the company, and then maybe go out there."

"If Wilcox picks someone else and they don't want you, what would you do?" James asked.

"Jan offered me a job in the States working for him," Bill said. "He's already got a couple of construction-related concerns here, and I know I could run them."

"Good to know that you've got options," James said.

"That's what I figured," Bill said. "So are we the first for the block?"

"You are," James confirmed. "I think Wilcox has a target number, and he'll keep selling until he meets that. So, I expect either HighRise or Marine to be next; I haven't been told which yet. When you get to the negotiating table with Wilcox, be careful, I wouldn't trust him not to agree then go back on his word if he felt that there was something else out there."

"Noted," Bill said. "Jan's got a really cool lawyer who's good at this stuff, and I'd take her with me. Wilcox doesn't need to know until the very end where the money's coming from, but we'll have to provide proper assurances that it's really there."

"What about the name of the company?" James asked. "I'm not sure J&B Industries wants a Waterford Ground Support out there."

"Evans Ground Support, EGS for short, logo looks just like the Waterford Ground Support logo, but with the letters changed," Bill replied. "Our lawyer looked at both and doesn't see an issue. When can I tell others?"

"Wilcox said that as soon as someone asks for a plant tour, then he'll send us a notice with blurb that we can share with everyone," James said. "My guess is that it'll have something about focusing on core businesses."

"Euphemism for dump what we don't want," Bill laughed. "I never thought that those classes we took and the mentoring that Hank Miller gave us would come in so handy."

"I think we were the lucky ones," James said. "I don't hear of many businesses doing something similar, the most some may stretch to is providing some funding for Master's degrees. I should get out of your hair, leave you to dream up a response to the bankers. I should tell you, in case you want to see what others see, we did put together a data room away from my office with all the documents relating to each division. If someone makes a serious offer, then they'll be directed to the data room for more information, and my guess is that a plant tour would only be offered to a successful bidder."

"Thanks, James, I wondered what the office guys in Irvine wanted all that stuff for," Bill said. "I'll stay in touch, and Jan said he may be in LA in the next couple of weeks; he may call you."

At home, later that evening, James and Katrina had a discussion about what to do with his folks over the weekend.

"Let's go up to Lake Arrowhead and have a picnic," she suggested.

"I think Big Bear Lake might be better," he said. "Lake Arrowhead seems to me to be swarming with docks and boats, no place to get near the water."

"Right," she said. "That place we stayed at when we first went up there, the Pine Tree Lodge, had cabins big enough for four. Why don't I check with them and see if there are any available on such short notice?"

"Good idea," he agreed. "If it's sold out, we can always go up early in the morning and come back after dark."

"I'll call right now," she said. She went to the telephone, consulted her book, then called and talked to Mary, the owner of the lodge.

"They can take us," Katrina told James. "I've booked us from Friday night to Sunday lunch time, so we can drive up after work on Friday. I'll ask your dad to make sure that the Jeep is full and tell them to take clothes for a couple of days. So, how was Bill Evans?"

"He's looking at things, and between him and Jan Hofmeyr, they'll put in a proposal," James replied. "I've no idea what Rosenberg and Davies will recommend to Wilcox and the board, my guess is the one with the funding that's most likely to be secure will be favoured."

"When does all this become public knowledge?" she asked.

"When the first potential buyer wants to take a plant tour," he said. "Then there'll have to be some kind of announcement."

"Do your folks know that you're probably selling yourself out of a job?" she asked.

"No, I'll tell them at some time, but I don't see the aerospace parts going for a while yet, so no hurry with that," he said. "My only concern is that Wilcox may argue that with fewer divisions, I have less responsibility, therefore should make less money."

"Would they do that?" she asked.

"Nothing would surprise me," he said.

"Sounds like Kasalia Copper all over again, bunch of bastards running the place," she said.

"I suppose they see their success as producing good numbers every quarter, and long-term thinking just doesn't come into things," he said.

"I wonder if anywhere in the corporate world is worth working for," she mused.

"I'm sure there are companies out there who truly do value their employees and don't just say so," he said. "I suppose it's just our luck that a change at the top of James & Brown undid all the good that Hank Miller did."

"Ah, well, we'll see what happens," she said. "I think it's bedtime, ready?"

"Always," he said.

James met with his divestiture team on Friday morning and told them what was happening with both J&B Construction and Waterford Ground Support. There were questions, of course, some of which he could answer, some he had been told not to answer, and some he said that he would get the answers to. That done, he called the divisions to see if there was anything he should be aware of, and there being none, he left early for the day. Katrina had also finished with her classes for the day, so they took off for the mountains at about two-thirty, so avoided much of the traffic.

"So, up to Victorville?" Katrina asked.

"That seems to be the best way," James agreed.

"Which way are we going?" his dad asked.

"We'll take the freeway up through the Cajon Pass to Victorville, and then we'll go east and drop back into Big Bear from the backside; it's an easier road than taking the winding route up the front of the mountains," James explained.

"How long?" his dad asked.

"It could be two hours, it could be four hours, it depends on the traffic," James replied. "Looking at things today, I'd say about two and a half hours. We'll stop for petrol in Victorville and grab a cup of coffee there too; there's a garage that actually makes good coffee."

"Victorville's also the home of the Roy Rogers museum," Katrina added. "Apparently, they have Trigger there, stuffed, as well as other things from the Rogers and Dale Evans movies."

"And Big Bear?" Mrs Martin asked.

"It was once the home of grizzly bears," Katrina replied. "But now no more grizzly bears, just an occasional black bear. It's a resort town in the mountains with a small permanent population, which could go up a lot with weekend visitors, like us. We've booked into a resort near the lake that we stayed at once."

"This is delightful," Mrs Martin said when they arrived at the lodge and were unloading the Jeep and taking things into the cabin.

"We've stayed in this one before," Katrina said. "It's got everything, and it does have a really great view of the lake."

"Does it snow here in the winter?" Mr Martin asked.

"It can do," James replied. "We were up here for Christmas, and they had just had 23 inches of snow, and there was some more after that."

"What can I get anyone?" Katrina asked. "I was thinking of a glass of wine on the deck at the front."

"That sounds super," Mrs Martin said. "Just give me five minutes for a trip to the loo and I'll be there."

"So, James, how's things?" his dad asked as they sipped on wine and drank in the view.

"All in all, not too bad," James replied. "We are selling off a couple of bits of the company, which may happen by the end of this year."

"Why, aren't they doing well?" his dad asked.

"No, they're all doing really well; it's the corporate office that wants cash for something new, so trim down what we have now to the really big bits and get some money for presumably another big bit," James replied.

"I've never understood why companies do that," his dad said.

"There are times when it makes sense," James said. "But my view is why sell what's doing well, but the decision is final, so I'll just do the best I can to get the best price."

"What happens to the people?" his dad asked.

"Usually there's some bland statement about the employees being the most valuable asset, then they go and start laying people off left, right and centre," James said. "There is a limit, and lay off the wrong people and you have no business at all, then they sell off the land, liquidate what's left and walk away."

"Very cynical," his dad said.

"Sad, isn't it?" James said.

"What happens to you?" his dad asked.

"I'll do fine, Dad," James said. "I have an employment contract that provides for me in case things all get sold, and I'm sure I could get another job fairly easily."

"Have you got enough put by?" his dad asked.

"Katrina and I are working on that," James said. "We'd like to have six months' worth in the bank, apart from any pensions, so that if we really don't like the job we can walk away."

"Will and Bridget seem to be enjoying their venture," his dad said.

"They are," James agreed. "They've had good bookings and people are rebooking to come back next year."

"That's what they told me," his dad said. "Alex is fine in Italy, it's good that you're all doing so well."

"What are you two talking about?" Mrs Martin asked as she and Katrina joined them.

"I was saying how nice it is that all three are doing so well," Mr Martin said.

"That's what a good education does for you," Mrs Martin commented.

"I was thinking about a barbecue for dinner. Does that suit everyone?" Katrina asked. It did, and James was told off to organise the fire and get ready to grill steaks.

They spent Saturday just enjoying the sunshine, the lake and the peace and quiet, only broken when someone went by in a motorboat. James could see that in time the number of people visiting would grow, the number of boats would grow, and that would drive people farther afield in their quest for relief from the population pressures of the Los Angeles Basin. Sunday was a repeat of Saturday, at least for the morning, then it was back to the smog of Orange County. From the tops, they could see the orange looking later beneath, and it was one of those things that caused James and Katrina to wonder what it was doing to their lungs. In the basin, it was hard to see the smog; it was only really evident when looking at the surrounding mountains that became more vivid when the wind changed direction and blew all the obnoxious fumes out to sea.

James had two telephone calls on Monday, the first from George Wilcox.

"James, I want you to handle the sale of Waterford Ground Support," he said. "The guys from Rosenberg and Davies will be out tomorrow and go through what we have so far. Have your chief legal eagle with you and forward us a copy of the final agreement for buy-off."

"I'll do that," James said, wondering how he was going to keep his friendship with Bill Evans separate from the negotiations, assuming, of course, that Bill had submitted a bid.

"We've had three bids," George said. "LHDLoaders, BagHandlers and the management, all pretty much in the same ballpark, the terms and conditions are going to be the deciding factor. We don't want to carry paper, that might knock BagHandlers out, and although the local guys say they have the money, they haven't said where from. Good luck."

"Thanks," James said, thinking that George was either very confident in his abilities or was setting him up to be a scapegoat if it all failed. It saddened James to have to work for someone whom he did not trust, and he wondered, not for the first time, if he should be looking elsewhere, but decided, again, not to at that time so that he could have a few years of experience to include in his CV, or résumé as it was known in the US. His second telephone call was from Jan Hofmeyr.

"James, howzit man?" he asked.

"I'm surviving," James replied.

"Look, I'm in LA now. What about dinner tonight? I'm staying in Newport Beach at the Marriott, bring Katrina with you," Jan suggested.

"What time?" James asked.

"Say six," Jan said. "I'd like to hear about your new job and also talk about the loaders."

"We'll be there," James promised.

When James went home that afternoon, he broke the news to his parents that they would be left to their own devices that evening, because he and Katrina were invited out for a business dinner. Katrina quickly showered and changed, and they left to fight traffic again, but eschewed the 55 freeway, instead using Jamboree, which had the benefit of running right by the hotel. Traffic was still slow on Jamboree, but was moving a little faster than the 55 traffic.

"Katrina, James, how are you both?" Jan asked as they joined him at the table.

"We're fine," Katrina replied for both of them. "James is busy with his job, and I'm taking a computer programming course. How have you been?"

"*Ag* man, we're doing really well," Jan said. "The country is in a mess, the government are idiots, we're embroiled in the war in South West, violence is increasing, sanctions are hurting, but for all that, we're doing well, and better yet, we've got money in Hong Kong and Singapore, which is why I'm looking to do something outside South Africa."

"Won't your government try and stop you from moving money out of the country?" Katrina asked.

"They'll try," Jan agreed. "But, there are still ways. We should just have an election involving everyone and get it over with, but the diehard racists don't want to hear of that, so afraid they'll lose their privilege and have to actually work for a living."

"How was your visit to Pueblo?" James asked.

"*Ag* man, it was good," Jan said. "We've made an offer, waiting to hear from the bankers."

"I've been put in charge of negotiations," James said.

"I see," Jan said. "Well, we'll try and not be too demanding."

"The only issue that Wilcox, the CEO, raised was where Bill Evans was going to get the money from," James said.

"I can set your mind at rest on that score," Jan said. "The financing will all be run through Marine Midland; they're part-owned by the Hong Kong and Shanghai Bank, which is where the money will come from."

"I'm afraid I can't tell you who else may have bid," James said.

"Of course," Jan said. "When can we expect to meet?"

"The bankers come out tomorrow to review the bids, and we'll set up a timetable for meetings," James replied. "How long are you in the US?"

"A month," Jan said. "Cecilia is joining me on Friday. She's looking forward to seeing you both again."

"I'll look forward to that," Katrina said. "Perhaps you could come for a *braai* on Saturday, James's folks are with us, so it'll be six of us."

"We'll be there," Jam promised. "Now enough of business, we should order and eat."

Chris Cohen from Rosenberg and Davies, along with Allen Landry and Robert Brant, arrived at the data room the next day and went through the offers with James and Jim Beatty. From their point of view, the offering amounts were fine, but there was always room for negotiation. Their greatest concern was the financing proposal put forward by BagHandlers, which called on Waterford to carry a loan of $20 million for five years. Both the bankers and James thought that was unacceptable and would be the main topic of discussion with BagHandlers. James suggested meetings the following two weeks with the three bidders, and the bankers said that they would be there. They also came armed with a draft copy of a sale agreement that James said he and Jim would review. James asked the bankers to contact the three bidders and set times for meetings to be held at the data room. That being done, the bankers left for their branch office in Los Angeles to make telephone calls. James and Jim then pored through the pages and pages of the draft sale agreement and both made comments and notes. James left Jim to make the amendments that they agreed upon and pondered his next move. He looked at the offer that Bill had made, $59,500,000 and wondered what his counter should be. The offer was based on financing arranged through the Marine Midland Bank and comprised equity of $20 million and a financing package for the rest.

James was surprised by the equity number; he had not expected anything that high. Normally, such acquisitions were done with the minimum of cash down, so the ratio of equity to debt was unusual. Perhaps Hofmeyr really wanted this to succeed and did not want to load it down with too much in the way of debt service; perhaps he just wanted money out of the country to be tied up in a going concern and not sitting as cash somewhere. Even the interest rates of the loans were favourable, and James was certain that if general rates went down, then they would refinance the package. BagHandlers was a different story; they offered $60,500,000 but were only putting $5 million down as equity, with a loan of $35,500,000 and the proposal that Waterford carry the other $20 million to be paid out in the next five years, with equal amounts per year, and only bearing interest of five basis points over LIBOR. That did not sit well with James, and he wondered why they had even submitted the offer. The LHDLoaders bid was for $60,000,000 and had a reasonable split between debt and equity, but did have some caveats and withholds for potential environmental issues and other litigation.

James found out later that day why BagHandlers had submitted a bid when Chris Cohen called him and let it slip that one of the people behind BagHandlers was a brother-in-law of Wilcox. Perhaps that explained why Wilcox had dumped it in his lap; even he could see the problems associated with selling to a relative. That would have to be handled carefully, as James was sure that chapter and verse would be conveyed back to Wilcox. He did wonder if it was a sly attempt by Wilcox to start quietly acquiring the businesses for himself by using a family member. Cohen also told him that they had dates set, the following Tuesday for BagHandlers and Monday the week after for LHDLoaders and Thursday of that week for the management team.

James met again with Chris Cohen, and they discussed what BagHandlers would probably want to do. They both agreed that they would probably want to go through all the materials in the offering memorandum and then review the supporting documents. So, James suggested that he have his team there to answer questions. Chris again let it slip that BagHandlers probably had the monthly reports that James submitted to George Wilcox, not that that complicated things in any way; the numbers all matched. Chris then left to go back to New York, promising to be back the following Monday to be ready for the Tuesday meeting. James returned to his office and called his team together, and told them what was happening and to be ready for the BagHandlers people. He spent some time with Dawn and Hermione and went through the procedures again that they would use for document control; he did not want anything walking out of the data room. If they wanted to make notes, that was fine, but no copies and no photographs.

James's parents left that weekend to fly back to London, and he and Katrina took them to LAX to see them off. As their flight was from the Bradley Terminal, they could only go as far as the passport and security checks, so said their goodbyes and watched until they disappeared from sight.

"I can't say I'm sorry they're gone," James commented to Katrina as they drove home. "My mother and I don't do well in the same house for too long."

"That's because you're too much alike," Katrina said. "So, what's the story for this week?"

"Meetings on Monday, Tuesday and who knows how many days after that, then again next week. Next week, more of the same, but later in the week will be easier because Bill and his people already know the business."

"And after that?" she asked.

"Then it's negotiations," he said.

"Well, I hope it all goes well," she said.

"So do I," he echoed. "Shall we stop somewhere and get some dinner?"

"There's that new place on Chapman," she suggested. "It's new enough that it's not overcrowded, and we can probably get a table."

Six people showed up on Tuesday from BagHandlers, all of them finance types. James did wonder about that. Who did they have to actually run the business, or did they assume that the current team would stay on after the divestiture? Chris, in an aside, identified Gordon Brown as the brother-in-law of Wilcox, but Gordon did not volunteer that information. The visiting team had questions, mainly about future prospects and how future earnings might be enhanced. That got into the mystical world of forecasting, and James was reluctant to commit the company to guaranteed forecasts because, as he pointed out, markets change, technology changes, even people change, so the best he could offer was a view of the future with upper and lower bounds that took into account various risks. Gordon wanted to know if the forecasts could be improved by the addition of other companies, and there was then a long discussion between him and Chris as to possible additions and how that might be best effected and what potential savings there might be with a larger base. James had heard much of this before, and his experience, limited as it was, and intuition was that it often sounded good but rarely worked in practice. Still, Gordon was not to be deterred, and he asked Chris for a list of possible future acquisitions. Chris did ask the obvious question: where was the money going to come from, and Gordon assured him that it would be forthcoming. For the rest of the week, Gordon and his team just skimmed through the pages of documents in the data room, but to James's mind, they had already made up their minds, and this was just to confirm that something really significant had not been missed. When they left on Thursday, it was with the promise of a definitive offer by the end of the month. Chris gave them a copy of the draft agreement of sale, and they said that they would review it and come back with their comments. Chris also told them that Waterford Industries would not carry any paper, and that just got grins and the comment that it had been worth the shot.

"So, how was the week so far?" Katrina asked James when he arrived home on Thursday afternoon.

"Interesting," he replied. "They've got money from somewhere, and they seem to want to splash it around. If I were Bill and these *ouks* land up being the ones, I'd bail out as soon as I could. I can see them just ripping the place apart to get whatever they can in as short a time as possible."

"Why?" she asked. "Why not buy a business and run it as a business?"

"I suppose it's the nature of funds and investing," he said. "Put as little in as you can, either build it up, on paper at least, then sell it for a higher price in three to five years, or strip out all the assets and recover as much as you can as quickly as you can."

"You don't have a very high opinion of those *ouks*," she said.

"I suppose it's the difference between being an operator or a financier; we'll never get really rich with me just running companies," he said.

"I don't need to be really rich," she said. "Just enough that I don't have to worry about a place to live or getting something to eat, plus a nice holiday once in a while. Is this the A stream, B stream thing you were told about in Zambia?"

"Probably is," he agreed.

"The stock options we have with James & Brown are they worth anything?" she asked.

"Not now," he said. "When they were issued, we were trading at $21.25; now we're trading at $19.35."

"Isn't one of Wilcox's jobs supposed to be bringing that up?" she asked.

"I'm sure it is," he said. "Perhaps that's what's behind all the sell-off, he wants something else that will make the markets look at J&B differently and start pushing the price up. I wonder what his incentive package is, earnings or stock growth."

"The one doesn't lead to the other?" she asked.

"Not necessarily," he said. "I'm sure your economics classes covered most of this."

"They did," she confirmed. "But this is real life, and it's interesting to watch it all unfurl in front of us. Anyway, enough of dreary business, let's go home, strip off and dance naked around the living room. It's been two days since we last got together, and I'm feeling deprived."

LHDLoaders were more interesting to talk to than BagHandlers; they at least knew the business, but it also meant treading carefully to not give too much away in case LHDLoaders were not the successful bidder. LHDLoaders really just wanted to check that the numbers in the data room matched those in the offering memorandum and then talk about the agreement of sale and terms and conditions. Chris and James spent a long time on the withholds and caveats, arguing about their lack of necessity, but LHDLoaders held firm in their desire to have them there. That in James's mind would move them down his ranking for the company most likely to win the bid. LHDLoaders did put a best and final number on the table before they left, but it was down to $58,500,000, which surprised both Chris and James.

The meetings with Bill Evans and his team all focused on the agreement of sale and the price. Bill introduced them to James, Mark Brooks, his own finance manager, Tamara Wilton, a lawyer for NewLoadCo, the company set up to acquire the business, Angela Norton, representing the bank and Nick Botha, representing the equity partner. They had no need to discuss forecasts or even the historical data; they were the ones who had provided it for the data room.

"Well, James?" Bill asked after he put his offer of $59,500,000 on the table.

"Not bad," James said. "But I was thinking more along the lines of $62 million, the business is certainly worth that, you've made it so."

"Nice try, James," Bill laughed. "I've got debt service to pay now, so anything over $60 is problematic."

"I'll take that to the board, $60 mil," James said. "If we get another offer that's higher, I'll make sure that you get the chance to better your offer. Now what about the agreement of sale?"

"There's a few things that we'd like amended," Bill said. "Section 3, subsection 2, clause C for one."

"That deals with patents," James said.

"I know," Bill said. "And I also know that J&B rolled over on that one for the sale of the construction business."

"I'll agree to including the patents if you go up by half a mil," James responded.

"Agreed," Bill said. "The rest of the stuff is legal language that we can leave Jim and Tamara to wrangle over. So, coffee and a wander outside?"

"Okay," James agreed.

"Any other bidders?" Bill asked as they sipped on their coffee.

"You know I couldn't disclose that," James said.

"I heard that Wilcox wants to keep it in the family, and I mean him," Bill said.

"You've got better sources than I do," James said.

"What do you figure are the chances?" Bill asked.

"I'll see if Wilcox means what he says when he said it was my pigeon," James said. "I wouldn't put it past him to overrule me."

"That's a lawsuit waiting to happen," Bill said. "If we come to an agreement and J&B reneges, then watch out."

"I'll bear that in mind," James said. "Did Jan tell you that we had dinner recently?"

"He did," Bill said. "Said you wouldn't tell him anything either. I can respect that, so can he."

"If you're not successful, what's your plan?" James asked.

"I'm going to go with Hofmeyr," Bill said. "He's got an interesting set of small businesses already in the US, plus whatever they've got in South Africa. I'd rather stay building the one I have now, but worst comes to worst, I've got a safe landing already set."

"With Jan putting up so much equity, are you and he partners?" James asked.

"We would form a partnership and I essentially do an earn-out over five years," Bill said. "Then we're equal partners."

"What are Tamara and Angela like?" James asked.

"Smart," Bill said. "I'd say that Tam is smarter than Jim Beatty, and I'd give my eye teeth to get Angela away from the bank and working for me. Nick is Jan's man, smart as a whip, he reports back regularly and keeps the bankers straight."

"We probably should get back and see how the lawyers are doing," James suggested.

The next two days were taken up with legal back and forth, until there was an agreement that both parties found acceptable. So, now James had two offers; all he needed to do was wait for the other. He decided that he would just tell Wilcox that he was in negotiation with the bidders, as he would not put it past him to pass on the offer prices to BagHandlers. Chris Cohen surprised James when he said the same thing, and James wondered if possible lawsuits had anything to do with that, or if Cohen was more honourable than he had given him credit for.

"James, if you ever fancy buying something for yourself, let me know," Chris said when he left to go back to New York.

"Thanks, Chris," James said.

"Or if you ever fancy coming to work with us, you'd be welcome, you'd bring an operator's perspective to things, seeing through all the bullshit the companies throw at us," Chris added.

"I'll keep that in mind," James said. "So, what's next?"

"We wait for the BagHandlers to send us their formal offer, then you and I meet to go over them, any issues we call the bidders in, otherwise it's the most money and cleanest deal," Chris replied. "Right now, it's looking like the management deal is the cleanest. I wonder where they're getting the backing from, that South African guy, Nick, ever met him before when you lived there?"

"No," James replied, quite honestly. "He's new to me."

"Sharp cookie, but then so are Tamara and Angela. I wouldn't mind either one of them on my team," Chris said. "Wonder how and where Evans found them."

"We could always just ask," James suggested.

"Might do that," Chris said. "Any road, see you soon, James. I'll be in touch."

James called George Wilcox and gave him the bare bones of the meetings and said that they were now waiting for the final offers. George wanted to know how much, and James reluctantly gave him the numbers, which favoured the management team slightly, and cynically, he had no doubt that when the BagHandlers offer came in, it would better that by a little. He also told Katrina all that had happened.

"So, now you wait?" she asked.

"We wait," he confirmed. "We need to see the best and final offer for both money and terms and then decide."

"And Wilcox, will he interfere, even though he told you it was your decision?" she asked.

"That I don't know," James said. "But, Bill did say that if they were the successful bidder and then it was pulled away from them, to expect a lawsuit."

"What's next after this one?' she asked.

"Probably access, the division in Tulsa," he replied.

"How soon before you sell yourself out of a job?" she asked.

"I would think four to five years at least," he said. "But, who knows, he might even decide to keep at least the aerospace. Anyway, how's the programming going?"

"Man, it's only fun," she said. "I've learned a lot, I'm still learning, and now I'm doing assembler, which is not quite ons and offs, but close."

"Which of the home computers that we have do you like the best?" he asked.

"They're different," she said. "The Macintosh is easier to use, but the IBM PC has its uses, and I quite like their new Word program."

"Which should I stick to?" he asked.

"I'd get familiar with both," she said. "My guess is that companies are going to favour one over the other, and for large purchases the IBM may have the edge because there are lots of compatible machines out there that are cheaper."

"I'll sound out Wilcox and see if he's got any thoughts. My guess is that he can't see a use for personal machines if we have a monster IBM mainframe and secretaries to type letters and such," James thought.

The final offer from BagHandlers came in two weeks later, and lo and behold, the offer price was $500,000 higher than the management offer. Chris Cohen flew out to meet with James, and they went through the offers carefully, looking at not only the cash involved but also the terms and amendments to the purchase agreement.

"Well, James," Chris said after a couple of hours of steady reading and not taking. "It looks to me that the management deal is the cleaner deal. The BagHandlers may have offered a little more cash, but there are a dozen clauses that I think Waterford and J&B would have a hard time with, and the LHDLoaders' offer is just too low."

"I came to the same conclusion," James said. "So, if we treat this as best and final, we should let the LHDLoaders and the BagHandlers guys know that they're not the successful bidders. I suppose it would be politic to tell Wilcox, even though he said it was my pigeon."

"Let's call him now, and I'll be on the call with you," Chris said. James dialled and Madeleine put them through.

"James, what's up?" George asked.

"I'm here with Chris Cohen, and we've just been through the best and final offers on Waterford Ground Support and based on the cash and the terms and exceptions to the terms, we've concluded that the management offer gives us the cleanest deal," James said.

"If you think so," George said. "It's a big enough chunk that we should run it by the board. Why don't you both come to New York, and I'll call a special meeting for next Wednesday."

"Okay," James said. "We'll be there."

"Okay then," George said. "What tipped the balance?"

"The Ts and Cs," James said. "LHDLoaders were too low with the cash, and BagHandlers had too many exceptions and caveats, and carve-outs for this and that. It would not have been a clean cash deal."

"And the management team has the money?" George asked.

"This is Chris, they do, I've been through it all with their bank, Marine Midland, and it's all there, equity and financing," Chris replied.

"I wonder how they did that," George muttered. "No matter, cash is cash, so let's get this approved next week, and we can move on to the next target. On another matter, James, the board has asked me to have you and your wife back here for a small get together next month on the twenty-second, fly in that day, stay overnight and either go home Saturday or stay and take in a show and go home Sunday. Use the company plane and fly into Teterboro, that's not too far from Manhattan."

"He's not happy," Chris remarked.

"Didn't sound it," James agreed. "Do you think he'll scupper things by prepping the board with the right answer?"

"I can't answer that," Chris said. "The board may all be his patsies, but if they hear the word lawsuit, they'll run a mile, so they'll want to be sure that they understand the Ts and Cs issues. In my view, the carve-outs drops of BagHandlers drops their offer to well below the management. The biggest one is the environmental. Do you know of any buried stuff or dumps that have been shut down?"

"None," James said. "It's not chemical processes of any kind, so there's scrap metals, cuttings, cutting fluids, hydraulic oils and such, but that's all saleable to various merchants, and I haven't heard about any of them being shut down."

"Carving out five mil in cash and only releasing it after five years is a bit steep," Chris said. "I'd rather have all the money in the bank now and not have to wait the five years for the rest. Any road, you'll have a presentation ready for next week?"

"I'll be prepared," James said. "Meet the night before to go over it?"

"Good idea, I'll pick you up at your hotel, just let me know where you'll be staying," Chris said.

"I've been asked to go to New York next week to explain to the board my decision on the sale of loaders," James told Katrina that evening. "I'll go on Tuesday and come back Wednesday afternoon. We've, that's you and me, been invited to a shindig in New York on the twenty-second of June. Fly there that day and back on Saturday. Wilcox did suggest we stay and take in a show and come home Sunday, anything you fancy?"

"I'll look and see what's playing," she said.

"I wonder who else is invited," he thought. "I should call Gene in Oak Creek and ask him."

319

"What do I wear?" she asked.

"Good question," he said. "This is an evening do, so something nice, not too lady of the night, not too aged spinster."

"Ou pas neefie," she said. "Not so much of the aged spinster. I'll talk to Dawn and Hermione."

"That's a good idea," he agreed. "I suppose I should just wear a grey suit, white shirt and tie, maybe maroon tie, maybe not, I'll go with an RSM tie, that'll confuse them."

"Do they need confusing?" she asked.

"Good question," he laughed. "I'm guessing that when it comes to finance and stuff, they're pretty good; when it comes to anything else, they may or may not have any experience."

James called Gene and learned that he, too, had been invited to the shindig. He also talked to the pilots, and they were happy to fly him to New York, even though it meant a Friday night away. Katrina found nothing that she really wanted to see, so they elected to come home on Saturday, leaving Teterboro at noon, so no need for a really early morning. Dawn and Hermione gave Katrina fashion advice, and she selected a simple black dress that had a silver thread running through it, and to go with it, a silver purse and black shoes with a silver motif on the heel. James had Megan make hotel and limousine bookings for them, and then they were ready to go.

James flew to New York the next week and met with Chris Cohen, and went through his presentation with him.

"You're sure you don't want to come and work for us?" Chris asked. "This is better than the one my office put together."

"Practice," James said. "I've made a lot of presentations over the years."

"Well, this should give the board more than enough to approve our recommendation," Chris said. "Do you mind if I use this tomorrow?"

"Not at all," James replied, thinking that that it had been really lazy and cheeky on the part of Chris to have him do the work.

320

"Here's a copy of mine, so you can quickly go through it and see how we did the analysis, not a lot different to yours, just a different slant, I like yours better," Chris said.

"Has George given any indication of which he'd like to do next?" James asked.

"HighRise," Chris replied.

"I rather thought that might be the case," James said.

"Any suggestions for HighRise?" Chris asked.

"I did meet this chap from the UK by the name of John Peel," James said. "He runs a business that is all construction-related and knew who we were and asked if we ever want to sell, to contact him. I'll send his details to you."

"Thanks, James," Chris said. "So, I'll see you tomorrow morning at nine at the office."

James and Chris were kept waiting for about fifteen minutes the next morning when they announced themselves at nine, then Madeleine came out of the boardroom and asked them to join the rest.

"Chris, James, morning, hope you've got some good news for us," George said.

"We have a recommendation," Chris said. "James and I have been through the offers, and the one from the management is the cleanest. I have copies here for each of you of a comparative analysis of the three offers so that you can see the differences."

"What's this carve-out stuff?" one of the directors asked after he had quickly scanned the report.

"BagHandlers assert that they're protecting themselves from future legal issues by the EPA in case there are buried hazardous wastes that can be tied back to Ground Handling," Chris explained.

"And are there any?' another director asked.

"None that we have knowledge of," Chris said. "And none that are in the folklore of the company."

"What do you mean by that?" the first director asked.

"Often we find that stories within the company have some basis in fact," Chris said. "But, we've heard nothing that suggests anything buried either on or off the site."

"I vote that we accept the management offer," the second director said. "It's clean, it's got no withholds or carve-outs, they do have the money, Chris?"

"They do," Chris confirmed. "I've talked at length to Marine Midland, and it's all set up."

"So, I'm putting a resolution forward that we sell Ground Handling to this Evans Ground Support," the second director said. James did wonder if he had another commitment and just wanted to be gone.

"Gentlemen, there is a motion on the table. Is there a second?" George asked.

"I'll second," another director said.

"All those in favour?" George asked. "Unanimous, okay, Chris, go ahead and process things and let us know as soon as it's done. James, Chris, thanks for coming. I'll be in touch with the next target. If you'll excuse us, we have other things to discuss."

"That was short and sweet," James said.

"Surprised me a little," Chris said. "I didn't realise how quickly Adams could read stuff and grasp the salient points. I think once he and Wilson had indicated they were in favour, the others went along, and George could hardly be the one nay vote."

"What do you need from me now?" James asked.

"Legal and HR support when we get to splitting off Ground Handling, you'll need to address the pension fund issues and ongoing litigation, such as it is," Chris said. "The banking and all that kind of stuff we can take care of quickly. I have the relevant account numbers for J&B Industries, so once you sign, money will change hands. Let's look for a signing in a month at the Pueblo site. I have everyone on hand and ready to go."

"Who informs BagHandlers and LHDLoaders?" James asked.

"I do that," Chris said. "And I'll also call Bill Evans. Here's a draft press release that we can put out after I've done that. Let me know if you've any issues with it. Then I'll run it by Wilcox, and we'll release next week."

"I'll look it over," James promised.

"Looking forward to working with you on the next two," Chris said. "It's been fun."

"I wouldn't say that," James said.

"Don't expect you would," Chris said. "Anyway, I'll be in touch."

"The first sale is all but done," James told Katrina that afternoon. "We'll sign documents in a month and then we'll see what happens next."

"Will you be flitting off the New York again?" she asked.

"Not as far as I know," he said. "The next time should be when we go to this shindig. So, tell me about programming."

"I've been through machine language," she said. "And we're into query languages now. I still think that not too long from now there's going to be a lot more emphasis on personal computers to do all the clerical stuff in offices, so we should make sure we stay abreast of Basic, MS-DOS and the Apple programming stuff."

"What are you going to do when you're done with the course?" he asked.

"I'm not sure," she said. "It may depend on what happens to you and if you get shifted again."

"I suppose that's always a possibility," he agreed. "Anyway, not for now, so let's go out and celebrate."

"You're paying," she said.

"I can afford it," he said. "When this closes, I get $150,000 in a bonus."

"I like that," she said. "We'll have to think of something sensible and useful to do with it."

"Maybe we should start a retirement home building fund," he said.

"Good idea," she agreed. "We just have to decide where that might be. In the meantime, we could use a few days away, so if you can get a week off, I've been reading about this place in Hawai'i."

"Sounds romantic," he said. "I'll check on things and perhaps the week after next. I'll confirm tomorrow."

"This has been an interesting couple of years," she said. "I wonder what the next couple of years hold for us."

"I suppose we'll find out," he said.